Shoulder the Sky

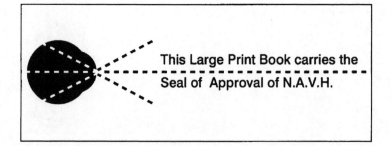

Shoulder the Sky

ANNE PERRY

Thorndike Press • Waterville, Maine

Published in 2005 by arrangement with Random House, Inc.

Thorndike Press® Large Print Basic.

The tree indicium is a trademark of Thorndike Press.

The text of this Large Print edition is unabridged.
Other aspects of the book may vary from the original edition.

Set in 16 pt. Plantin by Elena Picard.

Printed in the United States on permanent paper.

Library of Congress Cataloging-in-Publication Data

Perry, Anne.
    Shoulder the sky / by Anne Perry.
        p. cm. — (Thorndike Press large print basic)
    ISBN 0-7862-5763-6 (lg. print : hc : alk. paper)
    1. Great Britain — History — George V, 1910–1936 —
Fiction. 2. World war, 1914–1918 — Trench warfare —
Fiction. 3. World War, 1914–1918 — England — Fiction.
4. Journalists — Fiction. 5. Large type books. I. Title.
II. Thorndike Press large print basic series.
PR6066.E693S497 2005
    823'.914—dc22   2004027409

To my stepfather,
Major W. A. B. "Bill" Perry,
one of the last officers
to leave the beaches of Dunkirk,
June 1940

As the Founder/CEO of NAVH, the only national health agency solely devoted to those who, although not totally blind, have an eye disease which could lead to serious visual impairment, I am pleased to recognize Thorndike Press* as one of the leading publishers in the large print field.

Founded in 1954 in San Francisco to prepare large print textbooks for partially seeing children, NAVH became the pioneer and standard setting agency in the preparation of large type.

Today, those publishers who meet our standards carry the prestigious "Seal of Approval" indicating high quality large print. We are delighted that Thorndike Press is one of the publishers whose titles meet these standards. We are also pleased to recognize the significant contribution Thorndike Press is making in this important and growing field.

Lorraine H. Marchi, L.H.D.
Founder/CEO
NAVH

* Thorndike Press encompasses the following imprints: Thorndike, Wheeler, Walker and Large Print Press.

If here today the cloud of thunder lours
Tomorrow it will hie on far behests;
The flesh will grieve on other bones
    than ours
Soon, and the soul will mourn in other
    breasts.

The troubles of our proud and angry
    dust
Are from eternity, and shall not fail.
Bear them we can, and if we can we
    must.
Shoulder the sky, my lad, and drink
    your ale.
                        — A. E. Housman

Chapter

ONE

It was shortly after three in the afternoon. Joseph Reavley was half asleep in the April sun, his back to the pale clay wall of the trench, when he heard the angry voices.

"They be moi boots, Tucky Nunn, an' you know that well as Oi do! Yours be over there wi' holes in 'em!" It was Plugger Arnold, a seasoned soldier of twenty, big-boned, a son of the village blacksmith. He had been in Flanders since the outbreak of war in August. Although he was angry, he kept his voice low. He knew it carried in the afternoon stillness when the men snatched the three or four hours of sleep they could.

The German trenches were only seventy yards away across this stretch of the Ypres Salient. Anyone foolish enough to reach a hand up above the parapet would be likely to get it shot. The snipers seldom needed a second chance. Added to which, getting yourself injured on purpose was a court-martial offense.

Tucky Nunn, nineteen and new this far forward, was standing on the duckboards that floored the trench. They were there to keep the men's feet above the icy water that sloshed around, but they seldom worked. The water level was too high. Every time you thought it was drying out at last, it rained again.

"Yeah?" Tucky said, his eyebrows raised. "Fit me perfect, they do. Didn't see your name on 'em. Must 'ave wore off." He grinned, making no move to bend and unlace the offending boots and hand them back.

Plugger was sitting half sideways on the fire-step. A few yards away the sentry was standing with his back to them, staring through the periscope over the wire and mud of no-man's-land. He could not afford to lose concentration even for a moment, regardless of what went on behind him.

"They's moi boots," Plugger said between his teeth. "Take 'em off yer soddin' feet an' give 'em back to me, or Oi'll take 'em off yer and give yer to the rats!"

Tucky bounced on the balls of his feet, hunching his shoulders a little. "You want to try?" he invited.

Doughy Ward crawled out of his dugout,

fully dressed, as they all were: webbing and rifle with bayonet attached. His fair-skinned face was crumpled with annoyance at being robbed of any part of his few hours of sleep. He glared at Joseph. " 'Thou shalt not steal.' Isn't that right, Chaplain?"

It was a demand that even here in the mud and the cold, amid boredom and sporadic violence, Joseph should do his job and stand for the values of justice that must remain, or all this would sink into a purposeless hell. Without right and wrong there was no sanity.

"Oi didn't steal them!" Tucky said angrily. "They were . . ." He did not finish the sentence because Plugger hit him, a rolling blow that caught the side of his jaw as he ducked and struck back.

There was no point in shouting at them, and the sound would carry. Added to which Joseph did not want to let the whole trench know that there was a discipline problem. Both men could end up on a charge, and that was not the way for a chaplain to resolve anything. He moved forward, careful to avoid being struck himself, and grasped hold of Tucky, taking him off balance and knocking him against the uprights that held the trench wall.

11

"The Germans are that way!" he said tartly, jerking his head back toward the parapet and no-man's-land beyond.

Plugger was up on his feet, slithering in the mud on the duckboards, his socks filthy and sodden. "Good oidea to send him over the top, Captain, where he belongs! But not in moi boots!" He was floundering toward them, arms flailing as if to carry on the fight.

Joseph stepped between them, risking being caught by both, the worst part of which would be that then a charge would be unavoidable. "Stop it!" he ordered briskly. "Take the boots off, Nunn!"

"Thank you, Chaplain," Plugger responded with a smile of satisfaction.

Tucky stood unmoving, his face set, ignoring the blood. "They ain't his boots oither!" he said sullenly, his eyes meeting Joseph's.

A man appeared around the dogleg corner. No stretch of the trench was more than ten or twelve yards long, to prevent shellfire taking out a whole platoon of men — or a German raiding party making it through the wire. They were steep-sided, shored up against mud slides, and barely wide enough for two men to pass each other. The man coming was tall and lean with wide shoulders, and he walked with a certain elegance, even on the sloping duck-boards. His face was dark, long-nosed, and there was a wry humor in it.

"Early for tea, aren't you?" he asked, his eyes going from one to another.

Tucky and Plugger reluctantly stood to attention. "Yes, Major Wetherall," they said almost in unison.

Sam Wetherall glanced down at Plugger's stockinged feet, his eyebrows raised. "Thinking of creeping up on the cook, are you? Or making a quick recce over the top first?"

"Soon as Oi get moi boots back from that thievin' sod, Oi'll put 'em on again," Plugger replied, gesturing toward Tucky.

"I'd wash them first if I were you," Sam advised with a smile.

"Oi will," Plugger agreed. "Oi don't want to catch nothin'!"

"I meant your feet," Sam corrected him.

Tucky Nunn roared with laughter, in spite of the bruise darkening on his jaw where Plugger had caught him.

"Whose boots are they?" Joseph asked, smiling as well.

"Moine!" both men said together.

"Whose boots are they?" Joseph repeated.

There was a moment's silence.

"Oi saw 'em first," Plugger answered.

"You didn't take them," Tucky pointed out. "If you 'ad, you'd 'ave them now, wouldn't you!"

"Come on, Solomon." Sam looked at Joseph, his mouth pulled into an ironic twist.

"Right," Joseph said decisively. "Left boot, Nunn. Right boot, Arnold."

There was considerable grumbling, but Tucky took off the right boot and passed it over, reaching for one of the worn boots where Plugger had been sitting.

"Shouldn't have had them off now anyway," Sam said disapprovingly. "You know better than that. What if Fritz'd made a sudden attack?"

Plugger's eyebrows shot up, his blue eyes wide open. "At half past three in the afternoon? It's teatoime in a minute. They may be soddin' Germans, but they're not uncivilized. They still got to eat an' sleep, same as us."

"You stick your head up above the parapet, and you'll find he's nowhere near asleep, I promise you," Sam warned.

Tucky was about to reply when there was a shouting about twenty yards along the line, and a moment later a young soldier lurched around the corner, his face white. He stared at Sam.

"One of your sappers has taken half his hand off!" he said, his voice high-pitched and jerky.

"Where is he, Charlie?" Joseph said quickly. "We'll get him to the first-aid post."

Sam was rigid. "Who is it?" He started forward, pushing ahead of both of them, ignoring the rats scattering in both directions.

Charlie Gee swiveled and went on his heels. Joseph stopped to duck into the connecting trench leading back to the second line, and pick out a first-aid pack in case they needed more than the field dressing the wounded man should be carrying himself.

When he caught up with them Sam was bent over, one arm around a man sitting on the duckboards. The sapper was rocking back and forth, clutching the stump of his hand to his chest, scarlet blood streaming from it.

Joseph had lost count of how many wounded and dead he had seen, but each man's horror was new, and real, and it looked as if in this case the man might have lost a good deal of his right hand.

Sam was ashen, his jaw clenched so tight the muscles stood out like cords. "We have to see it, Corliss!" His voice shook in spite of everything he could do to steady it. "We have to stop the bleeding!" He looked at Joseph, his eyes desperate.

Joseph tore open the dressing and, speaking gently to the injured man, took his hand and without examining it, pressed the bandage and the lint over the streaming wound, then bound it as well as he could. He had very little idea how many fingers were left.

"Come on, ol' feller," Charlie said, trying to help Corliss to his feet. "Oi'll get you back to the doc's and they'll do it for you proper."

Sam climbed to his feet and pulled Joseph aside as Charlie and Corliss stumbled past.

"Joe, can you go with them?" Sam said urgently. He swallowed, gulping. "Corliss is in a hell of a state. He's been on the edge of funking it for days. I've got to find out what happened, put in a report, but the medics'll ask him what caused it. . . . Answer for him, will you?" He stopped, but it was painfully apparent he wanted to say more.

Suddenly Joseph understood. Sam was terrified the man had injured himself deliberately. Some men panicked, worn down

16

by fear, cold, and horror, and put their hands up above the parapet precisely so a sniper would get them. A hand maimed was "a Blighty one," and they got sent home. But if it was self-inflicted, it was considered cowardice in the face of the enemy. It warranted a court-martial, and possibly even the death sentence. Corliss's nerves may have snapped. It happened to men sometimes. Anything could trigger a reaction: the incessant noise of bombardment, the dirt, body lice. For some it was waking in the night with rats crawling over your body — or worse, your face. The horror of talking one moment to a man you had grown up with, the next seeing him blown to bits, perhaps armless and legless but still alive, taking minutes of screaming in agony to die. It was more than some could take. For others it was the guilt of knowing that your bullet, or your bayonet, was doing the same to a German you had never met, but who was your own age, and essentially just like you. Sometimes they crept over no-man's-land at night and swapped food. Occasionally you could even hear them singing. Different things broke different men. Corliss was a sapper. It could have been the claustrophobia of crawling inside the tunnels

17

under the earth, the terror of being buried alive.

"Help him," Sam begged. "I can't go . . . and they won't believe me anyway."

"Of course." Joseph did not hesitate. He grasped Sam's arm for an instant, then turned and made his way back over the duckboards to the opening of the communication trench. Charlie Gee and Corliss were far enough ahead of him to be out of sight around one of the numerous dogleg bends. He hurried, his feet slithering on the wet boards. In some places chicken wire had been tacked over them to give a grip, but no one had bothered here. He must catch up with them before they reached the supply trench and someone else started asking questions.

Morale was Joseph's job, to keep up courage and belief, to help the injured, too often the dying. He wrote letters home for those who could not, either through injury, or inability to put to words emotions that overwhelmed them, and for which there was no common understanding. He tried to offer some meaning to pain almost beyond bearing. They were already in the ninth month of the bitterest and most all-consuming war the world had even seen.

To begin with they had believed it would

18

be over by Christmas, but that had been December of 1914. Now, four months later, the British Expeditionary Force of almost one hundred thousand men was wiped out, either dead or injured, and it was critical that new recruits be found. Kitchener had called for a million men, and they would be fresh, healthy, not having endured a winter in the open in the unceasing cold and rain. They would not have lice, swollen and peeling feet, or a dozen other miseries to debilitate them.

Joseph crossed the reserve trench and saw men moving. A soldier was singing to himself, "It's a Long Way to Tipperary," as he poured water out of a petrol can, wrinkling his nose at the smell. He balanced the Dixie tin over a precarious arrangement of candles to heat it. He raised a hand to Joseph and smiled without distracting his attention from his task.

The men in this segment were from the Cambridgeshire villages around Joseph's home of Selborne St. Giles. Most of them knew each other by their local nicknames. Joseph was thirty-five, and for the years leading up to the war had been a lecturer in biblical languages at St. John's College in Cambridge. Before that he had been in the ministry. He knew most of these men's families. His own youngest sister, Judith, was twenty-four, older than many of these. He thought of her with a twisting confusion of emotions. He was intensely proud of her that she had volunteered to use her one distinctive skill, driving, to come here and work wherever she could help. She had been both a joy and a menace on the roads at home, but here she coped with the mud, the breakdowns, the long hours, and the horror of wounded and dying men with a courage he had not known she possessed.

The trench was climbing a bit, and drier. The slit of sky overhead was blue, with a thin drift of clouds, like mares' tails.

Joseph was afraid for Judith in many ways. The obvious danger of injury or even death was only a part of it. There was also the vulnerability of the mind and heart to the destruction around her, the drowning in pain, the loss of so many young men, and the inability of the ambulances to do more than carry them from one place to another, very often too late. He knew the questions that tormented his own mind. No sane person could be wholehearted about war, not if they had seen it. It was one thing to stand in England in the early spring with the hedgerows beginning to bud, wild birds singing and daffodils in the

20

gardens and along the banks under the trees, and speak of the nobility of war. It was an idea, at times even a noble one. Most people despised the thought of surrender.

Out here it was a reality. You froze most of the time. You were always cold and usually wet. All waking hours were occupied with monotonous routine: carrying, cleaning, digging, shoring up walls, trying to heat food and find drinkable water. You were always tired. And then there were the short interludes of horror: fear crawling in your stomach, shattering noise, and the blood and the pain, men dead, young men you had known and liked. Some would still be crippled long after the war passed into history; the nightmares would never be over for them.

Germany had invaded Belgium, and a matter of honor rested on it. Invasion was wrong; that was the one thing about which there was no question in anyone's mind. But the few German soldiers he had seen were in every way but uniform indistinguishable from the young Englishman beside him. They were young, tired, dirty, and confused like everyone else.

When a successful raiding party captured someone and brought him back, Joseph had often been chosen to question him because before the war he had spent time in Germany and spoke the language not only fluently but with pleasure. Looking back on those times now was a wrenching, muddled sort of pain. He had been treated with such courtesy, laughed with them, shared their food. It was the land of Beethoven and Goethe, of science and philosophy, of vast myths and dreams. How could they now be doing this to each other?

Joseph turned the last corner and went up a couple of steps where he caught up with Charlie Gee and Corliss, but the trench was still too narrow for him to help. Two men could barely walk side by side, let alone three.

The main dressing station was in a tent a few yards away. At least it was dry, and no more of a target than any other structure. It was quite spacious inside. After a bad raid they had to deal with dozens of men, moving them in and out as rapidly as ambulances could take them back to proper hospitals. Just now there was a lull. There were only two men inside, gray-faced, their uniforms bloodstained, waiting to be moved.

Charlie Gee gave a shout and a young

doctor appeared, saw Corliss and immediately went to him. "Come on, we'll get that fixed up," he said calmly. His eyes flickered to Joseph and then back again. It was easy enough to see in his haggard face, hollow-eyed, the fear that a hand wound was self-inflicted.

Joseph moved forward quickly. "We did what we could to help the bleeding, Doctor, but I don't know exactly what happened. He's a sapper, so I imagine something collapsed underground. Maybe one of the props gave way."

The doctor's face eased a little. "Right." He turned back to Corliss and took him inside.

Joseph thanked Charlie Gee and watched him amble back up the connecting trench toward the front line again.

An ambulance pulled up, a square-bodied Ford model T, a bit like a delivery van. It was open at the front, with a closed part at the back that could carry up to five men, laid out in stretchers, more if they were sitting up. The driver jumped out. He was a broad-shouldered young man with short hair that sat up on the crown of his head. He saluted Joseph then looked at the more seriously injured of the two men waiting, whose right leg was heavily splinted.

"Don't need ter carry yer," he said cheerfully. "Reckon an arm round yer and yer'll be fine. 'Ave yer in 'ospital in an hour, or mebbe less, if Jerry don't make too much of a mess o' them roads. Cut 'em up terrible around Wipers, they 'ave. An' 'Ellfire Corner's a right shootin' gallery. Still, we'll cut up a few o' them, an' all. Looks broke all right." He regarded the splinted leg cheerfully. "Reckon that's a Blighty one, at least for a while, eh?"

"Oi'll be back!" the soldier said quietly. "Oi've seen a lot worse than broken legs."

"So've I, mate, so've I." The ambulance driver pursed his lips. "But this'll do for now. Now let's be 'avin' yer."

Joseph moved forward. "Can I help?" he offered.

"Blimey! 'E don' need the last rites yet, Padre. It's only 'is leg! The rest of 'im's right as rain," the ambulance driver said with a grin. "Still — I s'pose yer could take the other side of 'im, stop 'im fallin' that way, like?"

Quarter of an hour later Joseph was refreshed by really quite drinkable tea. Unlike in the front trenches, there was plenty of it, almost too hot to drink, and strong enough to disguise the other tastes in the water.

He had almost finished it when a car drove up. It was a long, low-slung Aston Martin, and out of it stepped a slim, upright young man with fair hair and a fresh complexion. He wore a uniform, but with no rank. He ignored Joseph and went straight into the tent, leaving the flap open. He spoke to the surgeon, who was now tidying up his instruments. He stopped in front of him, almost at attention. "Eldon Prentice, war correspondent," he announced.

Joseph followed him in. "Bit dangerous up here, Mr. Prentice," he said, carefully not looking toward Corliss, who was lying on one of the palliasses, his bandaged hand already stained with blood again. "I'd go a bit further back, if I were you," he added.

Prentice stared at him, his chin lifted a little, his blunt face smooth and perfectly certain of himself. "And who are you, sir?"

"Captain Reavley, chaplain," Joseph replied.

"Good. You can probably give me some accurate firsthand information," Prentice said. "Or at least secondhand."

Joseph heard the challenge in his voice. "It's cold, wet, and dirty," he replied, looking at Prentice's clean trousers and only faintly dusty boots. "And of course you'll have to walk! And carry your rations. You do have rations, don't you?"

Prentice looked at him curiously. "A chaplain is just the sort of man I'd like to talk to. You'd be able to give me a unique view of how the men feel, what their thoughts and their fears are."

Joseph instinctively disliked the man. There was an arrogance in his manner that offended him. "Perhaps you haven't heard, Mr. Prentice, but priests don't repeat what people tell them, if it's of any importance."

Prentice smiled. "Yes, I imagine you have heard a great many stories of pain, fear, and horror, Captain. Some of them must be heartrending, and leave you feeling utterly helpless. After all, what can you do?" It was a rhetorical question, and yet he seemed to be waiting for an answer.

He had described Joseph's dilemma exactly, and the emotions that most troubled him, awakening a feeling of inadequacy, even failure. There was so little he could do to help, but he was damned if he would admit it to this correspondent. It was too deep a hurt to speak of even to himself.

"Nothing that is really your concern, Mr. Prentice," he said aloud. "A man's troubles, whatever they are, are private to him.

That is one of the few decencies we can grant."

Prentice stood still for a moment, and then he turned slowly and looked at Corliss. "What happened to him?" he asked curiously. "Bad ammunition exploded and took off his fingers?"

"He was down the saps," Joseph said tartly.

Prentice looked blank.

"Tunnels," Joseph explained. "The intention is that the Germans won't know where the tunnels are. They get within a yard or two of their trenches, then lay mines. If a mine had exploded there'd be nothing left of any of them."

"He's a sapper? I hear that men reaching their hands above the parapet level sometimes get hit by snipers." Prentice was watching Joseph intently.

Joseph drew in breath to reply, and then changed his mind. Prentice was a war correspondent, like any other. They all pooled their information anyway — he knew that. He had seen them meeting together in the cafés when he had been behind the lines in one of the towns at brigade headquarters, or even further back at divisional headquarters. Nobody could see everything; the differences in their stories depended upon

27

interpretation — what they selected and how they wrote it up.

There was movement at the entrance, and a sergeant came in. He saluted Joseph, ignored Prentice and spoke to the doctor, then went to Corliss. "What happened, soldier?"

Corliss stared up at him. "Not sure, sir. Bit of the wall fell in. Something landed on my hand."

"What? A pick?"

"Could be, I suppose."

"Hurts?"

"Yes, sir, but not too much. I expect I'll be all right."

"Sapper without 'is fingers is not much use. Looks like a Blighty one." The sergeant pushed out his lip dubiously, but his voice was not unkind.

Joseph took a deep breath and let it out, feeling his muscles ease a little. If Corliss had been as close to the edge as Sam feared, he might have been careless, might even have been partly responsible for the accident, but that was still not a crime. If someone else had been injured he should be put on a charge, but he was the one in pain, the one who would spend the rest of his life with half a hand.

"Nasty injury," Prentice remarked, taking a couple of steps over toward the sergeant. "Eldon Prentice. I'm press." He looked down at Corliss where he was lying. "Looks like you'll see home before the rest of your mates."

Corliss gulped and the fraction of color that was in his face vanished. His teeth were chattering and he was beginning to shake. Perhaps Sam had been right and his nerves were shot.

There was a long silence. Suddenly Joseph was aware of the tent being cold. The air smelled of blood, the sweat of pain, and disinfectant. There was noise outside, someone shouting, the faint patter of rain on canvas. The light was fading.

Should he say anything, or might he only make it worse? The doctor was unhappy, it was wretchedly clear in his tired face. He was a young man himself. He had seen too many bodies broken, too much hideous injury he could not help. He was trying to dam rivers of blood with little more than his hands. The shadows under his eyes looked even more pronounced.

Joseph knew the sergeant vaguely. His name was Watkins. He was regular army. He had probably seen most of his friends killed or injured already. He believed in discipline; he knew the cost of cowardice, even one man breaking the line. He also knew what it was like to face fire, to go over the top into a hail of bullets. He had heard the screams of men caught on the wire.

Joseph turned to Prentice. "It's a pity you won't get to go along the saps some time," he said, his voice drier and more brittle than he had meant it to be. "You could write a good piece about what it feels like to crawl on your hands and knees through a hole in the ground under no-man's-land, hear the water dripping and the bits of earth falling. A bit close to the rats down there, but it can't be helped. They're everywhere, as I expect you've noticed. Thousands of the things, big as cats, some of them. They feed on the dead, especially the eyes. You want to cover your face when you're asleep." He felt an acute satisfaction as he saw Prentice shiver. "But then you won't be able to go that far forward, will you? War correspondents don't. They'd get in the way. You only have to watch what other men do, and then go off somewhere safe and talk about it."

"And what do you do? Pray about it, Chaplain?" Prentice snapped. "God Almighty! You're a joke!" His voice was shrill with contempt. "You're no more use here than a maiden aunt in a whorehouse. If your God gives a damn about us, where is He?" He jabbed his hand viciously in the direction of the front line, and no-man's-land beyond. "Ask him," he pointed at Corliss, "if he believes in God when he's down one of his saps!"

"If you had ever been out there at night, when they're shooting, you would know there's nothing else to believe in except God," Joseph answered him with bitter certainty. "If there's any real, physical place to convince you there is a hell, try no-man's-land in winter. To sit in a nice warm pub with a glass of beer and write stories for the breakfast tables in England sounds like heaven in comparison."

"Look . . ." Prentice began.

He was cut off by the sergeant. "I think you'd better go back to your pub and your beer, Mr. Prentice," he said in a hard, level voice. "What the captain says is right. And you may believe in nothing at all, but you've got no place coming out here and making mock of other men's faith. When it gets bad, it may be all you've got. But you wouldn't know that, seeing as you aren't a soldier." He was a big man, heavier than Prentice, though not as tall, and he was seven or eight years older, probably nearer forty.

"Any officer can have you arrested at any time," he went on. "King's regulations. So it might be a good idea to be polite to the captain, don't you think?"

Prentice stood facing him, measuring his resolve.

Joseph waited without moving.

Prentice retreated, his face tight with anger.

The sergeant smiled. "Ambulance'll be here soon," he said to Corliss. "Take you back to a proper hospital, then Blighty in time." His voice was strong, comfortable, but Joseph knew from his face that he had no inner certainty that it was not a self-inflicted wound. He would not report it as such because Prentice had angered him. He was an outsider who had come in and tried to tell him his job. It was soldiers closing ranks against civilians.

Outside there was a splash and crunch as an ambulance drew up, and a moment later a loose-limbed young man came in. He was soaked and his dark hair dripped down his face. As soon as he spoke, it was obvious that he was American.

"Hi, you got anyone for me, Doc?" He saw Joseph. "Hi, Padre, how's it going?"

"Fine thank you, Wil," Joseph replied. "Yes, there's one for you there."

Wil walked over to Corliss. "Looks like it hurts," he said sympathetically.

Corliss tried to smile. "Yes, but not too much," he answered, his voice rasping between dry lips.

Prentice grunted, and smiled sarcastically.

"That's what everyone says!" Joseph told him, not bothering to suppress his anger. "If they're dying, they still say that!"

"But he's not dying, is he, Chaplain?" Prentice responded. "And he won't! In a week or two he'll be home in England, warm and safe!"

"So will you!" Joseph told him. "Only you'll have all your fingers." And he turned to help Wil Sloan get Corliss to his feet and out to the ambulance in the rain.

Matthew Reavley drove along the open road in the April sunshine. He was heading south from London toward the outskirts of Brighton and he had a sense of exhilaration to be out of the city and at last, after nine months of frustration and failure, to be on the brink of a real step forward.

The events of the previous summer, even before the outbreak of war, had altered his life irrevocably. At the end of June, on the same day as the assassination of Archduke

Franz Ferdinand in Sarajevo, Matthew's parents had been killed in a car crash, which at first had seemed simply an accident. On the previous evening John Reavley had telephoned Matthew to relate his discovery of a document that outlined a plan which, if carried out, would ruin England's honor and change the history of the world. It was in motoring from his home in St. Giles to Matthew in London that the accident had happened.

But when Matthew and Joseph had examined their father's possessions, taken from the wreck, there was no document. Nor was it in the shattered car. They had searched the house and found nothing even resembling such a thing.

The car crash had proved to be a careful and deliberate murder, although the police had never known that. John Reavley had also warned Matthew, in their last brief conversation, that the conspiracy touched even as high as the royal family, and he could trust no one.

Matthew and Joseph, seven years Matthew's senior, had uncovered the painful and ultimately tragic truth of what had happened. They had found the document where John Reavley had hidden it, and it was far worse than he had painted it. Even as Matthew sped between the hedgerows with their new leaves translucent green, a soft veil of rain misting the copse of woodland in the distance, he remembered the numbing horror with which he and Joseph had read the paper. It was beyond anything they had imagined: a treaty between Kaiser Wilhelm II and King George V agreeing that England should abandon France and Belgium to the German conquering army, in return for which England and Germany together would form an empire to divide the world between them. Most of Europe would fall to Germany, who would then help Britain to keep its present empire and add to it the old colonies of the Americas, including the entire United States. It was a betrayal almost inconceivable.

And yet it would have avoided the slaughter that was now staining the battlefields of Europe. The British Expeditionary Force of less than a hundred thousand men was already all but destroyed by death and injury. If England were to survive, it must raise a million more men to go voluntarily into that hell of pain and destruction.

They knew who had killed John and Alys Reavley, and why. The killer himself was now dead, as was his brother, but the instigator of it all, almost certainly the man who had believed he could convince King George to sign the treaty, was still unknown, and free to continue in whatever way he could to further the creation of his empire of subjugation and dishonorable peace.

Joseph was serving in Flanders and had no opportunity to pursue the Peacemaker, as they had called him. Hannah had moved back to the family home in St. Giles, with her three children. Her husband, Archie, was in the Royal Navy and at sea most of the time. She had been the closest to their mother, and in many ways was trying to take her place in the village, close to the familiar lanes and fields of her childhood, the families she knew, the routines of domestic care and the small duties and kindnesses that were the fabric of life.

Matthew himself had naturally continued in his career in the Secret Intelligence Service which his father had so deplored. It surprised him how much it still hurt that the one time John Reavley would have turned to him for professional help it had been too late, and he still, nearly a year later, could not complete the task.

Judith, five years younger than Matthew,

was using the only real skill she had and harnessing her aimless impetuosity somewhere in the Ypres area, as a VAD — Voluntary Aid Dispenser — driving ambulances, staff cars, whatever she was asked. Her letters sounded as if finally she had found a sense of consuming purpose, and even a fellowship, which gave her a kind of happiness in spite of the frequent danger and the almost perpetual physical hardship.

That meant it was only Matthew who was able to pursue the little knowledge they had in order to find the Peacemaker, not for personal vengeance or even some abstract of justice, but to stop him in whatever alternative way he was pursuing his goal. And none of them had ever imagined he would abandon it.

He drew up at the crossroads. A team of horses — heavy and patient creatures — were drawing a harrow over the field to his left and he could smell the turned earth, a rich, clinging fragrance. The rain had passed and the sunlight glittered on the dripping leaves in the hedge.

He accelerated and moved forward. He could trust no one outside the family, not even his own superior in the SIS, in fact possibly him least of all. He could only rehearse the facts that were indisputable and deduce from them what else had to be true.

John Reavley had finished his university education in mathematics in Germany, and had many German friends. One of them had been Reisenburg, the man whose calligraphic skills had been used to draft both copies of the treaty. Reisenburg had been appalled by what he saw, and stolen them, bringing them to England to the one man he trusted, and believed might be able to stop the conspiracy.

Reisenburg had passed the documents to John Reavley, who had within hours telephoned Matthew in London, saying he would bring them the following day. But he had got no farther than a few miles when he had been sabotaged on the road by Sebastian Allard, Joseph's favorite student at St. Giles. Sebastian was passionate, idealistic, and terrified of the destruction not only to life but to the very spirit of civilization that war would bring. He had believed the Peacemaker's plan to be the lesser evil. Then after he had committed double murder in its cause, and seen with horror the reality of violent death, he had found he could not live with it.

That had been followed by the murder

of Harry Beecher, Joseph's oldest and dearest friend. Reisenburg, too, had been killed, but they had no idea by whom.

And on August 4th Britain had been plunged into war.

Who was the Peacemaker? A man with allies who had access to the German royal court, almost certainly to the kaiser himself, and who also had private and personal access to King George V. No one would conceive of such a plan, let alone put it into action, without knowing both men. He was also quite obviously politically astute, had a soaring and utterly ruthless imagination, and yet in his own way a passionate morality.

He and his disciples had desperately wanted the treaty document back because there was neither time nor opportunity to redraft it and get the kaiser to sign it again before offering it to the king, but also it was imperative it did not fall into the hands of anyone who would make it public.

When they had discovered it was gone, they must have known it was Reisenburg who had taken it, but not in time to follow him. If they had, they would have taken it from him and killed him then. Similarly they could not have seen him pass it to

John Reavley, or again they would have acted at the time.

And yet they had instructed Sebastian to kill John Reavley the very next day; therefore they had to have known that he had it, and that he would be driving down that particular stretch of road that morning.

The Peacemaker could only be someone who knew John Reavley personally, and also knew that his second son worked in London in the Intelligence Services, and would be the obvious person to whom to take the document.

Who had contacted Sebastian Allard with information and instructions, in the few hours of the afternoon or evening after Reisenburg had given John Reavley the document, and knew that he had set out the next day to London?

Sebastian was dead, as was his brother, Elwyn. Their father, Gerald, was drowned even deeper in the brandy bottle, and their mother, Mary, was broken by the fury and shame of the scandal. She had changed her name and left Cambridgeshire with its unbearable past behind her. She had not adopted any family name, either on her parents' side, or Gerald's, but something totally unconnected. It had taken Matthew this long to find her where she worked as a voluntary aide in a military hospital outside Brighton.

It was early afternoon when he parked in the gravel space outside the entrance and climbed out, grateful to stretch his legs after the two-hour drive. He went up the steps and in the hallway inquired if he could speak with Mrs. Allan, and was directed to one of the wards. He passed a young man, looking no more than twenty, sitting in a wheelchair. The way the rug fell over his lap made it apparent he had only one leg.

Matthew did not want to look at it. He was twisted with pity, guilty for being able to stride out easily himself, and he was in a hurry. He was acutely aware that Joseph would have felt the same, and would have stopped. It often surprised him how much he missed Joseph. Since he had lived in London and Joseph in Cambridge, he had not expected to.

"Good afternoon," he said with a smile. "Am I heading the right way for Ward Three?"

"Yes, sir," the man assured him with a sudden light in his face. He looked at Matthew's uniform but saw no regimental insignia on it. "Straight ahead."

"Thanks," Matthew acknowledged, and

went the rest of the way and through the door. He saw Mary as soon as he was inside. She was wearing a gray skirt and blouse with a white apron over it, rather than the fashionable unrelieved black silk of mourning that he had last seen her in, but she was still gaunt-faced, her body almost fleshless, shoulders high and thin, backbone like a ramrod. She took no notice of him, concentrating on her task of rolling bandages. She was probably used to people coming and going in the ward.

"Good afternoon, Mrs. Allan," he said quietly, using her new name in order not to embarrass her. "Can you spare me a few minutes of your time?"

She stopped, her hands motionless, the bandage in the air. Very slowly she turned, but he knew that she had already recognized his voice. Her angular features were pinched with fear and her dark eyes shadowed. She stared at him without speaking.

"I'm sorry to disturb you, Mrs. Allan," he repeated her new name to let her know he had no intention of ripping away the mask she had so carefully constructed. There was such tragedy between them, wounds for which healing could not be imagined. Both his parents were dead at her son's hands, both her sons were guilty of murder and suicide, and the scandal had destroyed everything she cared about, and it was his brother who had exposed it. She had no dreams left, and the emptiness was there as she looked at him.

"I assume you have some reason, Captain Reavley," she replied without expression in her voice.

"Maybe we could walk outside?" he suggested, glancing toward the door which opened onto a terrace and then the lawn where he could see at least half a dozen young men in chairs of one sort or another.

"If it is necessary," she answered. She did not betray any interest in what he wanted, nor did she ask how any of his family were, although she must have known Joseph and Judith were both in Flanders, because it had been general knowledge in the area before she had left it.

He led the way, their footsteps hard on the wooden floor of the ward. He was aware of at least two men lying silently in beds watching them as they went.

Outside the air was mild and still, sheltered by the high walls covered with roses and honeysuckle, not yet in full leaf. The sky above was milky blue.

"What is it you wish?" she asked, stopping well short of any of the other occupants of the garden.

He had given a great deal of thought to what he would say to her, but nothing had ever been free from the desperate pain of the past. There was no clean or kind way of phrasing it. Perhaps simple was the best.

He had decided to tell her as much of the truth as he dared. She was owed that much, she had lost more than any of them, and he saw no added danger in it.

"Sebastian did not act alone," he began. "Someone taught him ideas and beliefs, then told him what to do. He obeyed, thinking it would avert war. That person, apart from individual guilt for death in your family and mine, is also still free to commit treason and sabotage of England, and to help Germany in any way he can. Their motives don't matter, they must still be prevented. I cannot ask official help in this because I don't know whom I can trust."

The faintest, most bitter humor touched her face for an instant, then vanished, her black eyebrows rising so slightly it could have been only a trick of the light. "And you imagine you can trust me?"

"I've told you little you don't already

know," he replied. "Added to which, I'm at a dead end. I cannot believe that you have any kinder feelings toward this man than I do."

The emotion was nowhere in her face except her eyes, suddenly sprung to smoldering life. "I would kill him if I could," she replied. "I would like to do it with my own hands, and watch him go. I would like to see the knowledge in him, and the pain. I would make sure that he went slowly, and that he knew who I was."

The implacable hate in her frightened him, but he did not doubt her words. He found his mouth dry. Could he ever hate like that? He had lost his parents, and the grief might never completely leave him, but their deaths had been swift and honorable. Both her sons, the passion and the hope of her life, had been turned into murderers, and died by suicide. And yet neither of them had been evil, he knew that as clearly as he saw the sunlight on the grass. They had been deceived and destroyed by others, and in the end, crucified by shame.

"Unfortunately I haven't yet found him," he said to her with a gentleness he was amazed that he could feel for her. She looked like some mythical fury rather than an ordinary twentieth-century woman standing on the lawn of a Brighton hospital. But then surely myth survived because it was a distillation of human truth? "You can help me," he added.

"How?" she asked, looking at the wheelchair-bound soldiers, not at him.

"Who contacted Sebastian the afternoon before the crash in which my parents died? In any way, telephone, letter, personally, anything at all."

"How excruciatingly delicate of you, Captain Reavley." There was a hint of mockery in her voice. "You mean the day before Sebastian killed your mother and father!"

"Yes. The morning would have been too early, anything from lunchtime onward."

She considered for a moment or two before answering. "He had two or three letters in the early afternoon delivery. One telephone call, I remember. No one visited, but he did go out. I have no idea whom he could have met then."

"Did the letters come through the post?"

"Of course they came through the post! What were you imagining? Letters by pigeon? Or a liveried footman dropping something off in a carriage?"

"A message by hand," he replied. "It is simple enough to put something in a letter box, but it wouldn't have a franked stamp on it."

She let out her breath in a sigh. "Do you really think this is going to help you find him? Or that it will bring any kind of justice if you do? You won't be able to prove anything. You will look ridiculous, and he will walk away. You'll be fortunate if he doesn't ruin you for slander."

"You underestimate me, Mrs. Allan. I didn't have anything so straightforward in mind."

She stared at him. It was not hope in her eyes, making them so alive, but it was a flicker of something better than the dead anger before. "There was a telephone call, from Aidan Thyer, and then half an hour after that, he went out."

Aidan Thyer. He was master of St. John's College in Cambridge, a position of extraordinary, almost unique influence. Many young men's dreams and ambitions had been molded by whoever had been master of their college in their first formative years as adults, away from home, beginning to taste the wild new freedoms of intellectual adventure. He could remember his own master, the brilliance of his mind, the dreams he had started, worlds he had opened for his students. Who better to teach Sebastian to be an idealist who would kill for peace?

If it were Thyer, it would hit Joseph profoundly. But pain had nothing to do with truth.

"Nothing between?" he asked aloud. "No one to the door, even at the back? No deliveries, no tradesmen?"

"No," she answered.

Was she being careful, or trying to avoid an answer that would hurt so deeply? But it had to be someone John Reavley had known, and presumably trusted. It had to be someone close enough and with the intellectual and moral power to have influenced Sebastian to kill two people he had known for years, the parents of the man who had tutored and helped him even before going up to university and even more afterward.

"Did he say anything about where he was going?"

"No. Do you think it was Aidan Thyer?" Her voice was crowded with disbelief. After Sebastian's death she had stayed in Thyer's house! He had witnessed her grief, and appeared to do all he could to help.

"I don't know," he replied truthfully. "There are lots of possible explanations. But it is at least somewhere to begin.

Someone told him what to do, and where my father would be."

"Why could it not have been at any time?" she asked, frowning slightly. "Why only in the afternoon of the day before? Why did he do it? Your brother was Sebastian's closest friend."

"I know. It had nothing to do with Joseph. It was political." That was as close to the truth as he would come.

"That's absurd!" she retorted. "Your father used to be a member of Parliament, I know, but he didn't stand for any convictions Sebastian was against. He didn't stand for anything out of the ordinary. There were scores of men like him, maybe even hundreds." It was possibly not intended to be rude, but her tone was dismissive and she made no effort to hide it.

Matthew pictured his father's mild, ascetic face with its incisive intelligence, and the honesty that was so clear it was sometimes almost childlike. Yes, there were many men who believed as he had, but he himself was unique! No one could fill the emptiness his death had created. Suddenly it was almost impossible not to snap back at Mary's callous remark. It required all his self-control to answer civilly.

"And had any of those hundreds been

the ones to learn the information he had, and had the courage to act on it," he said carefully, "then they would have been the ones killed." He deliberately avoided using the word "murdered."

Her face pulled tight and she turned away. "What information?"

"Political. I can't tell you more than that."

"Then go and talk to Aidan Thyer," she told him. "There's nothing I can do to help you." And without waiting for him to say anything more, or to wish him good-bye, she turned and walked back toward the door leading inside, a stiff-backed figure, every other passion consumed in grief, oddly dignified, and yet completely without grace.

Matthew remained outside, and went back to the car along the grass and around the footpath.

Chapter

TWO

"I don't know," Sam said wearily, pushing his hair back and unintentionally smearing mud over his brow. "It's such a bloody mess it's impossible to tell for sure. Looks like one of the props came loose and some of the wall collapsed. But what made it happen could be any of a dozen things. How much of his hand has he lost?"

They were in Sam's dugout, off the support trench. It was three steps down from the trench itself, a deep hole in the ground, duckboards on the floor, a sacking curtain over the door. It was typical of many officers' quarters: a narrow cot, a wooden chair, and two tables, both made out of boxes. On a makeshift shelf beside the bed there were several books — a little poetry, some Greek legend, a couple of novels. There was a gramophone on one of the boxes, and inside the box about twenty records, mostly classical piano music, Liszt and Chopin, a little Beethoven, and some opera. Joseph knew them all by heart. There was also a photograph of Sam's brother, younger, his face pinched with ill health.

"Two middle fingers, I think," Joseph replied. "If it doesn't get infected he might keep the rest."

Sam had brewed tea in his Dixie can, which was carefully propped over a lighted candle. He had a packet of chocolate biscuits that had come out of a parcel from home. He poured the tea, half for Joseph, and divided the biscuits.

"Thanks." Joseph took it and bit into one of the biscuits. It was crisp and sweet. It almost made up for the taste of the tea made with brackish water and cooked in an all-purpose can. At least it was hot. "There was a new war correspondent there," he went on. "Arrogant man. Scrubbed and ironed. Hasn't the faintest idea what it's like in a sap." He had only been in one once himself, but he would never forget how he had felt. It had been all he could do to control himself from crying out as the walls seemed to close in on him, and from the sound of the dripping, the scurry of rodent feet. Every shell he heard could be the one that caved in the entrance and buried them under the earth to suffocate. He was used to the *tap-tap* sounds of Germans doing the same. One could hear them in dugouts, even like this. In ways the silence was worse; it could mean they were priming their fuses. The mines could blow any moment.

Sam was watching him, his eyes questioning.

There was no avoiding the truth. "He thought it might have been self-inflicted," he admitted. "Somebody's been telling him stories, and he was full of it."

Sam did not answer. His curious, ironic face reflected the thoughts he refused to speak; pity for men pushed beyond their limits and the knowledge that this could have been exactly such a thing, fear of punishment for the man, and that he would not be able to protect him; and weariness of the dirt, the exhaustion and the pain of it all. He smiled very slightly, a surprisingly sweet expression. "Thanks for trying."

Joseph took a second chocolate biscuit and finished his tea. "It's not enough," he said, standing up. "Watkins wasn't going to charge him, but I'll make absolutely sure. Corliss looked a bit shaky to me. I'll go back to the field hospital and make sure he's all right."

Sam nodded, gratitude in his eyes.

Joseph smiled. "Maybe I'll get a decent cup of tea," he said lightly. "I've nothing better to do."

He walked as far as the first-aid post, passing Bert Dazely with the mail delivery for the men in the front trenches. He had a whole sheaf of letters in his hand and was grinning broadly, showing the gap in his front teeth.

"Afternoon, Chaplain," he said cheerfully. "Seen Charlie Gee up there? Oi got two for 'im. Oi reckon as that girl of 'is must wroite 'im every day."

"I think she does," Joseph agreed with a momentary twinge of envy. Eleanor had died in childbirth two years ago, and in one terrible night he had lost his wife and his son. In an act of will, he forced it out of his mind. There were things to do today, things to keep the mind and the emotions busy. "I've been with Major Wetherall. I don't know where Charlie is."

"Oi'll find 'im," Bert said happily, knowing he carried the most precious thing on the whole battlefield.

Joseph had only a quarter of an hour to wait before an ambulance showed up, and since the driver had only two injured to carry, he was able to beg a lift back to the Casualty Clearing Station, which was in effect a small mobile hospital. They had just recently come into full use.

He asked the first nurse he saw. She was a tall, striking-looking woman, but it was not until she spoke that he realized she was American.

"Can I help you, Captain?"

"Yes, please, nurse . . ." He hesitated.

"Marie O'Day," she told him.

"Irish?" he said with surprise. He must have mistaken the accent.

She smiled, and it lit her face. "No, my husband's people were, way back. He drives one of the ambulances. Who are you looking for?"

"Private Corliss, the sapper brought in with his hand crushed, yesterday."

The light in her vanished. "Oh. It's pretty bad. I think three of his fingers are gone. He's not doing so well, Chaplain. He's very low. I'm glad you've come to see him." She hesitated, as if to say more, but uncertain how to phrase it.

The fear tightened inside Joseph, knotting his stomach. This was exactly what he was supposed to be able to help, the shock, the despair, the inward wounds the surgeons could not reach. "What is it, Mrs.

O'Day? I need to know!"

"I don't know how it happened, and I don't care," she answered, meeting his eyes with a fierce honesty. "I don't understand how any of these boys have the courage to go over the top, knowing what could happen to them, or along the tunnels under the ground. They're terrified sick, and yet they do it, and they make jokes." Without warning her eyes filled with tears and she turned half away from him. "Sometimes I hear them saying . . ."

He reached out his hand to touch her arm, then changed his mind. It was too familiar. "What is it you want to tell me, Mrs. O'Day?"

She blinked several times. "There's a young war correspondent hanging around asking questions. I know they have to. It's their job, and people at home have a right to know what's going on. But he's heard something about self-inflicted wounds, particularly to hands, and he's pushing it." The indecision was still in her face, the need to say more, or perhaps it was the will that he should understand without her doing so.

He remembered Sam's fear, and his own. He had seen men paralyzed with terror, their bodies unable to move, or keep control of their functions. The underground tunnels were more than some men could take; the horror of being buried alive was worse than being shot for cowardice. He did not even know what Prentice was asking, or what he intended to write, and yet he came close to hating him already.

"I'll find him," he promised. "War correspondents don't have any rights to be this far forward. They're civilians; any officer can order them out, and I will, if he's being a nuisance."

She drew in her breath quickly to explain.

"I know," he assured her. "We don't know how Corliss lost his fingers, and I'm not certain that we want to."

She relaxed. It was what she needed. "Thank you, Captain. I'll take you to him." She turned and led the way out of the door, along a path of wooden boards and into another hut with cots along either side. Joseph knew from the past that it was immediately next to the operating theater. He saw Corliss on one of the beds, lying on his side, his face turned away. The fair-haired figure of Prentice was easily recognizable in the middle of the floor, by his clean uniform if nothing else. He was talking to a soldier with his arm in a sling.

He looked around as they came in and his face lit with anticipation.

"Ah! The chaplain again," he said eagerly, dismissing the soldier and moving toward Joseph. "Have you learned any more about how the sapper came to lose half his hand?"

"He did not lose half his hand!" Marie O'Day snapped. "And will you please keep your voice down! In fact, you'd better get out of here altogether. This is a hospital ward, not a café for you to stand around in the way, chatting to people." She was within an inch of his height and she was defending her territory and the men she cared about with a savage admiration and pity.

Prentice recognized that he was beaten, at least for the moment, and retreated.

Joseph gave her a beaming smile, then went over to Corliss's bed and looked down at him. He was lying with his eyes open, staring blindly into the distance, his face without expression.

It was situations like this that Joseph knew he should have some answer for, words that would ease the pain, take away some of the fear that twisted the gut and turned the bowels to water, something to make sense of the unbearable. Only the divine could serve; there was nothing human big enough to touch it.

But what could he say? Looking at Corliss now, he knew at least that he was aware of being suspected, and that he could not prove his innocence. He had lost his hand, and it might even become infected and he could lose his whole arm. If he was found guilty of causing it himself, he would be blindfolded and shot to death in dishonor. Could anything worse happen to a man?

The words died on his tongue. He simply sat on the bed and put his hand on Corliss's shoulder. "If you want to talk, I'm here," he said quietly. "If you don't, that's all right."

For a long time Corliss did not move. When at last he spoke it was hoarsely, as if his throat were dry. "What did Major Wetherall say? It hurts like a knife in my belly to let him down."

Joseph saw the tears on Corliss's face. "He sent me to keep the journalist out of your way," he answered.

" 'Cos he's after me," Corliss said. "He thinks I did it myself, on purpose. I heard him say so."

"He doesn't know a thing," Joseph replied. "I might see if I can take him down a sap, that'll give him a good idea of what it's like. If he wants a story, that would be a great one. Make a hero out of him."

Corliss smiled only slightly, and gulped.

"And Major Wetherall knows what it's like down there," Joseph went on.

Corliss blinked.

Joseph allowed the silence to settle.

"Thanks, Chaplain," Corliss said at last.

Half an hour later Joseph had spoken to each of the other men in the room, then went outside to find Prentice again. He needed to appeal to the man's better nature. If he understood what the losses had been, how many wounded and dead there were in every battalion, and no reserves to take their places, then he would not attack the morale of the men left who were trying desperately to stay awake day and night, sometimes to watch an entire length of trench from one dogleg to the next. They had been wet most of the winter, and frozen half of it. They lived on stale food, dirty water — and little enough of that. They slept in the open. Every one of them had lost friends they had grown up with, men they knew like brothers.

Many of them did not want to kill Germans. Some had blood-drenched nightmares from which they woke screaming, soaked in sweat, afraid to tell anyone — thoughts that might be seen as disloyalty, cowardice, even treason.

Prentice was talking to Sergeant Watkins. He looked relaxed, standing a little sideways next to a table with splints and bandages on it. His weight was more on one foot than the other, as if he had infinite time to spare. Opposite him was Sergeant Watkins, almost to attention, his jaw tight, his heavy face flushed.

"So morale is pretty low," Prentice was saying with assurance. "In fact about as low as it can be. I've heard that some men don't even want to fight the Germans. Is that so?"

"No sane man wants to kill another, if 'e don't 'ave to," Watkins replied in a low, angry voice. "But if Jerry fires at us, b'lieve me, mister, our boys'll fire back. You go up the front line some time, instead of 'anging around 'ere, an' you'll soon see. What d'yer think all that noise is, thunder? God Almighty moving 'is furniture? It's guns, boy, enough guns to kill every bloody thing in Flanders. Not that there is much left livin' around 'ere!"

"And you're short of ammunition, too, so I hear?" Prentice continued, not put off in the least. "Having to ration the men, even ask them to give back what they haven't used."

"None to waste," Watkins answered, glaring back. "Everybody knows that, just don't say so. If Jerry don't know, don't tell 'im."

"With the odds so heavy against us, and morale so low, it must be hard to make the men get out there and fight?" Prentice raised his eyebrows, his blue eyes very wide.

"You're talking rubbish!" Watkins said angrily, his face flushed dark red. "I got better things to do than stand 'ere listening to you rabbiting on. You get out an' see what it's really like, an' leave the sick 'ere to themselves." He turned half away.

"I thought you might have come to find out if the sapper's wound was self-inflicted," Prentice said very clearly.

Watkins froze, then turned back very slowly. "You what?"

Prentice repeated what he had said, his eyes challenging, his expression innocent.

Joseph's throat tightened, his stomach churning. This was exactly what he had come to prevent. He must say something now, before it was too late.

"Mr. Prentice, you know very little about it," he interrupted. "And military justice is not your affair. Sergeant Watkins is thoroughly familiar with his job. He's regular army. He doesn't need you to direct him."

Prentice turned to Joseph and smiled, a cold, satisfied curve of the lips. "I'm sure he doesn't," he agreed. "He'll do the right thing, for the good of the army as a whole, toward winning the war, whether he enjoys doing it, or it's personally difficult for him. He mustn't let like or dislike for a man stand in his way, or anybody else's civilian beliefs. Nor mine." He smiled even more widely. "Or yours, Chaplain. He'll find the truth. But then I imagine as a man of God, you're for the truth, too."

Joseph knew he had lost the argument as he felt it slip out of his hands, and he saw it in Watkins's face.

"What happens to a man who has deliberately injured himself?" Prentice went on. "You owe it to the rest of his unit to deal with it, don't you? The one thing I've noticed out here, even in a few days, is the loyalty, the extraordinary depth of friendship between men, the willingness to share, to risk and even to sacrifice." There was a note of envy in his voice, he hurried his words with an underlying edge of anger. "They are owed honor, and the loyalty of those who have the power to protect them, and the duty to lead."

Watkins looked at him in silent misery.

Joseph searched desperately for something to say, but what was there? Marie O'Day knew that Corliss's wound could have been self-inflicted, even Sam feared it. He had said Corliss was close to losing his nerve.

"It's a . . ." he started to say, looking for a medical excuse.

Prentice ignored him, keeping his eyes on Watkins. "Matter of military duty to collect the evidence," he finished the sentence. "Find the truth. There must be someone who saw it. The only reason not to speak to them is that you fear what they will say." He smiled for an instant, then it disappeared. "I'm sure that isn't the case . . . is it?"

" 'Course it isn't!" Watkins said tightly, his lips drawn into a thin line. "I'll look into it. If there's evidence, there'll be a court-martial. But it's none o' your business, mister! You get the hell out of here. Go do your job, an' leave us to do ours!" He swiveled on his heel and strode out past Joseph, too angry to speak, and perhaps ashamed that he had allowed himself to be trapped.

Joseph had failed. Far from protecting Corliss, he had been instrumental in allowing Prentice to force Watkins into investigating the incident, and Joseph already felt the sick fear that Corliss was guilty. People had different breaking points. A good commander could tell when it was coming. Sam had seen it and tried to protect him. It was himself Corliss had hurt, no one else. He had not left his post, or fallen asleep, or allowed anyone else to take the blame. It was one of those cases where turning a blind eye would possibly have saved him, given him time to recover at least his self-esteem, the control to build something out of what was left. Prentice had no idea what any of the men faced, let alone sappers. Joseph should have found a way to prevent this.

He went back and talked with Marie O'Day. She was furious with Prentice, but she could not help.

They could all hear the bombardment. The heavy artillery seemed to have a very good range tonight. The walls shivered and the lights swayed, casting wavering shadows on the walls. About ten o'clock the first casualties came in: some with broken arms and legs, a man with a deep shrapnel wound in the chest, another with a foot blown off. The surgeons operated in desperate haste. The smell of blood filled the air. Everybody seemed to be splashed and stained with red.

The night stretched on. The noise of the artillery stopped and started, stopped and started. Prentice was somewhere around. Joseph saw him half a dozen times; once he was carrying tea, more often he was helping a wounded man or lifting a stretcher. His clothes were now as creased and bloodstained as anyone else's, his fair skin pale from fatigue and perhaps horror as well, his voice rasping with emotion.

Then at about four in the morning Wil Sloan came in gray-faced, carrying one end of a stretcher on which Charlie Gee lay. His skin was almost blue, eyes sunken in their sockets, and there was a great scarlet streaming wound in the pit of his belly where his genitals should have been. Wil had tried to pad it with all the bandages he could find, but everything was soaked through.

"Help him!" he cried out, his voice close to a scream. "Help him! Sweet Jesus, do something!"

The surgeon dropped the needle he was stitching with, and an orderly picked it up and carried on. Marie O'Day let out a moan of anguish and lurched forward to help the other bearer ease the stretcher onto the table.

"All right, soldier," the surgeon said gently. "We'll look after you. We'll stop the worst of the pain, and stitch you up." He barely looked at the young VAD nurse who had come down from the other operating table. "Get water, plenty of pads, instruments," he told her.

She stepped closer and saw the wound, and in a hideous moment of realization understood it. Her face went paper-white and she staggered backward and crumpled to the floor.

Joseph saw the movement but he was too slow to save her.

Marie O'Day picked the girl up and dragged her to the corner, then went about collecting the things the surgeon had asked for.

Joseph knew Charlie had understood at least some part of the meaning of his blinding pain, and the wrenching panicky horror in other people's faces. He tried to look at Joseph. His lips moved but he had not the strength to make any sound.

Joseph thought of the girl who wrote to him every day, and felt so sick he was afraid he might faint, just as the nurse had done. But Wil Sloan was standing almost beside him, his eyes bright with tears, gulping to find enough air to sustain him, desperate, pleading without words, praying.

What God would let this happen to a young man? He would be better dead. He will probably die anyway, from shock and loss of blood, or from infection, but couldn't it have been without knowing what had happened to him?

Joseph put out his hand and grasped Charlie's, holding on to it, feeling the fingers move a tiny fraction. "Hang on, Charlie," he said hoarsely. "We're with you."

The surgeon was beginning to work already. The anesthetic mask was not there yet. Charlie was still conscious.

The wound was ghastly, still pumping blood, even though the first-aid station had done all they could.

Then Prentice was there, staring. "What's happened to him?" he asked. "God in heaven! His genitals have gone! There's nothing left!"

Charlie's eyes filled with tears and there was a gurgle in his throat. Joseph felt his fingers curl, and then loose again as the surgeon at last put the anesthetic mask mercifully on his face.

Wil turned around and looked at Prentice. His skin was gray, his eyes wild and he gasped and gagged for breath. He teetered for a moment, as if trying to keep his balance, then he lunged forward, swinging his fists, and caught Prentice on the side of the jaw.

Prentice went staggering backward, but Wil followed him, lashing out again and again, left fist, then right, then left. Prentice crashed into the far wall, sending a tray of instruments flying off the small table. He put up his arms to shield his face, but it was useless. Wil was in a red rage and he went on striking him on any part of his body he could reach, head, shoulder, chest, stomach.

The surgeon swore. "For God's sake, stop him! Somebody get hold of the bloody lunatic!"

Prentice fell over and slid down against the wall, half on top of the girl who had fainted. Wil grabbed his arms and yanked him up again, punching at him at the same time. Prentice gave a high-pitched scream as his shoulder dislocated with the twist of his own weight against the grip. Wil hit him again and he crumpled.

The orderly stood frozen. Marie looked around for something to hit Wil with, before he actually killed Prentice.

Joseph stepped forward, forcing the picture of Charlie Gee out of his mind. He stepped behind Wil and put his arms around his neck, throwing his weight backward so Wil was forced to let go of Prentice to save himself. But he struggled, trying to swing around and rid himself of the restraint.

"Stop it!" Joseph said fiercely. "You'll kill him, you fool! That isn't going to help anyone."

Wil jerked against him, almost pulling Joseph off his feet, then recoiled as his neck met the lock of Joseph's arm.

Prentice was clambering to his feet, his face streaming blood, his uniform torn and his left arm hanging limply, oddly angled at the shoulder. His mouth was a snarl of pain and fury, but he was equally clearly terrified.

Joseph kept his grip on Wil, but he met Prentice's eyes. "Back off." He waved. "Or I'll let him go."

Prentice was gasping, blood from a broken tooth running down his lip. "I'll have him court-martialed!" he choked out the words. "He'll spend the next five years in the glass house!"

"You can't have him court-martialed,"

Joseph replied coldly. "He's a volunteer. You can sue him in civil court, if you can get an extradition order. He's an American over here to help us in the war."

"General Cullingford is my uncle!" Prentice wiped his hand over his mouth and winced with a cry as it jagged his broken tooth. The gesture did nothing to stop the blood. "I'll see he's kept here!"

"For what?" Joseph asked, eyes wide. "Nobody here is going to have seen a thing! Are you?" he demanded, glancing sideways at Marie, working beside the surgeon, up to her elbows in blood, and the orderly passing instruments, swabs, needles threaded with fresh silk.

"Don't know what you're talking about," the surgeon said without looking up. "Get that bloody idiot out of here."

"You should take him out under arrest!" Prentice gasped, spitting more blood.

"Not him, you!" the surgeon snapped.

"I'm injured! He's broken my damn teeth!" Prentice said furiously.

"I don't do teeth." The surgeon was still working on Charlie, head down. "See the regimental dentist, if you can find him."

"You'd better tell him you got too near an explosion, and fell on one of the props." Joseph eased his hold on Wil Sloan, who

71

straightened up, coughing now that he could get his breath back.

Prentice glared at him. "You think I'm going to lie to protect you? There's military discipline for this sort of thing. You can't attack somebody and get away with it. He's a raving madman!"

"Really?" Joseph said, an exaggerated lift in his voice. "I saw nothing in particular. I was too busy thinking about a man shot half to pieces to worry about what was happening to a stupid journalist who didn't know how to keep his mouth shut in an operating theater."

"I saw nothing," the orderly added, his face twisted with anger and pity. "Did you, Mrs. O'Day?"

"Not a thing," she replied. "Nor did Janet." She gestured to the girl now climbing up slowly from where she had been slumped against the wall. The whole episode had taken only minutes. Janet stared at the scene in front of her, at Wil and Joseph, at the operating table, and then at Prentice. Her face was filled with shame, but it was only Marie O'Day's opinion she cared about, what had happened between the men barely touched her consciousness.

"Take them away." Marie O'Day gestured to the blood-soaked swabs in one of the dishes. "Bring me some more — quickly."

The girl moved to obey, grateful for a second chance, but still keeping her eyes averted from the operating table, in case her nerve betrayed her again.

"Out!" Joseph ordered Prentice. He pushed Wil in front of him also, and a moment later they were in the entrance, and then outside on the wooden walk. "You'd better get out of here," he said to Wil. "You're a volunteer, you can go wherever you like. If you've any sense, you'll go at least as far as divisional headquarters for a while. They'll find you something to do."

"What about Charlie? I can't leave him!" Wil demanded.

"You can't help," Joseph said gently. "You getting thrown out won't make it any better for him. Just lose yourself for a while. Go to Armentières, or somewhere like that."

Wil's eyes were still sunken with shock, and now, after the exertion, his rage having cooled off and the horror returning, he started to shake, but, stumbling and slipping on the boards, he made his way reluctantly along the line of the huts, and around the corner.

"Don't think I'll forget this!" Prentice snarled, blowing bubbles of blood through his bruised and rapidly swelling lips. One eye was already darkening with a huge bruise and the other cheek was blotched. His arm hung uselessly and obviously with pain.

"You can remember what you like," Joseph replied. "But you'd be wise to say and do nothing. If anyone hears about what you said in front of Charlie Gee, you'll get no cooperation from any of the men. And you may find you have other 'accidents' on dark nights. As you pointed out to Sergeant Watkins, friendship is about all we have here, that and loyalty to your unit and a belief that we're fighting for something that matters; honor, a way of life, people we love."

He looked at Prentice's face. The man was not used to physical pain, and he was obviously hurting pretty badly. "You'd better go up to one of the forward first-aid stations," he advised. "You're hardly a hospital case, but you could do with a little attention, a stitch or two, perhaps, and someone to put your shoulder back. It's quite a simple thing to do, but it'll hurt like hell." He said that with pleasure. "Wait your turn, and tell them anything you want. A shrapnel burst near you would probably be best. It looks as if you fell. There'll be lots hurt worse than you are, so you'll make a fool of yourself if you raise a fuss. People are hard on cowards." He gave a very small, tight smile. "And do it smartly, before I arrest you."

Prentice was furious. "That lunatic attacked me! I didn't even hit him back! Or are you going to lie about that, too?"

"For getting in the way of treating the wounded, and wasting medical officers' time," Joseph replied without hesitation. "You didn't hit him back because he didn't give you a chance. Be grateful I haven't arrested you already."

Prentice stared at him just long enough to realize he meant it, then turned on his heel and went off, shambling unevenly, feet slithering on the boards, physical and emotional shock making him dizzy.

Joseph went back inside the hospital hut to check on Charlie Gee's condition. It was too much, he thought. He remembered how alone and inadequate to the burden he had felt when his parents were killed, and suddenly he was the head of the family, expected to know the answers, and have the strength and the inner certainty to help.

That had been nothing compared with what he needed to do now. No teaching, no ministry prepared you to have answers for this. What kind of a God hurled you into this hell without teaching you what you were supposed to do, to say, even to think in order to keep your own faith?

There was no answer, only numberless men, young, broken, and in desperate need. He went up the step and in through the door.

It was several days after Matthew had returned from seeing Mary Allard in Brighton before he could take the time to go up to Cambridge and find an opportunity to speak with Aidan Thyer. It was a bright spring morning with a sharp wind and sunlight glittering off the wet cobbles of the streets. The porter let him into St. John's College. Apparently he had been told to expect him, because he walked with him across the outer quadrangle, under the arch and into the smaller, quieter inside quad where the masterlodgings were situated on the farther side.

"There you are, sir," he said respectfully. All men in uniform were regarded with a special dignity, whether he knew them or not, and he remembered Joseph with affection, and a peculiar awe for his part in the previous summer's tragedy. He did not want to be intrusive, and the indecision was in his face, but he had to ask.

"How is the Reverend Reavley, sir? We think of him often."

"He's well, thank you," Matthew replied.

"He's in Flanders, isn't he?" It was a statement, and there was pride in it.

"Yes, near Ypres." Matthew was surprised how much pride he felt in it himself. He realized how little he knew Joseph. He had half expected him to stay at home, or to find a post in administration, perhaps in one of the command headquarters far behind the lines. His language skills might possibly have been useful. He could very easily have avoided the worst of the violence and the pain, and no one would have blamed him.

The porter nodded. He was a quiet man, stolid, fond of a quiet beer in the evenings, and a walk beside the river. "We've got a few of our young men there. Many in France, too, o' course. An' Gallipoli. It isn't like it used to be. Don't hear young people laughing around the place like it was, playin' the fool, an' gettin' up to tricks." He sighed, his blunt face full of loss. "Daft, half the time. No harm in 'em,

77

mind, just high spirits. Dead now, some of 'em. Young Mowbray, what was studyin' history, lost both his feet. Frostbite, they said it was, then gangrene. Don't think of that in war, do you! Think of shots, and things like that." He took a deep breath. "That's the master's house, sir. He's expecting you."

Matthew thanked him and walked across the short space to the door. It opened the moment he knocked on it. A maid of about sixteen led him into the dining room where French doors opened onto the master's garden. It was presently filled with pruned rosebushes, bare-sticked, waiting for the spring, and gaudy splashes of late daffodils in bloom. Here and there were dense clumps of violets in the damp, shaded earth.

Aidan Thyer was sitting in his armchair, a pile of papers on the table beside him, presumably essays, theses on one thing and another. He stood up as Matthew came in. He was a little taller than average, but the striking thing about him was his flaxen hair, so fair it seemed to catch the light whichever way he moved. His face was long, his cast of expression a strange mixture of melancholy and humor, but both infused by a keen intelligence.

"Come in, Captain Reavley," he invited, waving to the chair opposite his own. "Can I offer you anything? Tea, or a glass of sherry?"

"Sherry would be excellent, thank you. It's good of you to make time for me."

"Not at all. You said it was important. How can I help?" As he was speaking, Thyer went to the cabinet, opened it, and poured two glasses of light, dry sherry. He carried one back to Matthew, and sat down with the other. "Have you heard from Joseph lately?" he asked with interest. "He writes occasionally, but I can't help wondering if he is putting a brave face on it."

"I'm sure he is," Matthew answered. "Sometimes it is the only way to deal with it."

Thyer smiled bleakly. He was waiting for Matthew to explain his visit.

Matthew hesitated also. It would take great care; he could not be as forthright as he had been with Mary Allard. Thyer was less emotional and a far better judge of other men's characters. Sitting in this quiet drawing room surrounded by the dust and stones, the wooden stairs hollowed by the feet of centuries of students, the strange mixture of wisdom and enthusiasm. He was acutely conscious that he might be facing a man who had deliberately plotted to betray and break it all on the wheel of idealistic militarism and bloodless surrender.

"I've been thinking about the deaths of my parents," he began, and saw the twist of pity in Thyer's face. "We know probably as much of the facts as we ever will," he continued. "And perhaps now they don't matter. But I still find myself needing to understand. It seems unarguable that Sebastian Allard deliberately caused the accident, and the evidence is strong as to how." He was aware of sitting unnaturally still. The silence in the room seemed like a tangible thing. "I still have no idea why, and I find that I need to know." He waited for Thyer's response, trying to read his face.

Thyer looked startled.

"My dear Matthew, if I knew why, I should have told you at the time. Or at least, to be more accurate, I should probably have told Joseph."

Matthew leaned back a little, steepling his fingers and gazing at Thyer over the top of them. "Would you? If it had been a painful reason, either to Joseph or to the Allards, for example? Or if maybe you had only guessed at something, perhaps later, in light of other events."

"I don't know," Thyer said, frowning. "The question is completely hypothetical. I know nothing about your family that could explain Sebastian's act, and I admit I have given it some thought myself and come to no conclusion at all. The little we know makes no sense."

"It wasn't personal and it could not have been financial," Matthew went on. He had weighed what to say on the drive from London. If he said too much he would betray to Thyer that he suspected him, yet if Thyer were the Peacemaker he would know exactly why Matthew was here and everything else that he knew about the document, and the murder of Reisenburg as well. The risk of learning nothing was too great to afford such caution.

"What are you suggesting?" Thyer prompted. His voice was level, his diction perfect. He had sat here, questioned by some of the most brilliant minds of more than a generation, men who would go on to hold many of the highest positions in the land, in industry, science, finance, and government. He molded them, not they him.

"Perhaps political?" Matthew suggested carefully.

Thyer considered for a moment. "I know Sebastian had some very strong beliefs, but so do most young men. Heaven preserve us from those who have none." He took a deep breath. "I'm sorry, I forgot for a moment what he did. I apologize. But knowing your family I find it extremely difficult to believe that your father held any conviction at all that would enrage anyone or make them feel threatened to the point of murder."

Was that a bait to provoke Matthew into proving himself correct? It was like a complicated game of chess, move and countermove, think three places ahead. He had already considered that. "I wondered if it had anything to do with my father's German friends." He watched Thyer's face. His expression barely changed, only a flicker of the eyes.

"You mean some German connection with the war?" Thyer asked a trifle skeptically. "I can't imagine what, unless it was built on a misconception. Your father was not for war, was he? I know Sebastian hated the thought. But then so did many young men. Since they are the ones who have always had to fight our wars, and give their lives and their friends to the slaughter, they can barely be blamed for that."

Matthew felt a faint prickling on his skin in the quiet room, so essentially English with its mahogany Pembroke table at the far side, its prints on the wall. He recognized one of Rievaulx Abbey in Yorkshire, ruins towering up like an unfinished sketch, more dream than stone. There were daffodils in the china vase, Connie Thyer's embroidery in a basket, the April sunlight on the flower garden beyond the French doors, centuries-old walls.

Beyond the quad in the other direction there would be students in cap and gown, exactly as they had been for hundreds of years, carrying piles of books, hurrying to class. Others would be crossing the Bridge of Sighs over the river, perhaps glancing through the stone fretwork at the punts drifting by, or the smooth, shaved green of the grass under the giant trees.

"Father was not for war," Matthew replied. "But he was not for surrender either. He would choose to fight, if pushed far enough." He kept his voice light, as if the words were quite casual.

"So would we all," Thyer said with a tight smile. "I really can't help you, Matthew. I wish I could. It makes no sense to me. Sebastian went to Germany that summer, I believe. Perhaps he became infected with strange ideas there. International socialism has become a religion for some, and can carry all the irrationality and crusading zeal of a religion, even the martyr's crown for those in need of a cause to follow."

"You speak as if you have experience of it?" Matthew observed. It seemed a world away from Cambridge, but ideas traveled as far as words could be carried.

Thyer smiled. "I'm master of St. John's; it is my job to know what young men dream of, what they talk about, whom they listen to, and what they read, both prescribed and otherwise. The best of them always want to change the world. Didn't you?" His face was gentle, at a glance no more than politely interested, but his clear, light blue eyes penetrated unwaveringly.

Was he a man who wanted to change the world — into an Anglo-German hegemony?

"It isn't the change that matters," Matthew answered, feeling his heart beat high in his throat. He must not give himself away. A clumsy word now would be enough. "It's the means they propose to use to bring it about," he finished.

"Sebastian was persistently against war," Thyer said with certainty. "He admired

German science and culture, particularly music. But that does not make him unusual. Find me a civilized man anywhere who doesn't."

They were moving around and around each other like a medieval dance, never touching. Matthew was learning nothing, except the extraordinary power over minds that the master of a college could exert, which he knew already. Thyer was simply reminding him. Intentionally? Did it amuse him to play?

"You spoke to Sebastian the day before he killed my parents," he said aloud.

Thyer was jolted at last. It showed only in the flicker of his eyes. "How did you know that?" he asked quietly.

"You took no trouble to conceal it," Matthew replied. "Was it meant to be secret?"

Thyer relaxed deliberately, the faintest touch of humor at the corners of his mouth. "No. Not at all." His face was almost without expression. "I called to remind him of his promise to give me a few quotes for a dinner with some friends. He could be forgetful. They were Greek scholars who could appreciate his translations of heroic verse."

It was another world, a year ago, and a

different lifetime. "And had he forgotten?" Matthew asked. Heroic verse! And the next day he had murdered John and Alys Reavley.

"No," Thyer replied. "He had prepared for it and was quite willing. As it happened, I canceled the dinner. It no longer seemed appropriate. Joseph would have been one of the guests, and in the circumstances none of us felt like proceeding." Thyer bit his lip and leaned forward very slightly. "I am quite aware of what you are seeking, Matthew. I find it almost impossible to believe that Sebastian was planning murder then," he said earnestly. "He sounded exactly like the young man we all knew: intense, charming, exasperating, brilliant, at times sublimely funny. And of course fickle."

Matthew was surprised. "Fickle?"

Thyer's face softened unexpectedly with a deep sadness. "He was very handsome. He had all life before him. He had a keen appetite for its pleasures, and he wanted to taste them all. I was unaware of his fiancée until she came here after his death, but I knew perfectly well of his dalliance with the girl in the pub along by the millpond, and others as well. He was fairly discreet about seeing her, but Cambridge is not such a big place, and he was easy to recognize also."

"I didn't know about others." Matthew was surprised, and disconcerted. "Who were they?"

"I have no idea," Thyer confessed. "I imagine he did not wish any of his — girls — to know about the rest."

"But you knew!" Matthew pointed out.

Thyer smiled very slightly. "A great deal is told to me that does not become general knowledge. As long as his behavior is within certain bounds, a student's love affairs are not my concern. I may not approve, but I do not interfere."

It still left a faintly disturbing taste. Sebastian had taken some trouble to deceive at least three women. It could not have been easy, it required planning, evasion, sometimes lies. Deeper than that, it required a degree of lying to himself. To his fiancée he had proposed marriage, or at the least, allowed it to be understood. To Flora in the pub along the river he had offered a deep and possibly intimate friendship, and now it seemed he had given time and at least a degree of affection also to other women. He had committed something of himself to each of them, and yet all of them would have sup-

87

posed themselves to be unique.

Was that kind of emotional deceit in a man the beginning of the duplicity that could betray his friends and eventually his country as well? Where does omission of the truth begin to be a lie?

The telephone rang on the wall beside Thyer. "Excuse me," he said, picking it up. Unconsciously he straightened a little as he listened, nodding his head and smiling. "Yes, of course," he said quietly. "I know your beliefs in the matter, but I think a compromise is necessary." He waited a few moments while the person on the other end spoke. He nodded again, giving occasional murmurs of agreement. He had not spoken the other person's name, and yet a certain respect in his manner made Matthew suppose that it was someone of considerable importance, and his mind was sharp to the power of a man in Thyer's position. What more perfect place for the Peacemaker? He would know men in government, the army, the royal household, the diplomatic service, he would know their dreams and their weaknesses, and above all, they would trust him.

He was still talking, giving gentle advice, the subtlest of pressure.

What had he really said in his conversation to Sebastian on that last afternoon before the murder? It need not have been anything more than an arrangement to meet. The knowledge of the document, the need for such horrific violence could not have been delivered that way, it had to have been face-to-face. He could hardly imagine the emotion there must have been, Sebastian's horror, recoiling from the savagery of it, the irredeemable commitment to a single act that was the violation of all he professed to believe. And the Peacemaker would have argued the greater good, the self-sacrifice to save humanity, the urgency to prevent the chaos of war — no time to delay, prevaricate. He might even have called him a coward, a dreamer with no passion or courage.

It had to have been face-to-face. Thyer had seen him that afternoon, or early evening. It was grotesque to sit here in the drawing room making polite conversation, playing games around each other, as if it were chess, not lives. There was a dreamlike insanity, the madder because it was real.

Thyer hung up the phone. He was standing near the instrument where it hung on the wall. Outside the morning sunlight was silent on the roses. In the far distance someone laughed.

"I don't suppose you saw him?" Matthew said aloud, his voice sounding unnatural in his ears. "Sebastian, I mean."

"No. I just spoke to him on the telephone," Thyer answered. "There was no need to say anything else." A very slight shadow touched his face. "Whatever prompted him to commit such a crime the following day, I believe it must have happened after that, but I have no idea what it was. I think you may have to resign yourself to the fact that you may never discover. I truly am sorry."

Was he a supreme actor? Or only what he seemed — a quiet, scholarly man, now watching half his students sent to the battlefields of Europe to waste their dreams and their learning in blood?

"What time was it you spoke to him?" Matthew asked.

"Almost quarter past three, I think," Thyer answered. "But I was with Dr. Etheridge from the philosophy department at the time. I daresay he would remember, if you think it matters?"

"Thank you," Matthew said with a strange mixture of honesty and confusion. He took his leave still uncertain if he had learned anything, or nothing. It would seem to be so easy to check all Thyer had told him, and yet if it were true, what had he learned? Who had spoken to Sebastian — where? How had he been contacted and given his orders to commit the crime that had destroyed his victims, and also himself, when there had been no other call, no letter and no message?

He left the master's lodgings and, after considerable inquiry, found Dr. Etheridge, who confirmed exactly what Thyer had said. Without difficulty Matthew also confirmed Thyer's whereabouts for the rest of the evening until after midnight. He had gone from dinner in the hall to a long conversation in the senior common room and finally back to his lodgings. He had never been alone.

Did that prove anything? According to Mary Allard, Sebastian had gone out, and been troubled when he returned. To see whom? All Matthew knew now was that it had not been Aidan Thyer.

He drove back to London knowing only that the master of St. John's was in a position of extraordinary power to do exactly what the Peacemaker planned, and that Sebastian had been seeing a third woman, perhaps a fourth, in a deceit that startled him. It was like a fog — choking, blinding, and impossible to grip.

Chapter

THREE

General Owen Cullingford stood in the center of the room he had turned into his corps headquarters in the small château a couple of miles from Poperinge, to the west of Ypres. The military situation was desperate. He was losing an average of twenty men every day, killed or wounded. In places there was only one man to each stretch of the trench and they were worked to exhaustion simply to keep sentry duty and give the alarm if there was a German attack. In the worst raids whole platoons of fifty men were wiped out in one night, leaving vast gaps in manning the line.

Ammunition was so short it had to be rationed. Every shot had to find a target; sometimes there was no second chance. Ironically, if a brigade did well, there was the difficulty of getting sufficient food up over the crowded and shell-cratered roads to reach them, and if they were decimated, the food was surplus, and wasted. Clean, drinkable water was even more difficult to find.

The other major challenge was evacuating the wounded. Those who could, simply had to walk. Kitchener had promised a million new men, but they were raised by voluntary recruitment, and were still too few, and too raw to fill the yawning gap.

The challenge he feared most was keeping up morale. An army that did not believe it could win was already beaten. Every day he saw more men wounded, more bodies of the dead, more white crosses over hasty graves. He could not afford to show emotion. The men needed to believe that he knew more than they did, that he had some certainty of victory that kept him from the fear that touched them all, or the personal horror or grief at uncontrollable pain. It was his duty to present the same calm face, squared shoulders, and steady voice whatever he felt, and to live the lie with dignity. Sometimes that was all he could do. He must never look away from wounds, or piles of the dead, never let a terrified man see that he was just as frightened, or a dying man think even for a moment that his life had been given for nothing.

Now the chaplain had come from the Second Brigade to complain about the war correspondent who had been crass and intrusive in the Casualty Clearing Station, and ended up in a fight. If it had been any other correspondent he would have told the chaplain to have the man arrested and sent back to Armentières, or wherever it was he had come from. But it was Eldon Prentice, his own sister's son, and characteristically, he had told everyone of their relationship, so they were reluctant to be heavy-handed.

Reavley was a decent man, considerably older than most of the soldiers, well into his middle thirties. Cullingford knew more about him than Reavley was aware of, because his sister, Judith, had been Cullingford's translator and part-time driver for several months. His previous driver had been severely injured and Judith had taken over at short notice because her language skills were excellent. Days had turned into a couple of weeks, and other considerations had taken over. She was an extremely good driver and, more than that, she knew the mechanics of a car better than many of the men.

Not that that was the reason he had made no effort to replace her with a regular army driver. Even as he stood in the middle of the room with his hands in his pockets, staring out the window at the overgrown garden, her face came to his mind, strong, vulnerable, full of emotion, the sort of face that haunts the mind, not so much for its beauty as for the dreams it awakens.

At first she had been full of anger. He smiled as he looked back on it now. She had been driving an ambulance and seen so many wounded men. She blamed the higher command, the officers who stayed behind and gave the orders, torn between cowardice and incompetence, sending younger and better men out to die. It had been a gradual thing, as she had driven him from one point to another, seeing the larger picture, slowly realizing how grave the situation was; understanding had come to her that he had no choice. One could not save a platoon, or a battalion, and in so doing lose a brigade. If they survived at all, it would be discipline and intelligence that saved them, not emotion, no matter how real or how easy to understand.

He found he could talk to her. With a male driver there was always the difference of rank between them. The man would be regular army, and regardless of conscience or loyalty, he would never lose sight of the difference in their station. An NCO could never argue with an officer, let alone a general, never even allow a difference of view to be seen. Judith had no such qualms. She was a volunteer, and could leave any time she chose. Strictly speaking, he had very little jurisdiction over her. He could dismiss her, but that was all. He could have no effect in her career because she had none. It gave her a kind of freedom, and he was amused to see her use it.

She was brave, generous, funny, and capable of the wildest misjudgments. But her innate honesty compelled her to admit it when she was wrong. It was on one of those occasions, weeks ago now, when he should have disciplined her, at least verbally, and he had found it painfully difficult to do, that he realized how dangerously his own feelings had overtaken him.

He had married later in life, only seven years ago, when he had been already forty-one. Nerys had been married before and it had ended in terrible tragedy. He had found her gentle, charming, and so utterly feminine that before he realized it she had become part of his life. Suddenly he had a home, a place of belonging where domestic order never failed him, where he was loved and comfortable. That he was not understood was something he had appreciated only recently.

He told her nothing of war; she had already suffered enough with her first husband's death. Even now she had occasional nightmares. He knew it when he saw her face white in the mornings, and her eyes full of fear. She did not speak of it, there were always vast areas of pain that neither of them touched — his of the war now, the men broken and lost, hers of the scandal and the suicide.

Judith was different. She saw as much of the present horror as he did, when she had been driving the ambulance perhaps even more. She might be angry, tender, exhausted, or wrenched with pity, but she confronted it. Her parents had been killed shortly before the war, and her own grief was still raw. Every now and then it spilled over and she reached out to other people who were shaken with loss of one sort or another, with a tenderness that woke new and profound emotions in him, hungers that were frightening, and too honest to deny, much as he tried.

So speaking to Joseph Reavley about Eldon Prentice had been difficult. Nevertheless, Reavley was right, and Prentice must be curbed in his diligence. No, that was the wrong word; Eldon was ambitious and crassly insensitive. He was Abby's only son, but Cullingford still found him impossible to like. He had tried, but there was an indelicacy in Eldon's perception of other people that offended Cullingford every time he observed it. It was as if he had an extra layer of skin, so he was unaware of levels of subtler pain in others, embarrassment or humiliation that a finer man would have felt, and avoided.

His words within Charlie Gee's hearing were unforgivable. His mere wounds were too hideous even to think of, mutilations worse than death. A decent man would not have looked. Reavley had said very little of what the American ambulance driver had actually done, knowing Cullingford would prefer not to know; all he wanted was to protect him.

There was a knock on the door.

"Come in," he replied automatically.

It was his ADC, Major Hadrian, who entered. He was a small, slender man, intense, efficient, and fiercely loyal. It had taken Cullingford a while to feel comfortable with him, but now habit had won and he accepted Hadrian's supreme efficiency as a matter of form. "Yes?" he asked.

Hadrian's face was tight, expression closed in and unhappy.

"A Mr. Prentice is here, sir. He's a war correspondent, and he insists on speaking with you." He did not add that the man was Cullingford's nephew, and that was a startling omission. Prentice would certainly have told him.

"He appears to have met with a slight accident, sir," Hadrian added.

"Did he tell you that?" Cullingford asked curiously. He dreaded having to listen to Prentice's complaints about Reavley, and principally about the American VAD driver who had attacked him.

"No, sir," Hadrian replied.

"Did he tell you he was my nephew?" Cullingford asked. Surely Hadrian would have dealt with the matter himself otherwise.

"No, sir. I already knew. Prentice and I were at school together, Wellington College. He was three years behind me, but I know him." He added nothing more, and his face was deliberately blank. Cullingford could not imagine that they had been friends, for reasons other than the difference in their ages.

"You'd better send him in," he said.

"Yes, sir." There was a flicker of understanding in Hadrian's eyes, then he turned on his heel and left.

A moment later Prentice came in, closing the door behind him. In spite of the fact that Reavley had warned him, Cullingford was startled at how bad Prentice looked. His fair skin had taken the bruising heavily, he was considerably swollen and the flesh around his eye and jaw was bruised dark purple. His lip was distorted out of shape and when he spoke it was with difficulty because one of his front teeth was chipped. His left arm was in a sling to keep it comfortable after the dislocated shoulder had been put back into place, a quick but intensely painful procedure.

"Good morning, Uncle Owen," he said almost challengingly. "As you can observe, I have been assaulted. You don't seem to have much discipline over your troops."

Cullingford had intended not to be annoyed by him, and already he had lost. He could feel his temper tighten. "I see men injured far more seriously, every day, Eldon. If you don't know the casualty figures, wounded and dead, then you are not doing your job. If you need medical attention, then go and get it. If you are looking for sympathy, mine is already taken up by soldiers who have had their arms and legs blown off, or their bellies torn open. It seems as if your worst injury is a chipped tooth."

"I assume your soldiers were wounded by enemy fire," Prentice said stiffly. "I was assaulted by an ambulance driver! An American, for heaven's sake!"

"Yes, we have a few American volunteers," Cullingford agreed. "They are here at their own expense, living in pretty rough conditions, they eat army rations and sleep when and where they can. They work like dogs. Some even get killed helping others. I think it is one of the highest forms of nobility I have seen. They give everything, and ask little in return."

Prentice hesitated, uncertain for a moment how to answer. It had taken the impetus out of his fury. "I suppose you have no power to exert any kind of discipline over them," he said finally.

"Never needed to," Cullingford replied straightaway, a tiny smile on his lips.

"Well, you need to now!" Prentice said in sudden fury. "The man has an ungovernable temper. He went berserk. Lost any kind of control."

"Who else did he attack?" Cullingford inquired.

The blood rushed up Prentice's uninjured cheek. "No one, but there was hardly anyone else there! It was only the chaplain who prevented him from killing me, and he wasn't in any hurry. Not much of a chaplain, if you ask me."

"I didn't ask you," Cullingford snapped. "You're not a child anymore, Eldon, to come running to your parents if someone picks a quarrel with you. Deal with your own problems. No one admires a sneak. I thought seven years at Wellington would have taught you that. And in Flanders I am not your uncle, I am the general in charge of this corps. I have one hundred and thirty thousand men, many dead or wounded, replacements to find, food and munitions to transport, and, please God, some way to hold the line against the enemy. I haven't time to attend to your squabbles with an ambulance driver. Don't come to me with it again."

Prentice was livid, but he forced himself to relax his body, shifting his weight to stand more elegantly, as if he were perfectly at ease. "Actually what I came for, Uncle Owen, was to ask you to give me a letter of authority to go forward to the front lines, or anywhere else I need to, to get the best story. I know correspondents are a bit limited, and pretty well any officer can arrest them, even the damned chaplain, who probably doesn't know a gun from a golf club. This one actually threatened me!"

"No," Cullingford said without needing even to consider it. "You have exactly the same privileges and limitations as all other correspondents." He was not going to be twisted by family loyalties into giving Prentice an advantage. Abigail should not expect it. The boy had lost his father a few years ago, but he was thirty-three, and indulgence would not help him.

"I imagine you know Captain Reavley," Prentice said without making any move to go.

"You're mistaken," Cullingford replied. "I've met him a couple of times. Two divisions is over a hundred and thirty thousand men. I know very few of them personally, and those I do are the fighting officers and the senior staff officers concerned with transport and replacements."

There was a slight smile on Prentice's face, no more than a sheen of satisfaction. "I was thinking of a more personal basis," he answered. "He must be related to your VAD driver, isn't he? Reavley's not such a common name, and I thought I detected a faint resemblance."

Cullingford felt a sudden wave of heat wash over him. There was really very little likeness that he could see between Judith and Joseph Reavley. He was dark and she was fair, her face was so much softer than his, so feminine. Perhaps there was something similar in the directness of the eyes, an angle to the head, and a way of smiling, rather than the structure of bones.

Prentice was watching him. He must answer. He was conscious of guilt, and being desperately vulnerable. He was not used to having emotions he could not control, or defend.

"They are brother and sister," he answered, keeping his voice level, not so casual as to seem forced. "If you think that means he is around here any more than his duties require, you have very little grasp of the army, or the nature of war."

"She's beautiful," Prentice observed. "In a kind of way. Very much a woman. If she were my sister, driving a middle-aged man around, I'd be over here pretty often — out of concern for her." He shifted his weight to his other foot, and smiled a fraction more. "In fact, since she's a volunteer, and could do or not do whatever she wanted, I'd make sure she didn't get into that sort of position."

Cullingford felt the heat rise up his face, and was furious with himself for not being able to hide it. He knew it was burningly visible because Prentice recognized it immediately. The triumph was brilliant in his eyes.

"But then perhaps the good chaplain doesn't know that you're married," he said quietly. "And I don't suppose for a moment that he'd connect Aunt Nerys's previous tragedy with you. After all, her name was Mallory then, and it was more her husband's name and poor young Sarah Whitstable whose names were spread all over the newspapers. They can be very cruel: Middle-aged man runs off with sixteen-year-old daughter of Tory peer; double suicide leap off cliffs at Beachy Head, or wherever it was. Bodies dashed to pieces on the rocks below. Poor Aunt Nerys! If she knew you were being driven around by a beautiful, hotheaded twenty-three-year-old, she'd start the nightmares all over again. But I'm sure Captain Reavley doesn't know that!"

Cullingford felt the room swim around him, as if it had been rocked by heavy artillery fire. It was a physical blurring, even though it was created by an emotional shock. It was real, Prentice was blackmailing him! There was no smile on his face, no wavering in his bold, clear blue eyes. He meant it!

There was also no defense. Cullingford had never said or done anything even remotely improper with Judith. He had never touched her, not even called her by her Christian name. It was all in his imagination, in the momentary meeting of eyes, things that had not needed words: a great sweep of sky across the west, gilded by the fading sun, cloud-racks of searing beauty that hurt and healed with the same touch; understanding of laughter and pain; the knowledge when to be silent.

His guilt was deeper than acts, it was a betrayal of the heart. And yet the loneliness had been slowly killing him. He had protected Nerys at a cost to himself greater than he had realized before. Perhaps it was his fault, too, for allowing her to live in a world cocooned from reality, but he had left it too late to change it now. Nerys was at home, in another life. Judith was here, she was the one who had seen the grotesque ruin of no-man's-land, the mud, the ice-rimmed craters with the limbs of dead men poking up as if in some last, desperate hold on life. He did not need to reach after impossible explanations for her, or speak with words that were too raw still to bear it.

"I only want a letter," Prentice was talking again, unable to wait. "Just something to stop them hedging me in. I'm doing my job! And of course I'll share anything I get with the other correspondents." He put his good hand in his pocket, in a possibly unconscious imitation of Cullingford's stance when he was at ease, moments he might have remembered before the war. "Thanks. It'll help a lot."

Cullingford would like to have thrown him out, possibly even physically, but he could not afford to. There was steel inside Prentice. He wanted to succeed. If he were prevented in a way he imagined unfair, he would bring down anyone he felt to blame. He would not care who else it hurt, but that it included Cullingford would please him. Cullingford had never liked him. He had tried, and failed. Perhaps he had not tried very hard; he was not a man to whom relationships were easy. Only Judith had crashed through his self-protection guard. She had put no artificial limits to her own feelings, no bounds at all to what she was prepared to know or to see. And then when she was hurt by it, her very hold on endurance, the courage to hope and purpose threatened, it was his strength she needed.

"I'll give you a letter of authority," he conceded, hating himself for such surrender. "But you can still be arrested if you get in anyone's way."

"I daresay that'll do," Prentice replied with the sharp relish of victory in his voice, making it high and a little abrupt. "At least for now. Thank you . . . Uncle Owen."

Cullingford did not look at him. It was only when the letter was written and Prentice had put it rather awkwardly in his pocket with his one hand, and then gone out, that Cullingford realized that his muscles were clenched with the effort of self-control and the anger inside him was making him hold his breath.

Hadrian was standing in the doorway waiting for instructions. His face was watchful, his eyes unhappy. How well did he really know Prentice? Well enough to have believed blackmail of him?

"If Mr. Prentice comes again," Cullingford told him, "I don't want to see him. In fact, so help me God, if I never see him again it will suit me very well!"

Hadrian stared at him, his face dark with emotion. "Yes, sir," he said quietly. "I'll see to it."

Cullingford turned away, suddenly embarrassed. He had not meant to reveal so much. "Will you tell Miss Reavley to get the car ready. I need to go to Zillebeke in half an hour."

"Yes, sir," Hadrian said.

Sam Wetherall sat on the fire-step in the sun, a packet of Woodbines in his hand. It was nearly five o'clock. He was smiling, but the sharp, warm light picked out the crusted mud along the line of his jaw, and the deep weariness around his eyes.

"There was Barshey Gee sitting there cleaning his rifle," he said wryly, "and holding this long philosophical discussion with the German captain, all very reasonable and patient, explaining to him how he was wrong. Apparently he'd been doing it for days. The German was lying with his head and shoulders sticking out of the ground about a foot below the top of the parapet."

"Days?" Joseph stared at him in horror.

Sam shrugged, grinning. "Oh, he was dead! No one had dared to climb over the top to dislodge him." He raised his eyebrows. "Which brings to mind, Jerry's awfully quiet this afternoon. Wonder what he's up to?" He cocked his head a little sideways, listening.

"It's been quiet for a while." Joseph realized he had heard no sniper fire for more than an hour. That was not unusual when there was a Saxon or South German regiment opposite them. They, like some of the English regiments, were inclined to live and let live. However there were others who were far more belligerent, and there had recently been a change on the German side, so this was unexpected.

Sam stood up, bending his head to keep it low, and moving over to Whoopy Teversham, standing on sentry duty. "What can you see?" he asked.

Whoopy was concentrating on the periscope in his hands and did not look away. "Not much, sir. Word is this lot's pretty tough. Oi 'aven't seen a thing. Could be all asleep, from anything Oi can tell."

Sam took the periscope from him and stared through it, his shoulders hunched and tense. Slowly he swiveled it around to look right along their own lines, then across no-man's-land again. He gave it back to Whoopy and stepped down onto the duckboards. "Wind's changed," he said with a shrug. "Blowing our way."

"I know that," Joseph answered ruefully. "Smells different."

Sam rolled his eyes. "You can tell one lot

of dead men from another?"

"Of course I can," Joseph replied. "You don't have to carry a rifle to have a nose. And the latrines are behind us, not in front."

"The subtlety of it," Sam expressed mock admiration.

"Oi can't see the trenches!" Whoopy interrupted sharply, his voice touched with alarm. "There's a sort of cloud! Only it's on the ground, and Oi think it's coming this way. Bit to the north of us, up Poelkapelle."

"What do you mean?" Sam demanded, his voice edgy. "What sort of cloud?"

"Greenish-white," Whoopy replied. "It's koind of drifting over no-man's-land. Maybe it's camouflage, hoiding a raiding party?" Now there was alarm in his voice as well, high-pitched and urgent. He swung around the butt of his rifle to clang on an empty shell case, and at the same minute gongs sounded along the trench to the north and west.

Men scrambled to their feet, seizing weapons, preparing for a wave of enemy troops over the top. Joseph saw Plugger Arnold with his odd boots, and Tucky Nunn. Then there was silence, a long breathless waiting.

Joseph stood as well, crouching a little, back to the wall. An afternoon raid was unusual, but he knew what to expect. There would be a shout of warning, shots, shellfire, wounded men, some dead. He would be there to help carry those they might save. Trying to maneuver a stretcher in the short, narrow lengths of duckboard, around the jagged corners was ghastly. But they had been built precisely so an enemy could not get a long range of fire and decimate a score of men in one raking barrage. It was worth the sacrifice. Most of them they would carry on their backs.

No one moved. Not a duckboard tilted or a foot squelched.

Then he heard it — not a fusillade, but gasping, a cry strangled in the throat, gagging.

Sam swiveled round, his face ashen. "God Almighty!" he said, his voice choking. "It's gas! Run!"

Joseph froze. He did not understand. How could any soldier, let alone Sam, give the order to run?

Then Sam's shoulder hit him hard in the chest and almost knocked him off his feet. He bent to a crouch, more by instinct than thought.

"Get up!" Sam shouted at him. There

were other noises now, yells of rage, terror, half words cut off in the middle, the terrible sounds of men retching and choking, and beyond them the rising barrage of gunfire.

"Get up!" Sam shouted again. "The gas sinks! It's on the ground."

"We've got to help!" Joseph protested, swiveling around and pushing against Sam's weight. "We can't leave them!"

"We can't help anyone if we're dead." Sam yanked him along by one arm. "In the supply trenches we'll have a moment."

Joseph did not understand him, but at least Sam seemed to have some idea what to do. Gas? Poison in the air? He stumbled to the next corner, and the next, bumping into the uprights, lurching left and right. He could already taste something acrid in the air. His eyes were watering. Men were stumbling everywhere. The shelling was getting louder. It must be closer. Any minute German soldiers would appear — towering over the parapet, shooting them like trapped animals.

He reached the supply trench and ran along it, his feet slipping on the wet boards, splashing mud, until Sam hit him from behind and sent him flying. He found himself on his hands and knees, rats scattering ahead of him.

"Take your scarf or handkerchief — anything, and piss on it!" Sam ordered. "Then tie it over your nose and mouth."

Joseph could not believe it.

"Do it!" Sam's voice exploded, high-pitched, close to panic. "For God's sake, Joe! Do it! It absorbs the gas, or at least the worst of it!" He suited the action to the word himself, tying the wet cloth around his face like a mask. "There's no time to look for stretchers, and there'll never be enough anyway."

Joseph obeyed, feeling sick, frightened, and absurd, but he was too accustomed to the smells, the physical indignity of trench life to be revolted. He followed blindly after Sam as they turned and made their way forward again, and down the slight incline. At the first opening they fell over the body of a soldier lying on his back, dead hands clawing at his throat, his face twisted in agony. There was froth and bloody vomit on his lips. It was Roby Sutter, one of Tucky's cousins. He had been nineteen. Joseph had bought cheese from his father's farm.

Ahead of him Sam was still moving, bent forward, head just below the parapet. The gunfire was heavier, and there were more shells. Earth and clay exploded up in huge gouts, shooting sideways, fan-shaped. The gas was drifting. He could see its dirty, green-white swathes in the air. If there was a raiding party coming over it would be any moment now. Sam turned raising his arms, swinging them round to indicate forward.

They found two more men still alive, one wounded in the shoulder, propped up against the trench wall. Blood was streaming down his chest and arm, but he was breathing quite well. The other was unconscious, his face already gray. Joseph bent to the wounded man just as there was another burst of shell fire, this time closer to them. The dirt rained down within a few yards.

"I'm going to get you back," Joseph said firmly. "But I'll have to carry you. I'm sorry if I hurt you." He had no idea if the man heard him or not. As carefully as he could, he eased him over his shoulder and straightened his back, not upright — in case he offered a target where the forward side of the trench had collapsed inward — but bent, as if heaving coal.

He heard Sam go onward, leaving the gassed man where he was.

About a hundred yards later, just as Joseph felt as though his spine was breaking, he met more troops coming in. Their faces were pale, frightened, their eyes wide. Immediately behind them were the stretcher-bearers.

He gave the stretcher-bearers his man — still bleeding, but alive — then turned and went back the way he had come. It was worse. More gas was drifting across the mud and craters between the lines. It was patchy, like a real fog, here and there in whorls torn rugged by the wind, leaving the dead trees poking up like gravestones above a drowned world. It lay like a pall, following the low ground until trenches that had been shelters became graves, bodies piled grotesquely, suffocated in their own blood and fluids.

The shelling went on, the noise deafening, shrapnel everywhere. Joseph found more men alive, struggling and wounded. He helped where he could, keeping the urinated scarf over his nose and mouth, tying it so it would not fall off while he used his hands. He lost count of the men he lifted, struggling to keep his balance in the mud, and carried or dragged back to medical aid, and some sort of cleaner air. His muscles screamed with the effort of their weight. Often he slipped and fell over.

His own lungs were bursting, but he could not stop, there were always more men down. Some he thought might live, some died even before he could get them help.

He did not know how long it was before he saw Sam again through the smoke and the gas. He lurched toward him, calling out. A shell exploded near them, knocking him off his feet. Part of the parapet caved in, filling the space between them with a cascade of earth and half-buried corpses, some weeks old. Now there was no shelter anymore.

"Help me dig him out!" Sam shouted through the gunfire, and Joseph realized there was a live man under the rubble as well.

If he was wounded, the shock of that would have killed him. If he was gassed there was no hope anyway, not under that slide of clay. He started to say so.

"Shut up and dig!" Sam yelled at him. "The poor sod was all right before that!"

Joseph's head was throbbing and his vision was blurred. The trench floor seemed to undulate, but the firing wasn't heavy enough to move the ground like that. The gas had a smell different from latrines or decaying bodies. He obeyed, digging clumsily with his hands, afraid that even if he could find a shovel, he might strike living flesh with it.

He was digging frantically, heaving great clods of wet clay and flinging them anywhere he could, aware of Sam a couple of yards away on the other side, doing the same. Then he felt the ground lurch and the inner side of the trench erupt in a flying wall of dirt that knocked him flat on his back. More weight landed on his legs, and staring upward he saw what looked like a row of giants with human bodies and the heads of pigs. It wavered as if he were seeing it all under water. The noise was deafening, and one of the pigs fell on top of him.

When he opened his eyes, his face was covered. There was something not only over his nose and mouth, but around his head and he could see only dimly. Panic seared through him. He put up his hands to tear it off, and received a sharp blow to his forearm, stinging with pain. One of the giant pigs was in front of him, staring with huge, baleful eyes. But his legs were free! He could feel them.

The noise was still intense: machine-gun fire, shells exploding, and the deeper roar of the heavy artillery far behind the lines.

Someone pulled on his arm and he had

no choice but to scramble to his feet or have his arm dislocated at the socket.

"Keep it on, you fool!" the pig in front of him shouted. "It's a gas mask! And don't just stand there! Take his feet!" It gestured to the blood-spattered man lying on the mud where the fire-step used to be.

Joy surged through Joseph like an incoming tide. Inside the surreal pig-mask it was Sam. Gasping and laughing, he bent to obey. It took a few moments to get hold of the man properly, then he straightened up again, grasping his ankles firmly, and setting off backward, head and shoulders stooped to keep them below the line of the fractured parapet. Breathing was easier. His head still pounded and he had no peripheral vision because the goggle eyes showed a view that was only straight ahead, but step by step they moved through a world like something out of a medieval painter's nightmare. Everywhere were mud and mangled bodies, some distorted into hideous forms by the agonies of suffocation. The greenish vapor still hung in drifts, sinking down the walls to sit in hollows, barely stirred by the wind.

On every side the guns barked. Heavy shelling shook the ground to the west, more sporadic eastward as the artillery to the rear tried to take out the enemy's biggest guns. Craters swam in mud and gas, foul-smelling as if hell beneath them had vomited up its bowels. Where the trench walls had caved in he could see the waste stretching out in broken tree stumps, lengths of wire, and the torn limbs, skeletons, and bodies of men until flesh and mud were indistinguishable.

They reached a supply trench and passed the man to stretcher-bearers, then went back for more. Neither of them spoke. What could there be to say? Somehow the world, in its political insanity, had descended another sharp step downward, dragging an innocent mankind in its wake. Young men Joseph had known all their lives were being destroyed in front of him, and he could do nothing even to explain it to himself, never mind to them. He was useless. All the study of his life evaporated here where hell was real. It swallowed everything.

Physical action was all that was left. He tore gas masks off dead Germans, stomach heaving, hands trembling. He propped men up and gave them a little water, sat with them a moment until they died, carried one here or there, took anyone he could reach. There was no time to cover the dead, let alone bury them. That would come in the days ahead, if they held the ground and could find them. If they were forced to retreat, then perhaps the Germans would do it.

Sometimes he lost Sam, but mostly they worked together, understanding each other without words, even without gesture, simply knowing. Two had more chance of lifting a wounded man than one, and with their gas helmets they could go where stretcher-bearers could not. Sam did not hesitate. He carried his rifle slung over his shoulder, bayonet fixed, and was ready to use it when they came around a corner suddenly and found themselves face-to-face with a German soldier. Sam lunged forward, spearing the man through the chest, and tearing off the soldier's mask to use on the next live man of their own they found.

There was no question of advancing. The relief poured in with terrible casualties, men falling forward as they were shot, faces in the mud, or floundering as the gas filled their lungs and they drowned from the inside, screaming and gurgling.

But at last the Germans fell back and the line held. By dark the guns and flares showed a landscape of torn wires, trenches barely recognizable in the cratered mud, and the still-lingering pockets of gas.

Joseph was at the dressing station, his head pounding, body so exhausted he could barely feel the pain of burning muscles, bruised flesh, and torn skin. He looked at the blood soaking his tunic and trousers with surprise, not even sure if any of it was his own.

Opposite him, sitting on another upturned box, Sam was stripped to the waist while a young VAD stitched the long gash across his chest and placed a bandage on it.

Sam's dark face was smeared with blood and smoke, his eyes bloodshot. "What a hell of a mess," he said with a slight smile. "Good thing it won't show. I'll tell you for nothing, I wouldn't let you touch my jacket with a needle."

"Sorry, sir," the VAD apologized. He looked about twenty, gray-faced with horror and exhaustion, and Joseph recognized his accent as Canadian, although he could not place it more closely than that.

Sam winced as the thread was cut, pulling the skin a little. "Don't worry. By the end of the war you'll be good enough to stitch shirts, I daresay," he said with a gasp. "If that's your idea of a straight seam, they'll fit Quasimodo."

The VAD looked puzzled. "Quasimodo, sir?"

"Hunchback of Notre Dame," Sam replied, moving his arm tentatively, then catching his breath with pain. "Bit before your time. French classic."

"Oh. Can I get you a shot of rum, sir? You look all in."

"You can. And one for the chaplain there. He frequents all the same pubs I do."

Joseph had only a couple of deep scratches; a little cleaning and bandaging were all that was needed. He drank the rum and tried to rise to his feet, but the tent swayed around him and he fell forward on his knees.

"No more rum for the chaplain," Sam observed. "He'll need to stay sober for weeks to bury this many dead." He watched as the young Canadian carefully helped Joseph to sit again. "On the other hand," Sam added, "perhaps he'll need to stay drunk to bear it! You'd better get him another, but get him something to eat at the same time." He turned to Joseph, his face suddenly tender. "Sleep it off, Joe. These poor devils deserve a priest who knows what he's saying, whether anyone believes him or not." He stood up himself, his face went ashen, and he toppled over just as the VAD caught him and eased him to the ground. "Stretcher!" he shouted, his voice rising sharply.

Joseph rolled over and lay down on the earth. If he tried to stand again he would only cause more work. Let them put him in a corner somewhere until he came back out of the black hole of oblivion. Please God it was a black hole, full of darkness without shape or sound, no agony, no awareness at all. He hoped they would leave Sam somewhere near him.

When Joseph opened his eyes again it was morning. He saw the sky above him delicate blue with the light pouring through it, still touched with the cool silver of dawn. Then he moved. Every muscle in his body hurt. He felt as if he had been beaten. He was lying on the ground outside the first-aid post. He must have been injured.

Then he remembered the gas.

He rolled over and sat up, his head pounding, his stomach knotted. Someone came to him with a cup of water, but he brushed it aside. Where was Sam? He stared around. The earth was littered with bodies, some bandaged, some splinted, some motionless. He saw Sam's dark head. He looked to be asleep. There was a bandage around his chest, under his tunic.

Now he remembered it all, the choking, the pall of death over everything, the struggle to save, the overwhelming failure. It came back with a taste of despair so intense he sank back to the ground, breathing hard, unable to force strength into his limbs. He was barely aware of it as somebody held the water to his lips. He drank only because it was less trouble than arguing.

He lay there for a while. He must have drifted off into sleep again, because the next thing he was aware of was someone easing him up into a sitting position and offering him food, and hot tea with a stiff lacing of rum.

Sam was sitting cross-legged opposite him, pulling a face of disgust at the taste of the drink in his hands.

"I wonder what else was in the crater they got this out of!" he said sourly. "A dead horse, I should think!" He took a deep breath, coughed, and then finished the rest of it. He grinned across at Joseph. There was nothing to say, no hope or sanity, nothing wise or clever. The only thing that made it endurable was the knowledge that he was not done.

Half an hour later Joseph was still sore, his body aching and skin torn raw where he had scratched it because of the fleas and body lice that afflicted everyone, officers and men alike. There had been no time or opportunity to try to get rid of them.

It was now nearly midday. There was an air of anxiety even more profound than usual, and Joseph became aware of it as he saw how many men there were still on the ground. Ambulances pulled up, were loaded, and drove away again, always five men or more in each. There was very little laughter; people were too stunned to joke.

Joseph stood up slowly, realized he could keep his balance, and set off to find the surgeon and see if he needed any help. But what could he say to a dying man, or one in appalling pain? That there was a purpose to all this? What? A God who loved them? Where was he? Deaf? Occupied somewhere else? Or as helpless as Joseph himself in the face of endless, senseless, unbearable pain?

There was nothing to say as he sat beside young, dying men. He repeated the Lord's Prayer, because it was familiar, and it was a way of letting a man already sinking into the blindness of death know that he was there. For some it was the sound of a voice, for others it was touch, a hand on a limb that they could still feel. Some wanted a cigarette. Though Joseph himself did not smoke, he had learned the trick early to carry a packet or two of Woodbines.

The bombardment picked up in the evening and went on all night. It was one of the worst he could remember; there were so many men gone that in places, sentries on watch were alone, exhausted, and fighting against falling asleep. Apart from the fact that it was an offense for which a man could be court-martialed and face the firing squad, no one wanted to let down their friends or themselves.

There were no reinforcements yet. The Canadians had suffered the worst along this part of the line, and the French Algerians farther east. Now, far from a shortage of food, there were no men to eat it, and it was rotting.

By dawn there was some respite in the attack, possibly because with the slackening of the wind, pockets of gas still lingered over the craters and in the lower lying trenches. As full daylight spread over the vast wasteland with its shattered trees and gray water, its mud and corpses, Joseph made his way back to his own dugout. He washed in cold, sour water, shaved, and sat down at his makeshift table with pen, ink, and paper, and a preliminary list of casualties.

He hated it, but it was part of a chaplain's job to write to the families of the dead and break the news. He tried not to say the same thing each time, as if one man's death were interchangeable with any other. The widow or parents, whoever it was, deserved the effort of individual words. Nothing would make it better, but perhaps a little dignity, showing that someone else cared as well as themselves, would make a difference in time.

Here in his dugout he had a few possessions from home, things he had chosen because they mattered most to his inner life: the picture of Dante from his study in St. John's, that marvelous tortured face that had seen its own hell and bequeathed the vision to the world; a couple of books of verse, Chesterton and Rupert Brooke; a photograph of his family, all of them together three Christmases ago; a coin his friend Harry Beecher had found when they had walked together along the old wall the Romans had built fifteen hundred years ago across Northumberland from the Channel to the Irish Sea. They were all memories of happiness, the treasures of life.

In the dugout the air was close and humid. Somewhere in the distance a windup gramophone was playing. The cheerful, tinny sound of dance music was at once absurd and incredibly sane. Maybe somewhere people still danced?

Outside he knew men were digging, shoring up trench walls, carrying in fresh timber and filling sandbags to rebuild the parapets. He could smell food, bacon frying, as well as smoke, the rot of bodies, latrines, and the faint lingering odor of the gas.

He had many letters to write, but the hardest was going to be of a captain he had held in his arms while he retched up his lungs and drowned in his own blood. It was one of the worst deaths. There was a horror and an obscenity to it that was not there in a shell blast, if it had been quick.

Of course many other deaths were appalling. He had seen men torn in pieces, their blood gushing onto the ground; or caught in the wire and then riddled with bullets, jerking as the metal tore them apart, then left to hang there, because nobody could get to them. They could be there for hours before death released them at last.

He wrote:

Dear Mrs. Hughes,

I am deeply sorry to have to tell you that your husband, Captain Garaint Hughes, was among the victims of last night's attack. He was a brave soldier and a fine man. Nothing I say can touch your grief, but you can be proud of the sacrifice he made, and the fortitude and good humor with which he conducted himself.

I was with him to the end, and I grieve for the loss of a man who lived and died with honor.

Captain Joseph Reavley, Chaplain

He looked on it and read it again. It still seemed formal. Should it be? Perhaps that was the only way to keep the dignity — if there could be any dignity in mud and blood and pain, and coughing your lungs up.

Then he picked up the pen again and added,

We sat in the lamplight together and he spoke to me with great frankness. He had

*the courage to call my bluff, and ask me
what I really believed. I think in trying to
answer him honestly, which he deserved, I
answered a few of my own questions also. I
owe him a gratitude for that, and I shall
not forget him.*

Joseph Reavley

Before he could think better of it, or feel
self-conscious, he folded it and put it in
one of the envelopes. Perhaps the fact that
it was personal would one day make her
feel closer to the man she had loved.

That afternoon Joseph went with Sam to
perform the duty he hated most of all,
worse even than writing to families of the
dead. The court-martial of Private Edwin
Corliss had been unavoidable. Since it was
a capital charge, it was presided over by
Major Swaby, from another division, with
two junior officers, Lieutenants Bennett
and MacNeil, neither of whom looked to
be over twenty-three. They were all pale-
faced, stiff, and profoundly unhappy.

They were all behind the lines. Such
proceedings were not conducted under
fire. One room of a café had been temporarily commandeered and it had an oddly
comfortable look, as if a waiter might ap-

pear with a bottle of wine any moment.

Swaby came over to where Joseph and Sam were waiting. He spoke to them briefly. "Your man, Major Wetherall?"

"Yes, sir," Sam said stiffly, his face pale and tight with anxiety. "He's a good man." He did not add any details of his service. This was not the time. Swaby understood.

"Don't worry," Swaby said calmly. "Straightforward case. We'll hear it and debate for a few minutes, then send the poor devil home. Wouldn't have brought it at all if the sergeant hadn't been pushed into a bit of a corner. Can't be seen to overlook these things."

"No, sir." Sam relaxed only a fraction.

Swaby went up to the front and sat down at the table. The proceedings begun.

Sergeant Watkins gave evidence, looking acutely unhappy, but he told the truth exactly as he saw it, standing to attention and facing forward.

Every accused man was entitled to ask an officer, usually of his own unit, to defend him, and Corliss had chosen Sam. Now Sam stood to question Watkins. He was courteous, even respectful. He knew enough to take great care neither to embarrass the man, nor seem to be condescending to him. Watkins was a career soldier. He would rather be abused than patronized.

Sam did not argue with the facts, he simply allowed Watkins to tell as little as possible, and choose his own words. It was apparent that if he had been allowed to, he would have let the matter go.

"Then why didn't you, Sergeant Watkins?" Sam said tartly. His face was pale, his eyes glittering with anger, his body stiff. He leaned forward a little and winced, probably as the bandage tightened over the gash on his chest.

"Civilian present, sir!" Watkins said bitterly. "Newspaperman. Couldn't let them write up that we 'ave no discipline. And 'e'd take it 'igher, sir!"

"I see. Thank you."

The surgeon looked so tired Joseph was afraid he was going to pass out before he was finished giving his evidence. Even Major Swaby seemed concerned for him.

"Are you all right, Captain Harrison?" he asked gravely.

"Yes, sir," the surgeon answered, blinking. "I really can't help you. I know Corliss lost two fingers in the accident, and we had to take a third off later, but I have no idea how it happened. Don't have time to think about such things, if it doesn't matter to the treatment. I certainly didn't ask him, and I've no idea if he said anything. People behave differently when they're in shock, and a lot of pain. There was an accident. That's all I know."

The prosecuting officer did his duty reluctantly. He had several of the men from Sam's command who had been present just before the accident, and those who were there immediately after. He may not have wished to question them, but he clearly had been given no choice.

Joseph sat in wretched unhappiness, aware of Corliss's misery and his strong sense of guilt, although whether it was because he had unintentionally injured himself, or because he felt he had let his unit down, it was impossible to tell.

The verdict was given within minutes. Surely they would understand that the case was only brought because of Prentice? They could find Corliss not guilty, say it was an accident, whether it was or not.

It was customary that the most junior officer on the panel should give his opinion on sentence first, so he might not be influenced by his seniors.

Everyone waited.

"Lieutenant Bennett?" Swaby asked.

Bennett looked everywhere but at

Corliss or Sam. Joseph had seen him fumbling through the handbook, his fingers trembling.

"Lieutenant Bennett?" Swaby repeated.

"I can't say anything else, sir," Bennett mumbled. "It's a capital charge, sir."

"I know what the charge is, Lieutenant. What is your recommendation for sentence?"

Bennett gulped. "Death, sir."

Corliss was already sitting. He was considered medically unfit to have to stand. His hand was very heavily bandaged and in a sling. Sam gripped hold of him, supporting him upright.

Swaby let out his breath, then gulped. "Lieutenant MacNeil?" he asked.

MacNeil looked as if he might be sick. "I . . . I have to agree, sir. I . . . I'm not sure that . . . I mean, is there . . ." He tailed off in profound distress.

"Would you prefer to suggest something else, Lieutenant?" Swaby asked.

MacNeil was clearly floundering. "No, sir," he said hoarsely. "The law . . . the law seems quite clear," he said, his hand on a well-thumbed red book, *The Manual of Military Law.*

Swaby was ashen. It was not what he had expected, but they had left him no way out.

He was too inexperienced in such things himself to know what latitude he had in reversing what his juniors had said, and there was no one to help him. The officers who usually conducted such courts-martial before were either dead or too badly injured to be here.

He gulped again, gagging on his own breath. "M-morale must be maintained. Any man who deliberately inflicts a 'Blighty one' on himself in order to return home and escape his responsibilities to his country and his fellow soldiers must be made an example of."

The room was breathless.

Sam was gray-faced.

Swaby looked like a man in a nightmare from which he could not escape. "Private Edwin Corliss," he said miserably. "It is the judgment of this court-martial tribunal that you have committed a serious act of cowardice in the field, and for this you should be sentenced to death. Major . . . Wetherall . . ." He gulped again. "Have you anything you wish to say in mitigation of the accused?"

Sam stood up. He looked so ill Joseph was afraid he was going to pass out himself. He half rose as if to help him, then realized the futility of it and sank back. Sam was almost as alone as Corliss.

"Yes, sir," Sam struggled to find his voice. "I have been Private Corliss's commanding officer for seven months and have seen him face conditions worse than those faced by the men in the trenches under fire. The saps are unique. It takes a very special kind of man to dig into any earth, and go into the tunnels he makes, but especially this. It's wet, it's cold, it's suffocating, and pretty often we come across dead bodies — sometimes Germans, sometimes our own men, men we've known, talked to, shared tea with or a joke. If such a man reaches the end of his concentration, sir, and makes a mistake that takes his hand off, I think he's more to be pitied than blamed! Especially by a civilian newspaperman, sir, who's never faced anything more dangerous than his editors' blue pencil!"

"Thank you, Major Wetherall," Swaby said quietly. "I shall take your plea for mercy into consideration when I pass our verdict on up the command. It will have to go right to General Haig, of course. All capital cases do. In the meantime, Private Corliss will be kept under arrest, and taken to military prison to await his sentence. This court is dismissed."

"Jesus wept!" Sam said between his teeth, his voice trembling.

"Actually, He's probably the one person who would understand." Joseph had not intended irony; he was sick, stomach clenched with misery as much for Sam as for Corliss, but it came to his lips unbidden.

Sam's mouth twisted with a terrible, bitter humor. "I suppose He would! He couldn't get Himself out of it either!" he said with despair, his eyes shadowed and hollow with pain. "I'll see Prentice in hell!"

Chapter

FOUR

"This way, Padre!" Goldstone said urgently.

Joseph had stopped bothering to tell Goldstone — or anyone — that he was Church of England, not Roman Catholic. It did not matter much, and he was happy to answer to anything well meant. "I'm coming," he replied, slithering in the mud. It was thick and clinging, wet on the surface after the day's fine rain. The raiding party that Colonel Fyfe had sent over the top earlier in the evening had been expected by the Germans and met with stiff opposition. There had been casualties, and Joseph and Lance Corporal Goldstone were among those who had volunteered to see if they could find anyone wounded and still alive.

"Not much in the way of snipers now," Goldstone went on, picking his way over a narrow neck of land between craters swimming in water. The occasional star shell showed the nightmare landscape in blacks and grays, quagmires of thick, gluelike clay, pools of water and slime, dead trees, dead men and now and then horses, dismembered limbs floating, or arms sticking up like branches out of the flat surfaces of ditches and holes. It was impossible to tell where it was safe to put one's weight. Any step could suck you in, hold you and drag you down, as if it were a vast, filthy mouth pulling you toward some primeval belly to be swallowed into the earth and become part of it.

The wind whined a little, shrill where it whistled through the wires. There was a cold edge to it. It was difficult to remember that it was spring, though now and again one heard skylarks, even here, and behind the lines, in the burned and ruined villages, there were still wildflowers.

"This is the way they should have come, and we're getting close to the German lines," Goldstone continued huskily, his black, slightly awkward figure alternating between stark silhouette and invisibility ahead of Joseph. "Can't go a lot further. God, this stuff stinks!" He pulled his boot out of the filth with a loud squelch. "Everything tastes of mud and death. I dream about getting it in my mouth. There's quite a big crater over there. Can you see?

Could be one of our boys in it. We'd better go look."

Reluctantly Joseph obeyed, his feet sliding as he missed his balance and almost fell forward onto Goldstone, who put up his hand to save him. Just as they reached the rim of the crater another flare lit up the sky. The standard advice was to freeze, because movement attracted attention, but instinct was to fling yourself forward onto the ground. Goldstone had already dived in and Joseph followed without thought.

He landed in the soft, stinking mud and visions raced through his mind of falling helplessly into the toxic fluid, every desperate lashing out at it only sucking him in deeper until it filled his mouth and nose and then closed over his head. It was a wretched way to die. He would rather be shot.

A wave of relief swept over him as he came to an abrupt stop, against a body crouched in the mud.

"*Shalom*, Shlomo ben-Yakov. *Baruch he-Shem*," the body said. "Have you any news about the Arsenal for me?"

"*Shalom*, Isaac," Goldstone's distinctive voice replied from the darkness. "Impregnable defense, in my opinion. I don't see any attack getting past."

A sickening shudder went through Joseph as he realized that Goldstone must know this German well and was giving away military information.

"Mind you, if Manchester United are on form, they could give them a spot of bother," Goldstone went on. "But Chelsea are a joke at the moment — defense like a sieve. Arsenal knocked four past them last Saturday, without reply. Do you follow football, Padre?"

Joseph burst out laughing with crazy, hysterical relief, the sound of it echoing over the squelching mud and the wind in the wires. He was in no-man's-land discussing football scores with two Jewish soldiers. "Not really," he gasped, choking on his words.

"Some of your men were through here earlier this evening, but they neglected to give me the latest football scores," Isaac continued. "Some were killed, but we captured three."

"Isaac, this is Captain Reavley," Goldstone told him as another shell exploded twenty yards away, drenching them all in mud. Joseph slid a little further into the ice-cold water. "He's a padre," Goldstone went on. "Captain, this is *Feldwebel* Eisenmann, a keen Arsenal supporter, but apart from that, a good man. He used to visit our jeweler's shop in Golders Green quite regularly before the war."

"*Guten abend, Feldwebel* Eisenmann," Joseph said, wiping the filth off his face with the back of his hand. "I did not expect to bump into you this way."

The next flare showed a slight smile on Isaac's face as he turned toward Joseph. "We Jews have a saying, 'Next year, in Jerusalem.' One day, Father, we will have our own homeland. You will not see Jew fighting Jew like this then. We do not belong here. You Christians have 'borrowed' our religion and persecuted us for centuries, but soon, we hope we will be out of your way. As the prophet said, 'They shall beat their swords into plowshares, and their spears into pruning hooks. Nation shall not lift up sword against nation.' "

"And in the book of Joel," Joseph replied, quoting in classical Hebrew, "is it not written, 'Beat your plowshares into spears, and your pruning hooks into swords'? I used to teach Greek and Hebrew at Cambridge University. Lance Corporal Goldstone, I think we had better get back to our own lines."

"So you speak our language, Father Yusuf!" Eisenmann said. "I hope we shall meet again. *Shalom. Leheitra-ot.*"

"Until we meet again, Smiling One," Joseph replied, translating the meaning of Isaac's name as he scrambled to the edge of the crater.

"One last thing, Father Yusuf?" Isaac added.

Joseph hesitated, clinging to the rim. "Yes?"

"Let me know how Arsenal are doing, please?"

Another flare made them flatten to the ground, but it showed them very clearly where they were, almost twenty feet from the German wire ahead of them. There were bodies distinguishable more by form than color. Some of them could still be alive, although nothing moved. But then it never did in the light.

The flare faded and it seemed even darker than before. It was overcast and drizzling slightly, an almost impenetrable gloom. It was a vague comfort to know they were roughly where they had thought they were. Men got lost sometimes, and end up blundering into the enemy's trenches, instead of their own.

Eisenmann raised his hand in salute, then scrambled forward and in moments was lost in the darkness and drifting rain.

"I met him at Christmas," Goldstone said softly, an edge of tragedy in his voice. He inched forward in the mud. "But it won't happen again. There'll be no truce next year. We are going forward into the night, Chaplain. Nothing for us to laugh at together." He was referring to the bizarre incident of the German pastry chef who had been baking on Christmas Eve. Infuriated at the French troops still firing across the lines, he had seized a branch of Christmas tree and, still wearing his white baker's hat, had rushed out into no-man's-land to shout his outrage at such ignorance. And ignorance it had turned out to be. The troops in question were French Algerian, and therefore Muslim, and had no idea what was going on. Telephones had rung up and down the lines, and then the firing had ceased.

The chef, Alfred Kornitzke, had put the tree down, taken out matches, and solemnly lit all the candles. Then he had bellowed at them in the silent night, "Now you blockheads! Now you know what is going on! Merry Christmas!" And he returned unharmed to continue stirring his marzipan.

Joseph remembered Christmas with an exquisite pain still twisted inside him.

Never had heaven and hell seemed closer than as he had stood on the ice-crusted fire-step and stared across the waste with its wreckage of human slaughter, and in the stillness under the blaze of stars, heard the voice of Victor Garnier of the Paris Opera singing *"Minuit, Chrétiens, c'est l'heure solenelle."*

Utter silence had fallen on every trench within earshot. Along the whole length of the line, whatever his nature or his faith, not a man had broken the glory of the moment.

But that was gone now.

Joseph and Goldstone moved on toward the wire, slowly in the dark, crawling on their bellies, slipping where the clay was wet, fumbling in the mud and water to gain a foothold. Whenever a flare went up they flattened themselves to the ground and for a moment the pockmarked land was lit, tangles of wire shown up black against the dun colors of the earth, bodies caught in them like giant flies in a web.

They found several men dead, and one still alive. It took them nearly half an hour, working between flares, to pull him out of the mud without tearing off his injured leg and making the bleeding fatal. Then between them they carried him across the cratered land with its crooked paths and stumps of trees, its pockets of ice-cold water still carrying the faint, ghastly odor of gas, until they reached the parapet of the front trenches. They answered the sentry's challenge, and slithered over and down, only to find that the man was dead.

Joseph was momentarily overwhelmed with defeat. The two men in the trench and Goldstone were all looking at him, expecting him to say something to make sense of it. There was nothing, no sense — human or divine. It was not fair to expect him to have an answer, just because he represented the church. No concept within man was big enough to find sanity or hope in this. It was just day after day of blind destruction.

"Chaplain?" It was Peter Rattray, whom he had taught in Cambridge. Thin and dark, he'd had so much imagination and poetry in the translation of ancient languages. They had walked along the grass under the trees together, looking at students punting on the river, and discussed poetry. Now his face was smeared with blood, his hair was cut short under his cap, and he was asking Joseph to find reason for him in this chaos of death, to untangle from it a meaning, as they once had with difficult pieces of translation.

"We had to try," Joseph said, knowing the words were not enough. "He might have made it."

"Of course." Rattray rubbed the heel of his hand against his chin. "If it were me out there, I'd need to think you'd come for me — whatever." He grinned, a desperate gesture, white teeth in the flare of a star shell. "Are there any more?"

Joseph nodded, and he and Goldstone turned back to go over the parapet again as soon as there was another spell of darkness.

The next one they brought back alive, and handed him over to the stretcher party.

"Thanks, Chaplain," he said weakly, his voice barely a whisper. They carried him away, bumping elbows against the crooked walls of the trench, slithering on the wet duckboards and keeping balance with difficulty.

It was toward dawn when Joseph saw the body lying facedown at the edge of the shell crater and knew even before he reached it that the man had to be dead. His head was half submerged, as if he had been shot cleanly, and simply pitched forward.

There was still time before daylight to get him back. Better he be buried somewhere behind the lines, if possible, than lie here and rot. At least his family could be told, instead of enduring the agony of missing in action and never knowing for sure, seesawing up and down between hope and despair. He refused to imagine a woman standing alone every morning, facing another day of uncertainty, trying to believe and afraid to think.

He knelt down beside the man and turned him over, pulling him back a little. He was well built. Carrying him would not be easy. But since he was dead, he would not suffer if he were dragged.

There was a smudge of gray in the sky to the east, but it was still not possible to see much until the flares went up. Then it was clear enough: the bright hair and — even through the mud — Eldon Prentice's face.

Joseph froze, a wave of unreality washing over him. What in God's name had Prentice been doing out here? He had no business even in the front trenches, let alone in no-man's-land. Now he'd been killed! Joseph should get him back before daylight made it impossible. He was so tired every muscle in his body ached, his legs would barely obey him. Goldstone was over somewhere to his left, searching another crater, and there was no way he could carry a body back by himself. He would have to stand even to get him in a fireman's lift over his shoulder, and it was already too light to risk that.

Why was he bothering to take Prentice, of all people? He wasn't even a soldier. He had been responsible for Corliss's court-martial. Without Prentice's intrusion, Watkins would have let it go. And his gross insensitivity into Charlie Gee's mutilation still made Joseph cringe in the gut with misery and rage.

But if Joseph's faith, even his morality, were about anything at all, it must be about humanity. Like or dislike had nothing to do with it. To care for those you liked was nature; it only rose above that into morality when your instincts cried out against it. He looked down at the body. Prentice was barely thirty. Now he was just like any other man. Death reduced the differences to irrelevance.

The pale smear of light was broadening across the dun-colored sky.

He started to pull him, on his back, not to drag his face through the mud if he should have to drop him when there was a flare.

It seemed to take him ages to get across the open space. There were tree stumps in the way, and the body of a dead horse. Twice he slipped, in spite of the broadening light, and the weight of Prentice's body pulled him into shallow craters full of dirty water. The stench of dead rats and the decaying flesh of men too shattered to reclaim seemed to soak through his clothes onto his skin. But he was determined to get Prentice back so he could be buried decently. The fact that he had disliked him, that he was heavy and awkward in death just as he had been in life, made Joseph doubly determined. He would not let Prentice beat him!

"I will get you back!" he said between his teeth as Prentice's body once again slid out of his hands and stuck fast. Where the devil was Goldstone? "I will not leave you be out here, no matter how bloody awkward you are!" he snarled, yanking him over half-sideways. Prentice's foot squelched out of the clay and Joseph fell over backward at the sudden ease of it. He swore, repeating with satisfaction several lurid words he had learned from Sam.

He covered ten yards before the next flare made him scramble for the slight cover of a shell hole. Only another ten yards to go. Any moment now and the sniper fire would start. The Germans would be able to see movement in this light.

His shoulders ached with the dead weight, sucked down as if the earth were determined Prentice would be buried here, in this stretch of ruined land that belonged to no one. Joseph wondered in a fleeting thought if anything would ever grow here again. How absurd it was to kill and die over something already so vilely destroyed! There were other places, only a thousand yards away, where flowers bloomed.

Then suddenly Goldstone was there, heaving at Prentice's shoulders. They covered the last few yards and rolled him over the parapet and landed hard on the fire-step just as a machine gun stuttered and the bullets made a soft, thudding sound in the clay a few yards away.

"He's dead, Padre," Goldstone said quietly, his face in the dawn light filled with concern, not for the body but for Joseph, the second time in one night struggling so fiercely to save someone, too late.

"I know," Joseph answered, wanting to reassure him. "It's the war correspondent. I thought he should have a decent burial."

Two hours later Joseph was sitting on an empty ammunition box in Sam's dugout, considerably cleaner and almost dry. The rations had been given out by the quartermaster and brought up to the front line, so they had both eaten a good breakfast of bread, apple and plum jam, a couple of slices of greasy bacon, and a cup of hot, very strong tea.

Sam was sitting opposite Joseph, squinting at him through the haze of cigarette smoke, but it was better than the smell of death, or the latrines, and completely different from the gas three days before.

"Good," Sam said bluntly. "We've lost better men than Prentice, and we'll lose a lot more before we're through. I suppose your Christian duty requires that you affect to be sorry. Mine doesn't." He smiled bleakly, there was knowledge in it, fear, and a wry understanding of their differences, none of which had ever blunted their friendship. He required honor, laughter, courage, but never a oneness of view. "You can say a prayer over him," he added. "Personally I'll go and dance on his grave. He was always a rotten little sod."

"Always?" Joseph said quickly.

Sam squinted through the smoke. "I was at school with him. He was three years behind me, but he was a crawling little weasel even then. Always watching and listening to other people, and keeping notes." The shadows around his eyes were accentuated by the lantern light inside the dugout. It was too deep for daylight to brighten anything beyond the first step inside the door, and the high walls of the trench blocked most of that. "I've got enough grief for the men I care about," he added, his voice suddenly husky. He brushed his hand across his cheek. "God knows how many there'll be of them."

Joseph did not answer. Sam knew he agreed, a glance affirmed it without words.

There was a sound outside, a child's voice asking in French if anybody wanted a newspaper: "*Times, Daily Mail,* only yesterday's."

Joseph stood up. "I'll get you one," he offered. "Then I'd better go and see to the bodies." It was his duty to prepare men for burial, and after a bad night there was often no time for anything but the briefest of decencies. Identification was checked, tags removed, and any personal belongings, then the bodies, or what was left of them, were buried well behind the lines.

That was the least one could do for a man, and sometimes it was also the most.

He stood up, Sam watching him as he went, smiling. Outside he bought a paper from the boy who looked about twelve, and told him to take it to Sam, then walked back along the supply trench to the Casualty Clearing Station where the bodies had been taken. It was a soft, bright morning now, mist burned off except for the wettest stretches where the craters were still deep. He could hear the occasional crack of a sniper's shot, but mostly it was only the sounds of men working, someone singing "Good-bye Dolly Grey," and now and then a burst of laughter.

He reached the Clearing Station and found three men busy. The casualties had not been heavy last night, and there were only five dead. Joseph went to help the burial party because he felt obliged to pay some respect to Prentice, for his own sake. It was a kind of finishing. He was the one who had found him, he had brought him back. To walk away now, and then return to say the appropriate words over the grave, seemed an evasion.

There were two orderlies in the makeshift room — Treffy Runham, small, nondescript, always tidy; the other was

155

Barshey Gee, Charlie Gee's brother. He looked tired, dark rings around his eyes as if he were bruised, no color at all in his skin. They worked quickly, cracking bad jokes to cover the emotion as they made the dead as decent as possible and retrieved the few personal belongings to send back to those who had loved them. They looked up as Joseph came in.

"Mornin', Chaplain," Treffy said with a slight smile. "Could 'ave bin worse."

"Good morning, Treffy," Joseph replied. "Morning, Barshey." He moved straight over to help them. He had done it often enough there was no need to ask what was needed.

Barshey looked at him, eyes haunted, full of questions he dared not ask. Joseph knew what they were: Should he wish Charlie dead, out of his agony of mind as well as body, or was life sacred, any life at all? What did God require of you, if there was a God?

Joseph had no answer. He was as lost as anyone else. The difference was that he was not supposed to be. He didn't fight, he wasn't a sapper like Sam, or a doctor, an ambulance driver or anything else. All he was here for was to give answers.

He looked at the bodies. One was

Chicken Hagger. There were tears in his tunic and his flesh, as much of it as he could see, and several bullet holes. He must have been caught on the wire. It was a horrible death, usually slow.

Barshey was watching him, but he did not say anything.

Joseph walked over to Prentice's body. They had left him until last, possibly because the others were men they had known and cared about, almost family. Prentice was a stranger. This was nothing like a usual civilian death, shocking and unexpected. Nor was anybody looking for someone to blame, as with Sebastian Allard, and Harry Beecher in Cambridge last summer. Here it hardly even mattered how death had happened; there was nothing to learn from it, no questions to ask.

Even so, Prentice's body was unusual in that there were no marks of violence on him at all. He had not been shot, or blown apart by explosive or shrapnel, he had simply drowned in the filthy water of a shell hole. There were no tears in his clothes, except from when Joseph had dragged him over stony ground. There was no blood at all.

Not that that made him unique. Other

men had drowned. In the winter some had frozen to death.

All Joseph could do was lay him straight, clean the mud off his face, and tidy his hair. The fact that he had drowned had distorted his features, and the bruises from the beating Wil Sloan had given him were still dark and swollen, his lip cracked. But then no one was going to see him, unless it was decided to ship him home. That was a possibility, since he was not a soldier. Perhaps he had better wash him properly, even his hair. Today there was time for such gestures.

He fetched a bowl of water and rinsed out the mud and the rank smell from the shell crater. Barshey Gee helped him, holding another basin underneath so they did not slop the floor.

"What's that?" he asked as Joseph put a towel around Prentice's head and started to rub him dry.

"What?" Joseph saw nothing.

"You left mud on his neck," Barshey replied, his voice was cold. Someone must have told him about the incident in the Casualty Clearing Station. They shouldn't have done. It was a pain Barshey could have done without.

Joseph unwrapped the towel and looked.

There were dark smudges at the back of Prentice's neck, just below the fair gold hair. But he needed only a glance to see it was bruised skin, not mud. Another look showed him very similar marks on the right as well. They were roundish shapes, two on either side. He heard Barshey draw in his breath quickly, and looked up to meet his eyes. He did not need to say anything to know that the same thought was in his mind. Someone had held Prentice down, keeping his face in the mud until it had filled his lungs.

"Could someone do that?" he asked, hoping for denial. "Wouldn't he struggle? Throw them off?"

"Not if you had your weight on 'im," Barshey answered, huskily, his eyes not moving from Joseph's. "Knee in the middle of his back."

Joseph rolled the body over, standing beside him to prevent him from falling onto the floor. He lifted the jacket and shirt and looked at the dead flesh of his lower back. The marks were there, just small, no more than abrasions, and little pinpricks of bleeding as if he had tried to free himself, and chafed the skin on fabric pressed hard against him.

Barshey swore quietly. "Here, Treffy.

Come and look at this! Somebody held 'im down with 'is face in the mud, on purpose, till 'e drowned. Whoi the 'ell would anyone do that? Whoi not just shoot 'im?"

"Don't know," Treffy admitted, biting his thin lips. "Maybe 'e loikes to be personal. Or he was close to our lines, and wanted to be quiet?"

"What's wrong with a bayonet?" Barshey demanded, his eyes angry and frightened. "That's what they're for."

"Maybe 'e'd just lost a friend, or something?" Treffy suggested. "Just needed to do it with 'is 'ands. Best not tell anyone, don't you think, Chaplain?"

"Yes," Joseph agreed quickly, pulling Prentice's tunic down and rolling him over again onto his back and smoothing his hair into place. He had not liked the man, he understood Barshey's feelings only too well, and Wil Sloan's too. Even better did he understand Sam's. The trial of Edwin Corliss had been a nightmare, and without Prentice it need never have happened. Sam at least would not grieve, he would probably bless whatever German had done this.

"Yes," he said again. "Better not tell people. There's no need."

Joseph left the Clearing Station to go to

speak with the other casualties of the night, the wounded and the bereaved, men who had lost friends. Almost everyone belonged to a household, groups of half a dozen or so men who worked, ate, slept, and fought side by side. They shared rations, parcels from home, letter and news, a sense of family. They wrote to each other's parents and girlfriends; often they knew them anyway. Sometimes they had grown up together and knew and loved the same places, had played truant from school on the same summer days, and scrumped apples from the same farmer's trees.

In the trenches they sat huddled together for warmth, told ridiculous jokes, shared one another's dreams, and pains. They risked their lives to save one of their own, and a death was personal and very deep, like that of a brother.

He sat in the trench in the sun with Cully Teversham, who was busy running a lighted match over the seams of his tunic to kill the lice. He did it with intense care, his big hands holding the fabric gently, keeping the flame exactly the right distance away not to burn the threads.

Joseph was listening, as he did so often, but now, more than in the past, he was afraid that he would not have any answers.

If he said there was meaning to it all, a God of love behind the slaughter and the pain, would anybody believe him? Or would they merely think he was parroting the words expected of him, the things he was sent here to say, by people who had not the beginnings of an idea what the reality was like? What kind of a man looked on living hell like this, and mouthed comfortable, simple phrases he did not even believe himself?

A dishonest man, a coward.

Cully let the match go and lit another. "Is Charlie Gee going to make it?" he asked. "It ain't roight. Oi just got to loike 'im. We never knowed the Gees till we come 'ere, Whoopy an' me. Tevershams and Gees never spoke. All over a piece o' land, years back, it was. Don't even know roightly what 'appened. Something to do wi' pigs on it. Dug up everything worth 'aving. But that's pigs for yer. Everyone knows that."

Joseph said nothing, just listening.

"But they're alroight, Charlie an' Barshey are," Cully went on, keeping his head bent, the sun bright on his ginger hair. "An' that newspaper man ought never to 'ave bin in that Casualty place, let alone go sayin' what 'e did. Whoi don't they do something about that, instead o' nailing that poor bastard what got 'is hand tore to bits, eh?" He looked up at last, awaiting an answer from Joseph.

What was there to say? The truth was no use, and lies were worse. He could not tell them that he knew no sense in it, he was just as afraid as they were, perhaps not of maiming or of death, but that all his life he had striven to have faith in something that was beyond his understanding, and at the very worst, was a creation of his own need? What did he worship, except hope, and a desperate, soul-starving need for there to be a God?

He worshipped goodness; courage, compassion, honor, the purity of mind that knows no lies, even to oneself; the gentleness to forgive with a whole heart; the ability to have power and never even for a moment misuse it. The grace and the strength to endure, the fortitude to hope, even when it made no sense at all. To be found dead at one's post, if need be, but still facing forward. That was the answer he gave himself, and pieces of it he gave to others.

"I don't think they have the answers any more than we do," Joseph told him. "Major Wetherall will do everything he can for Corliss, and it doesn't matter about Prentice anymore." He looked up at the narrow strip of sky above the trench walls, the wind whipping mares' tails of cloud across it. Sometimes it was all the beauty they could see, a reminder of the rest of the world and the glory and purpose they fought to hold.

"I'm glad that bastard's dead," Cully said, dropping the spent match in the mud and regarding his tunic skeptically. Apparently it satisfied him, because he put it back on again. "Is that wicked?" he asked anxiously.

Joseph smiled. "I hope not!"

Cully relaxed. "He was pretty damn unlucky! He must've run bang into the only Jerry around there, 'cos we were to the east of where 'e was and Harper's lot were to the west. Don't know how any Jerry got through."

Joseph was puzzled, but he thought little more of it until later in the evening when he was helping Punch Fuller light a candle to heat tea. He overheard a conversation that made it clear there had been a patrol between the German line and where he had found Prentice.

"What time?" he asked.

"Well, I dunno, Chaplain," Punch said,

his eyes wide. "Line held, that's all I know. We lost Bailey, and Williams got hit in the shoulder, but no one got past us. I'd stake my life on that!"

It was Prentice's life Joseph was thinking about. "But there must have been one German got through," he argued. There had to be. Maybe that is why Prentice was drowned rather than shot? It began to make sense. A German had been caught, probably out on a reconnaissance of the British lines, and he was alone so he couldn't afford to make any noise at all, or he'd attract the attention of the patrol.

"Why's that, Chaplain?" Punch asked.

"I found one of our men dead," Joseph answered. "About twenty yards out directly in front of Paradise Alley." He named the length of trench as it was known locally.

"Then you must have found the Jerry, too," Punch said with certainty. "No one got back past us."

"He must have waited till you went, and then gone."

"We didn't come back till dawn," Punch assured him. "That's how we lost Bailey. Too damn slow. If a Jerry'd got up out of the mud and gone back, he'd 'ave passed right through us. Believe me, that didn't 'appen. We'd all 'ave seen him, us, our sentries, and theirs." He turned to Stan Meadows beyond him. "Isn't that right?"

Stan nodded vigorously.

"I must be mistaken," Joseph told him, and bent his attention to the candle in the tin, and the mug of tea. He was not mistaken, but he did not want anyone else to start thinking what was now racing through his mind. It was ugly, bringing back hard, painful memories of Sebastian's death, the surprise and suspicion, the broken trust and the knowledge he had not wanted. Death was grief enough; murder was a destruction of so many other things as well. It stripped away the protection of small, necessary privacies, and exposed weaknesses that at other times could have been guessed at, and then left to be forgotten.

Was this murder again? In the general carnage of war, had someone taken the opportunity to kill Prentice, in the belief his death would be taken for granted as just another casualty?

Who? That was something he did not even want to think about.

What would happen now if he told Colonel Fyfe what he had found? Everyone would know. The trust between men would be destroyed, the friendships that made life bearable; the bad jokes, the teasing, the willingness to listen, even to silly things, anxieties that were foolish, dreams that would never happen, simply in the act of sharing. The certainty that one man would risk his life for another was what bound them into a fighting force.

Suspicion of murder, and the questions that went with it, would poison that, and the cost here would be even greater than it had been in Cambridge. If he told Fyfe, an investigation would begin, justice might be found, or it might not, but at what price? Wil Sloan? Even Barshey Gee? Or one of the sappers who had been Corliss's friends? And if it were not found, if they never knew, then what shadow would be over them all, perhaps endlessly?

But surely among all the things he could not help, could not even ease, this was one small certainty he could. Prentice had been killed deliberately, by one of their own. The morality of that could not be changed by the fact that Prentice had been arrogant, insensitive, even brutal. To say that it could was to set himself up as an arbiter of who could or could not be murdered with impunity!

The fact that justice was impartial was

one absolute in a world descending into chaos. Truth was one certainty worth pursuing, finding, and clinging on to. Whatever the work or the pain involved, he had a purpose.

He did not speak to Colonel Fyfe. When he knew the cause and could prove it, that would be the time to act.

There were many things he needed to know. The very first was the one he dreaded most, and perhaps in his heart was the reason he had to find the truth. He could not forget Sam's rage at the court-martial of Corliss. The whole thing had been merciless, and it would never have happened had Prentice not pushed the issue. Perhaps Corliss had lost his nerve. He would not be the first man to have been pushed beyond his limit, and for an instant cracked. Men covered for each other. The moment of terror was kept secret. There were few men who did not understand.

Corliss was Sam's man, his to punish or to protect. That was what loyalty was about, and Corliss had trusted him, as his other men did.

How could he ask Sam? How could he now protect him? Only by proving that he could not be involved, before he began any inquiry.

Sam looked up from cleaning his rifle. "Was he?" he said without emotion.

"Yes." Joseph sat down beside him, ignoring the mud. "I have to find out who did it."

"Why?" Sam lit a cigarette.

"You can't go around murdering people, just because you think they deserve it," Joseph replied.

Sam smiled, his black eyes bright. "Better reason than because they're German."

Joseph did not smile back.

Sam's face darkened. "Leave it alone, Joe," he said quietly. "Lots of people had pretty good reasons for hating Prentice. This isn't peacetime England. Better men than Prentice are being killed every day. We have to learn to live with it, and face the fact that tomorrow it could be our turn, or that of someone we love, someone we'd give our own lives to protect. Have you seen Barshey Gee lately? He knows what happened to Charlie. He's his brother, for God's sake!"

"Are you saying Barshey Gee killed Prentice?" Joseph's mouth was dry.

"No, I'm not!" Sam snapped. "I'm saying he'll be suspected. So will Wil

Sloan, or any of my men. Or me!" He stared at Joseph unblinkingly. "I'd see him in hell, with pleasure."

"I know." Joseph's voice was little more than a whisper. "That's why I'm here. I want to prove you couldn't have, before I begin. Where were you when Prentice went over the top?"

"Down a tunnel under the German lines," Sam replied. "But I can't prove it. Huddleston saw me go down, but he didn't come with me."

Relief washed over Joseph like a blast of warmth. He even found himself smiling. "I had to ask," he said aloud.

"Leave it alone, Joe," Sam repeated. "You don't want to know!"

Joseph stood up. "Maybe I don't want to, but I have to. It's my job. It's about the only certain thing I can do."

Sam's face was puckered.

"Hannah sent me some Dundee cake," Joseph offered. "Come and have some after stand-to."

Sam raised his hand in half salute, and acceptance, then went back to cleaning his rifle.

Joseph knew it would not be easy. No one else wished to know what had happened to Prentice. He had been either tolerated or positively disliked by all the men. They answered Joseph's questions out of deference to him, but unwillingly.

"Dunno, Captain," Tucky Nunn said bluntly. "Don't see much out there, 'ceptin' what Oi'm doing meself."

"Sorry, Chaplain," Tiddly Wop Andrews said bashfully, pushing his hair back, as if it were still long enough to get into his eyes. "Nobody loiked 'im. After what 'e done to that sapper, nobody gave 'im the toime o' day. Couldn't say where 'e went."

"Oi saw 'im earlier on," Bert Dazely said, shaking his head. They were standing with their backs to the trench wall. It was raining very lightly and the wind was cold. Joseph offered him a Woodbine and Bert took it. "Thank you, Captain." He lit it and drew the smoke in thoughtfully. " 'E were asking a lot o' questions about how it felt to kill Germans. Oi said it felt bloody 'orrible! An' so it does. You know Oi can hear them on a still day, or if the wind's coming our direction?" He looked sideways at Joseph with a frown. "They call out to us, sometimes. Oi even got a couple o' their sausages once. Left 'em out there, for us, an' we left them a couple o' packets o' Woodbines and a tin o' Maconochies."

"Yes, quite a few men do that," Joseph agreed, smiling. "I've even had the occasional German sausage myself. Better than a Maconochie, I think."

Bert smiled back, but his face was serious again the moment after. His eyes were intense on Joseph's. "If Oi swap food with them one day, an' the next Oi'm goin' over and killing 'em, what does that make me, Chaplain? What kind of a man am Oi going to be when I go 'ome — if Oi do? 'Ow am I goin' to explain to moi children whoi Oi done that?"

The easy answer was on Joseph's lips, the answer he had already given many times: that a soldier had no choice, the decisions were out of his hands, there was no blame attached. Suddenly it felt empty, an excuse not to answer, an escape from himself.

"I don't know," he said instead. "Would you rather have been a conscientious objector?"

The answer was instant. "No!"

"Then it makes you a man who will, reluctantly, fight for what he loves, and believes in," Joseph told him. "Nobody said fighting was going to be either safe, or pleasant, or that there were not only risks of physical injury, but mental or spiritual, too."

"Yeah, Oi reckon you're right, Chaplain." Bert nodded. "You got a way of cutting to what's true, an' making sense of it. A man who won't foight for what he loves, don't love it very much. In fact maybe he don't love it enough to deserve keeping it, eh?"

"You could be right," Joseph agreed.

"Oi s'pose it's a matter o' deciding what it is you love?" He lifted up his head and looked at the sky. In the distance there was a flight of birds, south, away from the guns. He knew all of them, every bird and its habits. He could imitate the calls of most of them. "Oi think Oi know what matters to me — England the way it ought to be," he went on quietly. "People comin' an' goin' 'ow they want, quarreling and making up, a pint of ale at the pub, seed time and harvest. Oi'd loike to be married an' buried in the same church what Oi was christened in. Oi'd loike to see other places, but when it comes to it, Oi reckon Cambridgeshire's big enough for me. But if we don't stop Jerry here, doin' this to the poor bloody Belgians, boi the toime he gets to us, if he wants to, it'll be too late."

"Yes, I think it will," Joseph agreed, the thought twisting inside him with a pain that left him breathless. To think of the land he loved so fiercely, it was like part of his own being had been desecrated. It was unbearable.

"Thanks," Bert said sincerely. "You koind o' make things plain, right an' wrong."

Joseph drew in his breath to answer, then did not know what to say. It was his job here, to make sense of the chaotic, to justify the descent into hell, even to make intolerable suffering bearable because it had meaning, to insist that there was a God behind it who could make even this all right in the end.

Men like Bert Dazely would not condone murder in any situation at all. What was there left to believe in if Joseph knew Prentice had been killed by one of them, and did nothing about it? It would tear that delicate, life-preserving thread of trust, and plunge them into the abyss beneath.

If personal murder for vengeance, or to rid oneself of embarrassment or pain, were acceptable, what exactly was it they were fighting for? Bert had spoken of country things like the church and the pub, a village whose people you knew, the certainty of seasons, but what he meant was the goodness of it, the belief in a moral justice that endured.

To allow Prentice to be murdered, and do nothing, would be a betrayal of that, and he would not do it.

"Did you tell Prentice how you felt?" he asked.

Bert shook his head. "None o' his damn business, beggin' your pardon, Chaplain. Don't talk to the loikes o' him about things loike that. He weren't one of us."

Joseph already had a good idea exactly who had been in the area, or could have been so far as they were not known to have been somewhere else. Most men would be able to prove where they were on the front line, and most stretcher-bearers, medical orderlies, or other troops would have been no further forward than supply trenches, more probably in an advance first-aid post, or dugout.

And someone must have seen Prentice, possibly given him permission and assistance to go over the top. Which raised the question as to why he had been there at all! Had it been his own idea, or had someone suggested it to him, or even lured him there? Whatever Joseph asked, he must do it so discreetly no one suspected anything but an interest in informing Prentice's family of what had happened, and of course General Cullingford in particular. He still had to do that, at least as a courtesy. Someone else might have given him the bare facts.

He must ask his questions quickly, or his reasons would no longer be valid. One did not pursue the fate of any one man for more than a few days, there were too many others. The whole regiment was his concern.

He asked Alf Griggs quite casually where Prentice had been the afternoon beforehand, almost as if it were of no interest to him.

"First-aid dugout, Plugstreet way," Alf told him, lighting a Woodbine and shaking his head. He was a small, dapper man with the art of finding anything anybody wanted, at a price. "Bleedin' nuisance 'e were," he continued. "Followed the quartermaster around like a starvin' dog for I dunno 'ow long, till 'e got told ter get out of it, or 'e'd be carved an' served up fer dinner 'isself. Dunno w'ere 'e got ter after that." He drew on his cigarette. "Wot does it matter, Chaplain? Poor sod's gone west anyway."

"Just to give his family some idea of how he happened to get killed." Joseph was horrified how easily the lie came off his tongue. "Not so easy to understand when it's a journalist rather than a soldier."

"That one is not so easy ter understand 'ow 'e didn't get trod on long before!" Alf said with a curl of his lip. "Nasty little sod! Beggin' yer pardon, Reverend, but bein' dead don't make a man good, just means 'is badness don't matter anymore."

Joseph thanked him and went along the relatively straight route of the second-line trench to the stretch known as Plugstreet, after the nearby village of Ploegsteert. He found the first-aid dugout where a couple of stretcher-bearers were sitting having a smoke. A third was dozing, his feet sticking out in the weak sun, his boots unlaced. Near him the mud under the duckboards was nearly dry. The rain had stopped and the sky overhead was hazy blue, and just at this moment the guns were silent. There even seemed to be fewer rats than usual.

Lanty Nunn opened his eyes. "Allo, Chaplain. Lookin' for someone?"

Joseph squeezed his way past and sat down, making himself comfortable. "Only trying to find out a bit more about how the journalist got killed," he replied. "I expect the general will want to know — and his family. It's not as if he had been a soldier."

"It's not as if 'e'd bin any damn use at all!" Lanty retorted.

Whoopy Teversham, who had been half asleep, sat up on his elbows. He had bright ginger hair and features like rubber, able to assume any expression. "Chaplain, you don't want to tell the poor bastard's mother 'e was a pain in the arse," he said cheerfully. "Anyway, Oi expect she knew! Hell-bent on getting the story that'd make his name," he went on. "Into everything, asking questions. Oi thought he was going to write it up like he'd saved the Western Front single-handed. He wanted all sorts of facts and figures; wounded, gassed, sent home to Bloighty, where and how the dead was buried. Guess he knows that now, eh?" He laughed abruptly, and ended up coughing.

"Don't mind him, Chaplain," Lanty said dourly. "He don't know no better!"

Doughy Ward blinked, staring at Joseph with a frown. "Tell his family he went too far forward and got caught in cross fire. What does it matter? He's dead."

"He was drowned, actually," Joseph told him.

"Yeah?" Doughy opened his eyes wide. "We don't know what he was after up there, an' to be honest, Chaplain, we don't care. He were always poking his nose in, asking things what wasn't none of his business."

"Did he say anything to you about going over the top?"

"Didn't listen to 'im. Told 'im to go to hell, actually." He smiled.

"Looks like he did, an' all!" Whoopy said with a grin. "I'd have told him sooner, if I'd have known he'd go an' do it!"

"Not in front of the chaplain!" Lanty shook his head, looking at Joseph apologetically.

Joseph thanked them and went on searching. No one was very eager to help, and he felt their irritation that he was spending his time trying to find out something which they saw as irrelevant.

"He's dead," Major Harvester said tersely, his strong, bony face showing his weariness. "So are many better men. Do what you have to, Captain Reavley. Say all the right things, you can even be sorry, if you feel it's your duty, but after that, get back to our own men. That's what you're here for. Prentice was a damned nuisance. He got under everybody's feet. Well, it looks like he was in the wrong place at the wrong time once too often. I don't suppose he'll be the last war correspondent to be killed."

"I would just like to know how he got so far forward," Joseph persisted. "He wasn't supposed to be up there."

Harvester's face hardened. "Are you saying someone was to blame, Captain?"

"No, sir," Joseph denied quickly. He was not ready yet to tell Harvester the truth. "I don't doubt Prentice himself was to blame. I'd like to be able to prove it, if anyone asks."

Harvester relaxed. "You have a point. Sorry for jumping to the wrong conclusion. But I've still no idea how he got past the second trench, let alone the fire trench."

Nor could Joseph find any sentry for that night willing to say they had recognized Prentice among the figures going over the top. In the brief flares, one man with a rifle in his hands looked much like another. And it was perfectly obvious that none of them cared. They were not insubordinate enough to tell him to leave it alone and attend to the living, but their smoldering anger was clear enough.

But someone had killed Prentice deliberately. It had not been accident or misfortune of war, but murder, and the wrongness of that was one certainty in the chaos and loss that Joseph could do something about. The difficulty of it, the fact that no one else cared, even his personal contempt for Prentice, if anything, sharpened his resolve.

Chapter

FIVE

Major Hadrian asked once more if there was anything he could do, then, tight-lipped and unhappy, he closed the door and left Cullingford and Judith Reavley alone in the room. Since the arrival of the British Army the small château, really what in England would have been called the manor house, had been used as divisional headquarters. It was late April, five days since the gas attack, and the situation was increasingly serious. The men in the trenches knew only their own stretch of a thousand yards or so, a platoon, a brigade, but Judith had driven Cullingford around the entire area, and she had seen how few men there were, how short they were of ammunition and the difficulty of getting it up to the front lines, along with everything else. The roads were jammed with troops, horses, refugees, ambulances, even wagons and dogcarts with household goods, terrified women and children seeing a lifetime in ruins.

Cullingford stood in front of the window. The rain drifted in silver sheets across the land, spattering against the glass one minute, the sun making prisms of it the next. The pale light showed the fine lines in his face and the weariness around his eyes and mouth. He stood upright, a little stiffly, but then he always did. It was not only habit, it was part of his inner defense. He had come so close to breaking it: Once he had knelt and spoken to a gassed man, and stayed with him while he died, talking quietly, telling him it was bad, but they would win. He had had no idea whether it was true or not. The other time it had been an injured horse that had moved him beyond his power to hide. He had been in the cavalry in his youth. The loyalty of an animal touched him where he could not allow the emotion of a man to reach.

He knew she had seen his tiredness, the times when he was too vulnerable to hide the fear of failure, the pain of guilt for other men's deaths, and the fact that he had no more knowledge than the rest of them about what to do to prevent more slaughter, even final defeat. But he had to pretend, their faith depended on it. That was the job of leadership, to endure being thought callous; to defend your mistakes, even when you know them to be mistakes.

They had never spoken of it. If they shattered the illusion of separateness with something as tangible as words, then it would have to be faced, and there was neither time nor strength for that.

"Miss Reavley," he said quietly, without turning toward her. "You told me that your father was killed just before the outbreak of war, and you implied that there was a conspiracy behind it, of great depth and dishonor. You said it was political rather than financial, and that if it had succeeded it would have altered Europe, perhaps even the world. I haven't been able to get it out of my mind. The loss . . ." He did not finish the sentence, it was too painful, too intrusive. "Were you exaggerating?" He asked only to dispel the last possible uncertainty.

She had told him only the barest outline, and then in such broken sentences she was surprised he had remembered so much. They had been stuck at Hellfire Corner, the engine had stalled and darkness was closing in. It had taken her a quarter of an hour in the rain, under sporadic fire, to change and re-gap the spark plugs and jury-rig the commutator to get them as far as Ploegsteert, where they could get proper parts to replace the old ones.

Afterward, when they sat drinking hot tea with rum in it, hands shaking, uniforms soaked and crusted with mud, she had realized just how close she had come to being killed. Heavy artillery fire had landed less than twenty feet away, sending earth and stones whining through the air, clanging against the car, and shrapnel landing within inches of them both.

He had said nothing, treating her as if she were a soldier like himself, and expected to remain calm. His absence of special treatment was the highest compliment he could have paid her. She knew it was not indifference; the warmth in his eyes made that thought ridiculous.

It was after that, when they could relax for half an hour, before she went to see to the car, and he to receive Hadrian's report on the other sectors, that she had told him about the fatal car crash, the missing document. She had not told him what it had said — that was too dangerous to repeat — nor that Matthew was still looking for the brilliant and terrible mind that had conceived it.

He turned around to face her at last. There was humor in his eyes, but it was only on the surface. "You were very circumspect, but I believe that you know a great deal more than the few details you spoke of," he said drily. But he was watching her, trying to gauge her pain and how far he must probe into it, and what harm that would do. "You said your father had been a member of Parliament. He would not lightly speak of England's dishonor, or a conspiracy that would alter the world."

"No." She stood very still. How profoundly everything she knew had changed in that time, less than a year. Last spring she had been in St. Giles, aimless, discontented, fretting against the bounds of a society basking in a golden peace she did not yet know to treasure. She had taken for granted the comfort of physical safety, clean linen, the smell of furniture polish, fresh milk, domestic duties, the boredom of the known.

Now it was like a lost world, a dream in the mind shattered on waking, the loneliness of being grown-up, separate, driven by duty and reality, looking back with longing when a moment of peace allowed.

He deserved honesty. "It was real," she said. "I imagine it still is. My brother Matthew is certain we inflicted only a temporary defeat. It is another war, different weapons from this, only a few people who know they're fighting it, the rest of us to be moved around like herds of animals, but it's a shadow of this one. Except I think that's not true, it is the real one, and we are the reflection cast, the unreality, pulled by it, not pulling."

"Eldon spoke of a new order." He was looking at her intently now. "He seemed to imagine he would have a place in it. He had a passion in him, as if he were a disciple rather than an adventurer, and certainly not simply a tool of someone else's cause. What political conspiracy could inspire that in him, Miss Reavley?"

"Peace," she replied quietly.

He was startled. "Peace!"

"At the cost of surrendering France and Belgium in return for German military help to regain our lost colonies, like America."

"God Almighty!" He was ashen. "Are you sure?"

"That is what the document said."

"But you don't know who is behind it?"

"No. We call him the Peacemaker, but we have only the vaguest idea who he must be." Was she telling him more than she should? Had she already broken her promise to Matthew and Joseph in telling

Cullingford this much? But he could not be connected with it! He had given his life to fighting to defend the country he loved and the way of life he believed in. If all of them were so distrustful they spoke to no one, that in itself would ensure the Peacemaker's victory.

Cullingford was waiting. He looked tired and so easy to hurt. Prentice was his nephew and she knew from Hadrian's expression, the odd words he had let slip to her, awkwardly, as if he wanted her help but would not ask for it, that the relationship was difficult, full of criticisms and resentments. Their values were different and they were too close to disagree with respect.

Suddenly she was furiously angry with Prentice for his supreme self-centeredness in allowing his petty family squabbles to make even one man falter in his step, let alone a general upon whom other lives depended.

"The Peacemaker has to be someone who had access to both the kaiser and the king, sir," she said firmly. "Someone with the total arrogance to assume that they have the moral right to make decisions that affect the rest of the world, without even telling us, let alone asking us. And he had to know both Sebastian Allard and my father personally. That narrows it down rather a lot, but it still leaves dozens of people — I think."

"Who is Sebastian Allard?" he said gently, as if he guessed, although he spoke of him in the present.

She forced herself to keep her voice steady, but it was difficult. Her breath was tight in her chest. "The student of Joseph's who killed my parents, to get the document back."

"And failed . . ."

"Yes."

"I see. I think we may assume that the Peacemaker has not given up his aim. The question is how has he redirected his forces, and what are his targets now?" He bit his lower lip. "He will want the war over as soon as possible, and presumably he does not care greatly who wins. No! No, it would be better for his purposes if Germany does. The kaiser must already have signed the treaty, because it was on its way to the king. We do not know if the king would have signed it or not." He began to pace back and forth, four steps and then turn, four steps and then turn, restless, caged in by more than the plastered and paneled walls. "Germany, he can rely on,

England he cannot. But if Germany wins, then a new government would be formed in England — one that would do as Germany told it — it would have no choice."

Judith stood still, watching him, cold inside. John Reavley would have liked him. They had the same kind of quiet, irresistible logic. It was utterly reasonable, and yet it never frightened her because the human warmth and the rueful humor were always there, an inner tenderness that once given was never lost.

"If I wanted England beaten quickly," he went on, concentrating with desperate intensity, "what would I do? Attack our weakest point . . ."

"Break through at Ypres?" Her voice was a whisper. "With more gas? Drive for the coast . . ."

"No," he looked at her, shaking his head. "Too costly. We are weak, but we're far from beaten. The use of gas didn't work. The men are more resolved than ever to fight to the last yard. It's a dirty war. They'll never surrender now."

"What then?"

"Attrition, but swiftly. Without reinforcements we can't last long. If I were in the man's place, I would attack morale at home, cripple Kitchener's 'new army' before it begins. Dry up recruitment."

"How?"

"That's the question. If we can find out how, we might stop him." His face tightened. "I need to speak to Eldon again."

"What can you say?" Now she was frightened he would betray them, unintentionally. Yet what could he say that the Peacemaker did not already know?

He smiled ruefully. "I have no idea," he confessed. "I . . ."

Before he could finish his sentence there was a sharp knock on the door and as soon as he answered, Hadrian came in.

"Is Colonel Fyfe here already?" Cullingford asked unhappily.

Hadrian was acutely unhappy. He was as immaculately tidy as always, but his face looked crumpled and he jerked his tunic down absentmindedly.

"No, sir, Captain Reavley, the chaplain from the second division. He says it's urgent, sir. I . . . I think you should see him."

A little of the color ebbed from Cullingford's face.

"I'm sorry, sir," Hadrian said with intense gentleness filling his eyes, and confusion, as if several emotions twisted inside him at once.

Unconsciously Cullingford straightened

his shoulders. "Ask him to come in."

"Would you like me to leave, sir?" Judith asked. She desperately wanted to stay. Whatever it was, she would learn of it sooner or later, why not now? Or was privacy kinder?

There was no time for him to answer. The door opened again and Joseph came in. He was thinner than the last time she had seen him, his face gaunt under the high cheekbones. He must have been aware of her, but he gave no sign, facing Cullingford squarely.

"Captain Reavley," Cullingford acknowledged. "What is it?"

"I'm extremely sorry, sir," Joseph said levelly. "But I have to tell you that Mr. Eldon Prentice, a war correspondent with the *London Times*, was killed in no-man's-land the day before yesterday. Colonel Fyfe asked me to tell you personally, since we believe he was closely related to you, rather than inform you in dispatches. He was buried with the other soldiers who fell that night, but if you believe his family would prefer his body to be shipped home, it could still be arranged."

Cullingford frowned. "The day before yesterday, you said?"

"Yes, sir. He was found in no-man's-land. I brought him back myself. I hoped that I would be able to tell you why he was there, and what happened to him, but I'm afraid I don't know yet."

"Yet? You expect to?" Cullingford was still confused, stunned by shock. He had heard of or seen the deaths of thousands of men, an average of a score a day, but it was still different when it was someone of your own family. The fact that one did not especially like the individual was irrelevant. It was blood that stirred the loss, the emptiness in the pit of the stomach, nothing to do with affection.

"I intend to, sir," Joseph said calmly. "It was extraordinary for a newspaper correspondent to be in the forward trenches at all, he should never have been in no-man's-land."

"No," Cullingford agreed. "It was a breach of discipline, but his, Captain, not the army's. If the army writes to his mother, I would be grateful if you did not make an issue of that. He was . . ." He stopped. He had been about to ask for emotional privilege, and he despised it in others. It was unprofessional. "I'm sorry," he apologized. "There is no need to ship his body home, any more than any other man's. Flanders clay is an honorable grave."

Joseph smiled, a momentary gentleness changing his features dramatically. "Of course. And as far as the record will show, he was a man of unusual courage, risking his life in pursuit of truth." There was an odd irony in his voice.

Cullingford picked it up. "I presume he was shot by the Germans, and you will tell her so. If he was caught on the wire, she does not need to know that."

"That's always how people die, sir," Joseph answered him. "But actually Mr. Prentice was drowned." He stopped. There was something pinched in his face, an unhappiness far more personal than the fact that he was bringing news of bereavement to someone. He was used to that.

Judith fidgeted, moving her weight, and for the first time Joseph turned to look at her. There was no smile in his eyes, only a kind of desperation. Judith felt it like something tangible in the room. She could not ask. She was merely a driver, like a servant. She was less even than a regular army private. She bit her lip, her breath hurting in her lungs. She knew Joseph too well.

Cullingford looked at her, then back at Joseph. "Is there something else, Captain Reavley?" he said softly.

"Not yet, sir."

Cullingford stood very still. "You did not say 'he drowned,' Captain, you said 'he was drowned.' Do you mean that some German soldier found him out there, and held his head under the water?"

Joseph said nothing.

Cullingford let out his breath very slowly. "Thank you for taking the time to come and tell me personally, Captain Reavley. If you could tell me where he is buried, I should like to pay my respects, for his mother's sake."

"Yes, sir. It is just beyond Pilkem. I can show you, if you wish?"

"Yes, please. Then I can go on to Zillebeke. Miss Reavley, will you fetch the car."

Judith drove, Joseph and Cullingford sat in the back. It was a bright, sharp spring day, sunlight one moment, drenching thundershowers the next, and the air was still cold with a cutting edge to the wind.

She drove in silence, aware of the crowding emotions that must be pulling Cullingford one way and then the other. She understood grief, confusion, anger, and how hard it was to fight through them without someone to listen, to help you find the reasons why you could miss someone so fiercely whom you have never missed in life.

She missed her mother. They seemed to have spent little time together, and much of that in quiet disagreement, pursuing different dreams, and yet the ache of loneliness that now she could never go back was deeper than she could have imagined. She missed all the comfortable little things that used to imprison her: time taken to cut and arrange flowers, the need to polish the silver or move the photographs when dusting the table. Now she thought of them as the cords of sanity that held her safe from the emotional violence of life. She caught herself thinking if only she could find a telephone she would hear her father's voice. And then she remembered, and the tears choked her.

They were driving slowly along the rutted road toward Pilkem. They passed supply trucks going the other way, and long wagons drawn by horses, mostly laden with the powder shells. There was nothing to do but move as they could, wait when they had to, overtaking would be both dangerous and pointless. There were others ahead anyway, as far as she could see along the flat, straight road.

They pulled up where an ambulance had lost a wheel and men from a small column of relief troops were helping replace it, working patiently in the rain. She looked back at Cullingford in the seat behind her, half in apology for not being able to do any better. He was staring at the windscreen, his eyes unfocused. Was he thinking of his sister and how she must be feeling, and that he could not be there to say or do anything to help her? Had she been proud of her son, knowing only what he said of himself?

Alys would have been proud of Judith, and terrified for her as well. But then every mother in Britain was terrified for someone. Probably every mother in Germany, too, and so many other countries.

Cullingford's face was impassive. He stared ahead. Only some delicacy of his lips indicated any feeling at all. She knew he had quarreled with Prentice because Hadrian had been furious about it. Hadrian was a quiet man, driven by duty and loyalty, meticulous in his job. The intensity of his emotion had startled her, as had the fact that he had refused absolutely to say what the quarrel was about.

Was Cullingford thinking of that, too, his mind racing over the reconciliation there could have been in the future, and now never would be? Did he think of Prentice as he had been when he was a child, times they had spent together when the world was so utterly different? They had been innocent, incapable of imagining the storm of destruction that had descended on them now. She still saw that bright, vulnerable look in the eyes of new recruits, when they did not know what the stench meant, and believed they could do something brave and noble that would matter. They had no conception how many of them would die before they had a chance to do anything at all, beyond the willingness, and the dream.

It took them half an hour to reach the place. The rain had stopped but the mud was still slick and in the pale sun the wet grass glittered with drops of water. Major Harvester met them, looking stiff, formal, and somewhat embarrassed.

"I'm very sorry, sir," he said, saluting smartly. "Please accept my condolences."

Cullingford looked at him with a flash of bitter humor. Judith wondered if he knew how Prentice had been disliked, and how much it hurt him. Whatever he had felt himself, Prentice was family. His loyalties must be torn.

"Thank you," he accepted.

Harvester remained where he was, standing to attention on the strip of mangled grass. Judith could see in his sensitive, bony face that he felt he should add something more, the usual remarks that the dead man had been good at his job, loyal, brave, well liked, all the things one says over graves. Decency, even pity, fought within him against loyalty to his own men, and the truth. It was a kind of betrayal to use the same words for Prentice as for a soldier killed in battle. He stood there tongue-tied, unable to do it.

Judith agonized for him, and for Cullingford. It was too late for Prentice to redeem himself now; he would be remembered as he was. Perhaps only his family would think of him as he could have become.

Cullingford rescued him. "There is no need to say it, Major Harvester," he said quietly. "Mr. Prentice was not a soldier. He does not warrant a soldier's epitaph." His voice shook so very slightly that probably Harvester did not even hear it.

"He . . . he was doing his job, sir," Harvester said, his face softening with gratitude.

Joseph spoke at last. "Would you like to come this way, sir?" he asked. "I'll take you to the grave."

"Thank you." Cullingford followed him.

Judith waited behind. She had disliked

Prentice. She had no right to go now as if she mourned him, and perhaps Cullingford would value a few moments of privacy for whatever grieving duty permitted him. She watched him go, stiff and upright, intensely alone.

A sergeant came over and offered her a mug of tea. Harvester went about his duties.

Twenty minutes later Cullingford came back, his face white, his eyes bright and oddly blind. He thanked Joseph and walked to the car. Joseph looked for a moment at Judith, his face shadowed with anxiety. She would like to have had time to speak to him, ask how he was, and above all, what he had meant by his strange remarks about Prentice's death. But not only was Cullingford her duty, he was her chief concern also. She smiled fleetingly at Joseph, and went to the car.

Cullingford was already seated, waiting for her, this time in the front passenger seat. Judith cranked the engine, climbed in and drove back onto the road toward Zillebeke.

She would like to have said something good about Prentice, but she knew nothing. To invent it would have been intolerably patronizing, in a way making it even more obvious that invention was necessary.

She was weighed down by a savage awareness of how alone Cullingford was. The men expected him never to show fear, exhaustion, or doubt of final victory. If he had weaknesses or griefs, moments when he was overwhelmed by the horror of it all, he must keep them concealed. There was no one at all with whom he could share them.

Joseph must have seen the conflict in him over Prentice's death. He might have understood it as grief for his family, pity for his sister, regret for all the possibilities now gone, and perhaps a thread of guilt because he had disliked Prentice and found him a professional embarrassment. He respected the ordinary fighting man, British or German. He understood their strengths, and their weaknesses, and he hated intrusion into their privacy, or their need. Prentice had violated both.

But she did not know how to find words that would not commit exactly that same intrusion, and let him know how much of his emotion she had seen.

"I'm sorry for Mr. Prentice's death, sir," she said finally.

The traffic was slowed to a crawl. He

looked at her. "Are you? It is unlike you to express a sentiment you do not feel, Miss Reavley, for courtesy's sake." There was the ghost of a smile on his lips. "Eldon was eminently dislikable, don't you think?"

She was startled by his frankness. Had she made her feelings so very obvious?

"I'm sorry, sir, I didn't mean to . . ." How could she finish? "To have been so . . ."

"Honest?" he suggested, his eyes bright and surprisingly uncritical.

"Undisciplined," she corrected him, looking away, the heat burning up her face.

"Discipline does not require that you swallow your own ideas of morality," he answered, turning sideways a trifle to look at her more comfortably. "You must have heard about the court-martial of the sapper, and the way Eldon behaved when Charlie Gee was brought into the Casualty Clearing Station?"

Of course she had heard. She knew it was Joseph who had restrained Wil Sloan from half killing Prentice. She was profoundly grateful for that. She liked Wil enormously. He was brave, funny, and generous. She loved the stories he told of working his way across half of America on the railroads in order to get passage to

England for the war. She also knew he had had to leave his hometown in the Midwest in an indecent hurry after losing his temper once before.

Cullingford was right about what she had thought. She hated being put in the position of not knowing whether she should deny it or not. He was Prentice's uncle, and had probably known him since he was born! He had to care, even if largely for his sister's sake. She would love Hannah's children, whatever they did. It was not a choice; she could not help it. But Prentice had still been an insensitive man who put his own advancement before basic decency in the face of human pain.

"Yes, sir, I'm afraid I did." The words were said from a depth of feeling, and she only thought afterward of how they might hurt him. "I'm sorry."

"Please do not keep saying you are sorry, Miss Reavley. It is growing tedious. And don't treat me like an aged aunt. Your honesty is one of your better qualities — along with your ability to mend a car."

She was confused, uncertain how to react, and she felt ridiculous that it mattered so much to her.

Then he smiled suddenly, which lit his face and took the tiredness from it. Images raced in her mind. What was he like away from war? What sort of man was he when circumstance did not force him into this hideous extremity of planning and executing death, having this unnatural power and answerability for the hope, morality, and survival of thousands of other men? What did he do when he was on leave? Did he like gardening, playing golf, walking? Did he have a dog, and did he love it, touch it with unbearable gentleness, as her father had? What music did he listen to? What books did he read? Who were his friends?

"A penny for your thoughts, Miss Reavley?"

Again she felt herself coloring. Thank God he could not know! "I wasn't thinking of Mr. Prentice," she answered.

"No, neither was I," he admitted. "If I had thought you were, I would probably have reduced it to a ha'penny."

She smiled back, and told him a half truth. "I was wondering what we would be doing if we were not here." She knew the answer for herself. She would be living the same rather purposeless life she had before the war. She would take part in all the usual village events, feeling unnatural and inadequate at it, watching time slip by having done nothing that made more than superficial difference. She could be wondering if she would settle for marrying someone she was merely fond of, someone who would be predictable, kind to her, who would behave with honor, whom she would probably even like, but never love with all the passion she could feel. Would he be someone she could live with, but not someone she could not bear to live without?

Cullingford fished in his pocket and put a penny on the dashboard.

"I would probably be driving," she said aloud, not meeting his eyes. "But not really going anywhere, just around the village, trying to do what my mother would have done. Do I have to find a penny for you to tell me what you would be doing, if there were no war?"

"You have a penny," he pointed out.

"Somewhere, but I don't know where."

"I paid you. That one is yours."

"Oh! Well, it's yours again, then. What would you be doing?" She wanted intensely to know.

"It's nearly May. I would be walking down to the woods to see the bluebells," he said without hesitation. "I would follow the path between the wild pear trees right into the middle of the flowers, where it all but disappears and you can hardly see where to put your feet without treading on them. It would be full of the sunlight and silence. I would stand there and let it sink into me until I was part of it."

She was seized with an overwhelming hunger to do all the same things, to do them with him, not to say anything, simply to be there.

"It sounds like a lot more use than anything I would do," she said quietly.

"If you would try to pick up the pieces of the things that your mother used to do for others, is that not useful?" he asked. There was a startling gentleness in his voice. "Isn't that what we do, when we miss someone almost beyond bearing?"

She looked away from him; his eyes were too tender, too probing. "I hadn't thought of it." She choked on the words. "I suppose it is. I miss my father more. He would have gone walking, only he would have taken Henry, our dog." She blinked rapidly. Her throat was so tight she could hardly speak. "I miss dogs — I miss dogs I could have as friends. You can't do that here, they're all messengers, or something. And I can't bear caring about them, because I know how many of them get killed."

Ahead of them the traffic was moving again, and she eased the car into gear and started forward. "It's bad enough to lose people. I can't cope with it when it's animals. Don't tell me that's stupid, and wrong. I know it is."

"I don't know how wrong it is to love anything, or not to love it," he replied, looking away from her and toward the traffic ahead. "I haven't learned how to prevent it." His voice shook a little. "With me it's the horses."

A dozen answers streamed through her head, and none of them were what she wanted to say. There had been a depth of emotion in him that was far more powerful than the simple meaning of the words. She put all her attention to driving, forcing everything else out of her consciousness, because she could not cope with it.

It was after they had returned to Poperinge, late in the evening, and extremely tired, that he spoke to her again. They were eating at their usual estaminet, Le Nid du Rat, in English the Rat's Nest, a small, comfortable place with half a dozen tables. They had stew, consisting mostly of vegetables, and good bread. Today she was acutely aware of how much better it was than anything Joseph would have. She had seen something in his face that troubled her, a kind of blind, painful purpose deeper than simply the duty to tell Cullingford of Prentice's death. He had suggested that he had been killed by someone who knew him, a British soldier, not a German one. If that was true then it was not an act of war, it was murder. And surely, after the past, Joseph of all people would not accept that unless he was forced to. There must be evidence he could not escape.

Could it be Wil Sloan after all? How violent was his temper? Before driving Cullingford she had driven ambulances nearly all the winter, much of it with Wil. There were ways in which she knew him even better than she did her own brothers. She was familiar with the rhythm of his work, exactly how he liked his tea, how he curled over sideways when he slept, the patterns of his speech, how he hated the lice and would scratch himself raw, and then be ashamed of it. She knew precisely which jokes would make him laugh, and which would embarrass him.

If Wil had been so appalled at Charlie Gee's injuries that the horror had overwhelmed him, maybe frightened him out of control, could he have gone after Prentice, out to no-man's-land, and pushed his head under the water? Perhaps they had quarreled about it again, and the misery had come back, the utter blinding helplessness of it. It would not be Prentice that Wil was lashing out at, just Prentice's blind, uncaring face; Prentice as a symbol of all that hurt too much to bear.

And if that were true, she would lie in her teeth to protect him. The law might require Wil to answer for it, justice did not, not to her.

She looked up and met Cullingford's eyes. He was watching her anxiously, and there was the same shadow in his gaze. But he did not know Wil Sloan. Who was he worried for? Or was it just the fear that someone had hated Prentice enough to kill him?

"I imagine your brother does not speak lightly?" he said, ignoring his food. It was a question that demanded honesty, even though they both longed for comfort, anything except one more burden.

"No," she answered. She could feel her stomach hurt. How was she going to answer him if he asked about Wil? Suddenly her loyalties were torn in a way for which she was totally unprepared. Cullingford was authority. He could not turn a blind eye. She could, and must. But she would hate lying to him. "But I don't think he knows anything," she went on.

His smile was sad, self-mocking, as if he understood her dilemma, and what she would do, and found a bitter humor in it. "Of course not," he agreed. "Not yet. But he sees a cause of truth there. He's a priest. He is used to thinking of morality in absolutes, and letting God take care of the broken pieces."

Now she was really frightened. She wanted to ask him what he meant, as if she were a child and he the adult to explain it for her and make it right. But if she wanted him to see her as a woman, in moments away from duty as something like an equal, then she must also accept the loneliness and the decisions, and the blame.

"Joseph will try to find out what happened," she agreed. "And if someone is responsible, who it is."

"I see." He picked up his fork, but he did not eat any more.

"Are you afraid it is someone you know?" she asked.

He looked up quickly. "Do you know?"

"No. But that is what occurs to me."

"Hadrian?" There was a wealth of

misery in his face, as if he himself were guilty of it.

She smothered her surprise, turning her gasp into a cough. It had never occurred to her that Hadrian's very clear dislike was anything more than a proficient soldier's contempt for a man who did not understand the army or its rules and conventions, and had no genuine respect for its men.

"Surely he didn't dislike him sufficiently to do that?" She tried to believe it, remembering the loathing in Hadrian's eyes as he had watched Prentice leave when he had come to see Cullingford a few days ago. Cullingford had given him written permission to pass almost anywhere he wanted. It was a defeat for Hadrian, who had told him such a thing was impossible.

A sane man did not kill for such a reason. Where was sanity here when a score of men could be killed in a night, for no worthwhile reason at all? Everything was exactly the same the day after, most times not a yard lost, nor gained. And it was all meaningless mud anyway, poisoned and violated beyond any conceivable use.

Yet looking at Cullingford's face, she saw the fear in his eyes was perfectly real — he believed Hadrian could be guilty, and it hurt him, with grief for the fact, and fear of what it would mean in the future.

She made herself smile. "I don't think so," she said with a conviction she imitated from him, thinking of him assuring injured men, lying with supreme ease. "He's too military to do anything so rash. He'd have had to leave his own post. He wouldn't do that on the night of a raid."

He smiled back at her, forcing himself to relax as well, let go of it as an act of will. "No. It was a foolish thought." He picked up his glass and sipped the rough wine. "I didn't like Eldon, but his death is . . . painful. I cannot return to England for some time, with things as they are. My sister Abby is a widow, and she is going to find this very hard."

She became aware of how acutely it embarrassed him to admit to such emotions. "You would like me to take some message to her?" she asked, to save him having to.

Then she was afraid she had presumed!

He looked at her with luminous candor. "Please? You know what grief is like. You could speak to her without being sentimental, which she would hate. Loss needs honesty. Nerys, my wife, would not . . ." He stopped, unable to finish the sentence without committing a betrayal. "She does not know a great deal of the reality of war." His hand fiddled with the small salt spoon on the table. "There is no need to harrow people with details of violence and suffering they cannot help. And certainly not of . . . of your brother's suspicions. It would add . . . to Abby's pain. She needs to think of Eldon as what he might have become, not what he was."

His words were very spare, little more than a sketch, but she saw in it an outline of loneliness that hurt too much to acknowledge. What part of his life did he share with Nerys if he could not tell her of the horror he saw, the fear, the overwhelming physical discomfort of the trenches; or the jokes, the friendship, the sacrifice and the sheer kindness as well? Now of all times, what was there left of meaning in the trivia of life, the things that floated past the windows of the soul but never touched the inner being, pictures without substance.

"Of course I'll go and see Mrs. Prentice," she said quickly. "I can tell her as much or as little as you like. I can say I met him several times, and that he was dedicated to his job, and brave enough to do it without fear for his own safety. I can tell her what it is like here — or conceal it, as you think best."

"Thank you." He broke a piece of bread off in his fingers and ate it slowly. He looked at her with intense gravity. "I shall leave it to your judgment what you say to her. I . . . I haven't seen her much lately. I . . ." He gave a shrug so slight his shoulders did not even pull his uniform. "I should have given her more time, especially after Allen died." He made no excuses.

"I can go the day after tomorrow," she offered. "If you give me the address and perhaps a letter to explain to her who I am, so she does not think I am simply intruding."

"Of course."

She thought he wanted to say more, but he was uncomfortable enough with asking her for help, and he was torn between loyalties. Everyone felt guilty for disliking the dead, especially when they were young, and the grief for them was something you ought to share, and couldn't.

"Thank you," he said softly. "It will make a difference to her."

They finished the meal without speaking again, but it was companionable, as if understanding made further words redundant.

Matthew closed the door behind him and looked at the four men sitting around the long, polished table. One of them was his own superior at the Secret Intelligence Service, Calder Shearing; another was the head of British Naval Intelligence, Admiral "Blinker" Hall, white-haired, fresh-faced, with the nervous habit that had given him his nickname. The third was Brand, a man with receding brown hair and nondescript features, an assistant to Hall.

The fourth man was dark-eyed, dark-haired, of medium height, and at present he looked so tired his skin had a withered, almost parchmentlike quality, shadowed around the sockets of his eyes and pinched near his mouth. The humor that was usually so clear in his expression was gone, as if stripped from him by shock.

"Come in, Reavley," Shearing directed. "Sit down. You know everyone here."

"Good morning, sir," Matthew answered, acknowledging Admiral Hall. He glanced around the table. "Kittredge not here yet?" The answer was obvious, but he was looking for an explanation. He looked again at the dark man with the ravaged face. He was wearing civilian clothing, a shirt that looked crumpled and an old Harris tweed jacket, too warm for the time of year.

"Kittredge is not coming," Shearing told him. "This is a closed meeting."

Matthew was startled. Kittredge was one of three other men recruited to the SIS at the beginning of the war as a cryptographer. Before that he had been an academic at Cambridge. Language and codes were his specialties. Matthew took his seat in the place indicated, and waited for them to begin. He knew what he was here for; the fourth man, Ivor Chetwin, had just returned from Mexico. The United States and its neighbors were Matthew's field of responsibility in SIS.

Of course Shearing did not know that Ivor Chetwin had once been a close friend of John Reavley, until profound differences over the morality of espionage work had divided them. It had driven John Reavley into the dislike and distrust of all intelligence work that had lasted until the evening he had telephoned Matthew to tell him of the Peacemaker's document given him by Reisenburg. He had been murdered the next day. It was only Chetwin's brilliance at gaining information, and his undoubted personal courage, that made it bearable to Matthew that they should work together.

Admiral Hall seemed to be in charge of

the meeting. He was courteous to Shearing, but he deferred to no one. At the beginning of the war, on the night of August 5, 1914, Britain had sent out a ship that had picked up the transatlantic telephone cable, so all communication between Europe to America since then had had to be made by radio. Germany had routed its messages to its diplomatic staff in the United States and Mexico through various neutral countries, particularly Sweden. Naturally, it had used code.

That code had been captured by British Naval Intelligence, and the fact that it had been broken was one of the most closely guarded secrets. Any action based solely upon information gained that way would betray to the Germans that their diplomatic exchanges were known, and the code would instantly be changed. All its value to Britain would be lost. Secrecy was vital. The German assumption that their codes could never be broken also helped!

"The situation," Hall prompted Chetwin.

"Even worse than the reports," Chetwin replied, his voice gravelly with exhaustion from weeks of fitful sleep, poor food, and the constant harassment of moving from place to place, only a step ahead of suspicion and arrest. "The whole of Mexico is in chaos," he went on. He spoke slowly, almost without emotion, as if it were exhausted out of him. "Zapata and Pancho Villa have gone crazy. They're dancing in the presidential palace like so many apes. They have no control over anything. Armed men roam the countryside looting and killing. They steal cattle, grain, horses, anything that can be moved. Bodies swing from the trees like rotten fruit."

No one interrupted him.

He ran his hand, neat and strong, over his brow. "There's nothing left to eat. Villages have been razed to the ground, roads and bridges have been torn up. There's death everywhere, like a pall over the earth. The cities are crawling with typhus and black pox, and there are more firing squads than queues for food."

"The Germans?" Hall reminded him.

Chetwin sighed. "Pouring in guns and money."

They all knew what that meant. If the Mexican armies crossed the Rio Grande the United States would mobilize all its forces to defend itself. There would be nothing left of men, munitions, or passion to consider what was happening in the rest of the world.

"How close?" Shearing asked.

Chetwin shook his head. "Not close enough," he answered the question they had not asked. "I told Washington everything I could, short of giving them our decoded messages. They've got explanations for half of it, and don't believe the rest. Nothing will persuade them that Germany is seriously behind the arming of Mexico, or the projected building of a Japanese naval base on their Pacific coast."

Shearing pursed his lips. "You know the kaiser, Chetwin. Is he serious about the 'yellow peril,' or is it just one of his ramblings?"

Hall jerked his head round. "You know the kaiser? Personally?"

"Yes, sir," Chetwin replied. "I spent a little time in the court in Berlin, before the war."

Did Matthew imagine it, or was there a faint, quite different discomfort in Chetwin as he answered? Something in his eyes had changed. His looks were no longer direct in exactly the same way as though he were guarding an emotion, something in which he felt a vulnerability.

Matthew watched more closely, his attention personal as well as professional. Chetwin had been John Reavley's friend, and in a sense enemy also. Unquestionably he had known him well. If he had been in the court in Berlin, not only had he apparently known the kaiser himself, he could have known Reisenburg. He was a man of acute intelligence and profound political knowledge, and possibly personal connection to the British royal family as well. John Reavley had believed him willing to use any methods, ethical or otherwise, in order to obtain the ends he believed in. That was the cause of their original quarrel.

The possibilities careering through his head made his stomach lurch as if he might be sick. He couldn't say anything. Dare he trust Shearing? Who else could he turn to for help? Hall would think him a lunatic. All he would achieve would be the loss of his own job, not only crippling him so he had no access to information with which to prove the Peacemaker's identity, or to block his future plans, but even to prevent any good he could do in his work with America. That was a measure of the Peacemaker's brilliance: His enemies were isolated from each other by distrust.

Hall and Chetwin were talking about the kaiser, his personality, his erratic mixture of desire to be liked by his cousins

George V of Britain and Nicholas of Russia, and his terror of being surrounded by enemies who intended war against his country. He veered between intimate, almost passionate friendship, and then outraged attack.

"I've no idea whether he will do it," Chetwin was considering. "Since he got rid of Chancellor Bismarck, he's about as predictable as the English summer. Last year was sublime, but I've seen snow in June."

Matthew listened as Chetwin told the rest of what he had seen, recounting his discoveries in Washington as well, but all the time his mind was racing over the possibilities of Chetwin's own complicity in German plans to have Mexico invade the United States, in the promise of regaining its old territories in the southwest, the price for keeping America out of the European War.

If Chetwin were the Peacemaker, then Germany already knew that British Intelligence had their code. Perhaps all the information gained was doubly compromised. What if it were the most magnificent double bluff in the history of espionage? It was not impossible. The uses of such a deceit were almost endless. Nothing they believed now was real!

As soon as the interview was over he was obliged to return to his own office and reconsider all his information in this light. Most of the ammunition used by Britain was purchased from America, all of it, of necessity, coming by sea. Sabotage was rife, loss to submarine warfare was a growing threat.

It was late afternoon before he had an opportunity to speak alone to Kittredge.

"I've heard Chetwin's report from Mexico," he said casually, stopping by Kittredge's desk. "It's as bad as we thought, possibly worse."

Kittredge looked up from the sheets of paper he was studying. He was thin and dark, in his early thirties, a man from the Peak District of Derbyshire, used to wild hills and the steep-streeted villages in his childhood, then the sudden intellectual liberties of university. He had not lost the keen edge of idealism, nor the richness of provincial accent.

"What do you know about Chetwin?" Matthew asked.

"Don't you trust him?" Kittredge looked surprised.

"Of course I trust his honesty, or we couldn't use him," Matthew replied. "I'd like a second view on his judgment."

Kittredge considered for a moment or two before replying. "Well, of course he speaks fluent German, but you know that, or you wouldn't have sent him into Mexico posing as a German. Did you know that before the war he was engaged to a German girl? Countess or princess, or something."

Matthew guarded his surprise. "No. I imagine Shearing knew, but he didn't mention it to me. Why didn't he marry her?"

"Sad business," Kittredge replied. "She died. Fever, or something. Don't know exactly what. He was very cut up about it. Beautiful girl, apparently. In her early twenties."

"But Chetwin must be nearly fifty!"

Kittredge shrugged. "What difference does that make? He's very well connected. One of his sisters is very beautiful, married to some descendant of Queen Victoria, and they all get along very well. And of course at his age he has proved his capacity to make a career and earn the respect of his countrymen. Without the war, he could have run for Parliament, or found a pretty decent job in the diplomatic service. Anyway, he was the one she wanted. It was a match of passion on both sides, and her family was quite agreeable. He got along very well at the court in Berlin. He has great wit and charm, you know, and he's a marvelous raconteur." He smiled a little self-consciously. "They say the Irish have the gift of the gab, and can charm the birds out of the trees, but I've yet to see anyone beat the Welsh. And for all his sophistication at times, Chetwin's heart is in the valleys of Wales. The music of his own language is always there."

"Does he speak Welsh?" Matthew was finding more surprises than were comfortable. He should have known these things.

"Oh certainly!" Kittredge raised his eyebrows. "He's no Englishman!"

Late that evening Matthew was sent for to the office of Dermot Sandwell, a senior cabinet minister with special responsibilities toward the intelligence departments.

"Come in, Reavley," he invited, waving an arm in the general direction of one of the large leather chairs in his office. It was a beautiful room decorated in cool earth colors and there were exquisite watercolor paintings on the walls. Matthew had been here once or twice before, and knew they were scenes of South Africa, by the artist and humorist Edward Lear. He was always hoping for an opportunity to look at them more closely, but he had been here only on the gravest business, and from the expression on Sandwell's abstemious face with its vivid blue eyes, this occasion was every bit as grim as the others. He was standing near the window toward Horse Guards Parade, the curtains drawn now.

Matthew did not accept the invitation to be seated. "Good evening, sir," he acknowledged.

Sandwell regarded him closely. "How are you? You look tired. I believe you have a brother on the Western Front. Heard from him lately?"

"Yes, sir. He's quite well, thank you."

"Good. I suppose you're inundated with stuff at SIS? I imagine you know as well as we in the cabinet do just how serious the situation is? Africa, Gallipoli." He winced as he said the second name. "The Balkans. There'll be an Italian front before long, I should think. France and Flanders are only part of it. I'm afraid the war is spreading across the world."

"Yes, sir." There was nothing for Matthew to say.

Sandwell jerked himself out of his thoughts and stared at him with sudden focused intensity. "Reavley, what I am about to say to you must not be repeated to anyone. Do you understand me?"

Matthew was startled. Who could he be referring to? All his fears about Shearing came flooding back. Did someone else know about the Peacemaker, perhaps even in the cabinet? Maybe he was not alone after all? Hope surged up inside him that Sandwell was going to say that he knew. The end was in sight!

"Yes, sir," he answered. "No one at all? Does that include Mr. Shearing?"

Sandwell turned away from the window, the light harsh on his face from the lamps on the wall, his body rigid. "Yes, that does include Mr. Shearing."

Matthew felt a coldness in spite of the mild April evening. "Yes, sir."

Sandwell drew in his breath slowly. "I have very good reason to believe that our enemies have turned one of our men in SIS against us. There is a traitor in your department. The evidence seems to be unarguable. Information has passed that can have come from nowhere else."

Matthew's stomach turned cold. He asked the question he had to. Sandwell would have thought him a fool if he had not. "Why are you trusting me with this, sir?"

Sandwell smiled, touched by the momentary humor of it. "Because some of the information is material that you do not have access to. For the time being you can trust no one with anything that you alone are privy to, anything that comes from sources that only you have. Report directly to me, but don't jeopardize your safety, or your position, by hiding whatever will be learned anyway. We have to know who this man is, Reavley. The situation is desperate." He did not add anything more or make any further emphasis to the danger.

"Yes, sir," Matthew replied. "Of course."

"Thank you, Reavley. That's all. Be careful. When you have anything to report, let me know. I shall make myself available."

"Sir." Matthew went out into the corridor without realizing quite how shocked he was until he tripped on the stairs and nearly lost his balance. He grasped the banister only just in time to right himself.

Was it Shearing, or Chetwin? Or God help him — both? It was reasonable to suppose that the Peacemaker would have gathered more disciples over the nine months since the outbreak of war: people who did not believe that violence was the answer to anything, whether from personal revulsion or ethical principle; people who believed they could not win against the power of Germany and Austro-Hungary; people whose businesses and fortunes were being ruined by the economic catastrophe of war and the sheer decimation of so much land; and people who were simply not prepared to lose any more young men they loved, no matter what the cause.

He went out into the evening air and the anonymity of the darkness. On Whitehall he caught a taxi home to his flat. He would collect his car tomorrow; it could remain where it was all night. He could not be bothered to drive. He would like to go to a bar or a club somewhere and have several stiff whiskies, but he dared not. His mind was bursting with fears and shadows, secrets he could not share, and which were too heavy to carry alone.

But there was no one to trust, absolutely no one at all. If he drank, and was vulnerable, forgot to watch and measure everything he said, then he must do it at home, and alone.

Several hours later, in a quiet house on Marchmont Street, the man Matthew referred to as the Peacemaker stared out of an upstairs window at the street below. He saw a taxi draw up about twenty yards along and a figure get out. In the distance and from this height he was foreshortened, but even so the Peacemaker recognized him. He was slender, about six feet tall, and he moved with an energy that marked him out from others on the footpath. He was dressed in a very ordinary suit, and wore a broad-brimmed hat that hid his features. But the man waiting knew exactly what he looked like, he did not need to see the thick, dark hair or the powerful, starkly emotional face with its broad mouth and wide cheekbones.

A few moments later he heard the doorbell, and the servant answering it, then the quick footsteps up the stairs.

"Come in," he commanded as they reached the landing.

The door opened and the man stood on the threshold, anticipation bright in his eyes.

"Close the door," the Peacemaker directed.

The man obeyed. They both remained standing. Richard Mason was perhaps the best war correspondent to emerge from this hideous conflict. His writing was lucid, concise, the force in it coming from simple language, a brilliant intellectual grasp of what was happening driven by a passionate anger at human suffering. Time and time again he saw the detail that brought a vast event into the grasp of the reader, making the experience immediate enough to hurt as does the death of one man, rather than overwhelm as does the destruction of a thousand. He gave the enormity of it a human face.

"I want you to go to Gallipoli," the Peacemaker said quietly. "The news is bad. They say the casualties are terrible. One observation pilot reported that the landing at Cape Helles beach was so fearful he looked down and saw the sea red with blood."

Mason's face was pale and his hands by his sides were clenched. He had seen war before, in South Africa. He would have given everything he possessed to prevent such slaughter and human misery happening again, but now, as then, he was helpless to do anything but watch. The Boer War with its civilian casualties, its concentration camps, its legacy of bitterness and destruction, had made him long for peace at any price, as a drowning man longs for air.

It had brought him together with the Peacemaker, and a few others who hungered in the same fierce and passionate way, in an attempt first to prevent this great engulfing conflict, and when that had failed, at least to make it as short as possible. God above knew how many men would die if it continued. He had seen the trenches, and the slaughter of tens of thousands of young men — and he had heard of the nightmare hell of gas.

"What about the Western Front?" he asked. "The Germans are breaking through at Ypres. They'll be to the French borders soon, and then Paris. What will be the point of Gallipoli if France surrenders?"

"I've got a man right there where the gas attack took place," the Peacemaker replied. "He's young and keen. He'll write a good piece. He actually saw it, and the casualties afterward. As of the moment, the Ypres Salient is still holding."

"For how long?" Mason said bitterly. "We're bent to breaking, right from Ypres to Verdun and beyond. Austria and Germany have got eight million men mobilized, the French have only got four and a half, and we've got barely seven hundred thousand! Now we've got the Turks against us as well."

"I don't know," the Peacemaker admitted. "But the story's in Gallipoli now. If it fails, eventually Churchill will have to go.

It may even bring down the government."

Mason stiffened, his eyes widening. There was a sudden flare of hope in him.

The Peacemaker smiled bleakly. "It's only a beginning," he warned. "And we'll pay for it in blood and tears long before it's over. But go out there and find the truth, then write it! I'll see it's published. I have editors in the small papers who have the courage to print an honest report, not the censored rubbish the rest of us get. People are being deceived. There is no choice without knowledge. Truth is the only freedom."

"Yes, it is," Mason said quietly. "But I wish to God sometimes I didn't have to see it in order to write it."

"I'm sure," the Peacemaker agreed. "It isn't cheap. Like everything else of value, it comes at a high price, sometimes everything we've got."

Mason did not argue. If he had to, he was willing to pay.

Chapter

SIX

Judith was on the deck of the transport steamer on the way back across the Channel. She stared into the luminous shadows over the sea and thought about Mrs. Prentice. If she was anything like Eldon, Judith would find it extremely difficult to be gentle with her or offer her any kindness to conceal how he had been disliked, and worse than that, held in contempt. It would cost her all the self-control she possessed to think only of the engulfing sense of loss any woman must feel for her son. Judith had never had a child, but she had watched many men die since coming to the Front, and she could still feel the raw pain of her own loss for her parents. There had been moments in the house when she had expected to hear her mother's quiet footsteps, or her father's voice talking to the dog. She had half listened for the car to come back, the old yellow Lanchester that was now so much mangled metal in some scrap yard, probably still stained with their blood. Surely that would help her say something to Mrs. Prentice that would be real between them?

The wind smelled of salt in her face and the slap of the water was swift, rhythmic. They were moving quickly. Surely the moonlight would catch the white line of the chalk cliffs of Dover soon?

What if Mrs. Prentice was like the general? She could picture his face very clearly, every expression, as if she had known him for years, whereas actually it was only a couple of months. Would Mrs. Prentice have the same gravity, and the sudden smile, and eyes that looked into your thoughts, and so seldom betrayed their own, but when they did it was as overwhelming as touch?

She heard the soldiers laughing, and then footsteps as one of them came closer. She turned, happy to be distracted.

"You a nurse, miss?" he asked.

"No, I'm an ambulance driver." Driving the general was not really her job, and they did not need to know about it. Anyway, she would rather not hear their opinion of him, even in their tone of voice on this dark, windy deck where faces were only pale blurs against the summer night.

There was a moment's appreciative silence, then they praised her, teased her and roared with laughter, exuberant with the joy of going home, to see family again, wondering what would have changed, saying anything to break the tension.

The boat landed around dawn and she went straight to the railway station for the London train. It was crowded, noisy, slow, like all troop trains, but by nine o'clock she was in London, broad sunshine already warming the pavements.

It was busier and shabbier than she had remembered. There were more cars and fewer horses. She refused to think of the dead horses around Ypres, limbs shattered, carcasses sometimes split wide open, but in spite of her will to blank it out, she remembered Cullingford's eyes when he saw them. In his cavalry days his life had depended on a good horse, and the trust never died.

She bought a newspaper and looked at it quickly, mostly just the headlines, and a few of the lead articles. The war news was first, of course. Most of it concerned the Western Front or the Dardanelles, but there was a little about East Africa.

The facts were there, at least some of them, but it was the words that fascinated her, the talk of courage, honor, and sacrifice, soldiers fighting for the right. And of course implicit all through was the conviction of ultimate victory. Casualties were given — they had to be — but it was nothing like the reality she knew. No one wrote of terror and dirt and pain. It was as if they had gone smiling into the night, clean and dignified.

It was probably necessary. Too much truth and one would scream oneself into paralysis and be no use to anyone. The only way to go on was to think whatever you had to, believe whatever you could, and take it five minutes at a time, then the next, and the next, help what you could reach.

She did not go immediately to the Prentice house. First she needed to find a hotel and take a bath, a luxury she had not enjoyed for a long time. She filled the tub as high as she dared, then climbed in and sank up to her chin in the steaming water. She let her mind become totally empty, thinking of nothing at all but the smooth, rippling heat over her skin. She put in soap bubbles and let them seep through her fingers and fall in dollops on her body, stretching her legs up, then down again. It was a big tub, an expensive bathroom, and she drowned her senses in every exquisite moment of it.

When the water was cooling she stepped out, wrapped herself in the big towel, and lay on the bed. She intended to dry off, then put on clean underwear and go to sleep. However, she drifted into a delicious haze, and woke with a start to find two hours had elapsed, and it was midafternoon. She was ravenously hungry.

She had already unpacked her dress and hung it up for the steam to get rid of some of the creases. She had bought it last leave. Like everything else in fashion, it was somber blues — no one wore bright colors — but it was very well cut, and had the full skirt to midcalf, then the slender skirt beneath to the ankle. The jacket was short, nipped to the waist, high at the neck, and had buttons all the way down the front. She looked at herself in the glass, and thought it was really very flattering.

Consequently, it was nearly five o'clock when the taxi dropped her in Hampstead and she walked up the path to the quiet house with the blinds drawn in the now familiar sign of mourning. She felt self-conscious, intrusive, guilty for being here at all when she had not liked Prentice. If she had not had General Cullingford's letter in her hand, which she had promised him she would deliver, she would have turned and gone back to the hotel. The only thing harder would be to tell him that she had failed. He might not blame her, he might even understand, but it would destroy a trust between them that she would not willingly live without.

She knocked on the door.

After several minutes it was opened by a girl of about sixteen in a long, black dress and a plain apron and cap. Her face was pale and her eyes pink-rimmed. "Yes, miss?" she said without interest.

"I am sorry to intrude," Judith said, "but I have a letter for Mrs. Prentice. My name is Judith Reavley, and I am General Cullingford's driver in Belgium. Would you ask Mrs. Prentice if I may see her, please?"

The girl hesitated. The message obviously confused her.

"Please?" Judith repeated. "I promised the general that I would deliver it in person."

"Yes, miss. If you come in, I'll go an' ask 'er." She pulled the door wide and led Judith across the hall into a sparse morning room. The mirrors were turned to the wall, the blinds drawn down even though it was still daylight, and there was black crepe on the mantelshelf. She left Judith there and went to find Mrs. Prentice.

Judith looked around, trying to imagine Eldon Prentice here. But this was not a room for the family; it was the formal place guests waited, or people came to write letters, or perhaps receive business callers. There was nothing personal.

She wondered what Cullingford's home was like. Was it comfortable, full of the physical things that spoke of his life: books, paintings, perhaps ornaments, pieces that had memories? Were there gardening gloves, or fishing rods, boots, binoculars for watching birds, a stick for long walks, hats for different occasions? Had he a dog, like Henry, that her father had loved so much?

The door opened and Mrs. Prentice stood in the entrance. Judith knew it was she because there was a likeness to Cullingford. It was not in her features; hers were less defined by experience, gentler and without the underlying fervor. It was the way her hair grew off her brow that was the same, a certain stillness about her, and something in her eyes. Now she was tired and the pain in her was desperately clear to see.

"Miss Reavley?" she said hesitantly. The intonation in her voice was like Cullingford's also.

"Thank you for seeing me, Mrs. Prentice," Judith answered, smiling very slightly. She was so used to death it no longer embarrassed her and the words came easily. "I know this is not a time you will wish for visitors, but I have a letter from General Cullingford. He also felt you might like to speak with me, because I knew Mr. Prentice a little. Sometimes it helps, at others it doesn't. I lost both my parents in July last year, and I don't always know whether I want to talk about them or not. At times I get angry when people are trying to be tactful, and skirt around it all the time as if they never existed."

"I'm so sorry," Mrs. Prentice said quietly. "That sounds awful. Both your father and your mother?" Her eyes were full of sympathy, and for an instant her own loss was forgotten.

"It was a road accident." There was no need to tell her it was murder, like her son's. She did not need to know that either. Judith smiled deliberately. "I'm really an ambulance driver, a lot of the time well behind the lines, but when General Cullingford's driver was injured I happened to be there, and he needed to go urgently to meet with the French, and I'm quite good at languages."

"You must be very brave. How is Owen?" The shadow was there in her eyes again, her own pain back, overwhelming her.

Judith knew she should answer with a good deal of the truth; it would make the other lies easier to believe. "He's quite well, I think," she said frankly. "But I can't imagine that he would complain about anything unless it were very serious." She saw the fleeting acknowledgment in Mrs. Prentice's face. "Of course he carries a terrible responsibility. He knows far more of what is really happening than an ordinary soldier would, and has some very hard decisions to make, and then the consequences to live with." That was more than she had intended to say, but a reserve in the other woman had prompted her to defend him. Had his own family any idea at all of the burden he carried? Did he, like a lot of men, write calm, trivial letters home, telling them what they wanted to hear, protecting them from reality? He had implied as much about his wife, was it true of his sister as well? Was there no one with whom he could trust his inner self, the

241

true, unguarded part?

"I imagine it is very hard," Mrs. Prentice replied, but there was no thought in her voice. She was being polite. "Have you come very far? Would you like a cup of tea?"

"I came from Dunkirk last night," Judith said. "I got to Dover this morning, and took the train up to London. I'd love a cup of tea, thank you."

"But — you must have eaten, surely?" It was a refuge in the practical, something uncomplicated to do.

"Oh yes, I ate at the hotel, thank you, but tea would be lovely," Judith accepted. She must give her the chance to ask questions, or simply to remember her son with someone who had known him.

Mrs. Prentice led the way into the drawing room. It had yellow-flowered wallpaper and windows looking out onto a lawn, and the last tulips in bloom beyond. The scent of lilac drifted in on the breeze. It caught Judith with a sudden ache of absurdity. It was all so normal, so terribly English, clipped lawns, the perfume of flowers, tea in the afternoon, as if life were the same as it always had been. And inside the void of loss was irreparable.

Mrs. Prentice rang for the maid, and requested tea. Twenty minutes later it came, with cucumber and egg and cress sandwiches and slices of Madeira cake.

"My daughter Belinda will be terribly sorry to have missed you," Mrs. Prentice said, pouring the tea and passing the cup across. "She and Eldon were closer than they sometimes appeared to be. She has found his . . . his death, very hard." It was difficult for her to say the words. Judith could see that she was deliberately forcing herself to, as if she had not been able until now.

"I have brothers," Judith tried to help her. "We disagree sometimes, but it's only on the surface."

"Yes, of course it is," Mrs. Prentice responded instantly. "I know what you mean. So often we just don't get around to saying what matters most. We suppose that people know, and perhaps they don't."

Judith wondered if she was thinking of Prentice and his sister, or of herself and Cullingford. Certainly Cullingford did not know. He wanted to reach out to his sister, and was aware with a sense of loss that she would not welcome it. But it was too delicate to touch now.

"Mr. Prentice was very brave," she said aloud. "I think we all knew that of him."

Mrs. Prentice smiled, blinking hard. "It's ridiculous now, I suppose, but we never thought being a war correspondent was a dangerous job. I imagined him talking to injured men, perhaps seeing ambulances, doctors, hearing from others what the actual battle was like. I thought Owen would look after him!" Without any warning the anger was there, the lashing out against unmanageable pain.

"He couldn't do that!" Judith retorted instantly, remembering passionately, against her will, Cullingford's anger at Prentice, and Prentice forcing him to write a pass for him to go wherever he wanted. "All our correspondents are ordered not to go to the forward lines, but Mr. Prentice wanted to see what it was like for himself, and he disobeyed." She heard her own anger harsh in her voice and tried to curb it. She was not the one bereaved. "He . . . he wanted to feel it, not just be told."

"Of course." Mrs. Prentice's anger was mastered again. "It's just that I know Owen didn't really approve of him. They used to be close, when Eldon was younger, but then they grew apart. Eldon didn't have much respect for the army command, and he wasn't always tactful how he said so." She was defending a wound too raw to touch. "But he was very clever, you know? He had a brilliant mind. He would have been a great writer." Her eyes were challenging, daring Judith to deny it, as if through her she were reaching Cullingford, too, forcing him to acknowledge her son, to give him now what he had withheld before, as if it could matter.

"That's one of the worst things about war," Judith replied, her throat tight with pity, aching inside herself. "It is so often the best who are killed. I'm so sorry."

Mrs. Prentice blinked away tears. Outside there was a blackbird singing as the light softened toward evening. "You are very kind to give up part of your precious leave to come here." Her voice was husky, fighting for control. Now she needed to talk of other things, hold the agony at bay until she could find the strength again.

"I know how it hurts when someone is gone," Judith said gently. "And no one will talk to you about them. People are afraid of hurting you, and embarrassed in case you break down."

Mrs. Prentice laughed very slightly. "You are right. Would you . . . would you stay to dinner, and meet Belinda? I know it is an imposition, but it would mean a great deal to her, and to me."

"Of course. Thank you. I was only going back to the hotel and I would probably have eaten alone."

"Don't you know anyone in London?"

"My brother Matthew, but he didn't know I was coming. I expect I'll see him tomorrow."

"You must be relieved he is not in the army."

"He is, sort of, but stationed in London."

"You said you had two brothers, or did I misunderstand you?"

"I have. Joseph is at the Front, not far from where I am. He's a chaplain."

"I thought chaplains stayed well to the rear, with the injured, advising people, comforting them and conducting services. Eldon said church attendance was compulsory."

"Yes, it is. But Joseph spends most of his time in the trenches."

"Eldon would have admired that." She said it with wistful pleasure.

Judith thought of how Joseph had despised Prentice, and was compelled by honor, not desire, to find out who had killed him. There were too many people who had wanted to, and in spite of himself he sympathized with them, but she must not say that here. She must walk a subtle, razor line between truth and evasion that concealed it.

She glanced around the room with its quiet memories, things of good quality, a little shabby with use. There were several photographs, images of a time only a year or two ago, and yet seeming now to be another age. Several were of Prentice, one of an older man. There was one of Cullingford, holding a horse by the head, its long face close to his. He looked happy. To judge by the unlined smoothness of his features it must have been nine or ten years ago.

Judith looked away quickly. Even in that small black-and-white image there was an intensity of feeling that shook her. This was part of his life she could not touch, except in imagination. He belonged to someone else — with whom he could share nothing of the torment of emotion that tore them apart, blistered with pain, removed them from the ordinary and changed them forever.

A group picture caught her eye: Cullingford smiling with a woman beside him. She had a gentle face and curling hair, a little darker than his, perhaps auburn from the soft freckles on her face, but it was impossible to tell. Prentice was beside them, and to his right a tall girl with startling, direct eyes that looked to be unusually light colored. Prentice was holding an oar in his left hand, upright like a spear, and he was wearing a straw boater hat.

Judith moved her gaze quickly, not wanting to see. It was absurd, but the sight of Cullingford with someone who was almost certainly his wife, reminded her of the reality of life outside the war, life the way it ought to be, and that she had no part in it with him. She belonged to battle, extreme hardship, not the way they longed for life to be again.

The clock on the mantelpiece struck seven. Beyond the windows a slight breeze stirred the leaves of a silver birch tree. At home in St. Giles there would have been starlings in the sky, swirling up behind the elms and swinging wide out over the fields. But that was in the past. It belonged in dreams, preserved where it was safe and the present could not touch it.

Twenty minutes later Prentice's younger sister, Belinda, came home from the volunteer work she had been doing making up parcels to send to soldiers at the Front. She resembled Prentice also, but she was darker, her face had the same intelligence and eagerness, but it was softened by a kind of inner calm he had not possessed.

When Judith was introduced her weariness vanished. "You're actually at the Front?" she said with fierce admiration, her eyes alight. "There with our men?"

Judith felt a mixture of pride and embarrassment. "I'm not actually in the trenches, although I know pretty much what they're like. We don't go further forward than the Casualty Clearing Stations where they bring the wounded back for us to collect."

Belinda's shoulders were tight, her face tense with her imagination. She had not yet sat down. "Is it very dreadful? I used to think of it as heroic, but Eldon said it isn't, it's filthy and degrading, and lots of the men are blown to bits without ever having a chance. He said that if we here at home had any idea what it was like, no one would join up to go there, because it's for nothing. It would be quicker to catch a bus to the local abattoir along with the cattle." She was searching Judith's face, hungry for an answer. It was easy to imagine the quarrels they had had over it, her dreams, his anger. Now she was left with nothing but confusion, and no one to help her resolve the truths she needed to know for herself, not only to help her grief, but to continue now.

There might be someone else she loved out there in the trenches; if there was not now, there would be.

Judith composed her answer carefully. "It can be pretty shocking when you first get there," she said to Belinda, avoiding Mrs. Prentice's anxious eyes. "The smell is awful, he's right about that. It tears your stomach, even when you get used to it. And there are rats, lice, fleas, all sorts of unpleasant things. Casualties are high, but we save most of the wounded."

Belinda sat down slowly, her hands folded in her lap. She did not take her eyes off Judith's face.

"But what it seems he didn't tell you about is the friendship," Judith went on. "The loyalty, the knowledge that the men beside you will share everything they have with you, food, warmth, shelter, jokes, laughter and pain, their lives if need be. Perhaps as a correspondent he didn't see that, but it's there in the front line. And the courage and sacrifice are there. That's not just propaganda. The difference is that it is real, not words; and no words can tell you what it's like, however passionate or clever. Maybe one poet will capture a little of it one day. Maybe the cold and the pain and the fierce, brave, kind, funny love of one man for his friends can't even be told."

There were tears on Belinda's face, and she was not ashamed of them.

"I wish he could have known that," she said, swallowing huskily. "I suppose he wasn't there long enough." Her words were brave, but her eyes betrayed her fear that it was not time but Prentice's own character that blinded him. "Are you going back?" she asked.

Judith had never even considered the possibility of not going.

"Of course! I . . ." She gave the faintest smile, but she felt it burn through her like heat. "I have to. My job is out there. That's who I am. And the people I love are there, too." The truth of that rang in her voice with a conviction that startled her.

Belinda did not say so, but her admiration was so intense it blazed in her eyes and in her soft, answering smile.

Dinner was served and Judith concentrated intensely, measuring every word so as to tell Prentice's family as much as she could about his life and his achievements.

She said no more about the details of trench life, there was no need for them to know. Let them sleep as easily as they could. Grief was more than enough to bear. She tried instead to say the decent things about Prentice himself. It was difficult to be specific, as if she had actually known him, without also mentioning his appalling behavior, which had ended with Wil Sloan beating him almost senseless. She could not think quickly enough to avoid lying, so she did, with embarrassing fluency.

When they spoke of Cullingford, with a remoteness that twisted inside her, she imagined how it must have hurt him and she changed the subject.

"But how did he get so far forward?" Belinda asked a second time. "I thought war correspondents stayed well behind the fighting? They all share the information anyway, don't they? That's what Eldon said."

"Yes, they do," Judith agreed quickly.

"Then why did Uncle Owen send Eldon out into no-man's-land? That's where you said he was found!"

"The general didn't send him." Judith denied it. Please God that was at least half true. Was it possible that Hadrian had heard his anguish and in loyalty done what Cullingford could not do for himself? The fear gripped hard and tight inside her.

King Henry II had cried out "who will rid me of this turbulent priest?," and his men in mistaken loyalty had murdered Thomas à Becket, and Henry had paid in guilt for the rest of his life.

"How could he do that? He knew Eldon wasn't a soldier!" Mrs. Prentice demanded accusingly. She was still seeking blame; it was so much easier to explode in anger than face the appalling void of grief.

Judith swallowed. "Mr. Prentice was very keen to see things the other correspondents hadn't and to gain his own experiences," she answered. "He insisted that he be given a wider permission, and he used the general's name to gain it. No one ever intended he should go 'over the top' with the raiding party." She saw the anger harden in Mrs. Prentice's face. "He was young and he was brave," she added hastily. "He knew the risks, and he still chose to go."

Mrs. Prentice's eyes filled with tears. "Thank you." She took a shaky breath. "It was very good of you to come."

"General Cullingford asked me to, and it was no trouble at all," Judith replied. "I'm so sorry for the reason."

Belinda smiled at her quickly, a flash of gratitude and understanding, then they turned to other subjects. It was late evening by the time Judith finally left.

She arranged to meet Matthew for dinner the following evening, and waited for him in a restaurant crowded with people all talking earnestly. She heard snatches of news about the war, but much of the conversation was about the latest play, the political news in Westminster, speculation of changes — even exhibitions of art and science. Two young women were excited about a moving picture starring Charlie Chaplin and Marie Dressler.

Ten minutes later she saw Matthew in the entrance. His uniform caught her eye before she recognized who he was. He was the same height as Joseph, but a little broader across the shoulders, and fair-haired. He had the same strong nose, and hint of humor around the mouth. He looked very tired, as if he also had been up too many nights and could not easily shake off the anxieties of knowing and caring more than he wanted to.

It took him a moment to see her, then he smiled and strode over to her. She stood up, eager to hug him, and feel his arms around her. It was a moment's break in a long loneliness. Friendship eased the heart and the mind, but there were times when the touch of arms around you healed an ache within that nothing else reached.

"How are you?" he asked, although he was looking at her face for the answer, and whatever she said would make no difference.

"I'm fine," she said with a slightly wry smile. She, too, was looking at him, trying to weigh what was merely weariness in his eyes, or the deeper lines from nose to mouth. What she saw was an underlying fear that did not vanish with comfortable words or a long night's sleep.

"Have you seen Hannah lately?" she asked. "Her letters say a lot about what she's doing, but not much about how she feels. I think that's a sign that she doesn't dare talk about it. Is it hard at home? Is everyone putting on a brave act, terrified it'll crack if they look underneath?"

"No, it's not that bad." He held her chair and she sat down again. He sat opposite her. "Some of us are afraid when we read the news because we tend to look between the lines, and dread what's worse that they aren't telling us. And of course pretty well everyone knows at least one person who's lost a son or a brother."

The waiter appeared. The choice of food

was still surprisingly wide and they ordered roast beef and vegetables and a full bottle of red wine. If there were shortages of anything it had been well disguised.

"How is Joseph?" he said when they were alone again. There was a loneliness in the question, almost an urgency.

Until this moment she had not been sure whether to tell him about Prentice or not, but now that he was here, his face, his voice, everything familiar about him reminding her of home, of the lost sweetness and safety of the past, the idea of not telling him was absurd. He would know she was lying, and fear something even worse than the truth. Also still gnawing at her mind was an anxiety that what Prentice had said about recruitment was true.

"He has a pretty rotten job," she said aloud. "Especially after the gas, trying to tell people that there's a God who's in control of everything, and He loves us. There's not much evidence of it."

"I don't think Joseph ever said God was in control," Matthew pointed out, sipping his wine even before he had tasted the food. "He doesn't control us, and we are the ones who've made the mess, not God. You'd better remind him of that." There was wry laughter in his eyes, but pity as well, and the concern was not any less than before.

"We had a young war correspondent up at the Front," she went on, watching him as she spoke. "Pretty rotten fellow, actually. Arrogant, intrusive, no sensitivity at all. He was General Cullingford's nephew. He's the one in charge of our stretch. . . ."

"I know." Matthew smiled.

She felt herself color a little, and went on quickly. "He persuaded the general to give him written permission to go all sorts of places other correspondents couldn't, including right into the front-line trenches."

Matthew was only mildly interested. "How on earth did he do that? I'd have thought Cullingford would have more sense, family or not." There was a thread of contempt in his voice.

Judith was stung by it. "Prentice didn't give him any choice. He was a total swine, actually. Major Hadrian, the general's ADC, was at school with him, and says he's an awful little worm. And actually I've just been to see his mother and sister, because he was killed, and took a letter to them from the general. Mrs. Prentice is his sister. Matthew, Prentice was saying that recruitment of men is dishonest, and if they had any idea of what it was really like on the front line, no one would go. Is that true? Are we losing heart at home?"

He heard the panic in her voice, but he did not answer with platitudes. "No. In some places there's even a renewed resolve, after the gas attack at Ypres. But I'm not sure if it'll last. Casualties are heavy, and people are beginning to realize that it isn't going to be over anything like as soon as they used to believe. Kitchener's right, we're in for a very long haul."

"Will we make it?"

He smiled, but he did not answer her.

"It's about morale, isn't it? If we think we'll lose, then we will."

"Pretty much," he agreed.

She looked away from him and concentrated on her food for a while. She could imagine the recruiting station if they heard the sort of things Prentice had apparently told Belinda.

"That isn't all," she said at last, her voice subdued, catching in her throat. "Prentice isn't just dead — someone murdered him." She ignored his response. "It wasn't obvious. He went over the top — nobody knows what made him do such a stupid thing, or what he went for, except bravado, but Joseph was the one who found his body in no-man's-land, and brought him back."

Matthew was appalled. His knife slipped out of his fingers onto his plate with a clatter. "What the hell was Joseph doing out there? He's a chaplain, for God's sake!"

"I know." Now at least she was on sure ground, filled with one moral certainty, and a hot, sweet pride. "But he takes that as part of his job — searching for people and bringing them back. Sometimes they're alive, but it matters to recover even dead bodies." She saw the reflection in his face of her own emotions. "But Prentice hadn't been shot, he'd been drowned in one of the craters still full of water. And Joseph worked out that there were no Germans anywhere near them at the time. It had to have been one of our own men. He was pretty rotten to a few people. . . ."

"Enough to kill over?" He was incredulous.

She looked away. "Lots of people are dying, every day. Unless you really care about someone personally, you have to get used to it, or you'd go mad. This is . . . different."

He reached out his hand as if to touch her, then changed his mind. It was not something he did naturally; this was born of a sudden, urgent understanding. "Are you afraid it could be the general?" he said very gently.

Lies would not do. "I don't know," she admitted, looking up at him. "And even if he didn't, I'm not sure he wouldn't be blamed for it. Not everyone likes generals."

He laughed outright: a short, bitter bark of sound. He did not need words to encompass the confusion of anger and fear, torn loyalties felt by the vast mass of people who knew only what they read, and the pain of losses, the day-and-night struggle between pride and terror for those they loved trapped and fighting in a horror they could only imagine. It was natural to blame someone.

He refilled his glass again, and she felt another flicker of worry brush her, as if someone had opened an outside door onto the cold again. "Matthew, have you learned anything more about the Peacemaker?" she asked, taking the bottle from him and adding a little to her own glass, even though she had barely touched it. "I wish we could be more help to you. We're doing nothing. . . ."

"There's nothing you can do," he said quickly, his face softening. "It's enough that you do your own job."

She searched his face, his eyes. "You

know something, don't you," she pressed. The darkness, the tension in him frightened her. "Do you know who it is, Matthew?"

"No. I think it could be Ivor Chetwin, but I need a lot more proof."

"Ivor Chetwin? But . . . but doesn't he work in Intelligence?" She was horrified, the betrayal could reach anywhere. "Matthew, please —"

"I am careful," he said quickly. "And I don't know that it is him. It could be lots of people. I've been working on how he contacted Sebastian to tell him what to do. It isn't the sort of thing you say in a letter, or explain over the telephone. It had to have been a fairly lengthy and persuasive conversation, in person somewhere. And it has to have been that afternoon. There wasn't any other time."

"Well, where did Sebastian go?" she reasoned. "Can't we find out?"

"I'm trying to."

"Be careful! We don't know who the Peacemaker is, but he knows us! Don't forget that! He'll be expecting you to come after him." She gulped, suddenly aware of how frightened she was. "Matthew . . ."

"I'm being careful," he repeated. "Don't gulp like that, you'll give yourself indigestion. If I'm paying for you to eat roast beef instead of corned beef and army biscuits, I'd rather you didn't ruin it by making yourself ill!"

She forced herself to smile, impatient with him, frustrated, aching to protect him and thoroughly afraid. "I'm going home tomorrow. I'd like to see Hannah for a day or so."

"Good idea. Rest for a while, at least. Now eat that before it's cold. Judith . . ."

"What?"

"Don't tell Hannah anything about all this — or the journalist getting killed. She doesn't need to know. She has enough to do looking after three children, and the losses in the village. Trying to help everyone keep up hope, and not be sick every time the postman arrives, dreading the telegram. They feel so helpless. That's a kind of suffering in itself."

"I know. I won't tell her anything I don't have to," she promised. "I'll be quite happy not to talk about it, believe me."

But it was not as easy as she had expected. She took the train to Cambridge, and then a taxi to St. Giles. The village still looked just as it always had, until she noticed the blinds half drawn in the Nunns' house, and another house a few doors down. There were no errand boys, no children playing by the pond. An old man walked slowly on the grass, a black band around his arm. She saw Bessie Gee carrying a basket of shopping, and looked away because she could not face her. It was cowardly and she knew it, but she was not prepared to see what she must be feeling, not yet, anyway.

The taxi stopped at her own door. She paid the driver and got out. She had to ring the bell and wait until Hannah came.

"Just for a couple of days," Judith said with a smile. It was absurd, but she was overcome with emotion to be on the familiar step. It looked smaller, shabbier than she remembered, and impossibly precious. It was peopled with memories of sounds and smells of the past so strong they were the fabric of all life that had formed her, the woven threads of who she was. This is where she had loved, and grieved, where she had been safest, and in most danger.

"Of course!" Hannah said, her face lighting with pleasure so the anxieties of the moment slipped away. "It's wonderful to see you! Why didn't you tell me you were coming? I haven't got any decent food in!"

Judith hugged her and they clung together fiercely for minutes. "I don't care!" she said, laughing at the triviality of it. "Anything's got to be better than army rations!"

"Are they awful?" Hannah said with sudden concern.

Judith remembered her promise to Matthew. "No, not bad," she claimed quickly. "I don't look starved, do I?"

Hannah's children came home from school, pleased to see her and a little shy, now that she was certainly part of the war. The conflict was not real to them, and yet it was the backdrop and the measuring stick of everything that happened.

"Do you think it'll go on long enough for me to join the navy, Aunt Judith?" Tom asked with a shadow of concern in his soft face. He was thirteen, his voice breaking, but no suggestion of down on his cheek yet. He was frightened in case he missed his chance of all that he thought of that was heroic, and the test and goal of manhood.

For a moment Judith could see nothing but the men she knew who had been blown to pieces, men like Charlie Gee — who had been boys like Tom only a few short years ago.

"I don't know," she answered, refusing to look at Hannah. "I don't think anybody knows at the moment. We just do our best. Take it a day at a time. Your job's here right now. A good soldier or sailor does the job he's given. Doesn't argue with his commander to pick and choose."

He stared at her solemnly, trying to work out whether she was treating him like a child or a man.

She gave him time, without pushing either way.

"Yes," he nodded, accepting. "But I will join the Royal Navy when I can."

"Good," she said lying in her teeth, and still avoiding Hannah's gaze. "As an officer, I hope?"

He grinned suddenly. "You mean concentrate on my schoolwork and do all the exams and everything," he said knowingly.

"Something like that," she agreed.

After the children had gone to bed, Judith and Hannah walked up the garden in the dusk. Appleton had gone to work on the land. Food was more important than flowers. Mrs. Appleton had gone with him, over in Cherry Hinton direction. Not far away, but too far to come back here to cook or clean. The weeds were high in the spring warmth and the long daylight hours.

"I can't keep it up," Hannah said, looking at it miserably. "Even the raspberries are overgrown. The children help a bit, but it isn't enough. There's always so much to do. There are fifteen families in the village now who've lost someone, either on the Western Front, or at sea. We heard about Billy Abbot just yesterday. His ship went down in the North Atlantic, with all hands."

Judith said nothing. She knew Hannah was thinking about Archie, but neither of them wanted to say so. There were some things it was better not to put into words, the silence helped to keep at least the surface of control. There was work that had to be done, children who needed to feel at least some faith in survival. As long as you did not give in to terror, neither would they. You had to be busy, to smile, if you must cry, then cry alone. Perhaps the women with children were lucky. They gave you a reason to force yourself to be your best, always. The act became a habit.

It was Hannah who broached the subject of the Peacemaker.

"Matthew won't tell me anything about his search for the man who killed Mother and Father," she said as they stood at the end of the lawn and looked west toward the last echoes of light in the sky. "Has he given up?"

"No." Now a lie seemed like a betrayal, and she was not in a mind to be able to deal in the loneliness of deceit. "He's trying to find out who Sebastian Allard spoke to the evening before."

"Why? Oh . . . you mean the Peace-maker . . . what a ridiculous name for him! The murderer must have told him what to do?"

"Probably not himself," Judith replied. "He wouldn't risk that. He has to be someone well known, very highly placed, and someone Father knew already, and trusted. He will have sent someone else to persuade Sebastian what to do. It couldn't have been easy. You don't just walk up to someone and say 'By the way, I'd like you to murder one of my friends tomorrow. It has to be tomorrow because the whole thing has become rather urgent. Will you do that for me?' You'd have to give him all sorts of reasons, and persuade him. Sebastian was a passionate pacifist. It will have taken some time to argue him into believing it was the only way to preserve peace in Europe."

Hannah was silent for several minutes. The last shreds of light from the west, no more than a luminescence in the air, caught her cheekbones and brow and the curve of her mouth, softening the anxiety and making her look as young as she had a year ago.

"I talk to Nan Fardell quite a bit. Her husband's in the navy, too. She lives in Haslingfield." She hesitated a moment. "Nan said she saw Sebastian in Madingley the afternoon before . . . he was with a girl. They seemed to be very close, talking earnestly, having an argument, which they made up before they parted." Hannah frowned. "She mentioned it because she knew he was engaged and she thought it was a bit shabby. She assumed he was trying to break it off with this girl, and she wouldn't let him, so he gave in, and apparently they parted in agreement. Nan said she was rather beautiful, nearly as tall as he was. I expect the Peacemaker's a man, but does the person who gave Sebastian his instructions have to be a man as well?" She turned to Judith. "He doesn't, does he? Lots of idealists who really get things done are women. They were in the past, and they are now. What about Beatrice Webb, or even more, Rosa Luxemburg? Nan said this woman was very unusual, she had remarkable eyes, pale blue and very bright."

Judith's mind whirled. It could be! It was a cold thought, and she had not the faintest idea who the woman was, or how to find her, and trace her back to the Peacemaker. But it was a beginning, or it might be. "I suppose Nan Fardell doesn't know who she is?"

"No idea at all. I asked her, just out of curiosity. She's never seen her before. Do you think it could have been she who gave Sebastian the order to . . ." She did not finish the sentence.

Judith shivered. "Yes, it could. It's possible. Matthew thinks the Peacemaker could be Ivor Chetwin, which is a horrible thought."

"It has to be someone we know," Hannah said quietly. "It's all horrible. Let's go inside. It's getting cold."

They turned and walked together slowly, not needing or wanting to discuss it anymore, but in Judith's mind was a photograph of an unusually tall girl with light, clear eyes, and she was standing next to Eldon Prentice.

Chapter

SEVEN

Days and nights continued their routine of alternating violence and boredom. Joseph helped with digging and shoring up in the trenches, carrying food, helping the wounded or dying, writing letters for people, often just listening when men needed to talk. They swapped stories, the longer and more fantastic the better. They made bad jokes and sang music hall songs with bawdy army lyrics to them, and laughed too loudly, too close to tears.

Little Belgian boys came by selling English newspapers, and they read voraciously to see what was happening at home. Joseph conducted the mandatory church parades, and tried to think of something to say that made sense.

But all the time at the back of his mind was the question of why Eldon Prentice had been in no-man's-land, and who had thrust his head under the water and held it there until he was dead. The thought was horrible, filling him with a revulsion quite different from the gut-turning pity of other deaths. There was a moral dimension to it he could grasp, a personal evil rather than the vast, mindless insanity around them all.

Nobody wanted to talk about it. To everyone else it was the one death that did not matter. Prentice had had a letter from General Cullingford giving him permission to come and go pretty well as he pleased, and he had used it freely. There was an impulsive feeling that he had got what he deserved. Grief was saved for other men, like Chicken Hagger, and now Bibby Nunn, caught by sniper fire.

Mail delivery was one of the best times of the day. Letters from home were the lifeline to the world that mattered, to love and sanity, the precious heart of what was worth dying for. For each man it was a little different, a different face, a different house that was familiar, but they shared them with the half dozen or so men who were their "family" here.

As chaplain, Joseph was uniquely alone. He was an officer, and apart. He belonged to everyone and no one. The nearest he had to a family was Sam. With Sam he could share Matthew's letters, even if they referred to the Peacemaker.

One witheringly cold night in January, he and Sam had crouched together on the fire-step in the trench known as Shaftesbury Avenue, the wind whining in the wires across no-man's-land, ice cracking on the mud, duckboards slick with it underfoot. Joseph had told Sam about his parents' deaths, and a brief outline of the Peacemaker's conspiracy, enough for Sam to understand at least the anger and the passion that drove him to seek the men who would still bring such betrayal to pass, if he could.

He could see Sam's face in his memory, sharply outlined for a moment in the glare of star shells.

The smile on his lips, the heaven and hell of irony in him. He had said nothing, simply put out his freezing hand and touched Joseph for a moment.

Now Joseph sat alone with the sheets of paper, the sun warming him in the stillness of the afternoon. Tucky Nunn and Barshey Gee were asleep a few yards away, faces at ease, their youth achingly apparent. Tucky half smiled, perhaps home again in dreams.

Further along Reg Varcoe sat bare-chested, holding a match to the seams of his tunic. In the distance someone was singing "Keep the Home Fires Burning."

For a moment Joseph thought of home: grasses deep in the lanes, woods full of bluebells, may blossom in bud. In Northumberland where he used to walk with Harry Beecher, the hills would be alight with the burning gold of gorse, the perfume of it like honey and wine. Sometimes it helped to think of the sanities of life, at others it hurt too much. He missed Matthew — he missed the easy conversation of trust, the knowledge of a bond that stretched back to childhood, a safety, before pain or failure were known.

He read Matthew's letter three times. There was nothing particular in it, just gossip about London, a short description of the countryside when he had been home, the weather, a few jokes. It was like listening to the voice of someone you loved. What they were saying was unimportant, the message through it was *I am here,* and that was what you needed to know.

There was a second letter for him, in a hand he did not know. He opened it with curiosity and read:

Dear Captain Reavley,

Thank you for your letter telling me of my husband's death. I know from the casualty figures that you must have this dreadful duty to perform very often. It was generous of you to write so personally to me.

I shall share your words with my brother-in-law who lives up in the family manor house a few miles away. Garaint was a quiet man who loved the land and the hills here. He would walk miles, even in the rain, and he sang beautifully, as so many Welshmen do. He seemed to be able to play any musical instrument if he turned his hand to it.

I find it hard to believe he is not coming back, but then there are many other women all over the country who must feel the same. Perhaps it is worse if it is a son, someone you have known and loved all their lives. That is a grief that won't come to me, and I am grateful for it.

I believe that you get newspapers quite often in the trenches, so perhaps you know as much news as I do. Some of it is very grim. I think the thing that saddens me the most is the death of Rupert Brooke. He died on April 23rd, off Gallipoli somewhere. It wasn't in action, it was blood poi-

soning. I feel horribly empty, because he was so wonderfully, vibrantly alive. Of course I never knew him in person, but I loved his poetry. He said all the things I wished I could. His dreams soared to the places I longed to be, passion and imagination and a fierce hunger for the intensity of life, as if you could touch it, taste it, for a moment hold it in your hands, as if you could stand in the sunset and in silence take its fire inside you.

The lights are going out, aren't they? What can we hold on to so that one day we can kindle them again?

Thank you for the strength of your faith that somewhere there will be meaning to all of this, if we have the courage to hang on. It does help.

Yours sincerely,
Isobel Hughes

He did not read it again. Perhaps he would later, at another time, when the words would matter. Now he was stunned and filled with loss, not for Garaint Hughes whom he had held as he died, but for a poet whose thoughts and words had woven themselves into the fabric of his own life. Rupert Brooke had been eight years younger than Joseph. He had studied at Cambridge and loved it with a passion he had made wild and beautiful in verse, to live beyond generations, let alone his own lifetime. But here in this mortal little space, they had seen the same stones and trees, the same burning sunset across the west from Harleyfield to Madingley, breathed the same air and watched the same birds in flight.

It was almost as if Sebastian had died again, only a better, brighter version of him, a man whose heart achieved the gold that Sebastian had tarnished.

The words of Brooke's poetry flooded his mind, painting with bone-deep nostalgia the beauty of the land they had both loved, familiar now in the pain of memory.

How could such hunger for life be gone, without warning? How many young men would have their promise shattered before it bloomed, their talents never more than a hope? Was it worth this price? He had told Isobel Hughes that it was, because it was what she needed to believe, but did he believe it himself?

Maybe the whole thing was just as tragic and insane as the Peacemaker had thought, the suicidal delusion of men who had more courage to die than to grasp reason, and unity and life. Was there a God somewhere weeping at this gigantic error? Or was life a blind chance anyway, and purpose only a dream created by man to comfort himself in the darkness of a universe without sense?

The soldier somewhere along the trench was still singing, a clear, true voice, caressing the melody.

How long before he was crushed as well?

He looked up to find Sam standing in front of him, a packet of Woodbines in his hand.

"No, thank you," Joseph said automatically.

"You look terrible," Sam observed. "Letter from home?" His voice was gentle, and for a moment there was fear in his eyes, not for his own pain but for Joseph's.

"No, not really. A widow I wrote to — to tell her."

Sam waited, squatting down in the sun, his back to the mud wall, his feet on the duckboards.

"Rupert Brooke's dead," Joseph said.

Sam did not answer, his eyes were far away, seeing something beyond the clay wall and the strip of blue sky above.

"Blood poisoning," Joseph added.

" 'Break the high bond we made and sell love's trust, And sacramented covenant to the dust,' " Sam quoted.

This time it was Joseph who did not answer. His throat ached and his eyes stung with tears, not only for Rupert Brooke, but for all the lost, the ones he knew and had cared for, and all the others he had not. He remembered walking along the Backs at Cambridge, watching the punts on the river in the evening light, the black fretwork of the Bridge of Sighs against the blaze of the burning sky, the gold on Sebastian's face as he spoke of all that war would destroy, not only of the flesh but of the spirit. And Sebastian was dead, too.

" 'The Great Lover,' " Sam said aloud.

"What?"

"Rupert Brooke," Sam explained. "That's what it comes from — the lover of life. 'Nor all my passion, all my prayers have power To hold them with me through the gates of death.' "

He smiled, and there was a strange sweetness in his face. "We have to make it count now, Joe. Maybe your God will sort it out in eternity, but I think He means us to do something here and now as well. There's enough that needs fixing for all of us to have a place."

"You're right," Joseph agreed. "Perhaps if I do something, I'll forget how much there is I can't do. I need a little forgetting. I can't afford a sense of proportion; it would crush me."

Joseph knew what he had to do, find justice for Eldon Prentice. It was something definite that could be forced into making sense, if he could learn who had done it. He might well discover that it was someone he liked, such as Wil Sloan, but his personal feelings did not alter the morality of the issue. It would be far worse if it turned out to be someone such as Major Hadrian, who had done it on General Cullingford's behalf. But that was unlikely. There was no motive powerful enough to prompt such an extreme action, especially since Hadrian was a staff officer, not a soldier actually carrying arms. He did not see death personally, only in numbers and reports. Joseph would need to know of something far more urgent, more visceral, than the fact that Prentice was arrogant and manipulative, and possibly something of an embarrassment to a general for whom Hadrian had a deep loyalty.

It was with great reluctance that he went to the Casualty Clearing Station to find out exactly where Wil had been on the night of Prentice's death. It was a warm

April day. The new grass was springing up lush and green in the few untrodden patches of earth. He passed a cart pulled by four horses, who squelched in the mud as they strained to heave it toward the ammunition depot. One man at their head, urging them on, gave Joseph a wave and called out to him.

Further along he ran into Snowy Nunn, the sun shining on his fair hair, making it look almost white. He was very grave, face tremulous, eyes confused since the death of his cousin Bibby. It was somehow different when it was so close. It was more than grief, it was as if death had touched your own body, not a grip, just a brush, which reminded you of its power.

Joseph stopped and spoke to him. There was nothing in particular to say, and he did not seek to find anything of meaning. He had given up believing there was anything, it was simply a matter of friendship.

Half a dozen huge black rats shot out of one of the connecting trenches, and they heard somebody swearing ferociously. Snowy's hand went to his gun, then away again. They were not allowed to shoot rats; there was no ammunition to spare for it. Anyway, it made no difference. There were tens of thousands of them. And their rotting bodies would only add to the stench.

Joseph reached the Casualty Clearing Station and found the American nurse, Marie O'Day, again. She seemed pleased to see him, her fair face lit with pleasure.

"Hello, Captain Reavley, what can we do for you? It's a bit quiet at the moment. Would you like a cup of tea?"

He accepted, partly to give him a chance to talk to her less bluntly. He asked general questions while she boiled the kettle, then took the tin cup carefully. It was hotter than he was used to — heated over candles in a Dixie tin. It actually smelled quite good, like real tea. He thanked her for it.

"What can I do for you, Captain?" she asked again.

He smiled. "Am I so transparent?"

She nodded, smiling.

"Do you remember that awful young newspaper correspondent?" he asked.

Her face darkened. "Of course. But if you're going to ask me if I saw Wil Sloan hit him, no I didn't. I know that's a lie, Captain, but I'm perfectly happy to tell it. What Mr. Prentice did was terrible." She bit her lip, and her eyes filled with tears. "Poor Charlie Gee died, and . . . and perhaps that was a release for him. I . . ." she swallowed hard and took a moment to compose herself. "I couldn't wish a young man to live like that. I wish the Lord had seen fit to take him immediately, without his ever having to know what had happened to him."

"I'd like to be able to say something wise," Joseph confessed. "But I don't know anything. I don't understand it either. It stretches faith very far. But I wasn't going to ask you if you saw Wil Sloan hit Prentice. I would rather not know. What I would like you to remember is if you saw Wil Sloan two nights after that."

"Why? Is he in some kind of trouble?"

"Prentice is dead, Mrs. O'Day."

"Oh. I'm sorry." She looked guilty rather than grieved.

"He was a correspondent, not a soldier," he said. "I need to find out why he was so far forward. It shouldn't have happened. Where was Wil Sloan?"

"You can't think he's concerned! Can you?" She was afraid, and he could see it in her eyes.

"I'd like to prove that he's not, Mrs. O'Day. You might be able to help me to, if you tell me where he was. That is, if you know?"

"He brought a badly wounded man in here, about four in the morning," she replied. "I don't know where he picked him up."

"Where is the man now? He's still alive, isn't he?"

"Yes," she said gravely. "But he isn't conscious yet. He lost a lot of blood. He was very badly torn up by shrapnel. He wouldn't be alive if it were not for Wil." The warning look in her expression was trying to guide him away from pursuing the subject at all.

He was uncertain how much to tell her. He needed her cooperation, and instinctively he liked her. He admired women like her, who left behind all that was familiar and comfortable and came thousands of miles to work in extreme hardship, for people they did not know, because they believed it right. It was a spirit of Christianity far more powerful than anything shown by most clergy who preached a faith of which they were only half convinced, accepted money and status for it, and considered themselves servants of God.

But Prentice's death was an absolute. He wanted to prove Wil Sloan innocent, but he could not turn away and refuse to see it if he proved him to be guilty after all. It would be painful, deeply so for himself, and because it would hurt Judith as well.

But it would have a certain cleanness to it in that no matter how Prentice had behaved, possibly beating him up was excusable, or at least an offense for which apology was sufficient. Murder was not.

And in silence, a confession of heart, uncertain if he was right or wrong, he thanked God for Charlie Gee's release.

Matthew had enjoyed seeing Judith more than he expected to. He had driven home to his flat after dinner with a sense of happiness, for once forgetting the vulnerability he had been so aware of since March's Zeppelin attacks on English east coast cities. Suddenly war had developed a new dimension. It did not require an army landing or a naval bombardment to be struck in one's own home; bombs could rain down from the air with fire and explosion almost anywhere.

As he pulled up outside his flat and parked his car, for a moment he envied her. Usually she would sleep wherever she got the chance to, often in the back of an ambulance. Her food would be army biscuit and tins of greasy meat. There would be terrible sights of death and violence, horror he could barely imagine. But there would also be a comradeship that was denied to him, a trust in her fellows, an inner peace he had not known since Joseph and he had found the document.

He unlocked the door and went inside. He turned on only a small light, just sufficient to see the shadow of the bookcase, but not the individual volumes. He knew what they were, poetry, a few plays, adventures from his childhood, not there to read again, just reminders of a different, more innocent time, a link to be looked at rather than touched. And there were books on current political and social history, warfare, and economics.

He poured himself a stiff whisky, drank it, and went to bed.

In the morning he had toast and tea for breakfast, his head aching, then he looked at the newspapers. They were full of more losses in Gallipoli, and of course all along the Western Front. It was discreet, no hysteria, no rage, only the long lists of names.

It was Churchill's plan to capture the Dardanelles and free the Russian Grand Fleet imprisoned in the Black Sea, then take Constantinople and give it back to the czar as a prize. They would be able to form a new battle line in the Austro-Hungarian rear, forcing them to fight a second front.

So far it was a chaotic failure, costing thousands of lives, French and British, and more particularly Australian and New Zealand volunteers.

The war had also been extended to Mesopotamia, and the Indian Ocean, Italy, and southwest Africa. An Italian ship had been torpedoed in the Mediterranean, and five hundred and forty-seven people had drowned.

He drove to work, and found a message waiting for him that Shearing wished to see him. He went immediately.

"Good morning, Reavley," Shearing said tersely, pointing to the chair on the other side of the desk from his own. "Sit down." He looked so tired his skin was like paper; his eyelids drooped as if he needed all his force of will to focus. His neat, strong hands clenched and unclenched on the desk.

Matthew obeyed, but he knew that had he taken the liberty of doing so before he was invited he would have been criticized for it. It was Shearing's way of establishing the rules of hierarchy before he allowed himself to break them. It was not in his nature to do the expected, even now when he seemed on the edge of exhaustion.

"The *Lusitania* is setting sail from New

York," he said bitterly. "The Germans have warned us that any ship flying the British flag, or that of the Allies, is liable to U-boat attack. We can't protect it! We're stretched too thin to protect our merchant shipping as it is. We need American steel in order to make guns. Without it we'll lose."

For the first time Matthew saw a flicker of fear in Shearing's eyes. Even the desperate battles of last autumn, the winter on the Western Front, then the gas attack at Ypres, had not stripped from him his outer composure before, and it chilled Matthew more than he would have believed. It was as if a step he thought certain had given way beneath his feet. He struggled to mask it in his face.

"Surely they'll never sink a ship everyone knows has American civilians on board, sir? It would force America into the war, and we know that's the last thing Germany wants." Or was that what they expected, a sudden and cataclysmic escalation of the war, involving all the world, like an Armageddon?

Shearing's face was bleak, the skin stretched across his cheekbones. "I think you are being naive, Reavley." Now his tone was critical, impatient. "You've read the correspondence from President

Wilson. He's a highly moral man with no understanding whatever of European character or history. In his mind he's still a schoolmaster who is going to arbitrate between two unruly children in the playground. He intends to be remembered as the honest broker of peace who brought Germany and the Allies together and saved the Old World from itself."

Matthew swore, and then apologized.

The faintest smile curved Shearing's lips. "Precisely," he agreed. "But unhelpful. Chetwin believes that even if the unthinkable happens, and the *Lusitania* is torpedoed and goes down, Wilson will still dither in virtuous inactivity, and his advisers will remind him of the very real threat to American copper and railroad investments, by Mexico's chaos. Their army is far too small to fight on two fronts, so their own border will naturally take priority. Unless we can persuade them of Germany's part in their troubles — which we cannot — Wilson will do nothing."

Matthew did not reply. He already knew every ploy the British ambassador had used to try to move President Wilson, and failed. America would sell Pittsburgh steel to Britain, as indeed it did to Germany. Individual Americans would come to Europe to fight, and sometimes to die, because they believed in the Allied cause. But there was also a large number of German-speaking Americans, and their heritage and loyalties mattered also.

To act upon any of the messages they had intercepted between Berlin and Washington would betray the fact that the code was known, and the Germans would instantly change it.

"Hoist on our own petard," Shearing said drily, as if reading Matthew's mind.

"Yes, sir."

Shearing looked very steadily at Matthew. "We need something to give us victory in the naval war," he said softly, his voice gravelly with weariness and the possibility of defeat. "German U-boats hold the Atlantic passages. We have skill, we have courage, but we are being sunk faster than we can replace men or ships. If it continues at this rate, we will be starved into submission before Christmas."

Matthew thought of Hannah's husband, Archie. He imagined what it would be like for the men at sea, knowing the elements were impartially violent, battering and devouring all ships alike. But uniquely for them, the enemy could attack from any direction, even the fathomless water below their fragile hulls. One could stand staring at the empty sea stretching to the horizon in every direction, silent but for the wind and water, and the throb of the engines. Then the deck beneath you could explode in destruction, fire, and flying metal. The sea would pour in, pulling you down into its vast darkness and closing over your head.

Shearing was talking. Matthew jerked himself to attention and listened.

"You know Shanley Corcoran, don't you," Shearing said.

Matthew was startled.

"Yes, sir. He and my father were friends since university days. I've known him all my life." He could not even say it without the old warmth returning, memories of a hundred occasions of happiness. "He's one of the best scientists we have."

Shearing was watching him closely, studying his face. "Do you trust him?"

For once Matthew did not have to think, and the pleasure of that was almost intoxicating. "Yes. Absolutely."

Shearing nodded. "Good. You'll know he's in charge of the Scientific Establishment in Cambridgeshire."

"Yes, of course."

A flicker of impatience crossed

Shearing's face. "I wasn't asking you, Reavley! I know where you live! I don't want to send for Corcoran, nor do I want to be seen down there myself. What I want done could win us the war, and if we are betrayed either intentionally or by carelessness, we will lose it in a space of weeks. Therefore what I say to you, you will repeat to no one else at all, in SIS or beyond it — do you understand me?"

Matthew felt the room swim. His head was pounding. It was almost as if he were back in Sandwell's office again, with fear of traitors within, suspicion, doubt everywhere.

"Reavley!"

"Yes, sir!"

"What the hell's the matter with you, man? Are you drunk?" Shearing demanded, his frayed temper unraveling. "The situation is desperate, a lot worse than we can afford to let the country know. We need to stop the German navy, that's where the real war is. The sea is our greatest friend, and enemy. We have to hold it to survive."

Matthew stared at him, mesmerized. There was a hideous truth to what he was saying, and yet it supposed defeat in France, and Europe dominated by Germany. Was he really preparing for that kind of disaster? The thought was deeply and painfully frightening. He pulled his attention together with an effort, waiting for Shearing to continue.

Shearing had not moved his eyes from Matthew's face. "We need something to stop the submarines, a missile that hits every time, instead of one in a score," he stated. "Ships are made of steel, so are torpedoes, and depth charges. There must be some way; magnetism, attraction, repulsion, electricity, something that will make a missile find a target with more accuracy. Imagine it, Reavley!" His dark eyes were blazing now, wide, almost luminous. His hands described a shape in the air, delicately, fingers spread. "A torpedo that changes course, if necessary, that searches out a U-boat through the water, and explodes when it strikes! Have you ever played with magnets on either side of a piece of paper? Move one, the other moves with it! Something like that must be possible — we just have to find the way. If any man can do it, it will be Corcoran!"

Matthew saw the brilliant possibility of it! Then at the same instant, like the crash of ice, he saw total surrender if the Germans obtained such a weapon. Never mind before Christmas, the war could be over in weeks.

"You see?" Shearing was leaning across the desk.

"Yes . . ." Matthew breathed out shakily. "Yes, I see."

Shearing nodded slowly. "So you will go to Corcoran and brief him to put all other projects aside, reassign them to his juniors, and give this priority. He must put each part of it to different people, so no one knows the entire project. All must be sworn to absolute secrecy, even so. I will see that it is funded directly from Whitehall, nothing through the treasury or the War Office. He will report only to me, no one else at all! Is that understood — absolutely?"

"Yes, sir." Matthew could see it was imperative, there was no need to add any explanations. He could also see, with a wave of nausea that made his gorge rise, what it would do if Shearing were the Peacemaker. It was an irony of exquisite proportions. He could be getting England's finest brain to create a weapon for German victory, and stealing it at the precise moment it was ready for use. And no one but Matthew Reavley would know, because he would indirectly have helped create it. The irony would be sublime; the vengeance for foiling his first plan!

He had no alternative. His heart was pounding, his tongue sticking to the roof of his mouth. "Of course I will." He could not refuse. At all cost he must keep it in his own hands. "I'll go tomorrow."

Shearing nodded. "Good."

Matthew drove to Cambridge, leaving London before six in the morning when the traffic was light, and he was well on the way north by the time he stopped for breakfast a little after eight. It was a bright clear day with white clouds riding the horizon and the sun bathing the landscape in an illusion of peace. Looking at the fat lambs in the fields, the cattle grazing, and the great trees towering into the air, green skirts brushing the high grasses, the whole idea of war seemed like an obscenity that belonged in the madness of dreams.

But in the village where he stopped there were only girls and old men in the pub, and their faces were strained, their eyes lonely. They looked on a healthy young man out of uniform with suspicion.

One old man with a black armband asked him outright. "You on leave?"

"Yes, sir," Matthew answered, with respect for his loss, which he judged from the band to be recent. "Sort of. I'm taking the time off for a duty, but I can't discuss it."

The old man blinked back tears. There was anger as well as grief in his face, and he was ashamed of them both, but his emotion was too strong to hide. "A healthy young fellow like you ought to be doing something!" he said bitterly, ignoring his tankard of ale.

"I know," Matthew admitted, his voice suddenly gentle. The old man was racked by loss, the details did not matter, the pain obliterated them all, he simply railed against the unfairness of it. "But some things have to be done secretly," he went on. "I lost both my parents. I think they were the first casualties of the intelligence war, which one can't afford to forget. My elder brother is on the Western Front, and my younger sister drives an ambulance out there." The moment the words were spoken he wondered why he had said them. He had never bothered to tell anyone before, and it was certainly not the first time anyone had looked at him with doubt, or even open blame. These days, coward was perhaps the ugliest word there was. One despised one's own who stayed at home and left others to fight, bleed, perhaps die, with far more passion than one ever hated the enemy.

Perhaps it had something to do with the pent-up despair he had seen in Shearing, or the fact that he was coming from the city and going home to the land he loved. In another hour or so he would pass along the very length of road where his parents had been killed. It would look just as it had on the hot June day when he and Joseph had first seen the gouge marks on the surface, and the broken twigs, the scars on the bark, mute witnesses of the violence that had cost so much.

And it still hurt to go into the house in St. Giles, with its familiar hallway, the furniture he had grown up with, the way the light fell in patterns he could see even with his eyes closed. But his mother would not be in the kitchen, nor his father in the study.

"My son," the old man said with choking pride as he touched a gnarled hand to the black band. "Gallipoli. They buried him out there."

Matthew nodded. There was nothing to say. The man did not want understanding, and there was no help to give. Platitudes showed one's own need to attempt something that was impossible.

He finished his meal and went back to the car. He was in Selborne St. Giles by ten past nine. The main street was quiet. Children were in school. The village shop was open, newspapers outside full of the same sort of thing as always these days, the Dardanelles, the Western Front, politics; nothing he was unaware of, and certainly nothing he wanted to read.

He turned off the main street and along the short distance to the house. It looked silent in the morning, almost unoccupied. In the imagination he still saw his father's yellow Lanchester that Judith had sneaked the chance to drive whenever she could. Hannah had never wanted to. Before the war she had had no need, there was always someone to drive her. Now few people had vehicles. Petrol was expensive. Tradesmen did not make deliveries anymore, the men who would have performed such a service were in the army. People walked, and carried. If they lived too far out, then there were dog carts, pony traps if you were lucky. God knew how many horses were in the army, too, poor beasts!

He switched off the engine, took his small case out of the boot, and went to the front door. It was unlocked. He hesitated before pushing it open. It was an idiotic

moment, but just for an instant time tele-
scoped and it was a year ago. Hannah
would be in Portsmouth, Joseph at St.
John's in Cambridge, but everyone else
would be here. His mother would be
pleased to see him, thinking about what
she could make for dinner that he would
like.

His father would leave his study and they
would take the dog and walk around the
garden together, deep in contemplation,
admiring the view across the fields without
ever needing to speak of it, knowing its
goodness with quiet certainty, the great
elms would stand deep-skirted, silent
above the grass. Starlings would whirl up
against the sky, and the poplars would
shimmer gold in the sunset breeze.

He pushed the door open and went in.
The first thing he saw in the hall was
Hannah's daughter Jenny's blue coat on
the hook by the cloakroom door. She was
eight, and possibly at school today, but it
was too warm for her to have needed it.

The dog came bounding up the hall,
wagging his tail, and Matthew bent to pat
him. "Hello, Henry! How are you old
fellow?" He straightened up and called
Hannah.

There was a moment's silence, then she

appeared from the kitchen. Her hair was almost the same color as her mother's had been, and she had the same wide, brown eyes. It cost him all the strength he had to make himself smile. He must love her for herself, for her griefs and joys, not because she reminded him of someone else. She was probably missing Alys even more than he was. They had been so close, and now she was in so many ways taking her place in the village, trying to pick up in the multitude of small duties, kindnesses, unseen things that Alys had done over the years. And she was living here in this house where the past was like an echo to every word, a reflection gone the moment before one glanced at the mirror.

Her face lit with surprise and pleasure. "Matthew! You didn't say you were coming! You just missed Judith, but I'm sure you know that!" She came toward him quickly, drying her hands on her long, white apron. She was wearing a plum pink dress with a skirt fashionably close at the ankle, but he knew enough to see that it was last year's cut.

He put his arms around her and hugged her closely, feeling how quickly she responded. She must miss Archie dreadfully. She probably was not even allowed to know where he was. It was her duty to keep up the façade of confidence for their three children, Tom, Jenny, and Luke, and hide whatever her fears were, her loneliness or the long hours of gnawing uncertainty. And it was not only about Archie, it had to be about Judith and Joseph as well. If she had very little idea what it was actually like in the trenches, of the horror or the daily hardship, so much the better. He hoped Judith had been as discreet as she had promised.

Hannah drew back in surprise. "You're squashing me!" she said with a smile, but her eyes were searching his, afraid he had come with bad news. The closeness with which he had held her awoke fear.

He smiled back broadly. "Sorry," he apologized. "It's just good to be home, and to find you here." She had moved up from Portsmouth a few months ago. Archie seldom had leave, and when he did it was for long enough to come to Cambridgeshire. It was foolish to let the house lie empty and none of them had wanted to lease it to strangers.

"Are you hungry?" she asked.

"No, but I'd love a cup of tea."

She led the way to the kitchen. It looked as it always had, blue-and-white china on the Welsh dresser, the brown earthenware jugs with milk and cream on them in white, the half dozen large plates hand painted with wildflowers and grasses on the wall. She had been making pastry and the mixing bowls, white inside, ocher on the outside, were still on the big wooden table.

She piled the coals in the stove then pulled the kettle over to the hob. For a quarter of an hour they talked of the village, and people they both knew.

"Bibby Nunn was killed," she said, gazing at him over the top of the cup she was holding in both hands, as if she were cold. "They heard yesterday. Mae Teversham was one of the first to go to Sarah. Ridiculous, isn't it, that it should take a death that could have happened to either of them, to bring that stupid argument to an end. Both Mae's boys are out there, too, and it could be her turn next. I think everyone feels that."

He nodded.

"And Jim Bullen from the farm on the Madingley Road lost his leg in France and he's now invalided home. Roger Harradine was missing in action. His father's grieving silently. He can't even speak of it yet, but Maudie still hasn't given up hope."

They had finished tea and were walking in the garden before he dared ask what she had heard from Archie lately.

She was staring at the weeds in the flower bed. "I miss Archie," she said quietly. "I can't keep ahead of it. The children do as much as they can. Tom's pretty good, although he doesn't like gardening. Luke is too young, but he tries." She blinked quickly, turning away. She would say nothing to him, she would consider it disloyal, but he knew how hard it was for her without Archie. They all missed him, but she was the only one who knew the danger he was in. She read the newspapers and knew every time a ship went down. She hid her fear from them.

She took a deep breath, still staring at the raspberry bed that was Joseph's favorite. He couldn't pass it without picking half a dozen, when they were ripe. "He says he's fine," she answered his question. "Tom is praying the war will go on long enough for him to join the navy, too," she said with an attempt at a laugh.

Matthew put his hand on her shoulder. "He's got a father to be proud of. You can't blame him for wanting to be like him."

"He's only thirteen!" she protested, her

eyes blazing, swimming in tears. "He's a child, Matthew! He hasn't any idea what he's talking about. He thinks it's all exciting and brave and wonderful. He doesn't know how many men get maimed or killed, or how many are blown to bits. And when a ship goes down, they hardly ever save anybody."

"I know," he agreed. "But do you want Tom to have the same nightmares you do?"

She turned away sharply. "No! Of course I don't!"

"Then you'll just have to put up with it, and thank God he is thirteen, and not fifteen," he said as gently as he could. "And be glad Luke's only five."

"I'm sorry," she apologized, her cheeks momentarily flushed. "It was good to have Judith here, even if it was only a day and a half. She's changed, hasn't she!" She laughed as if at herself. "She's so competent lately, so . . . full of purpose. She's just as emotional as ever, but now it all has direction. It seems almost wicked to say it, but the war has given her something. She's . . . found herself."

He smiled in spite of not wanting to. "Yes." It was unarguable. It had confused Hannah, divided her loyalties between the safety of the past and the needs of the present. It had faced Joseph with horror that stretched his faith beyond its limits, it had taken away all the old answers and left him alone to find new ones. It had destroyed Matthew's safety as well and filled him with suspicion of everyone. There was no trust anymore, he was totally isolated. But to Judith it had given maturity and purpose, something to do that mattered, and, for the first time in her life, people who needed her.

"I wish I could," Hannah said quietly. "I'm trying to help in the village, the way I know Mother would have. But everything is changing. Women are doing jobs that the men used to. I can understand that." She was staring into the distance. Clouds were drifting in, bright, silent towers in the sky. "But they like it! Tucky Nunn's sister Lizzie is working in the bank in Cambridge, and she loves it. She's found that she's really clever with figures and managing. She wants to stay on, even after the men come back! She wants to get a lot of us organized to push harder for votes for women. I can't even think of an argument against it, I just hate everything changing."

He put his arm around her shoulder and she leaned a little toward him, comfortably.

"It frightens me," she admitted quietly. "I hate everything changing, I mean any more than it has to."

He considered saying that it would probably all change back, after the war, but he had no idea whether it would or not; or even if they would win the war. Part of him wanted to comfort her at any price. This was Hannah, not Judith. He would never have lied to Judith. But Hannah did not deserve it either. "Let's get the men back before we decide who's going to do what," he said instead. "I have to go and see Shanley Corcoran this evening. I won't be here for dinner, but I'll come back for the night. If I'm late, I'll let myself in."

"Oh . . ." There was disappointment in her. He felt it as sharply as if she had spoken the words, and he realized again how lonely she was. There must be a million women over Britain that felt the same, and countless more over France, Austria, and Germany, too. He pulled her a little tighter, but there was nothing to say.

"Wonderful to see you," Shanley Corcoran exclaimed with enthusiasm shining in his eyes. He wrung Matthew's hands vigorously but with a familiar gentleness that awoke memories of childhood again, safety that seemed like another world, just accidentally placed in the same houses, with the same trees towering above, and the same broad summer skies.

"Sorry it's been so long," Matthew apologized, and he meant it. He had had to spend far too much time in London and old, safe friendships had suffered.

Corcoran led the way inside the high-ceilinged house with its spacious Georgian windows, wide wooden floors, and colored walls whose richness had mellowed into warmth.

"I understand," he said, indicating a chair for Matthew to sit once they were in the drawing room with its French doors onto the terrace. They were open, letting in the evening air and the sound of birdsong and the faint rustle of wind in the trees. Corcoran's face was grave. He was not handsome in a conventional way, but there was an intelligence and a vitality in him that made him more alive than other men, lit with more passion and more hunger for life. "We're all too busy for the pleasures we used to have. But what kind of a man grudges any blessing at a time like this?" He looked at Matthew with sudden concentration. "You look tired — worried. Is it bad news?" There was a shadow across his eyes, an anticipation of pain.

Matthew smiled in spite of himself. "Only war news," he answered. "Judith was home on leave briefly and I saw her the day before yesterday."

"And Joseph?" Corcoran asked, still watching intently.

"It's a hard job," Matthew answered. "I don't know how I would try to tell men out there that there really is a God who loves them, and in spite of everything to the contrary, He is in control."

"Nor do I," Corcoran said frankly. "But then I've never been sure what I really believe." He smiled, a warm, intimate gesture of self-mocking humor. "I couldn't bear the thought that it is all random and senseless, or that morality is only whatever our society makes it. And yet if I look at it closely, organized religion has so many contradictions in logic, absurdities that are met with 'Oh, but that's a holy mystery,' as if that explained anything, except our own dishonesty to address what contradicts itself."

His mouth pulled tight. "But far worse than that is the insistence on petty, enforceable rules to the exclusion of the kindness that is supposed to be the heart of all of them. If there is a God as the Christians conceive Him, there can be little room for blindness, hypocrisy, self-righteous judgment, cruelty, or anything that causes unnecessary pain, and there can be no place at all for hatred. And religion seems to nurture so much of it."

"Joseph would tell you it's human weakness," Matthew replied. "People use religion as a justification for what they wanted to do anyway. It isn't the cause, it's only the excuse."

Corcoran's eyes were bright. "Would he indeed?"

"For certain — it's exactly what he told Father, to the same argument." Matthew could remember it as vividly as if it had been last week, although actually when he counted, it was over seven years ago. Joseph had been newly ordained to the ministry, not medicine as John Reavley had wanted him to be. But he had still been proud of Joseph's honesty, and his dedication to serve others, even in a different path. They had sat in the study by firelight, rain beating on the windows, and talked half the night. He could see their faces in his mind, Joseph's so earnest, so eager to explain, John's calmer, with deep, slow growing satisfaction that the argument had logic as well as passion, that right or wrong, it was not blind.

Corcoran was looking into the past as well, at a long friendship stretching back to their own university days when he and John Reavley had studied together, walked the Backs along the river in the sun, or sat up all night sharing philosophy, dreams, and long, rambling jokes. "Are you worried about him?" he asked, bringing himself back to the present.

"Joseph?" Matthew asked. "No more than about anyone." It was not the truth, but he did not want to admit to Corcoran, or to himself, the weight of the burden he feared Joseph carried. "Tell me about yourself. You look . . ." He thought for a moment. "Full of energy."

Corcoran smiled broadly, lighting his uniquely vibrant face. "If I could tell you about the Establishment here, you'd understand." His voice had a sudden lift of urgency. He leaned forward in his chair. "We have excellent men, brilliant, and I use the term as your father would, the best minds in England within their fields. I think much of this war is going to be won or lost in the laboratory, with ideas, inventions that will change warfare, perhaps even stop some of this terrible slaughter of men. Matthew, if we can create a weapon more powerful, more destructive than anything the Germans have, once we prove it to them, they won't throw more and more men into the battlefield where they cannot win. At first the cost would be high, but for a short time, very short. In the end it would save hundreds of thousands of lives."

Matthew felt a sudden leap of hope. "Could you work on something to help in the war at sea?" he asked. "Our losses are mounting, men and ships, supplies we need desperately if we are to survive."

Corcoran did not rush into speech; he studied Matthew's face, the intensity in him, the measure of his words. "Is that why you're here?" he said softly. "You didn't come just because you're in Cambridge, did you?"

"No. I've been sent by my chief in SIS," Matthew answered. "The matter is so secret nothing is to be put on paper. He doesn't want you to come to London, and he won't be seen here. You are to trust no one. All the work you do is to be divided up among your men in such a way that no one person can deduce what the whole project will be."

Corcoran nodded very slowly. "I see," he

said at last. "What is it? I assume you can tell me that much?"

"Something to improve the accuracy of depth charges or torpedoes," Matthew told him. "At the moment it's a case of dropping a cluster and hoping you've outguessed the U-boat commander. If you're lucky one of them will go off in the right place, at the right depth, and damage him." He leaned forward. "But if we could invent something that would attach the depth charge to the U-boat, or perhaps even detonate it at a certain distance, then we'd have so much advantage they'd lose too many U-boats to make it worth their while anymore." He did not add how vital it was to keep some control of the sea-lanes. Like every Englishman, Corcoran knew that, never more so than now.

He sat in silence so long Matthew grew impatient, wondering if his request was somehow foolish, or out of place in a way he had not considered.

"Magnetism," Corcoran said finally. "Somehow the answer will lie in that. Of course the Germans will work that out, too, and we will have to think of a way to foil any guards against it that they use, but it must be able to be done. We must find the way, before they do! If they think of something first and can attach it to torpedoes before we do, then we are beaten." His words were lethal, catastrophic, but the energy in his face belied any sense of despair. He was accepting a challenge, and the fire of it already burned in him. "We need a budget," he went on. "I know everything does, but this is priority. I will come up with some specifications, things we have to have, who I recommend to work on the project. I need some figures from the Admiralty, but that shouldn't be difficult . . ."

Matthew took the papers out of his inside pocket and passed them across. "That may be most of what you want. But there are two conditions."

Corcoran was startled. "You said the work must be positioned out so no one knows the whole. What is the other?"

"You report to Calder Shearing and him only. It's top secret — no one else, not even Churchill, or Hall. Do you accept that?"

Corcoran looked at him quickly, a flash of appreciation in his eyes, then he bent to examine the pages. It was several minutes before he finished them. "Yes," he said decisively. "I have ideas already. Perhaps we can accomplish something to make history, Matthew."

His belief was contagious, uplifting. It was not a blind optimism but a faith rooted in possibility and endeavor. Looking at his face, the burning intelligence and the self-knowledge, Matthew found his own hope soaring. "I'll see you get the budget," he promised.

He was prevented from pursuing it any further, although there was little more to say, because Orla Corcoran came into the room and Matthew stood to greet her. She was slender, very elegant, her hair still dark. Conversation turned to other things. Orla was keen to hear of news from London; she had not been for nearly three months.

"There seems to be so much to do here," she said ruefully when they were seated at the dinner table. "Of course the most important thing in the area is the Establishment, but we have factories as well, and hospitals, and various organizations to look after people. We all try to pretend, but nobody's life is as it used to be. Everyone's got somebody they care about either on the Western Front, or at Gallipoli. We're all terrified to listen to the news, and when the mail comes in I see the village women's faces, and I know what they're dreading."

"I know," he said with a strange guilt for

his own part in spoiling the plans of the men who would have made peace, with dishonor, and prevented all this. He did not doubt that he was right, only he had not imagined at the time that the cost of it would feel like this, the individual loss over and over again, in a million homes throughout the land.

But then if the Peacemaker's plan had succeeded, what would have happened to France? A German province, occupied by the kaiser's army, betrayed by Britain whom it had trusted. And that would be only the beginning. The rest of the world would fall after, like so many bloodied dominoes, treason, collaboration, betrayals multiplied a thousand times, secret trials, executions, more graves.

No — this price was terrible, but it was not the worst.

The conversation went on about familiar things. As the evening deepened they spoke less of the present and more of happy things of the past, times remembered before the war.

Matthew left a little after eleven, and by midnight he was home at St. Giles, to sleep well for the first time in weeks with the silence of the country around him, the wind in the elms, and the starlight beyond.

In the house in Marchmont Street the Peacemaker was also speaking of Cambridgeshire, in fact specifically of the scientific Establishment there. The man opposite him was young, his face sharp, full of passion and intelligence.

"Of course I can get in," he said earnestly. "My qualifications are excellent."

"Don't be too eager," the Peacemaker warned. He was standing by the mantelpiece, looking at the younger man where he sat in the armchair, elbows on his knees, staring up. There was great confidence in him, extraordinary for one so untried in the professional world. He had a first-class honors degree in mathematics and engineering. He knew precisely what he wanted to achieve, and he had no doubt he would succeed. It was faintly unnerving to see someone with such blindness to the vagaries of fate.

"Every good inventor is eager," the young man responded. "If you don't believe in yourself, how can you expect anyone else to?"

The Peacemaker was irritated with the man for his arrogance, and with himself for allowing a form of words to be twisted against him.

"A man who knows his own worth is not eager to be accepted at less," he said coolly. "Insist upon a reward that meets your wishes, whether it's in money, honors, opportunities, or colleagues with whom you work. They must believe in you. Your opportunity may not come quickly."

The other man's face became suddenly very serious. "I know what I'm there for," he answered. "I won't forget it. World peace, an empire in which the creators and inventors, the artists, writers, musicians are not harnessed to the wheels of war and its insane destruction, but to the betterment of mankind!" The timbre of his voice was urgent. "In peace, order, and universal rule of law, we can build houses fit to live in, airplanes that can fly across continents and oceans without having to stop and refuel. We can conquer disease, perhaps even hunger and want. We will have the leisure to think, to develop great philosophy, write drama and poetry. . . ."

The Peacemaker felt the warmth of his enthusiasm and it refreshed the weariness in him.

The young man's face hardened into a cold fury. "We can't send our greatest visionaries and poets to be slaughtered like animals in a senseless waste, killing young

Germans who could also give fire and skill, art and science to the world — if they weren't lying facedown, bodies shattered, in the mud of some godforsaken shell hole." He rose to his feet, fists clenched. "I know what I'm here for, and I'll wait as long as it takes. You think you're using me to further your plans? You aren't! I'm using you, because I know what I do is right."

The Peacemaker smiled very faintly. "Shall we agree that we use each other? I shall exercise my influence to see that you are taken very seriously in the Establishment. Report to me seldom, and with the utmost discretion. Shanley Corcoran is a brilliant man. Earn his respect and his trust, and you will succeed — when the time comes."

The younger man smiled back, his eyes bright, his shoulders straight. "I will," he promised.

Chapter

EIGHT

The ambulance jolted over the rough road and Judith woke up and straightened in her seat. She had begged a lift from a lorry carrying supplies about thirty miles back in France, where the train had stopped. Now the familiar stench was in the air and she knew she was almost up to the lines. She looked out of the window and saw the flat country stretching out on every side, pale green poplars along the roads, here and there two or three dead and bare.

"Thought that'd wake yer," the driver said cheerfully. He was a man in his late thirties with a toothbrush mustache and a finger missing on his left hand. "Nose tell yer yer 'ome, eh?"

She smiled, pulling the corners of her mouth down. "Afraid so. It isn't exactly that you forget what it's like, but it has a renewed power when you've been away for a night or two," she agreed ruefully.

"Was Blighty good, then?" There was a

suppressed emotion in his voice, things he dared not allow too close to the surface of his mind.

She hesitated only a moment. If there was no home to return to, no ideal to fight for, what was the meaning of all this? "Wonderful," she answered firmly. "Same old traffic jams in Piccadilly, same scandals in the newspapers, same things to talk about: weather, taxes, cricket. I even got home for a couple of nights. The villages are just the same, too: farmers complaining about the rain, as usual, too much or too little; women quarreling over who's to arrange the flowers in church, but they always get done, and they're always gorgeous; someone's riding their bicycle too fast down the street; someone's dog barks. Yes, Blighty's just as it was, and I wouldn't change it, even at this price." Now she was intensely grave. "At least I'm pretty sure I wouldn't."

"Me neither," he answered, looking straight ahead at the road running like a ruler between the ditches. A windmill in the distance was the only break in the tablelike flatness of it. "Where yer want ter stop off then, love?" he asked.

"Poperinge," she answered without hesitation. "Or as near as you can get." She was going to find Cullingford, give him Mrs. Prentice's letter, and then take up her job as his driver again. She realized how eagerly she said it. She was sitting forward, already half prepared to get out, and they were still at least three miles away. She knew all these roads probably better than the driver beside her did.

He glanced at her. "Yer got a boyfriend here, 'ave yer?" he said with a grin.

She felt the heat wash up her face. He must wonder why she was pleased to be back when she had just been home. What other explanation could there be?

"Sort of," she answered. That was near enough the truth for him to believe her, and she did not want to be questioned more closely. There was no truth that she could tell, even to herself.

He laughed. "I bet he 'sort of' thinks so, too!" He took her all the way into Poperinge and she thanked him and got out in the square. It was a warm day, a few bright clouds sailing along the horizon, the sunlight gleaming on the cobbles. A couple of bicycles were parked against the tobacconist's shop window. Women were queuing at the bakery. She could hear the sound of voices from the Rat's Nest on the corner of the alley, and a snatch of song.

She walked over, and as the group of a dozen or so soldiers saw her, they sang more loudly, clapping on the beat, and finishing with a rousing chorus of an extremely bawdy version of "Good-bye, Dolly Grey."

" 'Oo are yer lookin' fer, love?" one of them asked her hopefully. He looked about twenty, with bright blue eyes and a lopsided face.

" 'Ave a glass o' beer!" another called out. "Drink enough of it, an' yer'll forget this is a bleedin' slaughter'ouse an' think if yer go round that corner you'll see a couple o' cows, an' a village pond wi' ducks on it, not some stinkin' crater full o' the corpses o' yer mates."

Someone told him abruptly to shut up.

"It would take more than beer to do that for me," she answered with a quick smile. "I'm looking for General Cullingford. I'm his driver. At least I was till I went on a couple of days' leave. But I'm back now."

One of the men looked her up and down appreciatively, and muttered something under his breath. Someone jolted him hard, and he did not repeat it.

"Sorry, love," the first man said. "Looks like yer lost yer job. The general went out of 'ere yesterday evenin' wi' a new driver.

Dressy little feller, 'e were, in a smart uniform an' a face like a schoolboy, but civil
enough, an' could 'andle a car like 'd built
it 'isself."

It couldn't be. She was stunned, as if she
had driven into a wall and she was bruised
to the bone. He wouldn't do that!

"Sorry, love. Looks like yer back ter ambulances, or whatever."

"What?" She looked at him as if she had
not really seen him before. He was slim and
dark, perhaps in his middle twenties, older
than many of the men, and the insignia on
his sleeve marked him as a corporal.

"What did you drive before you took the
general?" he asked. "Ambulances?"

"Yes."

"Then yer'd best get back to 'em. As a
volunteer yer can do wot yer like, I s'pose,
but that's w'ere yer needed most, if yer can
drive."

She nodded. It was ridiculous that it
should hurt this much. If she thought
about it honestly, she knew perfectly well
that she could not go on driving a general
around. It was a man's job. "Thank you,"
she added absently.

"Yer all right, love?" the corporal asked
with concern. "You look a bit — dunno —
off."

She forced herself to smile at him. "Yes, thank you. It's just funny — coming back. You have to get used to the smell again."

"In't that the truth! 'Ere, sit down a mo'. Wally! Get 'er a quick brandy, eh? We'd better get 'er right an' on the road. I couldn't drive them damn great ambulances, an' neither could you. We might need 'er — though please Gawd we don't!"

There was a bark of laughter, and a moment later a glass was put into her hand. The raw spirit burned down her throat, jolting her awake and into sharp attention. She realized their kindness, and felt slightly guilty for acting a lie as to the reason for her lapse. But the truth was secret — it had to be. She did not want to recognize it herself. She thanked them, finished the brandy, and went to look for a lift to the VAD ambulance headquarters.

She arrived in the early afternoon. It was a quiet time when most of the drivers were doing small maintenance and repair jobs on their vehicles. She found Wil Sloan standing over the engine of the ambulance she used to share with him, looking ruefully at the filthy commutator. His face lit when he saw her and he put the oilcan down and threw his arms around her.

"Hey, sugar! Where've you been?" He pushed her away from him, holding her by the shoulders and looking earnestly into her face.

"All around," she answered. "Then home to London for a couple of days."

"What's wrong?" They had shared too many experiences, good and bad, for him to be blind to her feelings. They had laughed together, told awful jokes, split the last piece of chocolate, read each other's letters from home.

"I went to see Mrs. Prentice, the mother of the war correspondent who was killed," she replied. "I had dinner with my brother, then I went home to St. Giles for a couple of nights. That's about all. I guess what really matters is, I had three hot baths. Let's get our priorities right!"

"And dinner in a restaurant where you couldn't hear guns?" he added. "What did you have?"

"I know I had ice cream for pudding!"

"Torturer!"

She smiled. In spite of driving Cullingford, she had missed Wil. "Yes," she agreed with a smile.

"So what's wrong?" he persisted.

"Are you going to clean that?" She indicated the commutator with a jerk of her head. "You won't get far with it as it is!"

He understood and handed her the oilcan, then bent his attention to cleaning the grit out of the commutator. They worked together for several minutes, put it back, then lubed the spindle bolts on the tie rods and oiled the steering post bracket. Finally the whole job was accomplished, polished and clean, and they were correspondingly filthy.

"So what are you doing back here?" he said at last, looking at her so directly she could not avoid his eyes.

"Driving ambulances, I expect," she answered, wiping her hands ineffectively on one of the discarded rags.

"Is that what's wrong?" he persisted.

"I suppose so. He's got a new driver, practically straight out of school, from what I hear. But I was only ever a short-term replacement anyway."

He looked at her, an oil smudge on his cheek. "You're sure burned about it. Why? That your pride speaking?"

She looked away. "No . . ." Then she did not know how to finish. She was afraid Wil knew her well enough to guess without words, but it was still something she would prefer not to make so honest between them. There were some things you did not discuss, even with your best friends.

With innate tact he assumed the truth, and evaded it. "You like the job, don't you. You're probably better at it than this guy anyway. What does he know?"

"Everything about cars, apparently," she replied.

A wide grin split his face. "That all? Well, we can fix his wagon any time! This is Ypres, not Piccadilly Circus."

"You've never been to Piccadilly Circus!" she pointed out. She was familiar with his adventures all the way from his hometown in Missouri where his explosive temper had lashed out one too many times, albeit in defense of someone smaller and weaker. But the ensuing fight had left two other young men hurt, one of them quite seriously. Wil had been advised he would be very foolish to remain around to face the unpleasantness that would undoubtedly follow. He should give people at least a year or two to forget.

The uncle who had given him the advice had also given him his sea fare to France, but Wil had had to make his own way to New England, and then New York itself. He had ridden the railways, worked where he could, and seen more of his own country than most of his fellows. But to serve in the war had been his goal, and although it had taken him nearly three months he had finally made it to Calais, and then north to Ypres.

Judith had listened with fascination to his stories of a vast land, of wonderfully varied people full of compassion and ingenuity. She had cried over their misfortunes, over those who had been injured in heart or body, laughed at their escapades. More than once during their bitterest nights, sodden, wind slicing across the unprotected land, she had realized that Wil was inventing things as he went along, to entertain her.

But the core of it was true, and it had not taken him to London. That was a dream he was keeping ahead of him, for before he finally went back to Missouri — London and Paris.

He was grinning at her now. "Aw shucks! I can read. I'll get there one day. You'll take me. You want your job back?"

"Yes." She had said it too quickly, and it alarmed her.

He raised his eyebrows. "Can't you make up your mind, then?"

She gave him a light punch on the arm, suddenly feeling tears prickle her eyes. "I can't have it, Wil. He's got a driver."

"A greenhorn!"

"A what?"

"A guy who knows nothing," he explained. "Still wet behind the ears. C'mon! Let's get cleaned up and onto the road. We'll find out where this guy is and get rid of him."

She had a sudden stab of alarm, thinking of Prentice, "Get rid of him! How?"

He half shrugged. "I dunno, but we'll think of something."

"Actually I do have a letter I have to take to the general," she said, walking beside him toward the water and soap. "And since it's personal, and I should tell him about his sister, I really do need at least to find him."

" 'Course you do," he agreed. "Never explain."

She flashed him a broad smile. "Never. We aren't army, right?"

"Right!" He saluted smartly. "Let's go look for the general!"

It was a long task. The day before there had been a large offensive that had failed and the losses had been very heavy. General Plumer had been forced to retreat and there was a considerable amount of disorder; it was hard to battle against anger and despair. The second German use of gas had made it even worse.

"General Cullingford?" Wil asked a harassed sergeant major.

The man wiped his sleeve across his brow, leaving a smear of dirt and blood. "Jesus, I don't know! Leave it to this lot and they'd 'ave all the bloody generals six feet under! And I'll not argue with 'em. What d'yer need 'im for anyway? The injured've bin evacuated from 'ere, and most of the dead are buried — at least those we can find."

Wil stood very stiff, his face pale. "Cullingford's not bad, as generals go. We have a message for him. Lost a member of his family."

The sergeant major's eyebrows rose. "Go on! You mean generals have families? An' here we was thinking they crawled up out of an 'ole in the ground."

"Someone should teach you the facts of life, Sergeant Major!" Judith snapped. "Unlikely as it may seem, even you had a mother once, who wiped your nose — and the rest of you. And probably even thought you were worth it."

The sergeant major blushed dark red, although it was impossible to tell whether it was shame for his attitude, or embarrassment at what she might be imagining about him. "Yes, miss. I 'eard he went toward Wulvergem, but I'm not sure."

"Thank you," she said stiffly.

The next person they asked was a major, and considerably less willing to help. Instead he directed them to take half a dozen men with shrapnel wounds or broken limbs back to Poperinge.

It was strangely familiar to be dealing with injured men again, ordinary soldiers who obey orders, made no decisions except to steel their nerves and go forward, live up to what was expected of them, not by the army or those at home who loved them, but by the men they lived with every day.

She had not meant to do it, except as a necessary act of obedience. Her mind was filled with finding Cullingford, telling him of her visit with his sister, the beginning of a softening in her, the first steps forward. She did not try to consider what she could do to replace his new driver, that was Wil's idea, perhaps his way of making her feel better.

Among the wounded was a ginger-haired man with a head wound. His right ear was torn off and there was a deep gash across his cheek, but the side of his face that was still visible under the bandaging was cheerful enough. If it cost him a terrible effort, he did not show it. He was busy talking to another man whose leg was shattered at the thigh. It was bound in a splint, but he looked gray-faced with pain, and his teeth were clenched together so tightly his jaw muscles bulged.

Two others bore shrapnel wounds, one in the leg, the other in the shoulder. They sat quietly, side by side, waiting their turn.

"I'll 'ave ter grow me 'air," the ginger-headed man was saying, talking for the sake of it, perhaps to keep the most badly wounded man's mind on something else, just to know he was not alone, or forgotten. "Me ma always said as I never listened anyway, so I s'pose an ear gorn won't make no difference. Yer all right, Taff? There's VADs 'ere, right enough. They'll get yer ter 'orspital where they'll fix that up for yer."

Judith smiled at him, and then bent to the man with the shattered leg.

"We're going to lift you up," she told him. "We'll be as gentle as we can."

"That's all right, miss," he said hoarsely. "It 'urts, but not too much. I'll be okay."

"Of course you will," she agreed. "But it could be a bit shaky for a while. I'll do my best not to hit the potholes."

"You drive that thing?" Ginger said with surprise. "I thought you was a nurse."

"I'm a better driver than nurse, believe me," she assured him. Wil was beside her, and one by one, with as much ease as possible, they loaded the wounded men in and drove back very carefully to Poperinge. There was a quiet companionship in doing their jobs together, working to exhaustion for a passionate common cause. They did not need to speak, but when they did it was almost in a kind of abbreviated language, references to past experiences, jokes they knew, a touch or a word of understanding.

It was nearly dark when they finally pulled into the central square in the town of Wulvergem and she saw the general's car outside the Seven Piglets. Judith's heart was pounding, her breath high in her throat as Wil parked the ambulance and she got out and walked over the cobbles, hearing her heels loud on the stones.

The laughter was audible even before she reached the door, men's voices raised, cheerful, calling out across the room, a shout, another guffaw. She pushed the door open and the smells of beer and smoke swirled around her. The inside was lit by gas lamps, old-fashioned ones with glass mantles. The tables had checked cloths on them and there were half a dozen men to each.

Few of them turned to look at her, supposing it to be just another soldier, then someone noticed it was a woman, and one by one they fell silent.

She saw the lamplight on Cullingford's fair hair and knew the shape of his head even before she saw the insignia of rank on his uniform. Opposite him sat a young man with a round, bland face. His skin was pale and his hands on the tablecloth looked soft and clean.

The boiling resentment welling up inside her was unreasonable and totally unfair. She knew that, and it made no difference at all.

The talk resumed again, but at a lower level. It was impossible now for her to retreat. However hard it was, she must go in, walk between the tables and speak to Cullingford, and give him his sister's letter.

He looked up as her shadow fell across the table. His eyes widened very slightly and his expression barely changed, but he could not keep a faint color from rising in his cheeks.

"Miss Reavley?" he said quietly. For an

instant she thought he was going to rise to his feet, as if they were both civilians, just a man and a woman met by chance at a dinner table. But he remembered the reality before he moved.

"Good evening, General Cullingford," she said more stiffly than she had intended to, as if she were guarding herself from hurt. But she realized with amazement that the hurt had already happened, perhaps months ago. Even this afternoon in the ambulance she had pretended to herself that she was only angry at losing a job she liked, though it was even harder to bear when she could see the whole picture and knew how serious the losses were, and the possibility of defeat. But there were also ways in which driving the general was easier than seeing individual men, real wounds not figures, blood and pain and fear you couldn't help, except to try to get the men back to the hospitals before it was too late.

Now, looking at him, seeing his eyes, his face, his hands on the table in front of him, she knew it was because she wanted to be wherever Cullingford was. She wanted to watch him as he talked with the men, see the hope rekindle in them as they listened to him, feel the shiver of pride because they believed in him. She had seen his unguarded moments; she had a close, painful idea of how much it sometimes cost him to maintain that façade when he knew numbers they did not, facts and figures that added up to something close to despair.

His odd, dry half-jokes made it bearable, the things he spoke of very seldom — walking, his dogs, horses he had loved, quotations that pleased him — made sense of the battle that cost so unbearably much.

Now he was waiting for her to explain herself, to tell him something about his family, the people he belonged to. She forced herself to meet his eyes and smile very slightly, as if she were simply a messenger and neither knew nor understood anything more than the facts of the errand. She was acutely aware of the new young driver sitting opposite.

"When I was in London I managed to call on Mrs. Prentice," she told him. "She wrote a letter and asked me if I would give it to you personally, sir. She was afraid it might take too long to get to you otherwise." She took the envelope from her pocket and held it out.

He reached up and took it. He did not mention the young man, or even glance at him. From the intensity of his gaze upon her it was as if he had forgotten the new driver's existence.

"Thank you, Miss Reavley. That is very good of you. Have you just returned?"

"Yes, sir. I went to Poperinge first, then to my ambulance unit." Would he understand from that that she had requested to resume her job? She heard the echo of accusation in her voice, and was embarrassed by it. She did not want him to know she minded. "Then I got ordered to drive a load of wounded men to Poperinge again," she added.

"Of course." There was every shade of expression in his voice, and she could not read any of it.

"Thank you for visiting Mrs. Prentice, and for bringing the letter," he repeated. He seemed to be about to add something, then changed his mind. It was pointless to ask how a bereaved woman was; she could only be racked with grief. The issue was only how openly she showed it, and that meant nothing. "You must be tired after your journey, and you have the care of your vehicle to attend to. Good night."

Was that as remote as it sounded? Or simply the necessity of the circumstances?

"Yes, sir." She stood to attention, then turned away immediately so he should not read in her anything more than a kindness accomplished, such as anyone might have performed.

Outside she found Wil waiting for her. She walked on, into the square toward the ambulance, furious with herself for the emotion boiling up inside her until she was choked with tears, and a rejection so agonizing it almost took her breath away.

Wil caught up with her, taking her arm.

"They're right," she said with an effort, keeping her face turned away from him, even in the dark. "He looks like a schoolboy."

"Then he shouldn't be too hard to get rid of," he retorted.

"General Cullingford may prefer to have a male driver," she said stiffly, opening the ambulance door and climbing in.

Wil went around to the front, cranked the engine to life, then got in on the driver's side and they moved off slowly. "My ma always reckoned my pa didn't know what was good for him, until she'd fixed it," he said casually, deliberately not looking at her, giving her the privacy of pretending she wasn't weeping. "Great woman, my ma." She could hear the warmth in his voice, the pride and gentleness, even though his face was hard to see in the sporadic light as they bumped over the cobbles and out of the square.

"Thank you, Wil," she said softly.

They were two miles down the road before he spoke again.

"I think I should make friends with him. In fact we both should."

She had been lost in her own thoughts. "With whom?"

"I love the way you folks speak! With the general's new driver, of course."

"I don't particularly want to make friends with him."

"Oh c'mon! Let's be nice to him. Take him out for a drink — or several. Give him some good advice. After all, he's new to this. He needs to know a few of the tricks. Help him on his way."

"Wil?" Had she really understood him correctly?

He was grinning. She could only see the gleam of his teeth in the fitful light.

"C'mon, sugar, you got to fight for what you want! If you don't, that means you don't want it enough to rate getting it! I didn't have you pegged for a giver-upper!"

"How could we do that?" she said reasonably, but wild ideas surged up inside her. "He'd be with the general all the time. I know I was. If I wasn't driving him somewhere, I was waiting for him."

"That'll make him the easier to find," Wil responded. "Wherever the car is, he'll be close." He had already pulled into the side of the road, and was now busy maneuvering the ambulance back and forth to turn it to face the way they had come.

"Now?" she said, aghast. She was not ready yet, she had not thought it through, or considered all the possible consequences.

"Of course, now!" He reached for the accelerator and the ambulance lurched forward. "Tomorrow could be too late. We could be busy with army things. You gotta do things when you can!"

She drew in breath to argue, then had nothing to say. A couple of days at home in England and she had lost the urgency of the Front, the knowledge that there may be no tomorrow. The only question was, did she want to get back her job as Cullingford's driver or not! Yes, she did.

"How much money have you got?" he asked.

"About thirty francs. Why?"

"Thirty!" His voice lifted in amazement. "What d'you think I'm going to feed him, Napoleon brandy?"

The edge of his excitement began to infect her. The ambulance was speeding along the road now, jolting over the potholes, lurching a little from left to right.

Twenty minutes later they were back in the square in Wulvergem, and they parked on the cobbles in the dark. Now the enormity of the plan struck her. She was a fool to go ahead with it! And a coward to back out. She wanted to drive Cullingford again. She would be more loyal to him than this new man could possibly be. She would see him more accurately, and believe in him more. She could feel the loneliness in him, the need to have one person to whom he could explain if he wanted, and yet to whom he did not need to.

She walked across the square after Wil. There were a few lights on in windows, a gleam here and there spilling out into the darkness. Someone else walked across the square, footsteps loud on the stones.

They were getting there much too quickly. And she was lying to herself. She wanted to be with Cullingford because she loved him. That was the first time she had admitted it. He was twice her age, and married. She was behaving like a complete fool. But what was sane in the world anymore? Was it wrong to love, if you didn't ask for anything in return?

They were at the door of the Seven Piglets.

"Wait here," Wil ordered abruptly. "Don't want you seen yet." Then he pushed the door open and disappeared inside.

Ten minutes later half a dozen soldiers came out, joking with each other, one of them laughing and staggering a little. She moved back into the shadows. They walked away and she was left alone. An old man crossed the far side of the square, pushing a handcart with something bulky in it. He moved as if he were infinitely tired. She felt a wave of pity for him, and tried to imagine how it would be if armies were camped in St. Giles, if foreign soldiers marched in the streets she had grown up in, and the peace of her own fields were shattered by shell fire, her own trees smashed. How it would hurt her if the familiar earth were gouged up and poisoned, soaked in blood, if generations ahead farmers would still plow the ground and find human bones.

Another half hour passed slowly, then the door opened again and finally Cullingford came out. He was alone. She recognized him instantly, even though she saw only his silhouette against the light.

The way he stood, the angle of his shoulders was unlike anyone else.

She thought of speaking to him: She could now, alone. But it would be absurdly undignified, as if she were running after him. The thought made her cringe.

He walked away, unaware that anyone saw him, and the moment was past. When he was around the corner, presumably to his lodging for the night, she went into the Seven Piglets again. It was far less crowded now and immediately she saw Wil sitting next to the new driver, both of them with glasses in their hands.

She hesitated, not knowing whether to interrupt them or not. Then Wil looked up and saw her. His face lit with pleasure and he waved enthusiastically. The driver turned to see who had drawn his attention.

Judith walked over.

"Of course she'll help you," Wil said encouragingly. "Judith, this is Corporal Stallabrass. He's an excellent driver. He knows everything there is to know about engines, but he doesn't know a damn thing about Flanders, at least not so far. Sit down." He pulled a chair out for her.

"I really don't expect . . ." Stallabrass began.

"We all help each other out here, Corporal," Judith told him, seeing from the corner of her eye, out of Stallabrass's sight, that Wil was topping up his glass with Pernod and very little water. It was lethal stuff. She had no idea what Wil was leading to, but she did her best to follow. "Share and share alike," she added.

"I could tell you stories. . . ." Wil embarked on a long and rambling account of a journey to Armentières. It was entirely fictitious, and incorporated just about everything that could go wrong with a vehicle, and several that couldn't.

"But . . ." Stallabrass started to argue several times, trying to assert his deeply studied knowledge. His face was earnest, and it apparently did not occur to him that Wil was deliberately embroidering the tale.

Judith got up quietly and went to the bar counter. She bought the rest of the bottle of Pernod and, with a jug of water, went back to the table. She would make her own mostly water, and surreptitiously refill Stallabrass's glass every time he was not looking.

Wil's account was growing wilder, and funnier every moment, and they were joined by a couple of other soldiers who were definitely a trifle happy for having imbibed generously most of the evening.

"I don't believe that!" Stallabrass said haltingly when Wil finished a particularly lurid tale of greasing an ambulance hubcap with ripe Brie cheese and ending up stuck in a field surrounded by a herd of cows.

One of the other soldiers, named Dick, tried to keep a straight face, but the tears were running down his cheeks.

"I like cows," his friend said sentimentally. "Beautiful eyes, cows have. Don't you think so, Corporal Stallabrass? Ever noticed the eyelashes they 'ave?"

But Stallabrass was staring into the distance, his mind locked in some dream of his own. "Beautiful," he repeated.

Wil glanced at Judith, then back at Stallabrass. "Is she?" he said with interest.

"Not everybody sees it," Stallabrass shook his head very slowly, as if he were nervous it might wobble and slide off. "They only see her as an ordinary woman, stamps and letters and money, and things." He sniffed and gave a genteel hiccup.

"Stamps and letters," Wil said, obviously no idea what he was talking about. "But she's not?"

"No," Stallabrass said with deep emotion. "She has ideas, dreams . . . she has passion!" He sighed. "She has the most beautiful . . ." He stopped, his hands clasping his Pernod glass, expression wistful.

Everyone waited with breath held for what he was going to say.

Judith was faintly embarrassed, in case it turned out to be too intimate.

Wil grinned. "Eyes?" he suggested to Stallabrass. "What about the letters? Does she write to you often?"

Stallabrass looked startled. "Oh no! Letters are part of her profession!"

"What?" Wil was totally lost.

"Letters," Stallabrass said patiently. "Stamps. She's the postmistress. That's what she does. It's very important. Where would we be without the Royal Mail? It holds the world together. King's head on every stamp. Do you know how serious it is to steal or damage the Royal Mail?"

"Oh yes," Wil agreed hastily. "Very important job for a young woman. She must be very special. What's her name?"

"Jeanette. She's forty-one. . . ."

Wil gulped and started to cough. The other soldier, partly to hide his own expression, patted him vigorously on the back.

"But she's beautiful?" Dick prompted gravely.

"Gorgeous." Stallabrass nodded, taking

Dick's Pernod absently and drinking it. "Gilbert Darrow thinks he's going to marry her, just because he's got a uniform and he's in the navy. Well, I've got a uniform, too!" He tried to square his shoulders, then changed his mind. "And I'm out here in France!"

"Flanders, actually," Wil corrected him. "But what's the difference, eh?"

"I'm here!" Stallabrass said carefully. "I shall see action! Front line — with the general. I shall win medals, and then we'll see what Gilbert" — he hiccupped — "Darrow has to show for himself." He blinked. "Say for himself," he corrected. "Nothing, that's what!"

"You're right!" Dick agreed with a broad smile. "You win a chestful of medals and go home and win Jeanette's hand. Sweep her off her feet! Or try anyway. Is she a big lady, with beautiful . . . eyes?"

"Yes, I'll do that!" Stallabrass said with another loud sniff. "I'll show them. I'll show them all!"

"To love!" Dick held up his glass.

Wil refilled Stallabrass's glass again and topped it up with a few drops of water. "To true love!" he said, lifting his own to his lips. "Always win in the end. Drink up, ol' boy!"

"To . . . true love!" Stallabrass emptied his glass all the way to the bottom, and slid off his chair onto the floor.

"Yeah, maybe," Dick agreed. "But not tonight, I reckon. Yer want a hand to get 'im up to 'is bed?"

"Thank you," Wil accepted, climbing slowly to his feet. "We'd better put him away nicely."

"Can't leave 'im 'ere, like nobody's child," Dick agreed, bending down to pick up Stallabrass in a fireman's lift. "Beggin' yer pardon, miss," he said to Judith. "But I think you'd better leave this to us. 'E's totally rat-arsed. Welcome to the army, Corporal!"

Judith stepped back. There was nothing more for her to do. It was three in the morning, and she had nowhere to sleep except in the ambulance. It would be chilly, but at least it would be dry, and she could lie down.

She woke in the morning to Wil shaking her urgently. She sat up, trying to remember where she was.

"You'd better get straightened up," he said in a hoarse whisper, as if they could be overheard, although actually there was no one else within fifty yards. The ambulance was parked in a side alley and it was not long after dawn. The cobbles still glistened with dew and the light had the hard, pale clarity of early morning.

She rubbed her hands over her face and pushed her hair back. Her head pounded and there was a vile taste in her mouth. Then she remembered the estaminet, Corporal Stallabrass, and the Pernod! No wonder she felt awful. She had not drank so much, but he had, and she was filled with guilt. How must he feel?

"Get yourself up, sugar!" Wil said firmly. "I don't think Corporal Stallabrass is going to win any medals today. In fact he just might not be safe to drive at all, and we wouldn't want the general to end up in the ditch, would we?"

She blushed and cleared her vision with an effort. She must find enough water to wash her face, a comb for her hair, and straighten her uniform so it wasn't so obvious she had slept in it. Then a hot cup of tea would help her to feel considerably more human. Actually, anything except Pernod would do.

Half an hour later she was standing in the square when General Cullingford came across the cobbles toward his car, beside which stood a bedraggled and deeply unhappy Corporal Stallabrass. He was only too obviously the worse for wear. His uniform looked as if he had put it on in his sleep, which he may well have done, and misjudged most of the buttons.

He attempted to salute, and looked as if he were a drowning man waving for help.

Cullingford stopped, a flicker of disgust crossed his face, then anger. Apparently the smell of alcohol was inescapable.

"Corporal, go and sleep it off," he said stiffly. "Then when you are sober, report to the duty sergeant for an assignment — not with me!" He turned away and saw Wil about twenty yards across the square, walking toward him with a fresh pastry in his hand.

"Good morning, sir!" Wil said cheerfully. He affected surprise and dawning concern. "Your driver not well?"

Cullingford looked at him coldly.

Wil gave the very slightest shrug. "You need someone?"

"How observant of you," Cullingford answered. "I don't believe you speak French."

"No, sir, I don't. But I've still got Miss Reavley with me, if you like? She knows the ropes, sir."

"Indeed." Cullingford took a deep

breath. "Then you'd better send her. I have to be in Ploegsteert by eight o' clock."

"Yes, sir!" Wil saluted, forgetting the pastry, and turned on his heel to march over to Judith.

Chapter

NINE

It was still imperative to Joseph that he learn who had killed Eldon Prentice, even though no one seemed willing to help with anything but the barest information that was so obvious as to be useless. Edwin Corliss remained in military prison awaiting the final verdict on his appeal. Any application of the death sentence was referred all the way up to General Haig himself, regardless of the offense or the circumstances, but the feeling against Prentice for having pushed the issue where Sergeant Watkins would have let it go, prevented anyone now from caring greatly how Prentice himself had died.

There was also his behavior over Charlie Gee's injuries, although that was less widely known. There was a searing pity for Charlie. Every man understood the horror of such mutilation, and their rage at Prentice's insensitivity was a release from the fear that it could happen to them. But it was rage, nevertheless, and the medical and VAD staff also were disinclined to give any information to Joseph that might help him discover a truth they were perfectly happy to leave alone.

Still, Prentice had been murdered by one of the British soldiers or ambulance drivers of this division, and he was becoming increasingly afraid that it could have been Wil Sloan. He could not forget Wil's uncontrolled, almost hysterical violence toward Prentice in the Casualty Clearing Station where he had brought Charlie Gee in, and Prentice had been so callous. If Joseph had not stopped him, he would have beaten Prentice senseless, perhaps even killed him there and then.

Could Prentice have been idiotic enough to have returned to the subject later, in Wil's presence, and Wil had somehow followed him, or even taken him, out into no-man's-land on the raid, perhaps on the pretext of looking for wounded? No one else seemed to have any explanation as to how Prentice had got there, or why.

The other alternative he could not escape was that it was one of Sam's men who was a friend of Corliss.

"Leave it alone, Joe," Sam said gravely. They were sitting in Joseph's dugout, sharing stale bread from rations, and a tin of excellent pâté that Matthew had sent in a parcel from Fortnum and Mason's in London, along with various other delicacies. For dessert they would have some of the chocolate biscuits Sam's brother sent whenever he could manage to.

"I can't leave it," Joseph said, swallowing the last mouthful. "He was murdered."

Sam smiled lopsidedly. "Aren't we all!" There was a bitter edge to his voice, the betrayal of a passion he rarely allowed to show through.

"Philosophically, perhaps," Joseph looked directly at Sam, watching his dark eyes with their sharp intelligence. "But for the rest of us it will be cold, disease, accident, or the Germans, all of which are to be expected in war."

"You left out drowning," Sam reminded him. "That's to be expected, too."

"Not by having your head held under it." Joseph heard his own voice crack. He despised Prentice, but it was a horrible thing to think of any man choking in that filthy water with the stench of corpses and rats and the lingering remains of the chlorine gas. He imagined the pressure on the back of his neck forcing him down until his lungs burst and darkness reached up and engulfed him.

Sam winced, as if it filled his mind as well. His face was tight, and the skin pale around his lips. "Don't think about it, Joe," he said quietly. "Whatever happened, whoever's fault it was, they'll probably be dead, too, before long. Leave it alone. Look after the living."

"It's the living I am looking after," Joe replied. "The dead don't need justice. They'll get it anyway, if there's a God. And if there isn't, it hardly matters. It's we who are left who need to keep the rules — for ourselves. At times it's all we have."

"You don't know the rules, Joe," Sam said quietly. "Not all of them."

"I know murder is wrong."

"Murder!" Sam said abruptly, jerking his head up, his eyes wide. "Jesus, Joe! I've seen men killed by snipers, shrapnel, mortars, explosives, bayonets, machine guns, and poison gas — do you want me to go on? I've skewered young Germans I've never even seen before, just because they were in front of me. And I've heard our own boys crying in their sleep because of the blood and grief and the guilt. I've seen them praying on their knees, because they know what they've done to other human beings, that could be ourselves in the mirror, except they're German. Dozens of them — every day! What rules are there to protect them, or give them back their innocence, or their sanity?"

He stared at Joseph intently, his eyes unblinking, a deep sadness in them for a moment allowing his own vulnerability to show. "Granted it wasn't a good thing to do, but hunting out whoever it was won't make it any better now. Morale matters, and that's your job. We have to survive. The men here need your help, not your judgment. We need to believe in each other, and that we can win."

Joseph hesitated.

"Leave it, Joe," Sam said again. "Belief can make the difference between winning, and not."

"I know." He stared at the ground. "We all need to have something to believe, or we can't forget it all. I wish I were surer of what I believe. There aren't many absolutes, but I'm supposed to know what they are."

"Friendship," Sam answered. "The best of yourself that you can give, laughter, keeping going when it's hard, the ability to forget when you need to. Have another chocolate biscuit?" He held out the packet with the last one left.

Joseph hesitated, then took it. He knew it was meant.

★ ★ ★

The corporal with the mail arrived, and Joseph went as eagerly as anyone else to see if there was anything for him from home. There were three letters, one from Hannah with news of the village. He could feel her tension through the careful words, even though he knew she was trying to hide it.

The second was from Matthew, telling of having seen Judith, and having visited Shanley Corcoran, and what a pleasure it had been.

The only other letter was from Isobel Hughes. He was surprised she should write again but he opened it with pleasure.

It was a simple letter, quite frank and comfortable, telling him about the farm, how they were having to make do with young women on the land where they had had men before they joined up and went away. She mentioned some of their exploits, and disasters. She had a robust, self-deprecating turn of humor and he found himself laughing, the last thing he had expected to do.

She described the spring fair, the church fête, life as it had always been, but with sad and funny changes, little glimpses of personal courage, unexpectedly generous help.

He read it through twice, and then wrote back to her. Afterward, when it was sealed and posted, gone beyond his recalling, he thought he had told her too much. He had written of his difficulty in trying to convince men that there was a divine order above and beyond the chaos they could see, a reason for all the senseless devastation. He felt a hypocrite saying it when he could give no reason for believing it himself. He should not have said that to her. She had made him laugh for a moment, feel clean and sane in the joy of little things, and he had rewarded her by talking of vast problems of the soul, which she could do nothing about. They would weigh her down, intrude into her grief, which she was trying so hard to control.

She would almost certainly not write again, and he would have lost something that was good.

He went to the hospital as soon as he had the chance, and asked Marie O'Day if the man Wil Sloan had brought in on the night of Prentice's death was conscious yet.

"Yes, but he's still in a lot of pain," she said guardedly. "Are you still after finding out if it really was Wil who brought him all the way?"

"Yes. I'd like to know."

"Well, don't push him! If he doesn't know, he doesn't," she warned.

But he did know, and he was happy to tell Joseph at some length how Wil had saved his life, at considerable risk, and how difficult the journey had been. His account was a little garbled, but it was clear enough to show that Wil could not have been anywhere near the length of trench known as Paradise Alley, where Prentice had gone over the top. He had been over a mile away, more like two.

Joseph left with a feeling of intense relief. Wil Sloan could not be guilty. For a moment he stood outside the Casualty Clearing Station in the sun and felt absurdly happy. He found himself smiling, and started to walk briskly back on the way to the supply trench again.

He was halfway along it, dry clay under his feet, rats scattering in front of him with a sound like wind in leaves, when he realized he had inevitably driven himself closer to the fear that it was one of Sam's men. It was a thought he was not yet ready to face. There were other things he could learn first. One of them was how Prentice had gained permission to go so far forward, and which officer had allowed him to join the raiding party, and on whose orders.

He was in a trench known as the Old Kent Road when Scruby Andrews came limping toward him.

"Gawd, moi' feet 'urt," he said with a twisted smile. "Must 'a bin a bloody German wot made moi boots! If oi ever foind 'im, Oi'll kill 'im wi' me star naked 'ands, Oi will! Sorry, Captain, but it's torture."

"Are you soaping your socks?" Joseph asked with concern. A soldier survived — or not — on his feet. It was an old trick to use bar soap to ease the rough parts of hard wool over the tender skin.

Scruby pulled a face. "Oi should've done that better. Barshey Gee says as you've bin asking about that wroiter fellow what got drownded out there?" He jerked his hand toward the sporadic sound of machine-gun fire.

"What I really need to know is what he was doing out there anyway," Joseph replied. "He shouldn't have been."

Scruby shrugged. "Shouldn't 'ave bin a lot o' things. Didn't listen, didn't care, an' got 'isself killed. Serve 'im roight." He sat on the fire-step and started to unlace his boots.

"I daresay in a way he deserved it," Joseph agreed with reluctance. "But which of us can afford what we deserve? I need better, don't you?"

Scruby looked up and grinned. "You're roight, Captain, but it don't work loike that. There's some rules we gotter keep. If we don't, there in't no point. We got nothin' left. It's rules what should 'ave kept Jerry out o' Belgium. It don't belong to 'im, it belongs to the Belgians, poor sods." He took his left boot off and rubbed his foot tenderly. "Oi seen an old man wi' a broken bicycle the other day, tryin' to push it up the road wi' a bag o' potatoes on it, an' a little girl trottin' along besoide 'im, carryin' a doll wi' one arm."

His face crumpled up, and he put his foot back in the offending boot, relacing it now loosely. "Oi didn't loike that bloke, Captain. Bastard, 'e were, but Oi s'pose rules is for them yer don't loike. Yer won't 'urt them as yer do. In't that what God's about, been fair to them as rubs your coat all the wrong way?"

"Yes, that's pretty well how I'd put it," Joseph agreed. "He rubbed my coat the wrong way, too, just about every time I saw him."

"Oi don't know for meself what's true," Scruby went on thoughtfully. "But Oi 'eard 'e were dead set on goin' over the top — more so 'e could say 'e 'ad, if yer get me? But 'e swung the general's name around summink rotten, loike the general were 'is pa, an' no one 'ad better stand in 'is way. Said 'e 'ad permission, written, an' all! Load o' rubbish, if you ask me."

"Actually the general was his uncle," Joseph replied. "But I can't imagine him giving a war correspondent permission to go over the top. I'd like to find out who he went with, exactly, and what this permission amounted to."

"Oi dunno, Captain. Reckon as you'll 'ave to ask the general 'isself. Oi don't see nobody else goin' to tell you, cos they don't care."

Joseph was forced to admit the truth of that. The captain who had led the raid had been killed, and everyone else had claimed that in the dark they couldn't tell Prentice apart from anyone else. He had been very discreet about it, but he already knew most of the sappers could account for each other. It was with a cold, unhappy doubt gnawing inside him that he finally begged a lift on a half-empty ambulance and went to Cullingford's headquarters in Poperinge to ask him outright. At this point he would like to have taken Sam's advice and let it go, but Scruby Andrews was right, if morality were to mean anything at all, it must be applied the most honestly when it was the most difficult, and to protect those everything in you despised.

But when he reached the house just outside Poperinge and asked if he might speak with General Cullingford briefly, Major Hadrian told him that Cullingford was not there.

"You can wait for him, if you've time to, Captain, but I have no idea when he'll be back," Hadrian said with brief apology. "Can I help you?"

Joseph was undecided. He did not want his inquiries to become the subject of speculation any more than they already were, but how could he decide the question one way or the other if he had not the courage to ask? It might be days before he had the opportunity to speak to Cullingford privately. And whatever he learned, he might have to ask Hadrian for verification anyway.

"Yes, perhaps you can," he said, choosing his words with care. They were alone in Hadrian's office; this was as discreet as it was ever going to be. "You may be aware that before his death, Mr. Prentice was keen to gather as much firsthand information as possible about the war."

Hadrian's face was pinched with distaste. He stood behind his desk, small and extremely neat, his haircut immaculate, his uniform fitting him perfectly. "Yes, I know that, Captain." He did not say that it was of no interest to him, it was in his expression. He was intensely loyal to Cullingford, and if Prentice had been an embarrassment to him, he would get no protection from Hadrian.

"He managed to get to several places much further forward than any other correspondent," Joseph went on. "He claimed to have General Cullingford's permission. Do you know if that is true?"

Hadrian looked carefully blank, his eyes wide. "Does it matter now, Captain Reavley? Mr. Prentice is dead. Whatever he did, it is not going to be a problem any longer."

There was no avoiding the truth, except by simply surrendering and going away. He could not do that. "The problem will not completely go away, Major Hadrian," he replied. "Mr. Prentice did not die by accident. He was killed, and at least some of the men are aware of it. For morale, if not for justice, there needs to be some accounting for it."

Hadrian frowned. "Justice, Captain?"

"If we do not believe in that, then what are we fighting for?" Joseph asked. "Why do we not simply leave Belgium to her fate, and France, too? We could all go home and get on with our lives. If promises to defend the weak are of no value, why is Britain here at all? Why sacrifice our men, our lives, our wealth on something that was in the beginning essentially not our business?"

Hadrian was stunned. "Are you likening Mr. Prentice to Belgium, Captain Reavley?" His abstemious face was filled with distaste.

"I did not like him, Major Hadrian," Joseph said. "And I gather you did not either, but that is hardly the point, is it? Most of the men who have died here in this mud had never been to Belgium before, and I daresay some of them couldn't have found it on the map."

Hadrian swallowed with a convulsion of his throat. "I take your point, but surely Prentice was killed by a German. If he was out in no-man's-land, then he was a perfectly legitimate target. Even if he were not, there wouldn't be anything we could do about it. He shouldn't have been there."

"No, he shouldn't," Joseph agreed. "Who gave him permission?"

Hadrian colored a deep red. "Is that your concern, Captain? If you feel you owe some kind of explanation to his family, General Cullingford is his uncle, as no doubt you are aware."

"Perhaps I didn't make myself clear, Mr. Prentice was not killed by a German soldier, he was killed by one of our own."

The color in Hadrian's face ebbed, leaving him pasty white. "Are you trying to say he was murdered?"

"Yes. Very few men know so far, but I would like to find out the truth and deal with it before they do. I would be obliged for your help, Major. I am sure you can see why. He was not a very pleasant young man, and he caused a certain dislike. People will speculate. I confess, in many ways I am more concerned with protecting the innocent than I am with finding the guilty."

Hadrian was silent, in acute discomfort.

The cold fear began to tighten inside Joseph until it was a hard knot of pain. If Cullingford had indeed given Prentice permission to go wherever he pleased, then why? It was an unprofessional thing to do. He would not have given such latitude to any other correspondent. Was it family favor, or had Prentice exerted some pressure? He thought of the bawdy laughter and the jokes he had already heard about Cullingford's replacement driver, the helpless Stallabrass, and his drunken confession to an unrequited passion for his local postmistress. The tale had spread like wildfire through the trenches. They needed to laugh to survive, and teasing was merciless. Every time the mail was brought to anyone within earshot of him, the jokes began.

Joseph also knew that Judith and Wil Sloan had deliberately got Stallabrass drunk so Judith could get her old job back driving Cullingford, and Cullingford had allowed it. All kinds of conclusions could be drawn, accurate or not.

"Did General Cullingford give Prentice written permission to go wherever he pleased?" he said aloud. "That is what he claimed."

Hadrian stared at him in undisguisable misery. He was obviously trying to decide whether he could get away with a lie, and if he could, what it would be to protect Cullingford.

Joseph put him out of his misery, partly because once he came up with a lie he would feel cornered into sticking to it, however openly he had been exposed. "I do not need to know the general's reasons for doing so," he said, meeting Hadrian's eyes. "Prentice was a manipulative man and not above emotional pressure where he perceived a vulnerability."

Hadrian's eyes widened.

"Before anyone makes any suggestions, I'd like to know where the general was on the night Prentice died," Joseph said firmly.

"You can't think he'd have anything to do with his death!" Hadrian's voice rose close to falsetto. There was outrage in it, but it was fear that put it there, not indignation. Joseph was now quite certain that whatever pressure Prentice had used, it had been powerful and effective.

"I don't," he said, trying to put more certainty into his voice than he felt. "But we need to be able to prove he had not, Major Hadrian."

"Yes." Hadrian swallowed hard. "I was at school with Prentice, Captain Reavley. He was not pleasant, even then. He had a knack for . . . using people. I am not being overly unkind. If you doubt me, ask Major Wetherall. He was at Wellington College also, in my year. Prentice used to keep notes on people then, in his own kind of shorthand. Cryptic sort of stuff. I never learned how to decipher it, but Wetherall was pretty clever, and he worked it out. He told me the sort of thing it was." Hadrian was stiff, his eyes fixed on Joseph's. He was apprehensive, and yet he felt he needed Joseph's cooperation. His anxiety was palpable in the air.

Joseph did not want to know how Prentice had treated his uncle, unless it was absolutely necessary, partly because it concerned Judith. It was a situation that was making him increasingly unhappy. "I didn't know that," he said aloud. "Where was the general that night?"

"The telephone lines were particularly bad," Hadrian replied. "They seemed to be broken in all directions. You'd get someone, and then lose them again before you heard more than a couple of words. Finally around midnight they went altogether. There was nothing to do about it but go along in person. The general went north and east, I went west. You can ask the commanders concerned, they'll all tell you where he was. Believe me, he was nowhere near Paradise Alley, which I understand is where Prentice was found?"

"Yes, it was. Thank you, Major. You

must have been Paradise Alley way then. Did you see Prentice?"

Hadrian was unusually still. "No. I . . . I was held up. My car broke down. I had to jury-rig it — use a silk scarf on the fan belt. Took me the devil of a time. It's not really my sort of skill. But no choice that time. No one else to ask."

"I see. Thank you, Major Hadrian." Joseph was not certain if he believed him, but there was nothing further to be pursued here. There might be a way to find out if he had been where he said, but he did not know of it.

He excused himself and was walking out of the building into the courtyard when the general's car drove up with Judith at the wheel. They stopped a few yards away. It was already dusk and the shadows were long, half obscuring the outlines of figures. Judith turned off the engine and got out. She was very slender, the long, plain skirt of her VAD uniform accentuating the delicacy of her body, her slightly square shoulders. She moved with grace, intensely feminine. In the headlights her face had the subtlety of dreams in it, and the fire of emotion. She was looking at Cullingford as he got out as well and slammed the door. It was necessary, to make sure the catch held.

He stopped for a moment. He said something, but Joseph was too far away to hear it, his voice was very low. But it was the look in his face that arrested the attention. He can surely have had no idea how naked it was; the tenderness in his eyes, his mouth, betrayed him utterly.

Then he straightened his shoulders, turned and walked over toward the entrance, his easy gait masking tiredness with the long habit of discipline, and disappeared inside.

Joseph moved forward into the pool of the headlights.

She saw him only as a figure to begin with, then suddenly recognition lit her face. "Joseph!" She dropped the crank handle on the gravel and came toward him.

He took her in his arms quickly and held her a moment. It was not perhaps strictly correct, but sometimes feeling was more important than etiquette. The touch of someone you loved, the instant of unspoken communication, was a balm to the raw need, a remembrance of the things that give reason and life to the man inside the shell. He could feel the strength and the softness of her, smell the soap on her skin and the engine oil on her hands. He was so angry with her for being less than she could have been, for twisting Cullingford's emotions till he was vulnerable to Prentice, and for laying herself wide open to contempt, or worse, that the words choked in his throat.

He pushed her away. "You shouldn't have done it, Judith!" he said hoarsely. "If it was someone else, I could excuse them that they might not have known any better! But you do!"

"Done what?" Her expression was defensive, but she could not make innocence believable. She tried, but an inner honesty belied it. "What are you talking about?"

He held her at arm's length. "That doesn't become you, but if you want it spelled out, you should not have coerced Wil Sloan into helping you get Stallabrass so drunk he lost his job, and you were waiting right there in the wings to take it back again. Do you imagine nobody knows what you are doing? They're laughing at the poor fool all around Belgium! He can't get a letter without the men making jokes about the wretched postmistress he's in love with!"

She bit her lip. "I didn't know. . . ."

"You didn't care!" he said furiously, the words pouring out now. "You didn't think about Stallabrass, he was simply in your way, and you didn't think about Wil Sloan. You knew he was your friend and would do anything he could to help you. You used him. God knows what you thought you were doing to Cullingford! This war is not for your entertainment, or to make it easier for you to have an impossible romance."

She was scalded by guilt, perhaps not so much for what she had done, but for the ideas and dreams of what she could do, might do, if opportunity were given her. She had not rebuffed Cullingford and it seemed she had no reservoir of virtue within to draw on, to restrain whatever hunger or need raged inside her.

Instead she picked on the least important detail. "I did not coerce Wil!" she said hotly. "It was his idea!"

"That's a shabby excuse, Judith," he told her bitterly. "He's your friend, and he did it to please you. If you have a passion to do something wrong, at least have the grace to stand by it. Don't duck behind someone else's skirts."

The accusation must have cut her like a whiplash, perhaps because part of it was true or because it was he who made it. "I am not hiding!" she said fiercely. "I was there with Wil! And Stallabrass drank because he wanted to! It's not my job to baby him!"

"It's your job to look after anyone who needs it," he replied without compromise. "You took advantage of Wil's friendship, of Stallabrass's ignorance, and of Cullingford's attraction to you, because you want something that isn't yours. Is Cullingford the sort of man who can have a love affair with another woman, and walk away from it without guilt, without knowing he had betrayed his wife, and more important than that, the best in himself?" he demanded. "And if he is, is he a man whose attention you want? What for? To prove you can get it?"

"I drive him!" She was raising her voice, possibly without realizing it, anger and guilt harsh in her. "That's all! You've got a rotten, vicious imagination, and as my brother, who's known me all my life, it makes me sick and disgusted that that's what you think of me. You think you can step into Father's shoes? You're not fit to stand on the same piece of ground!" She took a gasping breath and pushed further away from him. "Go and preach morality to your poor, bloody wounded who can't escape from you — because I can! And I will!" She turned her back, leaving him

373

alone on the gravel in the encroaching night, weary, angry, and disappointed.

But he could not afford to let it go. He still had no proof that Cullingford had not connived at Prentice's death, directly or indirectly. The last few minutes had shown how intensely vulnerable he was.

Joseph strode after Judith and caught up with her at the side door to the château. She must have heard his feet on the gravel because she swung around to face him. In the fast graying light he saw the tears in her eyes, but he knew it was anger as much as pain.

"What is it now?" she said between her teeth.

He glanced around to make certain there was no one else within the sound of their voices. There was no point in trying to be diplomatic with her, he had already made that impossible.

"Cullingford gave Prentice written permission to go wherever he wanted to, even onto the front lines," he said grimly. "No other war correspondent is allowed to do that. It meant none of us would arrest him and send him back, no matter what he did."

Her eyes blazed at him, her face was set in lines of defiance, but she said nothing, forcing him to continue.

"Prentice must have used pressure on him to force him into that," he said grimly. "Because of you."

She gulped. She wanted to say something, anything to defend herself, and Cullingford, but there was nothing. The helplessness burned in her eyes. "He was a bastard!" she said between her teeth. "Is that what you want me to say? You can stand there and be as holy as you like, Joseph, you can blame us all, and feel self-righteous and superior. You can make me feel as rotten and as frightened as you know how to, and you're good at it. I can't stop you. But what good does it do? Prentice is dead. You say people are laughing at Stallabrass, and . . . and talking about General Cullingford. Have you come to call me a scarlet woman — which I'm not! Or have you actually got something useful to say?"

He felt as if she had slapped him. His flesh should have been stinging hot. It was startling how deeply words could injure.

"Eldon Prentice was murdered by one of our own men," he replied in a low, grim voice. "I despised him for lots of reasons, for Edwin Corliss, for Charlie Gee, and for his moral pressure on General Cullingford.

But none of those things, repulsive as they are, make his murder acceptable. I need to know who did it, to protect those who didn't, if nothing else."

Her voice was husky, her face was paler. "Are you thinking the general did it? He wouldn't! Prentice was thoroughly rotten, but Cullingford wouldn't do that, no matter what it cost. You can't think . . ."

"No I don't, but that doesn't matter, Judith. It's what we can prove."

"If anybody killed Prentice over his moral blackmail, it would be Hadrian," she answered almost under her breath. "General Cullingford was far to the north and east of where you were, and that's easy enough to prove. I know it myself."

"Of course. No one thinks he crept out in the mud and shell holes himself, in order to push Prentice's head under the water," he replied. "I asked Hadrian. He was in the right area. He said he had a breakdown that he fixed with a silk scarf."

She must have heard the doubt in his voice. "You don't believe him!" she challenged.

"Do you?" he asked.

She hesitated too long, and realized it. "I don't know. He could have."

"But you have no way of knowing," he reasoned.

"Yes, I have," she said immediately. "It won't be difficult to ask the other men who drove the cars if he brought one back with a silk scarf in place of a broken belt. If there was one, somebody'll know. Then you can check everywhere he says he was, and see if it's true. You can, Joseph! Cars are too precious around here. We know what happens to each one. Do it!" Her face was keen now, she was leaning a little toward him. "If you really are trying to prove who's innocent as much as who's guilty, you can find out about Hadrian." There was challenge in her voice, and fear in case she was wrong. She was still angry, frightened and deeply hurt that Joseph blamed her, and was forcing her to blame herself.

"I'll find out," he replied. "But it doesn't change anything else. If Prentice gained permission to go forward from Cullingford, by blackmailing him over you, it was you who made that possible."

"There are times, Joseph, when you are insufferably pompous!" She almost choked on her words, spitting them at him, her fists clenched. "We were all devastated when Eleanor died. It was terrible. She was lovely, and you didn't deserve to lose her. But you've run away from feeling anything since then. You've become cold, detached, full of brains and emptyhearted. I'm not always right, but I'm not a coward! I'm not afraid to feel!" And without waiting either to look at him and see what pain she had caused, she swiveled round and stormed into the hallway of the building and through the far door, letting it slam after her.

He walked back outside into the darkness of the fast-falling night, numb inside from the weight of what she had said. She was wrong to stay with Cullingford when she knew he was in love with her, whatever his loneliness or the depth of his need for at least one contact of compassion, laughter, human tenderness, the hunger above all things not to be alone, even if it was only for an hour. An hour led to a day, a week, the ache for a lifetime.

He had meant to speak to her wisely, as their father would have done, in such a way that she would have seen her mistake for herself, and wanted to change it as much as he wanted her to. He had meant to come closer to her, so that in the wrench of giving it up, she would at least know that she had his support, and she was not alone either literally or emotionally.

Instead he had driven her so far away he had placed a barrier between them that he had no idea how to surmount.

But one thing he could do was trace the car Hadrian had used on the night of Prentice's death, and see if it had broken down as he had said, and he had indeed used a silk scarf to jury-rig it until he got back to Poperinge. He could also check to see if anyone else had seen him at the various points of his journey. It might prove that he could not have been in no-man's-land at the same time as Prentice.

He had almost completed his task when he spoke to the nurse, Marie O'Day, the following afternoon. It seemed incontrovertible that Hadrian had been where he had said, and Cullingford had certainly been ten or twelve miles in the opposite direction.

"It was a bad night," Marie told him. "I saw Prentice, but he was alone. Why are you asking about him, Captain Reavley? What is it you need to know? He's dead. Nobody liked him, and you know why. You were here when he did that to Charlie Gee, poor boy." Her face twisted with grief at the memory. "It's nobody's fault he went over the top. Nobody else made him go!"

"Nobody suggested it?" he pressed. "You don't know who gave him the idea?"

"Even if somebody egged him on, he didn't have to do it!" she pointed out.

"Did they?"

"No. He'd already made up his mind when he reached us." It was a statement of fact and there was no wavering, no over-emphasis in her as if she were urging a lie.

"Reached you from where?" he asked curiously. "Where had he come from?"

"I don't know," she admitted. "To the east a little. He was full of himself, said he'd already been right as far as the German wire, and he wanted to go again."

"Been as far as the German wire?" Joseph was incredulous. Had Prentice really been to another regiment, and gone over the top on a raid with them, and now he wanted to do it again, here? "Are you certain?"

"Oh, yes." Her face was full of contempt. "He was bragging about it. Said it was exciting and dangerous, a taste of the real war he could write something about that would grab everybody's attention. He wanted to add going over in a raid to what he already had! Maybe kill some Germans himself, then he could write as an actual soldier and tell people what it was really like, the feel of it, the smell of bodies, the rats, everything as it is, so they'd know." Her face pinched. "Maybe it's wicked of me, Captain Reavley, and you being a godly man, but I'm glad he didn't live to do that."

He was startled. He had not thought of correspondents writing so graphically. "Yes, I'm glad, too, Mrs. O' Day. Perhaps I'm not as godly as you think. Thank you for your help." He left her taking the mugs back inside, a tall, sad figure in a gray dress soiled with blood, busy with the small duties of habit and comfort.

He spoke later to Lucy Crowther, assistant to Marie O'Day. She was rolling bandages on the table in the first-aid station. Her dark hair was tied back severely and her knuckles were clenched and she avoided his eyes. "Yes. He was boasting that he was going over with the men," she answered his question.

"For the second time," he said.

She looked up at him. "No. He'd never been over before."

"He told Mrs. O'Day that he's been right up to the German wire!"

"Oh, that!" she said dismissively. "Any fool can do that, once the sappers have dug the tunnel!"

"You mean underground!" Again his belief was stretched to snapping.

Her face was twisted with contempt. "Yes, of course. You didn't think he went on top, did you?"

"He was back here from eastward somewhere," he asked, trying to piece it together in his mind.

"That's right. The sappers were working along at Hill Sixty. Major Wetherall and his men. Prentice went that way with them."

"Prentice went with Major Wetherall?"

"Yes." She finished the last bandage. "I don't know how Major Wetherall could stand him, but he can't have minded or he'd have got rid of him," she said. "Sappers don't have to put up with anybody they don't want to. It's pretty dangerous, with explosions, cave-ins, water, and all that." There was admiration in her now, an utterly different tone in her voice, a softness.

Joseph found himself smiling. He knew that what Sam did was dangerous, and vital. If a shell landed anywhere along the tunnel, they could be buried alive, crushed by falling earth, or perhaps worse, imprisoned and left to suffocate. And there was the moral hell of getting so close to the

German trenches that you could hear the men talking to each other, the laughter and jokes, the occasional singing, all the daily sounds of life far from home and in intense danger. You could sense the comradeship, the grief for loss, the pain, the loneliness, the whisper of fear or guilt, the hundreds of small details that showed they were men exactly like yourselves, and most of them nineteen or twenty years old as well.

They listened to overhear information. Sometimes they planted explosives to blow up the trench itself. More than once they accidentally broke in on an enemy sap and found themselves face-to-face with Germans doing exactly the same job, with the same fears and the same guilts. Joseph had sat listening to them, because listening was all he could do to help, and his admiration for them was intense. But there was still a sweetness seeing it in someone else. "Thank you," he said aloud. "Who would know what Prentice actually did do, and what was said, who he finally went with?"

"You could try Corporal Gee. Barshey Gee," she added, knowing how many Gees there were in the regiment.

He thanked her and went in the darkening air, now louder with gunfire, to look for Barshey Gee.

The gunfire increased, heavy artillery going on both sides. He moved from one stretch of trench to another, past men crouched over machine guns, others waiting, rifle in hand, in case there was a German raiding party coming. Eyes scanned the alternate glare and darkness of no-man's-land. It was easy to mistake the haggard outline of a tree stump for that of a man.

Then there was a bad hit at Hill 62, and he forgot Barshey Gee, Prentice, or anything else while he helped wounded men, mostly carrying them on his back. No one could carry a six-foot stretcher around the corners without tipping it over.

By midnight it eased off for a while, then there was another flurry, and the expected raiding party came. Star shells lit the sky and the running figures were momentarily silhouetted black. Against the glare bullets ricocheted everywhere. Several men fell, but the attack was beaten off. Two prisoners were taken, white-faced, stiff-lipped, only slightly injured. They looked to be about twenty, fair-haired and fair-skinned. Joseph was sent to talk to them, because of his fluent German, but he learned nothing except their names and regiment. It was all he expected. He would have both despised and pitied a man who gave him more.

It was close to the spring dawn when he finally caught up with Barshey, who was sitting on an empty ammunition crate smoking a Woodbine, oblivious of the blood crusting on his cheek and down his left arm.

"Hello, Reverend," he said cheerfully. "We won that one, Oi think."

"Raids are always rough on whoever crosses no-man's-land," Joseph agreed, squatting on his heels opposite him.

"Want one?" Barshey offered him a Woodbine.

"No thanks," Joseph declined. "Do you remember the raid the night Prentice was killed?"

"Who's Prentice?"

"The war correspondent."

"Oh, him!" Barshey shrugged. "Rotten little sod. Yes, of course Oi remember it. He didn't come back. They say he got drowned. Shouldn't ever have gone, stupid bastard." He drew in deeply. "Oi told him that, but he was hell-bent on it. He's been up the saps with Major Wetherall's men and thought he was a soldier." His lip curled in contempt. "Full of what he was going to write about it. Tell 'em all at home everything they don't want to know.

Oi moight've pushed him in a crater meself, if Oi'd 'a thought of it."

"I don't suppose you know who did?" Joseph said casually.

"No oidea."

Barshey stubbed out his Woodbine and lit another, cupping his hand around the match from habit, even though they were well behind the lines now. "Didn't you and Major Wetherall go out and look for some o' them as moight be still alive? You brought Captain Hughes back, didn't you? He didn't make it." He shook his head and his voice dropped. "Pity. He was a good man, even though he was Welsh."

"Yes. We found Prentice's body, too." Joseph said nothing about Hughes, even to defend the Welsh. That was Isobel's husband, and losing him still hurt.

Barshey shrugged. "Don't know whoi you bothered risking your neck for that one. He was dead anyway. No point, really."

"I'd have fetched him if he'd been anyone else," Joseph said.

Barshey grinned suddenly. "Oi reckon you're a fool, Cap'n, but it's a sort o' comfort. Oi'd loike to think you'd come for me, whether Oi were any good or not. Because sometimes Oi think Oi'm foine, but other days Oi wake up with dead Jerries in moi 'ead, and Oi think of their woives and mothers, and that maybe they're the ones Oi can hear singing sometimes? Or the ones that left the sausages out there for us, or that yell out asking for the football scores, an' Oi can't stand it. Oi need to think there's someone that'd come for me, no matter what." He was still smiling, but his eyes were brilliant, hurting with the intensity of his need.

"Don't think it," Joseph said softly. "You can be sure I would."

Barshey nodded, blinking a little. He looked down and squinted into the empty Woodbine packet to hide his feelings, not because he wanted another cigarette. "You know if you want to find out what happened to the stupid bastard, you should ask Major Wetherall. He was with him up the saps 'cos Prentice was bragging about it. Reckoned Wetherall thought he was some kind of soldier. Load of rubbish, if you ask me. Wetherall despoised him. But he came from the saps over to us during the raid, roight across no-man's-land. More guts than any other man Oi know. He might've seen the stupid sod fall in a crater."

Joseph was cold in the pit of his

stomach. "Major Wetherall came across no-man's-land during the raid?"

Barshey smiled. "Loike Oi said, he's one on his own."

It was the one answer Joseph had not thought of: any of the other sappers, Corliss's friends — but not Sam!

"You all roight, Cap'n?" Barshey said gently. "You look pretty bad. You didn't get hit, did you?"

"Hit?" Joseph said stupidly.

"Did you get hit — that last raid?" Barshey repeated carefully, searching Joseph's face. "You all roight? You look koind o' sick."

"Just bruised," Joseph replied. "Bruised inside, I think."

"Hurts, doesn't it," Barshey said sympathetically, even though he was not sure what he was referring to.

"Yes," Joseph agreed. "Yes, it hurts." He wished now that he had taken Sam's advice and not looked. He did not want to know, but you cannot undo knowledge. He knew who had killed Eldon Prentice. Thinking of Corliss still waiting to know if he was going to face the firing squad, perhaps it was not difficult to understand why. Maybe he should have known from the beginning. But he could not let it go just because it wounded him too deeply to deal with the pain of it.

There was no use hesitating. He would like to have avoided facing it altogether, but he knew that was not possible. Scruby Andrews's words were in his head, and the knowledge of the truth of them would not leave him. It would not now, and he knew it would not later.

At stand-to, Sam would be at his usual place. Breakfast was not the time for such a confrontation, and straight afterward they would both be occupied with other duties. It must be before. There was no choice but to waken Sam now.

He walked slowly along the damp morning earth. The trench walls were studded with beetles. A rat ambled away, unconcerned. He went up the steps and along the supply trench. It was eerily silent just at the moment. Both sides had stopped shooting. He could hear a bird singing somewhere high above in the morning sky of soft, unblemished blue.

He had walked this stretch of Paradise Alley so often he knew every bend and dip in the ground, where the posts and the hollows were. Every other time it had been with a sense of expectancy, even pleasure. Now he had to force himself because delay was pointless. It would change nothing.

He reached Sam's dugout and stopped. Every scar and nail hole on the wooden surround was familiar. There was nothing on which to knock, but one did not walk into a man's living quarters at this hour without making some attempt at courtesy.

"Sam!" His voice was rough, as if his throat were dry. "Sam!"

There was silence. Was he relieved or angry that he had to put it off after all? Perhaps Sam was at a very early breakfast? No. Stand-to had not been called yet. Maybe he was asleep. "Sam!" he shouted.

A tousled fair head appeared through the gap in the sacking. "You're looking for Major Wetherall? Sorry. He was transferred. Some sort of emergency along the line. No idea where."

Joseph stared at him. He could hardly grasp that this strange, blank-faced man was in Sam's dugout. Where were all Sam's things? How could this happen without warning?

The man blinked, recognized Joseph's insignia of rank and calling.

"Sorry, Chaplain. Not bad news for him, I hope?"

"No," Joseph said slowly. He took a breath. "No. No news at all, at least not now. Thank you." He turned away, tripping over a rut in the uneven ground. This was only a respite, it changed nothing, but for the moment he did not have to face Sam and deliberately destroy the friendship that was his lifeline to the laughter, the warmth of human touch, the hand that reached out and grasped his in the inner darkness of this seemingly universal destruction.

Chapter

TEN

The same evening as Joseph was talking to Marie O'Day, Judith was sitting in the kitchen of the château. She had been given an excellent dinner, but separately from Cullingford and the senior French officers with whom he had been conferring. She ate the last of the crusty bread, which was still warm, and the fresh Brie, finished her wine, then thanked the cook with an enthusiasm and a gratitude she did not have to feign.

Outside in the garden afterward in the balmy evening under the trees she could hear birdsong and smell the damp earth. To the north the glare of shells was marked against the evening darkness, and the sound grew louder as the firing increased.

Cullingford found her as the last light was fading in the sky. The heavy trusses of the lilac seemed more shadow than substance but the perfume was heady, snaring the senses and wrapping one around.

"Did they give you a good dinner?" he asked quite casually.

She turned in surprise. He was a couple of yards away and she had not heard his feet on the soft grass. "Yes, thank you. Best meal I've had in . . . since dining with Mrs. Prentice, actually,"

"What about with your brother, Matthew?" He smiled, his face toward the light, but there was no ease in it, and she thought no happiness. Was it because she had reminded him of his sister, and Eldon Prentice's death?

"Honestly, I hardly remember what we ate," she admitted. She wanted to ask him if everything was all right, but that would have been intrusive.

Perhaps he saw it in her face. He put his hands in his pockets, something she had learned he did when he was thinking deeply, and oblivious of his surroundings. It was relaxed, oddly intimate. He started to walk, quite slowly, and she fell into step beside him. Apart from the sound of guns in the distance, they could have been in an English garden, with fields of corn beyond the hedges.

"I have been thinking about what you told me of your father's death," he said, pulling a pipe out of his pocket and stuffing it with tobacco. "June twenty-eighth last year. And you said it was because he had discovered a conspiracy, but you didn't tell me much more. You mentioned your brother's friend who had actually caused the crash, but you said very little of the man behind it." He turned to look at her. "He's still free, isn't he? And with whatever power and liberty he had before?"

"Yes." Her voice was tight. The anger and the pain were still there, even the sense of surprise because everything that gave her life sense and value had been destroyed in one act. Perhaps she had deliberately sealed over some of the grieving, making herself too busy to allow it, but it was far from finished. She wanted to share it with Cullingford. He understood loneliness, emotions of horror and loss that form the shape of your mind, so powerful they were beyond control, deeper than words, consuming and too intimate to explain to those who had never felt such things themselves.

He had told his wife nothing of the reality of his own life here in Flanders: the daily, weekly risks, judgments, and duties that were his identity. Then what did they speak of? Household matters, mutual acquaintances, the weather? All that was passion and laughter and pain went unsaid, because she did not know his world, and he did not know hers? The loneliness of not knowing was sometimes like a weight crushing out the power to breathe.

"Yes," she said again, aware that he was watching her intently, and with a hunger in his eyes that he could not know she read. She did not look at him, but it made no difference; his face was in her mind exactly as if she did, whether first thing on waking or last thing before falling asleep.

"And he won't stop, just because he failed the first time," she went on. "Matthew thinks he could be attempting to destroy morale at home to damage recruiting, and prevent Kitchener from raising a new army." Then she remembered what Belinda had said about Prentice writing articles that would tell the truth about pointless deaths, and how it would affect those who were considering joining up. Perhaps Cullingford was aware of that. "I'm sorry," she apologized, aware of how family loyalty must tear at him, pity for everything that was too late now. "I don't suppose Prentice realized what he was doing with his articles. And it would have been censored anyway."

"My dear, I knew Eldon," he said gently. "He would not have taken the pains to find out. Too many men are dying now for us to pretend they were all good. That is a facet of decency that belongs to peacetime. Those of us who don't have to make decisions can indulge in dreams, but those of us who do cannot afford to. Please tell me what you know about this . . . creator of peace, at the price of slavery and dishonor," he asked.

In the growing dark she told him, as they walked along the paths which were now a little wild, since the gardening boys had been called up to the war. The unheeding earth had blossomed with its usual verdure as if oblivious that only miles away it was being poisoned and laid waste.

She had already told him something of the events themselves, and the search afterward as the fragments of meaning had come together, until finally, with Europe on the brink of war, they had discovered the conspiracy itself.

"Your father was a brave man," he said quietly when she had finished. "I wish I could have known him."

She was furious with herself because the tears filled her eyes and her voice choked when she tried to speak.

"I'm sorry," he said with deep contrition. He put his pipe away and pulled a handkerchief out of his pocket. He handed it to her.

She took it, wiped her eyes, which was almost useless, then blew her nose fiercely. She stood holding the handkerchief. She could hardly give it back to him now.

"I think Eldon may have been involved in the same thing," he said thoughtfully. There was immense sadness in his face, but he did not flinch away from the knowledge. "I've thought about some of the things he said to me last time I was on leave. He boasted about changing things. He often did that, as young men will, but he seemed surer of himself than before, as if he were speaking of something specific."

She said nothing.

He pulled on his pipe slowly and let out the smoke. She could smell it in the damp air.

"We had one of the stupid arguments we had so often. He hated the army and everything to do with militarism, as he called it. He said there was a better way than violence, way of peace and government that would supersede petty nationalism, and that I was fast becoming an anachronism, and I'd see!" He was standing still, the pipe in his hand almost as if he were not quite sure what to do with it. The light reflected on the polished wood of the bowl. "I thought he was just bragging at the time, but looking back, I think he knew what he was saying."

She turned to look at him, and he averted his eyes, even though in the twilight she could barely have read the expression in them. She knew it was shame, because he read Prentice so easily, the shallow and the vulnerable in him, the child that had needed to impress, and the man who had embraced an evil to do so, perhaps without recognizing it. She looked back at the trees against the sky, now little more than shadows in the afterglow.

"I saw photographs of him," she said quietly. "At a regatta. You were there. He looked young and eager, sort of excited, as if everything good lay ahead of him. I suppose there are thousands of young men like that. People must look at those pictures now, and . . ." She could not go on. She was hurting both of them, and it was pointless.

He put out his hand and touched her arm, his fingers strong, a steadying grip, just for a moment, then withdrawn again.

"There was a young woman as well," she

said, to fill the silence.

"I don't remember," he answered.

"She was unusual, very tall," she elaborated. "Dramatic eyes. They were pale, as if they might have been light blue or green." Then a memory came back to her of Hannah using the same words.

She stopped abruptly and swung back to face him, her heart pounding. "I think I know how the instructions were given to Sebastian to murder my parents! It couldn't have been a letter — you don't put that sort of thing down on paper. Anyway, you'd have to be certain that Sebastian was going to do it. You could hardly wait for him to write back! It had to be a conversation. Matthew said he didn't have a telephone call, except from Mr. Thyer at St. John's, and that was only a few moments. But he did meet a young woman in one of the local pubs." She was speaking more and more rapidly, her voice rising with excitement. "Hannah saw her! She was tall, with amazing light eyes! Of course it doesn't have to be the same woman, but it could have been! She might have drawn Prentice into it as well!"

Cullingford was staring at her, amazed, vulnerable, strangely naked in the last shreds of the light no more than a warmth in the sky. "Yes," he agreed gently. "Yes, it could. I'm going to London tomorrow. Just a couple of days. I'll look into it. See who she was."

She was surprised. He had said nothing about it before. She was startled how fiercely she would miss him, even for so short a time. She took the handkerchief out of her pocket and offered it back to him.

He laughed a little shakily. "Keep it," he said, reaching out very gently to touch her cheek with his fingers. "Be here when I get back. Please?"

"Of course I will!" The words were awkward, her throat aching so savagely she could barely swallow.

He leaned forward and kissed her, softly, on the mouth, hesitating a moment, then more fully. Then he let her go and turned to walk toward the house, without looking back.

Cullingford was in London by half past eleven. First he went to see Abigail Prentice. It was a stiff, highly emotional meeting, neither of them able to bridge the gulf of pain between them.

"Hello, Owen," she said with as much warmth as she could manage. There was an awkwardness in her that could not totally forgive him because he was a professional soldier, a man who had deliberately given his life to fighting, a thing she could not understand, and here he was, alive. Her son who fought with his mind and his beliefs, whose only weapon was the pen, had been drowned in no-man's-land, and buried where she could not even visit his grave. She had not been there to comfort him, or to mourn.

"Hello, Abby." He kissed her fleetingly on the cheek. It was all she offered him.

"Are you home on leave?" she asked, going ahead of him into the sitting room.

"A couple of days," he replied.

"I thought as a general you would have been able to have longer." She sat down in the old armchair near the fire. There were early yellow roses in a vase on the table. They were still in bud, short-stemmed, picked from the climber over the arbor in the garden. In a couple of weeks they would be glorious. "I suppose they can't manage without you," she added, both pride and resentment in her voice.

He wondered if he was sitting where Judith had sat when she was here. He glanced at the familiar room, the photographs of Prentice, one or two of himself, not many. There were several of Belinda, some of Abby and her husband. Then he saw the one Judith had referred to. He remembered the occasion. It was Henley, as she had supposed. It had been a hot day, dazzling sun on the water. There were young men in light trousers, straw boater hats, striped blazers, girls in dresses that were self-consciously nautical, or else all muslins and ribbons, and parasols against burning in the sun. The hallmarks of the day had been laughter, cold lemonade and beer and champagne, picnic hampers filled with fruit and sherbet, pheasant in aspic, and cucumber sandwiches.

And there was Laetitia Dawson with the startling eyes, almost as tall as Cullingford, a fraction taller than Prentice, but the young man had been fascinated by her. Had his involvement with the Peacemaker begun even there, the first introduction to the seductive and terrible ideas?

Was it she who had given Sebastian Allard his final, murderous instructions also?

"Would you like tea?" Abby asked.

"Thank you," he accepted, simply because it would be easier than sitting here doing nothing, and he would not go so soon.

"Will you stay to lunch?" she added.

"No, no thank you. I have to get into the city and see various people."

"Thank you for sending Miss Reavley," she went on awkwardly. "That was thoughtful of you. She was very nice. She spoke well of Eldon."

He pictured Judith here in this room, struggling for something kind to say, just as he was now. She had loathed Prentice and despised his insensitivity toward men for whom she cared with an almost unbearable tenderness. Thinking of her his heart raced, the room became too small, too imprisoning. He wanted to be back in Flanders, even with the violence and the grief, the noise and fear and dirt. In Flanders were the people he loved and the causes he understood.

"Good," he said aloud. "I'm glad she was of some help."

"Nothing helps, Owen," Abby answered. "I am just acknowledging your thought."

"Abby, I did not send him into no-man's-land," he told her. He wanted to reach out and touch her, but she was too stiff, too fragile, and he did not dare. "He took his chances, like any young man," he went on. "If you are angry with everyone who lives, because he didn't, you are going to hurt yourself intolerably. There are casualties in war, just as there are in life. We do the best we can, the best we understand. Sometimes we are wrong. Eldon was following his belief. Don't blame other people for that." He was lying to her. Hadrian had told him that Eldon had been murdered, which was different from war. But he had given many people sufficient cause to hate him, and Cullingford had no idea which of them had been offered the chance and taken it. He could not blame Charlie Gee's brother, if it had been he, or Edwin Corliss's friends. But there was no need for Abby to know that. She had grief enough.

She was staring at him, waiting, wanting to quarrel and not knowing if she dared to. The anger needed to spill out, but not at him.

He stood up slowly. "We haven't time to waste on hate, Abby," he said very softly. "Hold on to the good you have, while you have it. Time is so precious, and so short."

The tears spilled over her cheeks. Awkwardly, as if it were a gesture he had never made before, he knelt down in front of her and took her in his arms.

He had already given the subject considerable reflection, and he knew which friend he would speak to regarding the idea that was taking greater shape in his mind the longer he considered it. It made a hideous sense. If what he learned next fitted in with what Judith had told him, the identity of the Peacemaker was certain.

He walked along Piccadilly in the sun with a sense of dreamlike unreality. It all looked exactly the same as it had a year ago, and yet it was indefinably shabbier. Part of it was in the dress of the women. There were no bright colors, no reds, no oranges or hot pinks, as if they would be crass in the face of so many people's mourning.

Perhaps there were rather fewer horses and more cars, which might have had to do with the war, or simply the progress of time. Newsboys stood on the corners. There was nothing different: casualty figures from Flanders, France, Gallipoli; bits of news from other regions such as Africa and the Mediterranean. Oddly enough there were still theater flyers advertising musicals, dramas, the latest entertainment, and of course moving pictures.

He stopped to take his bearings for a moment, then crossed the street and went into a large block of flats, each one like a smart town house, with entrance foyer and a suite of rooms.

Gustavus Tempany was expecting him. He was at least fifteen years older than Cullingford. He was tall and thin, limping from the wound that had invalided him out of the Indian army ten years ago. He still stood like a soldier. His thoughts and dreams were with the men in France, but his own days of battle were over.

He welcomed Cullingford and offered him whisky, in spite of the hour, but he was not surprised when it was declined.

"Well?" he said gravely, looking at Cullingford where he sat opposite him, legs crossed as if he were relaxed, trying to appear casual. "Don't play silly beggars with me, Cullingford. Something's eating at you, or you wouldn't be here. This is not time for tittle-tattle."

"Do you know Laetitia Dawson?" Cullingford asked bluntly.

Tempany's eyes opened very wide, but he did not make any obvious comment. "Of course."

"Do you know what she is doing these days?"

"Socially? No idea. Don't care much about these things." Very carefully he did not ask why on earth Cullingford should be interested in such a superficial matter. He frowned. "Is it important?"

"It could be. She's still in London? Hasn't married, gone abroad, or anything?"

"No. Saw her at a dinner at the Savoy a couple of weeks ago, or perhaps it was three."

"Who with? Do you remember?"

"Somebody's brother. All very casual," Tempany replied.

Cullingford saw the curiosity in him, and smiled. He could have trusted his discretion, and his honor, but if Judith was right, such knowledge was dangerous, and Tempany had been his friend too long and too deeply to risk his safety.

"Can you put me in touch with anyone who knows her currently?" he asked.

"Cullingford, are you sure you know what you are doing?" Tempany said anxiously. "She won't be up to anything questionable, you know! You do know her family connections — who her uncle is?"

"Yes, I do. Please — it's important."

"Well if you must, I think she actually lives quite a bit of the time up near Cambridge. Family home, you know?"

"Yes, I know."

"You could try one of the young scientists up at the Establishment there. Can't remember the fellow's name, but supposed to be brilliant. All very secret stuff. War effort, and all that. Is that what you're after?"

Cullingford did not answer. It was fitting together too easily: Laetitia Dawson with first Eldon; presumably he had been the first? Then the message to Sebastian Allard. Now there was some young scientist in Cambridge. The connection was perfect. The passion was there, the idealism, the power. He would have to go up to Cambridge, of course. Every step needed proving, but he did not expect any difficulty. A society photograph of Laetitia was easy enough to find out of the Tatler. He would show it in the pub that Judith's sister had spoken of, and the chain would be complete.

He had a quick meal at the railway station, and went to Cambridge on the afternoon train, arriving a little after three. Fortunately the day on which John and Alys Reavley were killed was one that would be remembered in England as long as recorded history lasted. That day an assassination had occurred in the Balkans that had precipitated the last hectic plunge toward a war which seemed as if it must be the end of the world as Europe knew it, and the beginning of something unknown, perhaps swifter, darker, and immeasurably uglier.

It did not take long for him to find a driver to take him to the village, and the public house where Hannah had said Sebastian and Laetitia Dawson had been seen.

"A fine lookin' lass, all right," the publican agreed, looking from the picture to Cullingford with respect. He was in uniform, as thousands of other men were, but in his case because he had not had time, or inclination, to go home. He wanted to deal with this matter first, and if he was honest, he had no desire to see Nerys, and be obliged to put on the mask that for her sake hid his feelings. It was an effort he was uncertain he could sustain, and he was too tired, too emotionally raw to try.

"Do you remember her?" Cullingford asked patiently.

"Don't see 'er much these days," the publican replied. "Busy, I s'pose. Most folk are."

"I am trying to understand an event that happened a little under a year ago, in order to clear someone of a certain blame," Cullingford elaborated with something of a slant to the truth. "I'm sure you remember the day of the assassination of Archduke Franz Ferdinand . . ."

The publican rolled his eyes. "Do I ever? Hardly goin' to forget that!"

"I imagine no one is," Cullingford agreed. "Did you see this woman the day before that?" He remembered Judith's description of Sebastian Allard. "She may have been in the company of a young man, tall also, very good-looking indeed, fair brown hair, sunburned, looked like a poet, a dreamer."

The publican smiled. "Oh yeah! I remember him. Right handsome, he was. Odd, because I've never see'd 'im since. I s'pose he's gone to war — like most of 'em." His face flooded with sadness and he blinked several times. He polished the glass in his hand so hard he was fortunate not to snap it. "I'd like to think 'e weren't killed. 'E had such a look to 'im, as if 'e were alight with something inside 'isself." He shook his head. "An' it weren't love, like you see all the time in young folk. It were bigger than that, like you said, a dream. An' 'e and she were friendly, but no more'n that. An' she were proper 'andsome, too, but a bit tall for a girl, to my taste. Does that 'elp you?"

"Yes," Cullingford said quickly. "Yes, thank you." It was what he needed to know. He would take it to Matthew Reavley. It was his task to know how to arrest the Peacemaker, or what else to do about him. But at least now he would know who he was. His power would be curtailed forever. Perhaps they would do something discreet, no open accusation, certainly no trial.

He thanked the publican again and gave him a handsome tip for his time, then he walked outside into the sun.

Did people commit suicide out of honor anymore, if they were found in treason? Certainly the government could never let it be known. Would someone offer him a sword or a gun? It would be the best way.

The driver was waiting for him, and he went back to the station to catch the next train to London. He should have thought to ask Judith for Matthew's address, but he had not wanted to tell her what he intended to do. Any questions, and she might have guessed. Now he would have to telephone one of his friends in the Intelligence Services and ask. It was only a temporary setback.

The journey back from Cambridge was very pleasant. He let himself drift off into sleep. He woke with a start to find himself already on the outskirts of the city. He would have to find a hotel tonight, and perhaps go home tomorrow. Time to face that decision when he had to.

It was nearly seven o'clock and already the light was fading when he walked along the platform under the vast ceiling and out into the early evening air. It was warm, a softness to it as if summer were almost here.

He realized how hungry he was and looked for a restaurant to find a decent meal before going to see Matthew Reavley. Matthew was a young man, unmarried. There was no reason why he should be at home early, or for that matter, at all! Still, he must try, even if it took him all night, and he had to go to the SIS offices tomorrow. But tonight would be better for all sorts of reasons. It must be done in absolute privacy, where no one at all could overhear even a word. And Matthew might take considerable convincing that the Peacemaker was indeed who Cullingford now knew him to be.

The other main reason was that he wanted to do it urgently. Every hour the Peacemaker was free to make more plans, betray more people, might mean the deaths of other men, and bring defeat closer.

After dinner he made a single telephone call, and obtained the information he wanted. He hailed a taxi, and gave the driver an address a couple of hundred yards from Matthew's street. It was almost certainly an unnecessary caution, but he still did not wish Matthew's address known, even to a cabdriver, who might well remember a passenger in a general's uniform.

It was nearly ten when they fought their way through the traffic and he finally paid his bill and alighted. The evening was still warm, but it was completely dark now, and the streetlamps lit only pools like a string of gigantic pearls along the footpath.

Around the corner in the side street they were further apart. It was dark between them. He noticed a man standing a few yards beyond the lamp nearest where he judged Matthew's flat to be. He was on the curb, as if hoping to hail a taxi. He could not be waiting to cross because there was no reason why he should not. The street was silent. He hoped it was not Matthew himself! He was wearing a topcoat and hat, and carrying a stick. It was difficult to tell how tall he was. The shadows elongated him.

He turned just as Cullingford reached him, as if the sound of his footsteps in the quietness had drawn his attention. For a moment the light shone in his face, and he smiled.

"Good evening, Cullingford," he said softly. "I assume you have come to see Reavley. That's a pity."

Cullingford stared into the face of the Peacemaker, twisted with regret but without a shadow of indecision.

He actually saw the lamplight on the blade of the swordstick, then the next moment he felt it in his body, a numbing blow, not sharp at all, just a spreading paralysis as he fell forward into the darkness.

Joseph was sitting in his dugout, writing letters, when Barshey Gee came in without knocking. His face was white and he stared at Joseph without even an attempt at apology.

Joseph dropped his pen and stood up. In two steps across the earth floor he was in front of Barshey. He took him by the shoulders. "What is it?" he asked, his voice gravelly, steeling himself for the news that one of Barshey's brothers had been killed. It had to be a sniper, at this time in the afternoon. "What is it, Barshey?" he repeated.

Barshey gasped. "Oi just 'eard, Captain. General Cullingford's been murdered! In London. 'E were home on leave, an' some thief stuck a knife into 'im in the street. Jesus, Oi hope they hang the bastard!" He struggled for breath, his chest heaving. "What's 'appenin' to us, Captain Reavley? How can someone kill a general in the street?" His eyes were wide and strained. "Jeez, you look as bad as Oi feel!"

Joseph found his mouth dry, his heart pounding, not for himself but for Judith. It was like the past back again, death where you had never even imagined it, like your own life were cut off, but you were left conscious with eyes to see it, forced to go on being present and knowing it all. The end of life, but without the mercy of oblivion.

Judith was going to hurt so much! Cullingford was not her husband, but that had nothing to do with the pain she would feel. It was still love! It was laughter, understanding, gentleness, the hunger of the soul met with generosity and endless, passionate tenderness. It was the voice in the darkness of fear, when the world was breaking, the touch that meant you were not alone. She would grieve till she felt there was nothing left inside her. Then rest would restore her, and she would have the strength to hurt all over again.

"Thank you for telling me, Barshey. I must go to Poperinge, now! Help me find a car, an ambulance, anything!"

Barshey did not argue — he simply obeyed.

An hour later Joseph was at the ambulance post in Poperinge. First he went to Hadrian. He must be certain of the details. He even cherished some vague, ill-defined hope that Barshey had been wrong.

He had not. Hadrian was numb with shock, but he told Joseph that it was true. It had happened at night, in the same street where Matthew lived.

Joseph left Hadrian and went outside and across the cobbles to where he could see Judith and Wil Sloan standing together laughing. They must have heard his boots on the stone, because they turned to look at him. The laughter died instantly.

Judith came forward, the blood draining from her skin as she stared at him.

He put both his hands on her shoulders. She waited, knowing from his eyes that the blow would be terrible. Perhaps she expected it would be Matthew.

"Judith," he began, his voice catching in his throat. He had to clear it before he could go on. "General Cullingford was murdered in the street in London — just outside Matthew's flat. They didn't find who did it."

"What?" It was not that she had not heard him, simply that she could not grasp the enormity of it.

"I don't know any more than that. I'm sorry! I'm so very, very, sorry!"

"He's . . . dead?"

"Yes."

She leaned forward and buried her head on his shoulder and he tightened his arms around her until he held her as close as he could. It was a long time until she started to weep, then her whole body shook as if she would never get her breath, never ease the rending pain.

He kept on holding her. Wil stood where he was, horrified, helpless.

At last she pulled away. Her eyes were shut tight, as if she could not bear to see anything. "It's my fault," she whispered hoarsely. "He went after the Peacemaker, because of what I told him! I killed him!"

He pushed the hair off her face. "No," he said very softly. "The war killed him."

She leaned against him again, very still now, too exhausted to cry again, for the moment.

He just held on to her.

Chapter

ELEVEN

There was nothing Joseph could do to ease Judith's grief. She had to hide it from everyone except those closest to her, such as Wil Sloan, and possibly Major Hadrian. To permit its true depth to be seen by others would in a sense betray Cullingford's privacy, and perhaps his reputation. A new general was moved forward immediately, with his own driver, and she was returned to ambulance duty. It took a matter of hours, not days. War waited for no one.

Joseph knew that after that first brief and terrible encounter he would not see her again except by chance. He had been on or near the front line for weeks without leave and the stress was telling on him. He was due two weeks now, and he accepted it gratefully. Apart from anything else, it was important that he speak to Matthew as soon as possible. He believed Judith's assertion that it was the Peacemaker who had murdered Cullingford, either directly or indirectly, which meant that he had to have been close to finding him.

Watching the late spring countryside skim past him on the way to Calais, it seemed like an escape from the reality of mud and wasteland. Here the trees were in full leaf. At a hasty glance, the French farms and villages looked as they always had: uniquely individual, yet steeped in history, each with its own vines, cheeses, and livestock. It was afterward, on the boat across the Channel, that he realized he had seen only women, children, and old men. When they stopped to buy petrol or bread, there was a sadness in people's faces, and always a shadow behind the eyes, a knowledge of fear, probably not for themselves but for those they loved.

London was startlingly the same as before. After the loss of men he had expected a silence, some kind of mourning he could see, but it was full of traffic as always, motor and horse-drawn. There were men in uniform, some on leave as he was, some injured, hollow-faced with the gray pallor of the shell-shocked or inwardly crippled. He heard a man with a hacking cough; it was probably no more than a spring cold, but to him it brought back, with skin-chilling horror, the memory of gas.

He reached Matthew's flat a little after six, and the porter, knowing him well, let him in. He bathed, letting the hot water soak into his skin, although it stung the scratches where he had torn himself with his nails when the lice or fleas became unbearable. The bone-deep ease of it made him realize how tired he was, how many nights he had lain on the hard clay, or on duckboards, and slept fitfully. It was going to be strange to sleep in a bed with sheets, and waken knowing he was in England. It would seem eerily silent with only the distant sound of traffic, no gunfire, no shaking of the ground as the fourteen-pounders landed. No injuries, no deaths.

He toweled himself dry, examining the scraped and abraded patches of his skin, and dressed, borrowing clean underwear from Matthew's drawer. Then he made himself a pot of tea and sat down to wait.

Matthew came in a little before nine. The porter must have told him of Joseph's arrival because there was no surprise in his face. He pushed the door shut behind him and hesitated only a moment before flinging his arms around Joseph and hugging him briefly and fiercely. Then he stood back, looking him up and down.

"Hell, Joe, you look awful! And you're thin . . ."

"You know about Cullingford?" Joseph asked.

The joy in Matthew's face vanished. "Yes, of course I do. It was only a few yards from here, practically on my doorstep. He was the one Judith drove, wasn't he? Is she all right?"

Joseph found himself torn with all kinds of emotions. A few days ago he had been furious with her, so certain that regardless of temptations, she was morally wrong. Now nothing was so certain. He understood the darkness where, without a human touch, you drown. Perhaps Cullingford had needed that to survive, whether Judith did or not. Who else could he turn to? Not his wife in England, certainly not his junior officers. Maybe right and wrong did not move, but understanding of them did. The wrenching pain of walking the same path, even for a short space, tore away the willingness to judge.

"I don't know," he answered Matthew. "She loved him."

Matthew's eyes flickered wider open. "I didn't know that!"

Joseph shrugged. "It's not only that," he went on. "She told him about the Peacemaker, all she knew." He saw Matthew's start of surprise. "Apparently Prentice was something of an idealist as well, with a lot of the same beliefs, and a driving compulsion to do something about them. Judith's convinced Cullingford found the Peacemaker and that's why he was killed, which to her makes it her fault!"

Matthew sat down slowly in the largest chair, running his hands through his hair, scraping it back off his brow.

"Oh, God! You mean he was on his way here to tell me when they caught up with him?"

"Probably." Joseph sat opposite him.

"I think it's Ivor Chetwin." Matthew looked up at him. "Everything I have points to him. He has the knowledge, the political ability, the family connections in England, and we know he has the brains." He pushed his hair back, dragging it off his brow. "It's absolutely bloody, because he knows our codes in SIS, and other things I can't tell you! I just need a few last details from a fellow called Mynott, who used to be a military attaché at the embassy in Berlin before the war. That should settle the last doubts there are. Unfortunately he's ADC to Hamilton out in Gallipoli. I've got a berth on a troopship leaving tomorrow night. But you can stay here, as long as you like! Thank God at least Mynott wasn't a naval attaché, or I'd never find him. I'm sorry, Joe, but I've got to go out and ask him the last questions. He knows for sure what Chetwin was doing in Berlin. If he knew Reisenburg, that'll be enough."

It twisted inside Joseph that it should be Chetwin, for his father's sake, but it had to be someone he had known, or at least had known him. He knew Matthew had even feared it was Shearing himself. Joseph had been afraid it was Aidan Thyer. There was no answer that would be painless, and after Cullingford's death, there was a new bitterness to it.

Matthew stood up and poured himself a generous glass of whisky. "I don't suppose we'll ever prove that. But I'll be happy to see Chetwin swing high just for Mother and Father." He drank the glassful in one draft. "Do you want some?"

"No." He looked at Matthew with anxiety. He seemed to have drunk the whisky with unusual ease. A few months ago he would have sipped it, made it last the evening.

Matthew turned back to look at him, the glass still in his hand. He frowned. "Exactly what did she tell Cullingford, Joe? How could he find the Peacemaker in a couple of days when we haven't in a year?"

"What's the connection between Chetwin and the woman who spoke to Sebastian in the pub the day before he killed Mother and Father?" Joseph asked.

"I've no idea. Could be anything: relatives, lover, disciple, possibly just a paid messenger, a mercenary. If we get him, she won't matter."

"That's how Cullingford trailed him, I think." Joseph tried to remember exactly what Judith had said. She had been certain it was her fault, and he thought it was not hysteria but a deep and terrible knowledge. "There was a photograph of Prentice in his mother's home that Judith saw when she was there, taking Cullingford's condolences, as it were," he explained. "Prentice was with a young woman who answered pretty closely to the description of the woman Hannah says was seen with Sebastian the day before the murders. If it was the same woman, perhaps Cullingford knew who she was, and knew her connection to the Peacemaker."

"Then go to Mrs. Prentice tomorrow and look at the photograph!" Matthew said urgently. "I can't, I have to go on the early train to Portsmouth in time to get on board the troopship. Look at the picture, and for God's sake, Joe, do nothing! Just remember what the woman looks like, and get out." He finished the whisky, pulling a face as if he disliked the taste of it. His voice was hoarse, fear in his eyes, and more emotion than he could control. "I don't want to come back from Gallipoli and find you dead, too." He tried to smile. "Apart from anything else, what would I tell Judith? Just go and tell Mrs. Prentice that you were the man who brought her son back, and buried him. Say something nice about him. . . ."

"Matthew!" Joseph exclaimed. "I understand! I'll just look at all the photographs of Prentice, then I'll come back here. I may go home for a few days, see Hannah. . . ." He saw Matthew's face fill with alarm. "And I won't go asking questions in any pubs! I swear!"

He was prevented from any further persuasion by the telephone.

Matthew stood up to answer it. He listened in silence for several moments, his body rigid, his hand holding the mouthpiece shaking a little, then he said "Yes, sir," and replaced it on the hook. "That was Shearing. The Germans have sunk the

Lusitania," he said with a gasp. "Over eleven hundred people drowned, including Americans. I'm . . . I'm sorry, Joe, but I've got to go in to the office. Washington can't overlook this! It could turn the war!"

Joseph was stunned. "The *Lusitania*! I thought that was a passenger liner! How could that happen? Where?"

"The Irish Sea. It *is* a passenger liner, and I don't know how it could happen, just that it did."

"What about Chetwin . . . and Gallipoli?"

"I can't go. Can you?"

"Me?" Joseph was startled.

Matthew's face was white. "If you don't go to Gallipoli, and I can't, and Mynott's killed before he can give us the proof, then the Peacemaker goes on, and England loses the war."

Joseph leaned forward, head in his hands. "All right. I'll go in the morning," he whispered.

"I'm sorry," Matthew said with sudden gentleness. "I know you haven't had leave in months, and God knows, you deserve it. But I can't trust anyone else."

"I know," Joseph agreed. "I'll be all right. Tell me about Mynott, and what I need to do."

The sea journey was, as Matthew had said, roughly three days, steaming at full speed south through the Straits of Gibraltar, then east across the Mediterranean. The weather was perfect, blazing sunshine and warm, blue seas.

At first Joseph was glad simply to sleep as much as cramped and shared accommodation allowed him to. The ship was full of men going out to fight on the beaches and landings at Gallipoli, and they must have heard of the storm of casualties there already. Many of them would not come home, and most of them who did would have sustained injury and loss.

Joseph made himself available to offer what support and encouragement he could, but they were raw recruits, and he had already seen nearly a year of war in the trenches of the Western Front. It was better he tell them nothing. There were truths too overwhelming, too shattering to the mind and the hope, to be faced all at once. A step at a time was all the mind could bear. He thought it was not cowardice that kept him silent when he heard their laughter and their talk of heroism in battle, of honor and sacrifice and the glory of courage.

The Dardanelles were among the great legendary places of the world, a crossroad for the nations of history: Persia, Judea, Greece, Rome, Islam, and the vast empires of the East beyond. Alexander the Great had left Greece to conquer the ancient realms of India and Egypt. Xerxes had crossed the Dardanelles in his attempt to crush the rising Athens. Leander had swum the Hellespont to be with Hero, and died for love. And in the mists of time Homer's Greeks had come that way bound for the siege of Troy: Helen, Menelaus, Achilles, and Odysseus on his long return to Ithaca.

In even older dreams, Jason and the Argonauts had pursued the Golden Fleece through these same straits up into the Black Sea.

Now he heard young Englishmen talking of it as if this were another great heroic saga, and they would return with the honor of war. He stared across the dancing blue water, and felt his eyes sting with tears. He, too, had grown up with the poetry of the wine-dark seas of Homer flowing through his dreams. He had wanted to walk the ruins of Troy in the magic light of the Mediterranean, hear in the silence of the wind in the grass the echoes of the wars between men and gods that laid the dreams of Western man and built the cities and laws, the philosophies and poems, upon which Europe had nourished its heart for two thousand years.

And he would see it, but now it would be amid the slaughter of today, and perhaps out of it he would find the truth of a betrayal he had to know, however much he did not want to.

The ship dropped anchor in the Aegean Sea, north of the Dardanelles, opposite the landing beaches of Anzac Cove. All the men crowded to the side to stare at the shore and the pale, steep hills behind, jagged right down to the shore. The bay was dotted with ships, but far out, beyond the firing range of the Turkish artillery from the fortresses and placements on the crown of the ridge above. Men crowded the beaches, hundreds of them, wounded and sick waiting to be escorted out to hospital ships. Medical orderlies were trying to help, fighting units huddled under the brief stretch of rocks and outcrops, making a slow and bloody way upward, surrounded by fire on all sides except the sea.

Joseph had told the commander that he was on Secret Intelligence Service work, backed up by the documents Matthew had given him. He was quite open that he was here to find a particular officer who might have information, but he did not give any name, until he was on the tender, making its way through the pale Aegean. The water should have been a limpid blue, but here it was turgid with sand, and blood, and the dark figures of men struggling to help the wounded into makeshift carriers of any sort, just to get them off the beach.

Above in the distance the Turkish guns occasionally raked the sea with shot, but most of the boats were just out of range, and the warships returned fire with a roar of shelling.

The score of men in the same boat with Joseph were huddled together, pale and excited, wanting to appear brave and not having any idea what to do. The fact that they wanted to do anything at all made their innocence heartbreakingly obvious. Seasoned men would have been happy to do nothing, knowing the time would come.

The prow of the boat scraped the sand and the foremost men leaped out. Joseph scrambled ashore with them. The water was warm and the sand soft under his weight. He ran through the gentle surf and floundered up to a pile of ammunition crates where a couple of medical orderlies were passing around water. One of them noticed Joseph's uniform with its clerical collar.

"We don't need you yet, cobber!" he said cheerfully. His accent was broad Australian, his face sunburned and lantern-jawed.

Joseph gave him a gesture of salute. "I'm looking for General Hamilton's headquarters," he said. "At least I'm actually looking for his ADC, Major Mynott. It's urgent I find him."

"Yeah?" the soldier was unimpressed. "Pass me that splint, will yer? Everything's urgent here, including that bleedin' water!"

Joseph reached for the canteen and handed it to him, and the splint, then looked around slowly. As far along it as he could see, the beach was crowded. Long lines of the injured stood waiting for medical attention. Others, more seriously hurt, lay in silent pain, faces crusted with blood and sand. There seemed to be flies everywhere.

Another soldier saw Joseph's expression and sauntered over to him. "Welcome to Gallipoli, mate," he said with a shrug. His face was round with wide blue eyes and ginger-gold hair. His smile was cheerful, as if he were determined to find something, anything, to like about the chaos around him. "Don't worry, I'll look after yer." He led Joseph up the sand past the makeshift medical unit where a nurse was creating as much order as she could.

"Never mind, darlin'!" one of the men called out to her. "We love yer!"

Someone else made an extremely bawdy comment about love. There was a loud burst of laughter.

The nurse was dark-haired and slender, perhaps twenty-five. "Back of the line!" she ordered, pointing her finger at the offender.

He groaned loudly. "Aw c'mon! Don't be such a . . ."

"Do you want to go to the back twice?" she asked ferociously.

There was more applause.

"Sorry!" the soldier yelled.

"Good!" she called back. "End of the line!"

Grudgingly he obeyed, to still another burst of clapping and catcalls.

Joseph and his guide reached a group of soldiers sitting on the grass eating rough bread and tinned bully beef. A Dixie can of tea hung over a smoldering fire.

One of them looked up. "Wot yer got there, Blue? Reinforcements from Blighty?"

There was a guffaw of laughter again

from the half dozen men.

"Only if yer feelin' like the last rites," Blue replied, sitting cross-legged in a spare patch without too many small stones. "Sit down, mate," he invited Joseph.

"Bleedin' 'ell!" one of the men said, his eyes widening as he realized Joseph was a chaplain. "Are things that bad?"

Another man crossed himself elaborately. "Here we are stuck on the edge of being wiped out, and what do the Pommies send us? One bloody preacher! You going to bury the lot of us then? Or are you the real thing?"

Joseph blushed. "The real thing?"

"Part the waters and we can walk to the other side!"

There was more laughter.

"No use," Blue said cheerfully. "We don't want to be on the other side, dumbo!"

"Speak for yourself, mate! I'd love to be on the other side!" He turned to Joseph. "What are you here for, Rev? Maybe you can turn the stones to bread?"

"How about turning the water to wine?" another suggested.

"Actually I'm no use at all," Joseph said candidly. "I need you to help me."

"Too right, you do!" three of them replied in chorus.

"What's yer problem, sport?" another asked, squinting a little at him. "Apart from that yer here, o' course. We all got that one." He grinned, showing a gap tooth at the front.

"You couldn't wait to get 'ere, yer stupid bastard!" the man next to him pointed out. " 'We gotter go!' yer kept sayin' — 'We gotter go!' "

The first man lifted his hand dismissively. "Well, we have gotter."

"So what d'yer want then, mate?" Blue faced Joseph, his wide eyes curious.

"I'm looking for a Major Mynott, General Hamilton's ADC," Joseph replied. "He has important information about a traitor." He used the word intentionally, since he knew it would burn their emotions. They were young men who had heard the need of their mother country, dropped what they were doing and come from the other side of the world, in their thousands, to shed their blood in France and on these hell-raked beaches. Surely to them there would be no uglier word?

"So you're not a holy Joe for real?" A flicker of disappointment crossed Blue's eyes. "You're a spy, or whatever they're called."

Joseph smiled with a little grimace.

"Actually I'm very much a holy Joe. My name's Joseph Reavley, and I'm a chaplain on the Western Front. I was home on leave and the intelligence officer who was supposed to come was called away since the Germans just sank the *Lusitania*. Over eleven hundred civilians were drowned, men, women, and children. I was on leave from the Ypres Salient, where my regiment is, so he asked me to come in his place. I need to be back in time to return to Flanders in ten days."

Blue let out a low whistle, his eyes round. "Well, I'll be . . . ! So you're a dinkum priest! What's Flanders like, sport? Is the gas as bad as they say?"

"Yes. Whatever they say, it's as bad. Can you help me find Mynott?"

" 'Course we can, eh?" He looked around the group, and everyone replied with vigorous agreement. "Mind it feels in the air like there's going to be another raid up the hill soon," he added. "Maybe we'd better start asking now. If Mynott's the geezer I think he is, he's a real scrapper. He'll be up there with the men."

"Best not waste time," they agreed. "C'mon then, mate."

They rose to their feet carefully, ever mindful of Turkish snipers on the escarpments above the beach.

It was not as warm as Joseph had expected, and the terrain was appalling: rock and clay, open hillsides, gullies with trees and — incredibly — wildflowers. Everywhere there were smells of earth, latrines, creosol, tobacco, cordite, and the sharp fragrance of wild thyme. As in Flanders there were dead bodies no one had had the chance to bury, and clouds of flies, black, blue, and green ones. Joseph did not have to be told that dysentery and similar diseases were almost as big a danger as the Turkish guns.

The Australians were unceasingly helpful, although while their ferocious lack of respect for British army regulations caused occasional setbacks, it also swept away some of the impediments of officialdom.

At sundown the huge sweep of sky was stippled with mackerel clouds shot through with light. The Aegean Sea was a limpid satin blue beneath it, though still dotted with ships and struggling men.

Joseph sat on a patch of stony ground a hundred feet or so above the beach, shivering a little with cold and exhaustion.

For four hours he had scrambled over ridges and scree, floundering, tripping rather than falling into trenches that were little more than scrape holes in the earth. Once he had had to duck and run to avoid the raking fire of Turkish machine guns, before he had reached the place where he had been told Mynott would be.

Apparently he had led a raid uphill, hoping to capture a Turkish position and take a few prisoners. It was hopelessly against the odds, and it had failed, but the attempt had improved morale greatly.

Now Major Mynott sat opposite him on the thyme-scented earth, his arm wrapped in a blood-soaked bandage, his face gaunt. He was a man of medium height with a prominent nose and slightly hooded eyes that at the moment were shadowed with the horror of so much violence, disorder, and sudden death.

"What can I do for you, Captain Reavley?" he said with barely concealed impatience. "I really know nothing of use to military intelligence. As you may have noticed, it is something we have very little of around here."

"We don't have any to spare in Ypres either," Joseph replied. "But this is to do with something that happened before the war, in Germany, and I've been told that you are familiar with the details."

"I was in Germany before the war," Mynott agreed, frowning. The sky was fading at his back, the color bleached out, silver bars of light on the water interspersed with pools of shadow, the vast horizon melting into the night.

"You knew a man named Ivor Chetwin," Joseph went on, forcing his concentration back to the present. They were on a long escarpment where the ground was too hard to dig more than a few inches. How anyone, even a madman, had thought soldiers could storm up these hills in the face of shells, mortars, and machine-gun fire was beyond imagination.

"Not very well," Mynott answered. "Met him perhaps half a dozen times."

"He was betrothed to Princess Adelheid von Gantzau."

"Yes." Mynott's expression was guarded.

"Can you tell me something about her father?" Joseph asked. "He and Chetwin were close, I believe, and Gantzau was a friend of the kaiser."

"Do you suspect Chetwin of something?" Mynott was blank.

"I can't tell you. Please, the matter is of the greatest importance."

Mynott regarded Joseph with curiosity and it was quite a long time before he answered. "I don't know what you have been told," he said slowly, seeming to pick his words with deliberate care. "But most of the story is true. Gantzau was a friend of the German royal family, and certainly he knew Schenckendorff and many of the others like him who had political ambitions and strong ideas." He winced slightly as he moved and the pain in his arm shot through him. "But in Europe before the war all sorts of people knew each other. I knew many of them myself. After all, our king and the kaiser are first cousins. Don't read anything into that."

"And Reisenburg?" Joseph asked.

"Yes. Why?"

"Chetwin knew Reisenburg? Are you sure?"

Mynott squinted at him. "You said it as if you want the answer to be *no,* but you're afraid it's *yes.*"

Someone walked past them in the dark. The smell of tobacco smoke was sharp in the air, and crushed wild thyme where their boots trod on it. He passed, not much more than a shadow. There was sporadic gunfire. Were it not for the starlight over the sea, and the sharp slope of the hill, Joseph could have imagined himself back in Ypres.

"I need to know," he said aloud.

Mynott caught the urgency in his voice. "Look, Captain, Chetwin fell in love with Adelheid. She was young, beautiful, and full of life. He was older, but he was vigorous and highly intelligent. Her family were reasonably happy about it."

"I heard he was engaged to marry her?" Joseph asked.

"Do you want the story, Captain, or just the end?" Mynott said testily.

Joseph apologized.

Someone coughed a few yards below them on the hill, and the smell of smoke drifted up in the air. Seabirds were circling high overhead, riding the currents of warmer air in the very last light.

Mynott resumed the tale. "The affair became serious, and indiscreet. Adelheid was with child. That was the point at which the family insisted Chetwin marry her. It grew unpleasant." Mynott shrugged, but Joseph could see only the faintest movement in the near darkness. "Chetwin refused."

"He refused?" Joseph was horrified, not only for the dishonor of such an act, but because it made no sense of the information Matthew had given him. "What did Gantzau do?" He leaned forward. "Why did Chetwin refuse? Surely he didn't doubt the child was his?" The situation seemed uglier with every new fact.

Mynott's voice was tired and strained with pain.

"I don't know. But he told me that Adelheid did not want to marry him, and he believed there had been someone else she cared for far more, but who couldn't or wouldn't marry her."

"But he was engaged to marry her!" Joseph insisted. Surely Matthew could not be mistaken in so simple a fact?

"Her parents insisted," Mynott replied. "I don't know whether the child was his or not. The parents thought it was and they forced him into an engagement."

"Forced?"

"He would have been politically ruined if they made it known he had taken advantage of a noblewoman, twenty years younger than he, got her pregnant, and then abandoned her." Mynott was impatient with Joseph and contemptuous of Chetwin. "It would ruin her, and her father would make damn sure it took him down, too."

That was easy enough to believe. "But he didn't marry her!" Joseph pressed.

"No. She miscarried the child. It was very bad. She bled to death." Joseph could

441

not see Mynott's face in the darkness, but he could hear the pity rasping in his voice, and for a blinding moment all his own loss returned to him, as if the carefully nurtured skin had been ripped off his wound. It was as if Eleanor and his own child had died only yesterday. It seemed absurd to sit here in this harsh grass of Anzac Cove, where the earth and the sea were stained with the blood of thousands of men, and still feel such overwhelming sadness for individual losses from a past that seemed to have disappeared into a life that was like a dream from which one had permanently awoken.

"What happened to Chetwin?" He forced himself back to the present.

"He left Germany, and would be a damn fool ever to go back there," Mynott answered. "Anyone near the court would string him up by the . . ." He left the sentence unfinished.

"I see."

"Is that helpful?"

"It . . . it proves the theory is wrong," Joseph said with surprise, and a strange, dizzy sense of relief, which was absurd. They must find the Peacemaker, for John and Alys Reavley, for Sebastian, for Reisenburg, and now for Cullingford. He had not been beaten because the treaty was taken from him before it could be presented to the king. No one knew if the king would even have signed it! The Peacemaker would have other plans, and they needed desperately to know what they were. All kinds of sabotage, betrayal, and deceit were possible, and the very fact that he would murder Cullingford showed he was still powerful, and dangerous.

But something in Joseph still shrank from finding it was a man he had liked. The face of evil should not be familiar, it should be strange, terrifying, unknown before the instant of confrontation.

The Peacemaker was a man who would sell a nation of forty million people into oblivion, betray into bondage their history, their culture, their language, and everything they had created over a thousand years. French in all its wit, color, sophistication, and pride would become a dead language. And after France and Belgium, one by one the other nations would fall, subjugated to the iron control necessary to keep them obedient, afraid, and unable to move against the center.

And England would be worse, not the betrayed but the betrayer! That was the ultimate sin.

He stared out to sea where the rising moon barely glimmered on the faint ripples of the water. It was becoming difficult to see the black outlines of the ships, or the boats plying between them. Around him he could hear the clang of iron shovels on the rock in the earth as burial parties worked.

The army had not been long here. Blood was still fresh. There were no rats like those at Ypres — at least he had not seen any. The latrines smelled much the same, but there was not the stench of corpses — so many of them weeks and months old. There you could hardly dig a trench or shore up a broken wall without slicing into a limb.

If the Peacemaker's plan had worked, all those men would still be alive. This hill would be empty of everything but wild irises and the purple-flowering Judas trees. There would be silence but for the lap of water, and perhaps the odd bleat of a goat or two.

These men would be at home with their families in the far corners of the earth.

But which was the greater madness, and which the sanity — to fight and die by the tens of thousands for what you believe, not knowing if you could win, or to surrender before the bloodshed, and save all the lives, the young and brave and so passionately innocent, to live out their days a conquered people, prisoners to someone else's will?

"I don't know anything else about Chetwin," Mynott said apologetically.

"No . . . no, I think that's probably enough," Joseph answered him. "We were wrong. It couldn't be what we thought."

"Does it matter a lot?"

"Yes. It matters a hell of a lot." Of course Matthew would have to check that it was true, but Joseph believed it. The Peacemaker had intended to succeed. Setting up a double bluff like this, at the expense of a young German noblewoman's life, was absurd, disgusting, and above all completely self-defeating. "Thank you. I'll see if I can get a lift on the next ship going home again."

"Well, there's nothing going out tonight. You might as well get a little sleep," Mynott observed. "Tomorrow look for a fellow called Richard Mason, war correspondent. He's down to go either tomorrow or the next day. If you can find him, you can probably thumb a lift with him."

"Thank you. I'll do that."

Joseph slept on the earth about fifty feet up. It was hard and cold and only exhaustion gave him any rest at all. Perhaps a few nights on the ship had made him soft?

He woke quite a while after dawn and looked down on the beach full of activity. Men were moving about as if on the scene of some busy factory yard, digging, carrying, piling up boxes and crates. The smell of smoke drifted up from cooking.

Joseph thanked the Australians with whom he had camped for the night.

"Hooray, mate!" Blue answered cheerfully. "Holy Joe! I like that!" He laughed till the tears filled his eyes.

"G'day, sport," Flanagan called out. "Mind where you go!"

"You, too." Joseph refused to think what their chances were. He would choose to believe they would be among the few who would survive. "Thank you," he said again.

He set off along the ridge and down on the grass toward the level, in roughly the direction he had been told he might find the correspondent Richard Mason. Actually he was looking forward to it — he had seen his name on many of the best and most honest articles he had read. The man had an ability to catch the experience of a small group in all its passion and immediacy, and make it represent them all. There was something clean and unsentimental in his use of language, and yet the depth of his feeling was never in doubt.

It took him nearly two hours, by which time his feet were sore and he was horribly aware of the flies everywhere.

"Over there, mate," a lanky Australian pointed. "That's the Pommie writer feller."

"Thank you," Joseph said with profound relief. He could see only the man's back. He wore a plain khaki-colored jacket and trousers and a wide-brimmed hat jammed on his head.

"Excuse me, are you Richard Mason?" Joseph asked when he reached him.

The man turned around slowly. He had an unusual face, with wide cheekbones and a broad, full-lipped mouth. It was a face of high intelligence, but far more striking was the brooding emotion in it, the sense of will. Joseph was certain he had found the right man; such features belonged to one who would write with blazing honesty.

"Yes," Mason answered. "Who are you? A chaplain!" He looked surprised and very slightly amused.

"Joseph Reavley," Joseph told him. "I had a mission out here, which I have completed. I understand you are shortly leaving for England. I need to return as soon as possible, and if there is room in your transport I would be grateful."

Mason's eyes flickered for a moment of puzzlement, then he looked beyond them both at the milling men on the beach and up the slope at the dugouts, the shallow trenches, the makeshift shelters of stones and boxes. Finally he looked back at Joseph. "Your mission is finished, you said?" His implication was clear.

Joseph regarded him levelly and a little coldly. "Yes, it is. I have only a few days more leave before I have to report back to my regiment at Ypres."

Mason colored faintly. "I'm sorry." It was said frankly. His diction was perfect, a little sibilant, but there was a beauty in its exactness as if words were precious to him.

Joseph offered his hand.

Mason grasped it. "There's a ship going back toward Malta tomorrow. Probably about dawn. They'll find room for you. Won't be hard to get a troopship home from there." His eyes searched Joseph's face curiously. "Yours must be a rotten job a lot of the time. How the hell do you tell people they can make sense out of all this?" He gestured toward the rock escarpments almost six hundred feet above them where the Turkish guns commanded most of the bay. "Fever, dysentery, gunshot and shrapnel wounds, seasickness, overcrowding. One hospital ship out there has eight hundred and fifty wounded, and two doctors to look after them all. And one of those a bloody vet!" The anger was profound and so deep inside him it showed only in the lines of his face and the rigid tension of his shoulders, there was no surface fire anymore. It had long since worn itself out.

"I don't try," Joseph answered. "I deal with people one at a time. I can only address the small things."

"In other words you can't make sense of it either," Mason concluded with a certainty that obviously gave him no pleasure. "You've given up on telling them this is some kind of divine destiny, and necessary furnace of affliction, and they should cling onto belief, and just endure?"

"Actually I don't tell people much of what they should do at all," Joseph answered. "Most people are doing their best anyway. The big choices are taken away from us, it's only how we react that's left."

Mason turned away. The sunlight was harsh on his face, showing the lines of strain around his eyes. He looked about Joseph's own age, but the knowledge and the rage inside him were timeless. "It would have been nice if you could have given some great cosmic answer," he said drily. "But I wouldn't have believed you anyway. Have you had anything to eat today?"

"No. I wanted to be sure to find you."

Mason hesitated, as if to ask another question, then changed his mind. He turned and led the way through the wiry grass and the tumbled clay and rocks along toward a makeshift field kitchen. Half a dozen men were cooking and a group was already lining up for breakfast.

Joseph waited his turn, and was glad to walk away with a plate of stew, a couple of hard biscuits, and a mug of tea. He sat next to Mason on the ground in the shelter of a rock to eat, aware of the tensions around him, the constant glances up at the headlands where the Turkish guns were dug in and commanded almost all the advances up the slopes.

There was a lot of good-natured banter. The men were mostly Australians and New Zealanders, but there were just the same sort of robust and colorful complaints he would have heard at Ypres. Only the accents were different, and the individual terms of abuse. The subjects were the same: the food, the officers, the general impossibility of doing what was commanded. Men had sore feet, bellyache, only here they tried bathing in the sea to get rid of the ever-present lice. It didn't work any better than the matches in Flanders.

It was early afternoon and Joseph was up the incline a dozen yards away from Mason, observing him writing notes, when the attack started. Men poured up the hill, charging the Turkish positions. Gunfire was incessant: The heavy artillery dug in behind the trenches and gullies; the machine guns' rapid, staccato fire; and the boom of ships' guns from the battleships in the bay.

Joseph followed Mason up to the lowest line of the dugouts and shallow trenches. The wounded came rapidly. A few were carried on stretchers, but most were floundering on their own feet, staggering and falling. Some were more seriously hit, and carried by their fellows. At times it was hard to tell which were the injured men; there was blood everywhere.

Once Joseph looked up from a rough piece of field first aid he had been performing to find Blue on his knees in front of him. His tunic front was scarlet with blood, his hair matted, his face almost gray.

Joseph felt a lurch of horror so intense for an instant he was unable to move.

"Y'all right, sport?" Blue said hoarsely. "Look like you seen a ghost! Here." He half hauled a blood-soaked body forward. One arm was shattered, the hand gone altogether, and its left foot was blown away. "See what you can do for him, will you? He . . . he was a good bloke." His eyes pleaded to be told something better than the truth he already knew.

"Of course," Joseph gulped, dizzy with a surge of relief that it was not Blue, although it was senseless. Blue was going straight back up into the fire, and it could be him next time, or the time after. Only a fool would imagine any of them had much of a chance of coming out of this without some fearful wound. Perhaps those who died quickly were among the fortunate. Their families would grieve, but that was secondary to the hell that was going on here, now.

He took the dying man from Blue and told him to go back. There was no need for him to remain and watch.

Blue waved his hand and, ducking low,

started back up again, rifle slung over his shoulder, feet scrabbling on the stones.

Joseph bent to the man on the ground. He was gray-faced, but still breathing. There was no way of knowing if he was conscious enough to feel the pain, or understand what had happened to him, but Joseph spoke to him as if he did.

"Hang on there," he said calmly. "You're in the first-aid station now. We'll patch you up. Give you something for the pain, as soon as we get a bit further down."

The man's eyelids fluttered. It might have been because he heard, or just a response to the agony in his body.

Joseph took a wet rag and cleaned the man's face gently. It was a totally pointless gesture in every practical sense, but it showed someone cared. If he was even half conscious he would at least know he was not alone.

Ten minutes later he died, and Joseph moved to the next batch of wounded brought down. He helped medical orderlies, most of whom had little training. One was a veterinary surgeon from somewhere in New Zealand. He was skilled and worked with frantic dedication and an air of confidence. It was very reassuring to those who did not see his moments of panic as he reached for medicines and equipment he did not have, and fumbled now and then in human anatomy.

"Thanks, Padre," he said as Joseph handed him a bandage, then held the injured man's white-knuckled hand while the wound was bound up. "Where'd you come from?" he went on conversationally. "You speak like a Pommie." He finished his bandaging and eased the man up.

Joseph leaned forward quickly to help, taking the man's weight. "That's right," he agreed. "Cambridgeshire."

"You mean where they have the boat race?" His face lit up. "I'd like to see that." He washed the bench down with creosol.

"Actually they have it on the Thames, near London, but we row against Oxford, every year."

The vet grinned. "Don't always win, though, do you!"

"Not always," Joseph conceded. He held the next man while the vet straightened a dislocated limb, but there was no time to wait for the waves of agony to pass before moving the man and starting on the next.

"Train a lot of horses in Newmarket, don't you?" the vet asked, jerking his head to indicate that he needed Joseph's help lifting a dead man so he could reach the living. "Love horses. God, I hate to see them hurt!"

Later Joseph helped carry the injured down to the beach and onto tenders to take them out to the hospital ships. It was there that he met Mason again, who was also exhausted and covered with blood. He had lost his hat, and his black hair was falling over his face. There was a gentleness in his hands as he lifted the wounded and eased them into half-decent positions of comfort that momentarily masked the savage rage inside him.

It showed again later when close to exhaustion he stopped for an hour. He and Joseph sat together drinking scalding tea with rum in it, their backs against a pile of ammunition crates. Joseph was so tired every muscle in his body ached as if it had been wrenched and his bones had been bruised. Like Mason, he was caked in blood and his skin abraded by sand. It was an effort to hold the mug, but the rum in the tea was worth it.

"The bastard who thought of this bloody fiasco should be made to be here!" Mason said through clenched teeth. His eyes stared far away, as if he could see something out toward the horizon, and everything closer was a blur.

Joseph did not answer. Agreement was unnecessary. He sipped again and felt the fire slide down his throat and hit his stomach. This whole expedition was a nightmare from which he did not know how to waken. Perhaps life was the nightmare, and death was the awakening? Did the men who were slaughtered here open their eyes to some quiet place where they were whole again, with the people they loved around them, and no pain? Or was this all it was — hope and then disaster — and finally oblivion?

Mason climbed to his feet stiffly and looked at the water, then slowly he started to walk toward it, taking his boots off, then his clothes as he went.

Joseph did the same and followed after him, only half certain what he intended to do.

Mason reached the edge, and without hesitation, waded in. When he was waist deep he bent and scooped it up in his hands and then poured it over his head. He did it again and again, as if to wash away more than the blood and dirt.

He turned to look at Joseph, a couple of yards away.

"Tell me, Chaplain, how much of this can be washed off? I could scrub down to the bone, but would all the seas of the earth take it out of my mind? I wonder if Churchill has read Macbeth? What do you think? Would his hands 'the multitudinous seas incarnadine' with this bloody slaughter? There's no victory, no sense, just death and more death."

He walked back to the shore, dragging his feet against the tide, and put on his clothes again. Joseph did the same, the fabric sticking to his wet body.

"We'll be out of here in the morning," Mason said, his words terse. "In three days, if I'm not torpedoed by some bloody U-boat, I'll be back in London and I'll write a story that'll get this insane carnage stopped. Once the nation knows what the truth is they'll throw this government out."

"You can't tell them what it's like," Joseph replied flatly. "Even if you could write a piece that would describe this . . ." He was too stiff to point, he just glanced around. "They wouldn't publish it. It's all censored. It has to be, or it would break the spirit at home. We'd get no more recruits."

"You want more men to come out and be slaughtered like this?" Mason asked, his eyes burning with accusation, but it sprang from his own raw, hurting anger, the inner wounds bleeding, not a desire to hurt Joseph.

"I'd rather not have war at all," Joseph replied. "But I didn't get to choose."

"None of us did!" Mason said bitterly, bending to tie his bootlaces. "If we were told the truth, then perhaps we would have! At least we'd have gone into it with our eyes open."

"You can't tell all the truth, only part of it," Joseph pointed out. "Anything you say is going to be your judgment, what you see and feel. Do you have the right to decide what other people must know, when they can't do anything to change it?"

"I have more than the right," Mason replied, straightening up. "I have the duty. We are a democracy, not a dictatorship. You can't choose if you don't know what the choices are." He half turned to face Joseph, wincing as a strained muscle in his shoulder shot through with pain and he moved gingerly to ease it. "Tell me that you believe any sane man or woman in England would choose *this*," he said the word with a savagery that tore the sound out of him, "if they knew what it was. Is this glory? Are these Rupert Brooke's heroes, 'swimmers into cleanness leaping' from this life to some mythical Valhalla?

God in heaven, man! If you've any humanity at all, look at it! It's worse than barbarity, it's a hell only a civilized imagination could conceive! It's a refinement of madness beyond the merely bestial."

"And is telling people at home going to help anything?" Joseph asked with quiet pain.

Mason's eyes blazed.

"Of course it will! Men won't volunteer for this if they know the truth. There's nothing glorious in it! There's nothing even useful! They're dying because of incompetence! We aren't going to take the Dardanelles, we aren't going to take Constantinople, and we aren't going to liberate the Russian Grand Fleet! The Eastern Fronts are going to be against the Italians, poor sods, and the Russians in the north — if anyone's insane enough to try that. Napoleon failed. That should be a lesson to anyone."

Joseph smiled with a downward twist. "Now who's being naive?"

They reached the spot where they had sat before. Their mugs were still there. Mason picked up his and looked at the dregs. "You don't think the kaiser will march against the tsar? This whole abattoir is a glorified family feud! They're all bloody cousins!"

"I meant," Joseph corrected him, "that I don't think anyone is instructed by the lessons of history."

Mason smiled at last, a curiously honest expression that suddenly shed years from his face. "Have another cup of tea? At least the rum's real. Then we'll go and see if we can get some of these poor devils out to the hospital ships. Not that they'll be that much better off there! They can exchange being shot at for being seasick. Personally, I think I'd rather stay here and take my chances." Without waiting for Joseph to answer, he took both mugs over to the field kitchen.

Joseph relaxed a little. There was still time to try to make Mason see the terrible damage of what he intended. When they were at sea, away from this horror, he would be able to convince him that it would be wrong.

They spent the rest of the daylight helping the wounded men who could walk, carrying those who couldn't. It was back-breaking and heartrending work. Another three times Joseph struggled up the hillside himself to help more men down. He stepped in blood, tripped over bodies, sometimes only limbs or torsos, riddled with bullets or blown apart by shells. In the shallow trenches British, Australians, and Turks sometimes lay together, indistinguishable in the blood and earth. The smell of slaughter filled his mouth and throat and lungs. The wild thyme was gone; even the sharp sting of creosol couldn't penetrate through the sick sweetness of blood.

It was after midnight when he sank into a dazed exhaustion and the oblivion of sleep overtook him until dreams invaded it, full of torture and screaming.

He awoke with a jolt to daylight and someone throwing a bucket of seawater in his face. Its saltiness was exquisitely clean. He gasped and sat up, struggling for breath.

"There y'are, cobber!" a voice said cheerfully. "An' there's plenty more where that came from. But if yer ain't broke your legs, yer can fetch it for yerself."

"Hey! It's Holy Joe!" another more familiar voice added. "Let's get the poor bleeder some breakfast. For a Pommie he wasn't too bad last night."

Joseph clambered to his feet, pushing his hair off his face and wiping the water away. His body ached appallingly. "Thanks, but I need to find the journalist. He's shipping out today, and I'm getting a lift with him. Thanks all the same."

"No you aren't, sport! He left a couple of hours ago!"

Joseph froze. "What?"

"Guns got your ears? He left a couple of hours ago — at least! He's long gone — over the horizon on his way to Malta by now. You'll have to take the next ship — whenever that is. Have a cup o' tea!"

Chapter

TWELVE

It was another twenty-four hours of frantic effort before Joseph could find a ship going as far as Malta that would take him as a passenger. He had to use all the persuasion he had to gain it, including his letters of authority from Matthew.

He paced the deck as the shores of Gallipoli faded behind him and became an indistinct blur, Anzac Cove and Suvla Bay no longer distinguishable. Even the sound of guns was finally lost in the wash of the sea. The island of Samothrace towered to the south, its corona of mist gilded by the setting sun. Today the beauty of the past, the heroes, the love and hate of Troy, which used to be a safe island of retreat, were simply a legacy of epic words, with no healing left in them. The pain of the present drowned out all memory. The urgency of catching up with Richard Mason before he could hand his work to some irresponsible publisher made chaos of any other thoughts.

If Joseph could just have time to talk to him, explain rationally the damage it would do! If he could make him understand what Ypres was really like, repeated over and over again through hundreds of trenches right across the Western Front, the courage and the loyalty of the men, the idea of putting off even one man from taking up arms to support them would be abhorrent to him.

Men did not go into battle in cold blood but in the fever of the moment. The price was terrible, but the cost of failure was higher.

He paced back and forth, unable to sit down, too tense to eat, too filled with nervous energy to sleep, until at last exhaustion overtook him lying in a narrow cot in a crewman's quarters, while the man was on duty.

Malta was ancient, fascinating, full of colors, eclectic architecture, and a cultural mixture that reflected every tide that had swept the Mediterranean in five hundred years, and yet was unique to itself. Explorers, merchants, and Crusaders had stopped here. Now the harbor of Valetta held British warships and the liners, the yachts, the racing skiffs were silent and unseen.

Joseph barely saw any of it; he looked only for signs of where Mason could have gone. He asked the British seamen he met, the loaders and dockers, and eventually the harbormaster himself.

"That would be the English gentleman from the newspapers," the harbormaster replied. "Very fine writer. Read his stuff myself. Admire those chaps." He said it with profound feeling. "Never afraid to go where the danger is, if they can get the truth. He took the ship out to Gibraltar this morning. I arranged it for him myself."

"Gibraltar!" Joseph exploded with burning frustration. "How can I get there? It's urgent! I have dispatches for London. I have to get there in three days, at the outside!" If he did not catch him, Mason would deliver his work, with his damning descriptions of chaos and pointless death. Again so many of them were men who had volunteered, come willingly from the other side of the world, because they had felt it was the right thing to do. Their lives were squandered, uselessly and terribly.

At least that was what Mason would write. Whitehall would try to censor him, but he had seemed sure that he had a way to evade that. And once he had published it, and it was spread by pamphlet and word of mouth, could anyone prove him wrong?

He wasn't wrong!

Joseph could not explain that to anyone because he dared not use Mason's words, they were too easily repeated with all the irreparable damage they could do. He used Matthew's letter of authority again, arguing, pleading, hearing the panic inside him burn through.

Finally as he stood once again on the deck of a steamer, this time bound for Gibraltar, watching the lights of Valetta fade into the soft Mediterranean night, emotional and physical exhaustion overcame him, and with it a feeling close to despair.

Now Joseph was racing across the Mediterranean trying to catch Mason, a brilliant journalist, a man of passion and his own kind of honor. Joseph had seen the searing tenderness in him as he had done what pitifully little he could for the wounded, body hunched with tension, rage almost choking him at the waste, the disorganization, the needless vulnerability of men exposed to shellfire on all sides.

And yet Mason's passion and horror were irrelevant to the harm he would do if he published what he had seen. Perhaps people would rise up and try to change the government, by ordinary civil means? There would be a vote of no confidence in the House, forcing a general election. But that would leave Britain in turmoil, no one to make decisions, just as the Germans were lunging forward in Belgium, France, northern Italy, and the Balkans. It would pile chaos upon chaos. And who else was there to elect?

It would shatter faith, the only strength left when defeat stared the armies in the face, and it offered nothing but anger and doubt in return. All those who had already died, caught in the wires, drowned, frozen or blown to pieces, choked with gas, or those shell-shocked, maimed and mutilated by war, would have suffered for nothing, a surrender because no one else would come forward to take their places when they fell.

The thought choked him with a tearing grief for all those he had known, whose deaths he had watched, and for the countless others lost, and for those who loved them and whose lives would never be the same again. It seemed the ultimate blasphemy that their sacrifice should be thrown away. He could not bear it.

He ate, slept fitfully, and paced the deck, shoulders tight, hands clenched, as the ship made its way across the Mediterranean at what seemed to him a snail's pace.

He imagined what German occupation would be like for the Belgians and the French. The laws would be changed, there would be a curfew imposed so no one could go out after dark. Travel would be restricted, you would have to have passes to go from one place to another, and explain your reasons. All newspapers would be censored. You would be told only what they wanted you to know. Food would be rationed, and all the best would go to the occupying forces, the good cheese, the fresh fruit, the meat.

But the physical inconveniences would be small compared with the change in people. The brave would be hunted down and punished, interned in camps, perhaps like those in Africa during the Boer War, women and children as well. The collaborators would be rewarded, the betrayers and profiteers; the vulnerable, the weak, the bribable, deceivable, the terrified would drift with sheeplike obedience.

What would Joseph tell the suffering Belgians to do, those quiet men and women he saw around Ypres and Poperinge and the sheltered villages and farms, refugees from their homes, leaving behind a broken land? Would he tell them they were beaten, and should now put up with it in peace, and that to attack the occupying forces or countries was actually murder? Turn the other cheek, or retaliation? Render unto the kaiser what is the kaiser's? If you attack your oppressor, does it have to be the individual soldier attacking you, or do you use intelligence, and strike at the head? Use the most effective weapon you can, when and where they are not expecting it, against whom it will do the most damage?

They were moral questions to which his instinct said one thing, and his doubts said another. He had little privacy in which to pray, but it was only convention that said you had to do it on your knees, or with your hands folded. A few minutes alone on the deck, a forced quietness of his racing mind, and he began to see more clearly, if nothing else, at least the need to stand for his own beliefs. It should be his wish to defend others, and it was certainly his duty. How could you argue with Christ who was crucified that it might hurt, or even cost you your life?

Was there any faith at all, Christian or otherwise, that would excuse you on these grounds?

Actually it was only three days before he saw the jagged teeth of Gibraltar on the skyline, and then by midafternoon the ship was docked in the harbor below the almost sheer rise of the great rock itself.

He went ashore immediately. The air was close and there was hardly any breeze. It felt warm and clammy on his skin. The slurping water smelled of oil and refuse, fish, the heavy salt of the sea.

The rock towered above him, dense black, blocking out the pale sky littered with stars. The lights of Irish Town crowded close to the shore, with its narrow streets, cobble-paved, winding upward so steeply there were flights of steps every so often. A hunting cat slithered past him, with economic, feline grace, soundless as a shadow. A laden donkey clattered up the incline, panniers on its back sticking out so far they bumped occasionally against the alley walls.

Church bells tolled. It must be a call to evensong, or the Roman Catholic equivalent. A glance at a few streets, church towers, statues of the Virgin Mary, or Christ with the Sacred Heart, showed that Catholicism was the predominant faith, in spite of the ancient Moorish architecture of the buildings silhouetted farther up the hill.

Ships crowded the water and Mason could be on any one of them, or he could already have gone. Joseph was frantic even to know where to begin to look. Hysteria welled up inside him and it took all his effort of will to control it and start asking sensible questions of people. He began with the assistant to the harbormaster, who told him the ships due to leave in the next twenty-four hours, and then when he produced his identification, the names of those bound for Britain that had left over the last two days. There was only one, and that had been yesterday. There was no way of knowing if Mason had been aboard.

He spent a wretched night walking the docks asking, pleading for any kind of passage to England. Twice he was taken for a deserter, and got short shrift from men contemptuous of anything that smelled like disloyalty. They had no time for cowardice and he was lucky to escape with nothing more than verbal abuse.

A little after midnight he found a friendly Spaniard who seemed less inclined to leap to conclusions as to what an Englishman was doing in uniform seeking to go home instead of toward a battle front. They sat in an alley in the warm darkness and shared a bottle of some nameless wine, and half a loaf of coarse bread not long from the oven. To Joseph it was an act of supreme kindness, and he began his search again at dawn with new heart, and a sense of urgency rather than overwhelming panic.

He found a cargo steamer willing to take passengers, but it cost him almost all the money he had left. He found himself on the afternoon tide, once again at sea.

They made good headway north up to the Bay of Biscay, although the weather was rougher than the Mediterranean, even though it was spring.

There were other passengers: an elderly gentleman of Central European origin who spoke quite good English, although he discussed nothing but the weather. The other passenger Joseph saw was an adventurer who did not acknowledge any nationality. He stood on the deck alone and watched the horizon, speaking to no one. Perhaps he had no country anymore, no home where he belonged, and was loved.

Joseph slept in a cabin no bigger than a large cupboard. He was barely able to lie with his legs out in the hammock provided, but he could have slept on the floor, had it been necessary. It was warmer and drier than a dugout in the trenches, and definitely safer. And it had the advantage of neither rats nor lice. He was less sure about fleas! But it was a luxury to lie still without the constant patter and scrabble of rodent feet.

He had time to think. Over and over again he rehearsed in his mind what he would say to Mason when he caught up with him, and each time the power of it was beyond him to frame in words. A year ago he would have expected them to come to him. Putting the most passionate beliefs into speech was his profession, and he had thought himself good at it, at least at that part of it.

But since then he had lost sight of intellect and became a man of emotion, which was the last thing he had intended. He was a stretcher-bearer, a digger of trenches, a carrier of rations and sometimes ammunition. He was even a medical orderly at times of extreme emergency. He had been up to his armpits in mud and water, struggling to pull out a body, or soaked in blood trying to stop a hemorrhage. There was no time for thought. It was emotion that drove him, the one thing he had intended to avoid. He had started out determined to do the best he could, to give every act or word of comfort, honor, and faith that he knew, or prayer could yield him, but keep his strength by protecting his emotions.

He seemed to have failed pretty well everywhere.

The passengers ate with the crew, but they spoke very little. The food was unimaginative, but perfectly palatable. By the second night he was relaxed enough to sleep quite well.

He woke with a start to hear feet in the passage outside, then a loud banging somewhere very close. He sat up, for a moment forgetting where he was, and feeling the hammock swing, almost tipping him out. He scrambled to regain his balance as the door burst open and a crewman shouted at him.

"Out! U-boat's stopped us!" He was almost invisible, but his voice was sharp with fear. "We've got to abandon ship. Don't hang around or you'll go down with it. They're giving us a chance." He withdrew and Joseph heard his feet thudding along the short passage and then a banging on the next door.

A U-boat! Of course. They must be well into the English Channel by now.

The man's feet were returning. He slammed the door open again, this time holding the lantern high and his face yellow in the glare of it. "Come on!" he ordered. "Get out! They'll torpedo the ship. You'll go down with it!"

Joseph reached for his clothes and pulled them on. He was used to sleeping in them, but here he had thought he was safe. He slid into his trousers, fingers fumbling with buttons, and grabbed his jacket. He pushed his feet into his boots without bothering to do them up, and lurched out of the door and along the passage.

It was oddly silent. It was a moment before he realized that the ship was rolling as if it were dead in the water. Of course. The engines were off.

He went up the gangway steps clumsily, his boots slipping because they were not tied. The outside air struck him in the face, cold, wind fresh and tasting of salt.

It was light on deck, because of searchlights from the U-boat. He could see its sleek, gray hull low in the water, only twenty yards away. There were men on the deck, just dark forms beyond the glare, maybe seven or eight of them. The sticklike silhouettes of guns were clear enough.

The captain of the steamer was standing stiffly near the rail. His face was bleak in the yellow beam, features almost expressionless, mouth pulled a little tight. He was in his late fifties, gray-haired, thick-bodied, a little stooped in the shoulder.

"Get your crew off, *Kapitan!*" The voice came drifting across the choppy water, clear, precise English with only a slight accent. "You have lifeboats!" That was a statement; they were clear enough to see in the lights.

"We need time," the captain answered. He had no power to bargain and he knew it. The U-boat could sink the steamer whenever it wanted to, and then the lifeboats afterward as well, if they wished.

"You have ten minutes," the answer came back. "Don't waste it!"

The captain turned around, moving awkwardly, shock slowing his movements.

Joseph bent to tie up his boots. This was not the time to lose or fall over one's laces. He worked quickly, his mind racing. Where were they? If they were allowed to escape in the lifeboats, which shore would they make for? Was there food? Water? How many people?

He looked across the water toward the submarine. It was an ugly thing, but swift, strong, silent beneath the waves, a wolf of the sea. The lights sparkled on the crest of the waves. They curled over, sharp ridges white-tipped, full of bubbles.

He stood up slowly. His body still ached from carrying the wounded on the Gallipoli beach. He turned toward the other men on the deck, and came face-to-face with Richard Mason.

Mason smiled. His face was white, his hair wet with spray and slicked back over his head. The flesh on his high cheekbones shone in the light and his eyes were brilliantly readable. There was bitter humor in them, and a suppressed rage, a will to live, but no enmity at all. If anything, he could see the irony in their both facing a common foe in the U-boat, and possibly the sea.

The crew were lowering the two lifeboats. The captain moved toward the open gangway. There was a shot, a loud crack, sounding different out here on the water from the way it did in the trenches. It hit something metal and ricocheted.

The captain stopped abruptly.

"Very noble to go down with your ship, *Kapitan!* But not necessary," a voice called out. "Back to the rail, if you please."

The captain hesitated.

"If you don't, I shall shoot one of your men. Your choice."

The captain returned slowly. In the glaring light he looked like an old man, too stiffly upright to be able to bend.

The lifeboats hit the water with a series of slaps as the waves banged against them with jolting sharpness. The sea must be rougher than it looked, even from the small height of the deck. They were not yet given permission to get into them.

Joseph realized with surprise that he was cold. Neither he nor the other man had had time to bring coats. He estimated there were about a dozen of them, including Mason, and the other two passengers. The light played over their figures, as if trying to identify one from another. The quiet man who had stared at the horizon put his hand up to shelter his eyes. The mid-European was shifting impatiently from foot to foot.

The U-boat also had launched a small boat into the water and it was now coming toward them, a hard black shape against the serrated edges of the waves, alternating light and darkness in the path of the lamp. It was easy to see two men rowing and two more standing in the bow, guns at the ready.

No one spoke while they crossed the short distance to the side of the ship, and the two with guns climbed up and on board.

"Kapitan." The first one stood to attention, but not for an instant altering the aim of his gun at the captain's chest. "You will come with us. Please bring your ship's papers. You will be interned in Germany, unless of course you prefer to be shot." It was not a question. He assumed the answer.

"Let my crew go," the captain replied. He made no mention of passengers. Perhaps that was a deliberate omission. Sailors might be treated with more respect than civilians. Had they been neutral nationals perhaps he would have said so.

"That is already agreed," the German told him. "Come now." He turned to the others. "You will wait here until the captain is on board our boat, then you will get into your lifeboats and move away. If you do not, the vortex of the ship's going down may suck you under."

The man in the overcoat made a wild, swinging movement with his right arm. Something in his hand shone in the light, like black metal. A shot rang out from the U-boat and he fell forward, quite slowly, as if he were folding up.

One of the crewmen lunged forward to help him, and a volley of shots followed. The second German clutched his shoulder and spun around, sagging to one side.

A handgun fell on the deck and slithered toward the rail. Another crewman dived for it, caught it, and fired toward the man in the boat.

Then there was a another volley of fire, bullets cracking, ricocheting around. Joseph fell to the deck instinctively, crouching on his hands and knees behind the shelter of the housing over the hatch. People were shouting, in anger, fear, and there was more shooting. The lights were harsh, now raking over the whole boat and the sea at either end.

Someone fired back from the deck. There was an explosion in the direction of the U-boat, and the light went out.

Silence.

Then the captain's voice came very clearly. "We surrender! I'm coming over! Let my crew get into the lifeboats and they'll leave!" Then he must have turned around to face his own deck, because his voice was louder. "Put down the gun! They'll torpedo the ship and we'll all be lost. Do it now!"

Silence again.

Joseph lifted his head very carefully to peer over the hatch. He saw in the dim starlight and the sickle moon the black shape of the U-boat against the slight shimmer of the water. A group of men were clustered around the dead light, two bent over as if working to get it mended, at least temporarily, but they were keeping low; two others stood separately, their guns trained toward the steamer.

The wind was cold and the ship was rocking as she lay without help of engines. By the rail the captain stood facing his own men.

Joseph could see two bodies sprawled on the deck, motionless. They might be wounded, or dead, or they might simply be too frightened to move. He could see the glare of a gun barrel on the wood almost a yard away from the outstretched arm of one of the bodies. It was perhaps twelve feet from the hatch beside which he lay. If anyone else reached it and started firing, the Germans would torpedo the ship, and they would all go down.

He started to move sideways, quickly, around the casing and onto the open deck. Before he got as far as the gun he stood up, aimed a kick with his right foot, and sent the gun over the side. It fell into the water with a plop. He held both hands up high. "The gun's gone!" he called out, more to the U-boat than his own captain. "It's over the side!"

Silence again, except for the wind and the slap of the waves.

"Thank you," the captain said quietly, then he turned back to the U-boat. "I'm coming!" He climbed over the rail and started down. "Good luck!" he said gravely. "There are compasses on the boat. Go northwest." And the next moment he was gone.

The other crewmen appeared, only shadows. One of them held his arm awkwardly as if it were injured. They were indistinguishable one from another in the darkness. The two bodies on the deck still did not move.

"Into the boats," someone ordered, his voice steady with authority. "There's no time to argue, just do it!"

There was sudden, swift obedience, fumbling now to see without the light. At least two of them seemed to be hurt, and there was another lying behind the engine housing forward. There were nine men alive. They divided four into one boat, five into the other. It was awkward, slippery, knuckle- and shin-bruising work climbing and then dropping into the shifting, swinging boats, unshipping the oars and pulling away from the steamer.

Joseph had one oar, someone he could

not distinguish had the other. The man with the injured arm was in the stern, his good hand on the tiller, and someone apparently more seriously hurt lay on the boards at the bottom. Joseph pulled as hard as he could, trying to fit in with the rhythm of the other man, but it was difficult. The boat bucked and twisted in the choppy sea.

He started to count aloud. "Pull!" Wait. "Pull!" The other man obeyed, and suddenly the oars bit and they began to create a distance between them and the steamer. He had no time even to think where the other boat might be.

Then it happened. The cannon on the U-boat fired and the steamer erupted in a gout of fire. The noise was deafening and the shock of the blast seared across the water. An instant later there was a second shock, far greater as the boat exploded, yellow and white flames leapt up into the sky. Metal, wood, and burning debris flew high in the air, lighting up the waves, the stark outline of the steamer, broken-backed, already beginning to settle deeper. The other boat was fifty yards away off the bow. Mason was pulling at the oar beside Joseph. The U-boat beyond was temporarily hidden.

In the glare Mason smiled. "Can't seem to lose you, can I?" he said wryly. "I suppose I should be grateful, at least you saved us all going down with the ship. You're more use than most priests. Keep pulling!"

Joseph put his back to the oar again. The ship was still burning fiercely, but already the sea was rushing in and it would plunge within minutes, creating a vortex that would suck in everything close to it.

"If you're waiting for me to say something nice about war correspondents, keep hoping. I'll try . . . when I have time," he answered.

Mason gave a bark of laughter and threw his weight against the oars again.

They rowed in silence, skirting wide around the sinking ship, which exploded twice more, sending steam hissing high in a white jet, then erupting in red flames just before it tipped and slid with a roar into the black water, and within moments was gone, nothing but a few pieces of wreckage remaining. The U-boat had vanished. The other lifeboat was just visible, about half a mile away.

The two other men in the boat had not moved appreciably, neither had they spoken. Now the one with the injured arm bent over awkwardly and spoke to the man who was half propped up against the side, his head resting against one of the ribs of the hull.

"How are you doing, Johnny?" he asked, his voice strained, gasping with his own pain.

There was no answer.

"Somebody help me!" he begged. "I think he's out cold! We've got first-aid stuff in the locker, and there should be a lantern, and food and water, and a compass."

Joseph handed the oar to Mason, who moved to the center of the seat and took over. The boat slowed a little, but it was possible for one man to manage, as long as the weather got no worse.

Joseph opened the locker, feeling in the dark, fumbling a little until he located the lantern and, shielding it from the wind with his body, got it alight. Then he could see that indeed there was a first-aid box, several bottles of water, hard rations of biscuits, dried beef, and bitter chocolate, and even a couple of packets of Woodbines. The matches he already had, from lighting the lamp.

The first thing was to see how badly the crewmen were injured. He looked first at the man lying on the boards. He had been shot twice, once in the upper thigh and once in the shoulder. Both wounds had bled badly and he was barely conscious.

"Can you do anything for him?" the other crewman asked anxiously.

"I'll try," Joseph replied. He had very little real medical knowledge, but this was not the time to say so. He certainly would not even think of attempting to take a bullet out by lamplight on the floor of a pitching boat, but he could roll up cloth into pads and do everything possible to stop the bleeding. It might be enough.

"Hold up the lantern," he asked. "What's your name?"

"Andy." In the yellow light he looked no more than nineteen or twenty, fair-haired, a blunt freckled face, now pasty white.

Joseph worked as well as he could, but it was difficult and the clothes around the wounds were soaked in blood. Even when he pressed on them, the injured man barely groaned. He was sinking deeper and there was nothing they could do about it. When he had bound him up, Joseph tried to get him to take a little water, even just to moisten his mouth, but he was too far gone to swallow.

After that he did what he could for Andy.

His upper arm had been shot through and it was bleeding badly as well, but the bone was intact. When he bound it as tightly as he dared without cutting off the circulation, it seemed to stanch the bleeding, even if it was no help for the pain.

He returned to take the other oar from Mason. The wind was stronger and they were having to work much harder to keep the boat moving, and headed against the waves so it did not turn sideways to them and risk being swamped.

There was a faint paling in the northeast of the sky, as if dawn were not far off. The other boat was nowhere to be seen.

"I suppose you've still got your story about Gallipoli?" Joseph asked.

"Of course," Mason replied.

"And you're still determined to hand it in?"

"You've already argued that one, Reverend." He used the word with mild sarcasm. "You preach your gospel, I'll preach mine. You want to protect people from the truth, for what you think is the greater good. I think they have the right to know what they're signing up for, what the battle will cost them, and what chance they have of winning anything worth a damn." He dug into the water and pulled, hurling his weight against the oar.

"You're going to tell them the truth about Gallipoli, how many men are dying, and how?" Joseph pressed.

"Yes!"

"And what you think our chances are of winning and making it through to Constantinople?"

"No chance at all. Nor of getting the Russian fleet out of the Black Sea. And even if we did it would make no damn difference in the end. We'd probably give Constantinople to the Russians anyway," Mason said.

"And that our generals out there are ill informed and for the most part incompetent?"

"For the most part, yes. You want to protect them? That's naive, Reverend, and dangerous. Your pity for them, God knows why, is getting in the way of your intelligence. Maybe your religion requires you to be compassionate and see the good in everyone, but He gave you a brain as well, presumably in the hope you'd use it! Do you really think any man's reputation is worth what those soldiers are paying for it?"

"I'm not trying to protect reputations!" Joseph dug just as deeply with his oar. It was taking all his strength and the exhausted muscles in his back and arms to hold the boat to the wind. Mason must feel the same. He had carried just as many wounded men. "I'm trying to keep up hope and courage at home, for very good reasons, and a rather longer view than you have! Few men set out on a battle they don't believe they can win."

"Few of them are stupid enough," Mason agreed tersely.

"And are you going to tell them what will happen if they don't fight?" Joseph had to raise his voice against the rising noise of the wind and the water in order to be heard. The light must have been broadening a little behind him to the northeast because he could see the stippling on the backs of the waves and the pale crests were creaming now and then. His feet were numb with cold.

"With no army we'll be forced to surrender," Mason answered him. "The slaughter will stop. It's a war we should never have got into. England has no quarrel with Germany."

"Whether we should have or not doesn't matter now," Joseph told him. "It's past. Right or wrong, we can't undo it. Germany has invaded Belgium, the land has been bombed and burned, the people driven out, thousands of them killed, their farms and villages destroyed. Are you going to tell them to surrender to the soldiers that have despoiled them, bury their dead, then carry on as before?"

"Of course I'm not going to tell them anything so damned stupid!" Mason said angrily. "Belgium will suffer, it already has, but isn't that less evil than the whole of Europe plunged into chaos and death? We are on the brink of destroying the finest young men of an entire generation for what? Can you justify what's happening?"

"I'm not trying to." Joseph was staring at the two crewmen in the stern. Andy seemed to be asleep, although he stirred now and then, and once Joseph had seen him open his eyes. The other man was lying next to him, half cradled across his knees, Andy's uninjured arm supporting his head, but he had not moved in over half an hour.

"Take the oar," Joseph said abruptly. It was light enough now to see Mason's face, the weariness and the strain in it, wet from spray. He understood what Joseph was thinking. He took the oar.

Joseph moved forward carefully. The boat was pitching and if he stood he might lose his balance, perhaps even go over the side. On his hands and knees he reached the wounded man.

Andy opened his eyes: wide and frightened, full of pain.

Joseph put the back of his hand to the other man's neck. He could feel no pulse at all. His skin was waxy-white in the creeping daylight.

Andy's good arm tightened around him. His face asked the question, but he did not speak.

"I think we could let him lie on the bottom," Joseph said, having to speak loudly to be heard above the sea. "Be more comfortable for you. That weight would send your legs to sleep."

"I don't mind!" Andy protested.

"You might need your legs, when we reach land," Joseph answered. "And it won't help."

Andy blinked, his face crumpling.

"I'm sorry." Joseph touched him briefly. "Come on."

Andy still hesitated, then slowly eased himself sideways and helped Joseph move the dead man's body so it lay out of his way and where the oarsmen would not bump it. Then he inched back to where he had been before, careful to take exactly the same position, and pulled the piece of canvas over himself. "I'm sorry I can't help," he apologized.

Joseph broke off a piece of the chocolate and gave it to him. "There are only two oars anyway," he replied.

He went back to his place again and he and Mason rowed in silence for a while. The white light spread across the horizon behind them, still without color. The wind was harder, and rising. It was getting more and more difficult to make any headway against it.

"Where do you come from?" Joseph asked Mason. He was anxious to know, and he needed to find some opening, some corner of emotion in Mason he could use to carry his argument. He must not give up, no matter what it cost. This was the ultimate test.

"Beverly," Mason replied. "Near Hull, in Yorkshire. Where do you?"

"Selborne St. Giles, just outside Cambridge," Joseph said. "Have you always been a journalist?"

"Nothing else I ever wanted to do." Mason smiled bleakly. "Don't tell me you always wanted to preach, I couldn't bear it! Some time, even if it was in the cradle, you must have wanted to do something else!"

"My father wanted me to be a doctor. I tried, but I felt so useless in the face of the pain, and the fear."

"So you chose the pain and fear of the spirit instead?" There was surprise in Mason's face, but it was not without respect. "Was your father upset?"

"Yes. But he's dead now."

"So is mine. He died while I was in Africa . . . reporting on the Boer War." He said the words with anger and a grief that clearly still hurt him. He was looking not at Joseph but at the sea rolling away behind them, now beginning to be touched with color, but a heavy gray, only undershot with blue.

"That's where you learned to hate war," Joseph observed. It was barely a question.

"It's not a noble thing," Mason said, his lips tight. "It's vicious, stupid, and bestial! It brings out the worst in too many men who used to be decent. There is immense courage, pity, honor, and all the things that are finest in human nature in some, but at the price of losing too many. The sacrifice is immeasurable. And it's a cost we have no right to ask of anyone — anyone at all!"

Joseph was quiet for a while. It was becoming difficult to hold the oars. The boat was bucking as the waves caught it from different angles and his strength was failing. He began to think of all the things he valued most, not what ought to matter, but what really did: his family, the people he loved who formed the frame of his life within which everything else took meaning. What was laughter or beauty or understanding if there was no one with whom to share it? What was achievement alone? So many things were made only in order to give them to someone else.

Friendship was at the root of it all, the honesty without judgment, the generosity of the spirit, the tenderness that never failed. In a way it was the end of fear, because if you were not alone, everything else was bearable.

He thought of Sam. If he and Mason didn't make the shore, then at least he would never have to go and find Sam and tell him he knew he had killed Prentice. He was surprised how much of a relief that was.

His hand slipped on the oar, as if he had already half let it go. Mason jerked around, fear in his face for an instant, until he saw Joseph tighten his grip on it again.

What would Sam have said to try to persuade Mason not to write his article on Gallipoli? What arguments were there left?

He had tried everything he could think of. None of it was enough. What if he failed? Finally he faced the thought he had been avoiding for the last two hours. There was only one way to be absolutely certain that Mason did not publish his piece, and that was to kill him. Could he wait until they were within sight of land, and he could manage the boat alone, then calmly take the oar and strike Mason with it, so hard it would kill him? He had no need to ask himself, he knew the answer. But was that humanity, even godliness? Or was it cowardice?

What if a ship were to see them before that, while he was still dithering, and pick them up? The decision would be taken out of his hands. No. That was dishonest. He would have left it too late, and missed his chance. Anyway, justification or excuses were pointless. If morale in England were destroyed, the reason Joseph Reavley failed to act would be utterly irrelevant.

"You would tell all of the men who might enlist and go," he said aloud. "And then many of them would change their minds. Their families would be relieved — at least most of them would. How about the families of all those who are already there? Or who have died in France, or

Gallipoli, or at sea? How do you suppose they would feel?"

"Probably angry enough to demand that the government answer for it," Mason replied, struggling to keep hold of the oar. "Pull, damn it!"

"We can't pull against this," Joseph replied, jerking his head at the waves. "One misjudgment and we'll be tipped over. We need to turn and go before it."

"Where to, for God's sake?" Mason demanded, his voice higher pitched, exhaustion and panic too close to the surface. "Out into the middle of the Atlantic?"

"Better there, and above the water, than the English Channel, and under it," Joseph replied. "Even south of here we'll still be in a shipping lane. We don't have a choice."

"Can you turn it without capsizing?" Mason demanded.

"I don't know," Joseph admitted. "But we can't go on like this. We can't hold it. We'll have to be fast."

"What about the wounded man? If he goes over we've lost him!"

"If the boat goes over we're all lost!" Joseph shouted back. "Together! When there's a lull. Wait for it! You lift out, I'll pull."

"A lull?" Mason yelled with disbelief.

The wind gusted, then dropped.

"Now!" Joseph bellowed, lifting his oar high, digging it round and feeling the boat turn, yaw wildly, pitch almost over as the wave slapped against the side, then as Joseph dug again, throwing his weight against it, come round with the wind and the current behind it.

Mason gasped, pushing his hair out of his face with one hand and grabbing at the oar to plunge it in the water again. Now the boat was running before the wind, but it still needed both of them with all their weight and strength to keep it from turning again.

Joseph's heart was pounding so hard he felt giddy. He had come within feet of drowning them all, Andy as well as Mason and himself. Relief left him shaking. He clung to the oar as much to regain his control as to wield and pull it. But something in him had resolved.

"I can't let you publish that piece," he said clearly. "That is, if there really is a publisher?" He had to know.

"Of course there is," Mason said without the slightest hesitation. "Some of the provincial newspaper owners believe as I do. They think people have a right to make their own decisions, knowing what they're going to face."

"Aren't they afraid of being charged with treason?" Joseph asked. "The Defense of the Realm Act is pretty powerful. Or are they going to do it anonymously, so they won't have to answer for it?"

Mason was angry. "Of course they're not going to do it anonymously!" he retorted. "What the hell kind of truth is that?"

"Are you sure?" Joseph let disbelief burn through his voice.

"Yes, I am sure!" Mason shouted. "I've known the owner all my life! He won't let the editors take the blame, he'll answer for it himself."

Joseph believed it. The certainty in Mason's face, the passion in him and his sense of honor and purpose, mistaken as it was, lit him with an intensity no lie could carry.

"I'm sorry," Joseph said, and meant it sincerely. He liked Mason, indeed admired him. "I can't let you do that."

"You can't stop me." Mason smiled — a warm, unaffected expression.

Joseph shipped his oar. "Yes, I can."

The boat jerked sideways until Mason lifted his oar out of the water also and the boat tossed and slapped without help at all.

"For God's sake!" Mason shrieked. "We'll sink! What the hell's the matter with you?"

"I can't kill you," Joseph answered. "But I won't help save you either." He looked at Andy. "I'm truly sorry. But if this piece is printed it'll be picked up by other underground papers, and will get round the country like fire. Well-meaning pacifists will pass it around out-side recruiting stations, and fifth columnists, pro-Germans will slip it through doorways and hand it out in meetings. In the end thousands of people will be affected by it. Fewer men will volunteer for the army, and our men in the trenches in France and in Gallipoli will be left to fight alone, until they're beaten. I can't let that happen, to save my life, or yours. I'm sorry."

"I understand," Andy said quietly. "Maybe we wouldn't have got home anyway. At least this is for a reason."

Mason pushed Joseph violently, knocking him off the bench, and seized his oar, pulling on both of them and righting the boat to send it in front of the wind again.

Joseph settled in the stern, next to Andy. It was a relief not to be straining his aching back against the oar anymore. Drowning was supposed to be not too bad a way to die. He had heard that you lost consciousness pretty quickly. Not like being caught in the wires in no-man's-land and left there for hours, even days. Prentice had died comparatively easily.

Pity Sam would not know. He would have appreciated the irony! Even more of a pity that he couldn't tell Matthew where the newspaper editor was. He didn't know the name, but it would be easy enough to find. Someone Mason had known all his life, who owned several papers, and was against the violence and waste of war.

He did not want to think of Matthew, or Judith or Hannah. It was too hard, too filled with pain. It hurt with a deep, gouging ache he could not control.

"You're a fool!" Mason was shouting at him, struggling to keep the boat straight with the wind behind it. "Surrender could mean peace! A united Europe. Isn't that better than this insane carnage, and the destruction of all our heritage, the poisoning of the earth itself? Europe's becoming an abattoir! There isn't going to be anything but ruin and madness left for the victor. Can't you see that?"

"You want peace?" Joseph asked, as if it were a real and urgent question. They were being pitched sideways, one direction then the other as Mason fought to keep control, his face sheened with water, his muscles clenched.

"Of course I want peace!" he shouted furiously.

Joseph braced himself not to land his weight on top of Andy, who was watching him intently. "And you think that surrender will bring peace?" He allowed his own disbelief to ring through. "Maybe to us! But what about Belgium that we proposed to protect? We gave our word. And what about France?"

"We didn't promise France," Mason retorted.

"What the hell has that got to do with it?" Joseph demanded. "Do we only protect people if we've got treaties that say we must? Do we only do the right thing if we are forced to?"

"The right thing?" Mason's voice rose in outrage. "It's the right thing to crucify half the youth of Europe in a quarrel about who governs which strip of land, and what language we speak?"

"Yes! If the right to have our own laws and our own heritage goes along with it. If anyone conquers us and lays down the rules for us, then bit by bit anything that makes us free and unique will be taken away."

The wind was still rising and Mason was finding it more and more difficult to hold the boat, even with the storm at his back.

"Free and unique! You're a madman! They're just dead! Bodies piled on bodies; tread on the earth in Flanders and you're standing on human flesh! Tell them the truth, and let them choose what they want! It's an unpardonable sin to lead them blind to the slaughter." He yanked at the oar, his face contorted with the strain. "You're supposed to believe in good and evil — to deny knowledge is to deny freedom — that is evil. Who the hell do you think you are, you supremely arrogant bastard, to decide for the youth of Europe, whether it will fight your damned war or not? Answer me, Reverend Reavley."

Joseph's mind raced. Mason's argument was the Peacemaker's, and he was so nearly right, so close to pity and humanity.

"You told me I was naive," he shouted back. "You want peace? Don't you think we all do? But not at any price, no matter how high. Belgium was invaded, and France. If we give up, do you think that's going to bring peace? Do you think the Belgian and the French people will simply lay down their arms and surrender?"

The wind tore Mason's answer from his lips.

"The government might give up, even

some of the people!" Joseph went on furiously. "But do you think the army will? The men whose brothers and friends have already died in the mud and gas, on the wires and in the trenches? The men who've frozen, drowned, and bled for what they loved! They've paid too much! So have we!"

Mason stared at him. His face reflected the pain of his tearing muscles as he strained against the oars. The boat bucketed and slid in the troughs. He was losing. He began to realize Joseph was going to die for his conviction, and take Andy, too, if that was what it cost. The knowledge woke admiration in him, reluctantly, angrily, but totally honestly.

"There'll be mutiny," Joseph went on, conviction growing in him. He was so cold now that he was not moving and he could hardly feel his legs below the knee. Andy must be beginning to suffer from exposure. It grieved Joseph to sacrifice him. "In the army, and at home," he went on. "What could the government do? Arrest all those who want to resist? Hand them over to the German occupying force? You know human nature, Mason! The brave men will flee to the hills, the forests, anywhere they can hide and regroup. Those who can't —

the old, the sick, women with children —
will pay the price. There'll be mass trials
for treason, if they're lucky; if not, then
just executions. There'll be collaborations,
of course, and betrayals, counterbetrayals,
groups of vigilantes, informers, and secret
police. . . ."

"All right!" Mason yelled. "There won't
be a bloody thing if you don't help me
keep this boat ahead of the wind! We'll all
be dead!"

"No, we won't," Joseph told him, leaning
forward to make himself heard above the
roar and crash of the sea. "You and I will
be, and unfortunately Andy, but no one
else. The other crewman is dead anyway."

Andy struggled to sit up. His face was
ashen white in the cold morning light. The
hard gray sea was racing around them,
waves spume-topped, foam flying.

"Do you agree with him?" Mason demanded, staring at Andy. "Is this what you
want, really? Because if it isn't, you'd
better tell him." He jerked his hand toward
Joseph. "And quickly. I can't hold this
much longer."

"It's what I want," Andy answered, his
eyes screwed up against the wind, but un-
wavering. "You've got to fight for what you
believe, an' die for it, if that's the way it

goes. An' you fight for your mate, same as he'd fight for you."

"And is Belgium your mate?" Mason asked savagely.

Andy gave him a crooked smile. "Yeah. S'pose he is. Your mate's whoever's beside you. The Germans've got no right to go through Belgium doing what they're doing. Nor into France neither. We'd fight if it was England. It isn't different, just 'cos it's somebody else." He said it simply, as if it were obvious.

Joseph felt a sting in his throat. It was the whole philosophy of the British "Tommy" he knew. Are you your brother's keeper? Yes, you are, at the price of your life, if that's what it takes. All his and Mason's arguments were academic, deciding for others. It was Andy, and a million men like him, whose lives were the cost.

He looked at Mason's face and saw the amazement in him, and the grasp after a new understanding.

"You throw that thing overboard and swear as you won't write it again, or we'll all go down," Andy told him. "I reckoned I'd give up my life for my country, if I had to — well, this is having to, that's all. Never thought it'd be to stop a traitor, but at least there's some point in that."

"For God's sake, man, I just want to stop the bloody slaughter!" Mason shouted back at him. "Do you know how many men are dead already, and the war isn't a year old yet?"

Joseph ached to be able to help him, but he could think of nothing else to say. Any hour, any minute now, Mason would be unable to hold the boat alone and it would go over, and they would all be in the sea, floundering, battered, struggling as long as they could until it overwhelmed them, and they swallowed water, it filled their lungs, bursting. Could it be as bad as being gassed? He remembered that with a sickening horror! And what about Prentice, drowned not in the clear sea but in the filth of a shell crater. Sam had done that, Sam, whom Joseph loved as much as a brother. He reached out his hand and grasped Andy's and felt his fingers respond, stiffly, too cold for more.

"I don't care!" Andy gasped. "I stand fast!"

Mason struggled with the oars. He was weakening. His face was tight with the strain, but it was in his mind as much as his aching body. He looked at Andy for another moment, then at Joseph. "It's in my pocket inside my jacket," he shouted.

"Take the oars from me, and I'll throw it overboard. You could be right, England might be full of suicidal idiots like you."

Joseph grinned hugely, even though he did not know how much the victory was really worth. They could well drown anyway. It was a triumph of the spirit at least. He fell forward onto his knees as the boat tossed and jolted again, swinging round and slamming against the waves. He took the oars from Mason and threw his weight and all his strength into pulling the boat straight, safe from the trough. It tore at the muscles on his back and shoulders, but he was rested, stronger than Mason now, and he could hold it, at least until Mason had thrown the papers away.

"Tear them up," he added aloud.

Mason made one more attempt. "It won't make any bloody difference! I'm not the only one."

"The only one what?" Joseph asked.

"Writing the truth, and who'll get published."

"You're the one writing about Gallipoli," Joseph responded. "You're the one who'll do the damage."

Mason gave a bark of laughter. "Don't you believe it! We've got a new young chap at Ypres. He was actually there for the first gas attack. He's got an almost photographic memory, but he took notes of it all, the panic, the horror, the way the men died."

Joseph froze. "Notes?"

"You'll never find them, they're all in a code he developed when he was at school."

Suddenly the hard, white light and the waves were as clear as midsummer, burning from horizon to horizon. "Eldon Prentice," he said aloud.

Now it was Mason who crouched as if turned to stone. It would have been impossible to deny it — his face betrayed him.

"He's dead," Joseph told him. "Dead in no-man's-land, drowned in a shell crater full of filth. Don't even think to argue. I carried him in myself. Or to be more accurate, I dragged him most of the way. He's buried near Wulvergem. I don't know what happened to his notes, but I can guess."

Mason blinked, still without responding.

"I have a friend who was at school with him. He could read them. You're on your own. Put your papers over the side."

Slowly, Mason took the carefully wrapped package out of its safety pouch and let the waves take it, then, as if infinitely tired, he lay back in the stern and Andy passed him the bottle of water.

Mason moved back to the other oar and silently they pulled together. Joseph took count of time. The wind chopped and by midday the sun was high, but there was no sight of land.

Joseph sat back. He was exhausted. Every inch of his body hurt and he was so hungry he would have welcomed even the worst of trench rations, but there was very little left in the emergency store, and they must make it last as long as possible. It was the lack of water that worried him most. They were restricting themselves to a mouthful each, every hour or so. Even then, there was perhaps another twelve hours left.

Mason looked haggard, and Andy was so white his skin seemed almost gray, but the bleeding had stopped some time ago.

"There's no point in rowing," Joseph said quietly. "We might as well ship oars and take a rest."

Mason did not argue. Together they completed the stroke and lifted the oars in. They laid there along the bottom of the boat, careful not to knock the dead man.

"You should rest, too," Joseph said to Andy. There was nothing on the horizon in any direction, no land to row toward, no ship whose attention to attract, not that that would be easy, lying so low in the water themselves.

Andy nodded, and carefully, to avoid bumping his arm, he slid down into the floorboards more comfortably. He smiled at Joseph, then closed his eyes. Nestled a little sideways, as if asleep, it was easy to see in him the child he had been a few short years ago.

Joseph glanced at Mason, and saw the recognition of exactly that in his face. His eyes burned with the blame, and the challenge.

Joseph did not speak, but he was as sure of his answer as Mason of his question.

He made himself as comfortable as he could and must have slept for quite some time, because when he woke Mason was sitting up, and the sun was low and murky over the water to the west.

"There's a fog coming," Mason said grimly. "Do you want some water?" He held out the canteen.

Joseph's mouth was dry and his head was pounding. He took the canteen, and could feel by the weight of it that if Mason had drank any at all, it was not more than his rationed mouthful. He smiled, drank his own gulp, and passed it back. "No point in waking him," he said, nodding toward Andy. He checked that he was breathing, and then sat back again. "We should row," he said to Mason.

"Where to?" Mason glanced around. "America?"

"Northwest," Joseph answered. "The storm blew us south. However far we've come, there should be the south coast of England to the north of us, and even if we were beyond that, which we aren't, there'd be Ireland. We'd better row while there's still light."

"What the hell do we need light for?" Mason said bitterly. "We're not exactly going to hit anything!"

"Fog," Joseph replied. "We'll only know which direction we're going as long as we can see the sun in the west."

Mason did not reply. Silently he unshipped his oar and put it in the rowlock, then, in time with Joseph, he began to row.

It was the hardest physical work Joseph had ever done. His body ached with every pull, his hands were blistered and he was so thirsty it took an intense effort of will to keep from plunging his hands into the sea, even though it was salt, and would only make him sick. Its slick, smooth water was cold and in its own way, mesmerizingly beautiful.

Andy woke and drank his mouthful of water. The sun was so low and the fog thick enough now that the west was barely discernible, but he understood what they were doing.

"There's no need to sit up," Joseph told him. "We'll just go as long as we can."

Andy smiled.

Joseph lost count of time. It grew so dim, the light so diffused, it was hard to tell anything but the broadest directions. No one spoke.

Then suddenly Andy stiffened and pointed with his good arm.

Mason swiveled around, oar out of the water. "A ship!" he yelled. "A ship!"

Joseph turned to look as well. Out of the gloom to their left there was a high, darker shape.

Mason pulled his oar in and started to climb to his feet.

"Sit down!" Andy cried shrilly. "You'll capsize us in their wash!" He started forward as if physically to restrain Mason, but he was too weak and fell forward onto the floorboards.

"Ahoy!" Mason bellowed, standing upright now, waving his arms. "Ahoy!"

"Sit down!" Andy screamed.

Joseph lunged for Mason just as the wash hit them. The boat bucked, the bow high and sideways. Mason lost his balance and fell just as the boat slapped down again and pitched the other way, throwing him backward. The side caught him behind the knees. He folded up, hitting his head on the gunwale, and slid into the sea.

Without waiting, Andy went in after him.

The boat swiveled and tossed on the wake and Joseph grabbed after the oars, desperately fumbling as Andy and Mason slipped astern. He got them both at last and turned the boat, heaving with all his strength, his muscles burning, to get back to them. It seemed to take forever, stroke after stroke, but it must have been no more than a minute or two before he was there. A hand came up over the side and he shipped the oars and reached to pull Mason up and on board. He was almost deadweight, streaming water, and gasping.

Then he turned for Andy. He saw him for an instant, just the pale blur of his face, then he was gone.

"Andy!" Joseph shrieked, his voice hoarse, piercing with despair. "Andy!"

But there was no break in the gray sea,

nothing above the surface.

He was sobbing as he flung himself on the oars again and sent the boat lurching forward, all his weight behind each stroke. He called out again and again. He was aware of Mason clambering up and going into the bow, peering ahead, calling as well.

It was Mason who finally came back and sat down in the stern. Joseph could see no more than an outline of his body in the darkness now.

"It's no good," Mason said, his voice raw with pain. "He's gone. Even if we found him now, it wouldn't help."

Joseph was weeping, the tears running down his face and choking his throat. There was no point in telling Mason he was a fool — he knew it. The guilt would never leave him.

"That's what he meant," he said, struggling to speak, even to get his breath. "You give your life for your mates — whoever they are. It's nothing to do with them, it's to do with you."

Mason bent his head in his hands and wept.

Chapter

THIRTEEN

Joseph lost track of time altogether. There was no point in rowing, but he was too cold and thirsty to sleep. He drifted in and out of a hazy unconsciousness, grieving for Andy, touched with guilt that it was his decision not to row with Mason that might have cost them a possible landfall, although it was unlikely.

More than that he was worried for Mason, who was not only wet, and therefore suffering far more from exposure than Joseph, but also because of the guilt that tormented him.

Joseph felt a terrible pity for him. He could not get out of his mind the memory of Mason on the beach at Gallipoli, struggling up and down the gullies with the wounded, under fire when he did not need to be, working through exhaustion when every muscle hurt, to rescue others. He worked for the Peacemaker, but he had done it because he honestly believed what he was doing was for the greater good. No man can do more than the best they understand, the utmost they believe.

But the Peacemaker was responsible for the deaths of Joseph's parents, indirectly of Sebastian, and now of Cullingford as well.

Yet Joseph could not hate Mason personally. And alive, Mason might lead them to the Peacemaker, intentionally or not.

He sank back into a kind of sleep again, too cold to be aware of discomfort, only of thirst and a gnawing emptiness inside himself.

He woke with a jolt to feel hands lifting him and he heard voices, cheerful and urgent. Someone forced a cup between his lips and the next instant the fire of rum scalded down his throat, making him cough and then choke. He was too stiff to help them as they carried him up into the trawler and wrapped him in blankets.

"Mason?" he asked between cracked lips.

"Oh, he'll make it!" a voice assured him. "I reckon."

The next hours passed in a haze of the pain as circulation returned to his limbs, the blessed sensation of warmth and food, blankets at first, and then clean sheets.

When he finally awoke to sunlight shimmering through a hospital window, Matthew, white-faced, was sitting beside him. "God, you gave me a fright!" he said accusingly.

Joseph managed to smile, but his skin still hurt. "I'm all right," he said huskily.

Matthew poured him a glass of water from the jug and lifted him up with intense gentleness to help him drink it. "What the hell happened to you?" he demanded savagely.

Joseph sipped the water, then lay back again. "Ran into a German U-boat on the way back," he answered, his throat easier. "I found Mynott. Decent chap. He told me about Chetwin in Berlin. It wasn't him. I'm sorry."

"Damn!" Matthew swore. "I thought we had the bastard." He was still regarding Joseph with profound concern. "What else? Was Gallipoli hell? Surely it couldn't be worse than Ypres?"

"No, about the same," Joseph replied. "But I met a journalist out there, brilliant fellow — Richard Mason, actually. Matthew, he was going to write a hell of a story about Gallipoli, tell everyone the truth of what it's really like." He saw Matthew's face darken and his body tense. "I tried to persuade him what it would do to morale, but I failed before we left. I think I tipped my hand too far." The chaotic beach was in his mind as if he had barely left it, the Australian voices, the smells of blood and creosol and wild thyme, the light across the high, wind-stippled sky and the sound of water.

"He was going to write about it, tell everyone at home what a senseless slaughter it is." He looked at Matthew's blue eyes. "It would have been even worse than someone like Prentice going on about the gas attack at Ypres. He's a better writer, a far bigger name. And we couldn't help the gas. Gallipoli's our fault." The words choked in his throat, but they were true enough he could not swallow them. He longed for someone to trust, not just with facts and the things that words could frame easily, but with the grief inside him for all the broken men he had seen, the pain, and for the fear inside himself. He had been prepared to die in order to take Mason with him.

Had Sam felt like that, faced with Prentice, whom everyone hated? Joseph didn't hate Mason, but he would in effect have killed him.

He felt Matthew's hand warm and strong on his wrist, and looked up at him.

"Joe, what happened?" Matthew said insistently. "Where's Mason now?"

He was afraid! Joseph realized it with amazement. Matthew was afraid because something in Joseph had changed irreparably. An innocence of decision had gone. Nothing was as simple as it had seemed, not Judith and Cullingford, not Sam and Prentice, not himself and Mason.

"You're right," he agreed quietly. "I would have drowned him rather than let him publish his piece." He started to shake his head. "I would have let it go down." He blinked as tears filled his eyes. "But he can't do it now. I tried to tell him the reason for it all, explain to him, but I didn't have the words. Andy showed him."

"Who's Andy?" Matthew asked.

"Tommy Atkins," Joseph replied, then in simple, choking words he told Matthew what had happened. Matthew listened in silence, his hand held tight over Joseph's.

"Where's Mason now?" he said when Joseph fell silent.

"In the next room," Joseph replied. "He was colder than I was, because he was wet. But he's all right. He made it."

"There's no one in the next room," Matthew said with a frown. "I passed it as someone was leaving. Tallish fellow, with dark hair. He looked pretty rough."

Joseph felt himself cold again.

"You must find out who was going to print it," he said urgently. "If the Peacemaker gets hold of him, he just might write it again. I don't think so — but we have to be sure!

"Mason comes from Beverly in Yorkshire. When he thought we wouldn't make it, he told me he'd known the newspaper owner all his life. The man has several papers, all in Yorkshire and Lancashire. He could kill recruiting right across the Midlands. You ought to be able to find him. Politically he's a pacifist for a united Europe, doesn't care at what cost, or who's in charge." He closed his eyes, his mind and his heart aching with understanding for Sam. He wished to God he had never told anyone at all that Prentice was murdered. "Bloody Prentice was working for him as well," he said aloud. "Mason told me."

"The Peacemaker?" Matthew's eyes filled with understanding. "The original plan couldn't work, so his plan now is to bring about British surrender because we haven't the army to defend ourselves any more. God damn it, Joe! We have to stop him, whatever the cost!

"And you're sure it's not Chetwin?"

"Absolutely. It seemed so . . . inevitable. But it's not." He repeated to Matthew what Mynott had said about Chetwin's German fiancée, her death and her parents' grief and anger. "It would have been impossible for Chetwin to have any connection with the document," he went on. "The kaiser wouldn't let him into the palace grounds to deliver the coal, never mind to take a secret document of state to someone here to carry to the king. I think he was lucky to get out of Germany alive."

"Father would be pleased," Matthew said with a very slight smile. "He didn't want to hate Chetwin. Although I don't think he would have admired that story! Poor girl."

"And her parents. She was their only child." For a moment memory of Eleanor came back again. He saw in Matthew's eyes that the same thought had come to him. His sorrow was there naked, his ache to be able to help, and the knowledge that he could not.

Joseph found himself smiling, not that the memory was much easier, but because Matthew understood it. "We've paid too much to give in now," he said aloud. "How could we face those who've given everything they had, and tell them it was for nothing? We haven't the stomach to go on! We asked everything from them. They gave it and we took."

"I know." Matthew bit his lip. "We won't give in. But we're a long way from the end. I'm glad it wasn't Chetwin, but I wish to hell I knew who it was. We need to, Joe, whoever it is. He's ruthless. Killing Cullingford like that shows he'll destroy anyone he thinks stands in his way." His face was bleak. "Gus Tempany died, too. I don't know if it has anything to do with the Peacemaker, but he was a hell of a fine man, and a friend of Cullingford's. Died the day after Cullingford. Accident of some sort, in his flat. I actually went and asked the porter if Cullingford had been there the day before, and he said he had."

The coldness seemed to be in the air of the room. Joseph felt Cullingford's death more deeply than he had expected to. His mind turned automatically to Judith, and meeting Matthew's eyes, he knew his had also.

As if in answer, Matthew spoke. "I write to Judith, pretty well every day. She writes back, but she doesn't really say much. I feel so damn helpless."

"Letting her know you're there is about all you can do," Joseph replied. "It does help, at least after a while."

Matthew nodded very slightly. "Our losses are appalling," he said bleakly. "And the war at sea is getting worse." He shook his head with a slight, self-deprecating smile. "I suppose I hardly need to tell you that! And you've seen more of the carnage than I have. No one could know better how little we can afford to be betrayed from within as well. We've got to find him and destroy him, before he takes our faith in ourselves away from us."

"You'll find the newspaper owner?" Joseph pressed.

"Yes. But that won't be all the Peacemaker is doing."

"No. No, of course not. I suppose if Mason's well enough to get out of here, I must be, too." He sat up slowly. He still ached, but his head was clear. "I've got to get back to Ypres," he added. "I must see Judith. And I have to do something about Sam."

"In a day or two," Matthew agreed gently. "Come to my flat for a while first. Give yourself a chance, Joe. You're no use to anyone like this."

"I don't know if I can afford it. What day is it anyway?"

"May nineteenth. I've told your unit;

you've got till the end of the week at least, more if you need it. I don't know what you're going to do about Sam. I can't help you with that, but Judith will be all right. We're all going to lose people. She'll hurt, but she'll recover. You need a day or two here first. I'll take one or two early nights. We'll go to the music hall, or see a Charlie Chaplin film. You need to think of something absurd, that doesn't matter a damn, before you go back. So do I."

Joseph looked up. "I'm sorry. I didn't even ask how you are!"

"That's all right! I wouldn't have told you anyway," Matthew said with a sudden, beautiful smile.

In Marchmont Street the Peacemaker was stunned. Mason looked appalling. His eyes were hollow, and his face had a haunted air as of a man whose dreams make sleep worse than waking. He stood straight, but there was an overwhelming weariness in him, and when he moved it obviously hurt him.

"You lost it?" the Peacemaker repeated. "You said it was wrapped in oiled silk!"

"I didn't lose it, I destroyed it," Mason repeated. "I took it out of its wrapping and threw it into the water. Actually I had very little choice, if I wanted to survive. He would have let us all drown rather than have it published."

"Drown himself? And the other crewman?"

"Yes."

The Peacemaker stared at the man in front of him and saw in his wide-boned, passionate, stubborn face an immovable certainty that he was right. And there was something more than facts, there was a difference in emotion, a change in his eyes. "Joseph Reavley? The biblical language teacher from Cambridge?" he asked, still finding it difficult to believe.

"Yes," Mason replied. "He's serving as a chaplain in Ypres now. He's seen a lot of action. I watched him helping the wounded in Gallipoli. He's done a lot of it before."

The Peacemaker swore. He was not often wrong about men. He could not afford to be, and this was an expensive mistake. That was two brilliant pieces of propaganda, opportunities to tell the truth in its horror, that had been snatched from him. He looked steadily at Mason, trying to read beyond the weariness; the emotion that Gallipoli and the sea had stirred in him. How long had he been adrift in an open boat with a blind and suicidal chaplain? Mason was a good man, he abhorred the waste, he cared for the individual, but he could also see beyond sentimentality to the greater good, which only too evidently Joseph Reavley could not. . . . Damn Joseph Reavley! He was far more of a nuisance than could have been foreseen!

"Never mind," he said aloud. "You can write it again. It might not have the immediacy of the battlefield, but write the truth! Say you were pursued across the Mediterranean, that you took ship in Gibraltar but it was sunk and you only just survived crossing the Channel in a lifeboat, and you lost your original draft. It will make even more compelling reading." He went on urgently. "And it will heighten people's awareness of how vulnerable we are at sea."

"Possibly," Mason agreed flatly. "But I won't."

"Reavley can't . . ."

"It's nothing to do with what Reavley would do," Mason replied, a flare of anger in his eyes. "Or to save my life. It's because I don't believe it's the right thing to do. It won't bring peace, only a betrayal of the ordinary soldier who now believes that he's fighting a just and necessary war. I won't do that."

The Peacemaker's temper flared because he was losing control in a startling and unexpected way. It took him a supreme effort to mask it and keep his expression bland. "Even Gallipoli?" he asked. "What was it like? What happened to you there?"

"I helped the wounded," Mason replied. His voice was filled with pain, but there was a finality in it, closing off search for detail.

The Peacemaker stared at him. His words were true, but he was concealing something deeper. He could feel it. He could also feel the emotional tension in Mason, a passion just below the surface that consumed him, but he was too frightened of it to allow it through.

The Peacemaker would have to wait, move gently. Mason was too valuable to lose. He must be won back, persuaded, whatever it needed to change his mind again. Perhaps this was not the time to raise the subject of U-boats and torpedoes anyway! He would like to have turned his attention to those plans that included undermining and ultimately destroying this government, but he was not at the moment sufficiently certain of Mason's loyalties in that direction.

"You've had a grim experience," he said

with some warmth. "And perhaps you are right about some of the issues of morale." It was difficult to say, and he saw the surprise in Mason's face, but he would come back to it later, slowly and with greater subtlety. "There are other matters of importance," he went on with a smile. "The situation in the United States is of the utmost interest. Mexico is in turmoil and could invade any day. Unfortunately no one there is to be relied on. They are at war with each other as much as with any outside force."

Mason's eyes were wide, stunned with total incomprehension. "Why in God's name did the Germans sink the *Lusitania*? I thought even Wilson would go to war over that!"

The Peacemaker pushed his hands into his pockets. "It seems nothing will bring him in. The Mexican move was even more successful than we hoped. We'll keep working on it. Let me tell you what the exact situation is now, who we have there and what is next to be done." He indicated that Mason should sit down. "It's detailed," he began. "Complicated. You need to understand the people."

Mason listened, his attention held at last, almost as if he were relieved to have something to fasten his intellect on and rest from the turmoil inside him.

The Peacemaker did not tell him about the mole he had placed in the Scientific Establishment in Cambridge. He would keep that secret. It was as well to give only the information you had to. Trust no one.

Joseph ate and slept and did little more than wander around Matthew's flat for two days. Then in the evening of the third day Matthew answered the telephone, and Joseph, watching him, saw his face light up, and an intense concern fill his expression.

"How are you?" Matthew said earnestly. He waited for the answer, listening with obvious sympathy. "I can't," he went on. "Although I expect Joseph would move for you. He's been through a pretty rough time. He went out to Gallipoli, and came back by sea. His ship was sunk, and . . . yes, yes, he's all right!" He glanced at Joseph as he spoke. "He's here, now. I wouldn't tell you like that, for heaven's sake! But he did spend a bit of time in an open boat, rowing the thing. Yes, of course he is! I swear!"

There was another silence.

Matthew smiled. "Of course. That

sounds like a good idea. Do you want to speak to him? Right." He held out the telephone receiver. "It's Judith. She's in London."

Joseph took the receiver. "Judith?" He was terribly afraid of what he might hear — the pain in her he still had no idea how to help.

"Are you all right," she said urgently, "Joseph?" She sounded as if she were afraid for him.

"Yes, I'm fine," he answered. "I was only cold and wet . . . and terrified."

She laughed a little jerkily. "Is that all?"

"Where are you?" he asked. "If you want to stay here, I can move to a hotel."

"No . . . thank you. I wanted to stay with Mrs. Prentice, and she invited me. I'm going to a dinner at the Savoy tomorrow evening, a sort of government thing, to get some kind of organization into voluntary help. There are people all over the country doing things; knitting, driving around, packing parcels, writing letters. It needs to get some order, or we'll be falling over each other. It's Dermot Sandwell's idea, I think. Anyway, I need to find a dress."

"Who's taking you?"

"Taking me?" She drew in her breath quickly, a little shakily.

"May I?" he asked before she had time to think.

"If . . . if you want to? Yes. Thank you."

"Where shall I pick you up, and when?"

She gave him the address. "About six, to give us time in case the traffic is bad."

He heard the hesitation in her voice. "What is it?" he asked.

"Nothing! At least not . . . Joseph, this is Eldon Prentice's family, you know. And . . . and General Cullingford's sister . . . they've lost . . ." She did not know how to finish.

"Are you saying you would rather meet me somewhere else?" he offered.

"No! I was saying perhaps you could come a little earlier, and say something . . . decent about Prentice at least. It . . . Joseph, it's terrible for them. . . ."

"Of course." He responded immediately and without wondering how he would do it, especially now that he knew what Prentice had really been intending to do. "And no one has anything to say about Cullingford except good." He took a deep breath. "Are you all right, Judith?"

"No," she said a little huskily. "But then is anybody?"

"No. It's only a matter of degree. How about five, or is that too early?"

"Five would be excellent. Thank you."

"The only thing I have to wear is a uniform. Is that all right?"

"It'll be perfect. Good-bye."

"Good-bye." He passed the receiver back to Matthew. "She's got a dinner tomorrow evening. I'll take her."

Matthew smiled. He did not say anything, but his pleasure was like a brightness in the room.

Joseph still looked haggard when he surveyed himself in the mirror in Matthew's bathroom, but he was almost as presentable as any other soldier home on a brief leave.

He borrowed Matthew's car, and by the time he pulled up outside the Prentices' house he was decidedly nervous. He was being faced again with the duty of trying to say something of comfort to people who had lost someone they had loved long and intimately. It hardly ever made sense, in peacetime or war. The wound was gaping, full of all kinds of regrets, wishes, guilt over things said, and unsaid, all sorts of hopes dashed. Mrs. Prentice did not know her son had been murdered, but Joseph did. He remembered Mary Allard's terrible, consuming grief. Nothing could limit it, nothing attempt to heal.

Would Mrs. Prentice be like that? Was he going to feel just as helpless? Or more so, because he had despised Eldon Prentice. Worse than that, Sam, who had killed him, was Joseph's dearest friend, and he understood heart deep, bone deep, why he had done it. He had come close to doing something very like it himself.

He rang the doorbell. It was not a maid who answered, but Judith. He was startled because she looked so beautiful. She was utterly different from the healthy, rather coltish country girl, full of shy grace, that she had been a year ago. Now there were shadows in her face, a sculpting under the cheekbones. She looked far older, a woman, one who had seen passion and tragedy and understood at least something of each. She looked even more vulnerable than before, but also, oddly, she was stronger.

She was wearing a blue dress, which was quite deep in color, muted like the sky at dusk. It had a wide waist, emphasizing how slender she was, and the skirt was swathed and fell to below the knee, then another skirt beneath it to above the ankle, keeping the fashionable line.

"Thank you," she said under her breath,

then after giving him a quick kiss on the cheek, she turned as another woman came into the hall. This was obviously Prentice's mother. She had the same fair skin and hair, although now it was leached of all vitality, almost as if she were a drawing the artist had forgotten to color. She was wearing dark gray, not quite the full black of mourning.

"Captain Reavley," she said quietly. "How nice of you to come early. Judith said you might. Please come in. Perhaps you would join us in having a drink before you leave for the party?"

"Thank you." It was unreasonable to do anything but accept. This was what he had come for. He thought ruefully how difficult he had imagined it was to sit in his dugout and write letters to mothers and widows of the men who had died, especially those he had known little, and about whom he had to invent something. It was nothing compared with facing someone like Mrs. Prentice, seeing the grief in her face, finding it hard even to envision what she had been like when there had been light in her eyes, when she could have laughed and meant it. He had disliked Prentice deeply, and now, knowing what he had intended to do, he regarded him as a traitor to his own land. And Sam was his friend, with all the warmth, the laughter and gentleness, the trust that that word encompassed.

He followed Mrs. Prentice into the quiet sitting room with its family photographs, slightly worn carpet, and unmatched antimacassars on the backs of the chairs. There was a bowl of early roses on the Pembroke table by the wall, golden reflections shining in the polished mahogany. A silver-framed picture of Eldon Prentice stood next to it. He wondered where the one of Owen Cullingford was. Or had she room for only one bereavement at a time?

He thought of what Judith had said about seeing the photograph of Prentice and Cullingford at Henley, with the unusual girl, then mentioning it to Cullingford later. She believed it was that which had led him to the Peacemaker, and his death.

He looked again at the photographs. One of them was of a group at Henley; Cullingford, Prentice, a couple of other youths, and a tall girl with fair, wavy hair. Later he would ask who she was. There was no time now, without being rude.

There was someone else in the room, a girl in her early twenties, slender, dark gold hair. She looked too like Eldon Prentice not to be his sister, but the steady look that in him had been arrogant, in her was merely candid.

Mrs. Prentice introduced them. "This is my daughter, Belinda. Captain Reavley has been kind enough to come early, to talk with us. It was he who . . . brought Eldon back to . . . from no-man's-land." She was having difficulty retaining her composure.

"How do you do, Captain Reavley," Belinda said gravely. "Please don't feel you need to tell us about it again. Judith already did, the first time she came. We are terribly grateful to you." She glanced at her mother, as if warning her, then back at Joseph again. "It is our maid's evening off. We're lucky still to have her. We expect her to go and work in a munitions factory any day now. May I get you a sherry? Or would you prefer something else? Whisky, maybe? I think we have some."

He had to accept something. "Sherry would be excellent, thank you."

"Are you sure?"

"Absolutely." He made himself smile. "It's very civilized. We get raw spirits in the trenches — navy rum. This would be far better."

She smiled back at him, relief far more

obvious in her face than she could have realized.

Mrs. Prentice invited him to sit, and they
all accepted, but awkwardly, not leaning
back in comfort. It was his responsibility to
carry the conversation. He was the priest,
they were the bereaved, the ones he was
here to comfort, to offer some pattern of
sense. Except that there was no sense he
could share with them. And you never
knew how much people wanted to know,
what healed, and what only made the
wound deeper.

Mrs. Prentice was watching him, her
blue-gray eyes desperately hungry for any
kind of gentleness at all, any hope of good.

"What would you like to know?" he
asked her.

"I . . . I'm not sure," she said awkwardly,
looking down at her hands and then up
again quickly. "I so much wanted you to
come, and now that you are here, I'm not
sure what to say. I know Eldon was . . .
abrasive sometimes." She smiled, and her
eyes were full of tears. "He could irritate
people, because he had no patience with
lies. He didn't understand that people have
to . . . to defend themselves, not only what
they say, but what they can find the
courage to believe."

Was she talking about Prentice, or was she also asking him not to tell her a truth that would destroy the illusions she needed in order to survive?

"Of course," he agreed, keeping the smile in his eyes. "People who tell the truth have never been popular with everyone, regardless of the fact that some truths have to be told, and others can be concealed for a while, or perhaps forever. It's the judgment that's so difficult. And the horror of the front line is not an easy place."

"He would have . . . mellowed." She gulped the words. "He was slow to learn tact. He was so angry at the loss of life, at the way the men were treated."

"He believed the whole war was wrong, Mother," Belinda put in, speaking for the first time since she had been introduced.

"Nobody but a lunatic wants war." Joseph turned to look at her, seeing the anxiety, the confusion in her face. "It's just that some alternatives are worse. Whatever the cost, there are some things that are worth fighting for, because life without them is a different kind of death, without hope for the future."

"I know that, Captain Reavley," she said with a very slight edge to her voice. She was struggling to defend her brother, as well as her own conviction, and yet not tear her mother's loyalties apart. "Eldon felt he could change things, make people stop talking and thinking about it as some glorious crusade, and realize how terrible it really is." Her face tightened with anger. "You should read some of the pieces that are written — words like *courage* and *honor* and *noble sacrifice*. Eldon said it's nothing like that! It's mud and rats and body lice, filthy food, stinking latrines . . ." She ignored her mother's gasp. "And terrified men being slaughtered for no gain at all!"

Joseph thought of the men he knew, men like Sam, Barshey Gee, Wil Sloan, Cullingford himself, and Andy.

"He wasn't there long enough to see all of it," he answered her, not avoiding her eyes or offering pity. "All those things are true, and worse. But the best is true also. The courage is there, and it's real, not fairy tale. It's going forward to face what turns your bowels into water and makes you sick with fear, knowing the shrapnel could hit your body any moment, but you do it anyway, because it's the right thing to do. Above all there is the friendship, in things as big as giving your life to save someone else, and as small as sitting up all night telling bad jokes and sharing your chocolate biscuits." His voice was rough with emotion, remembering talking with Sam all night, about anything, everything, and surviving hell, because he was not alone. "It's about cold and terror and death all around you, and finding someone reaching out his hand to you, thinking of your pain — not his own."

Mrs. Prentice heard it and bit her lip.

There was a moment's silence. There were tears on Belinda's face.

"He had someone willing to publish his work, didn't he?" Judith intervened, her voice harsh with her own grief. She was speaking to wrench her mind away from it. "Because most national newspapers wouldn't."

"Oh, yes!" Mrs. Prentice said quickly. "If anyone had found his notes, we would have forwarded them on."

"It probably wouldn't have helped," Belinda put in. "He used to write in his own kind of shorthand. Unless they could decipher it, it would be meaningless."

It was absurd. Joseph thought of Sam, and his knowledge of the schoolboy cipher. A week ago he would have given almost anything to have known where to find the publisher. Now, because of Richard Mason, Matthew would find out

540

and it no longer mattered.

"It wouldn't have made any difference," he said to Mrs. Prentice, mostly so Judith would know. "If it would be against the Defense of the Realm Act it would be suppressed. The Intelligence Services know who it is." Then as her face crumpled in confusion he wondered if he should not have said it. It was Judith who needed to know that it did not have to be pursued. Mrs. Prentice could have kept her dreams, if they were of comfort. But could he retrieve it without being obviously patronizing, and destroying everything else he had said? How could you touch such grief without adding to it?

"It was secret," she protested. "He meant to do so much good! He said no one tells the real truth, and people have the right to know. You can't ask men to give their lives, and lie to them how it will be."

"Sometimes we can only take bits of the truth, and still survive," he reminded her. "We have to fight, and for that we need courage, and hope. By the time he got back to England, he might have realized that, especially if he had spoken with you."

She turned away quickly, her voice choking. "Do you think so? I'm sorry." She stood up. "Please excuse me." And she hurried from the room.

"I shouldn't have said that," Joseph apologized with contrition.

"Oh, it's all right!" Belinda said hastily, her face white. "Eldon was too arrogant to listen to anyone, but it's nice to imagine he might have. It's all we have now."

Joseph said nothing. Perhaps Prentice might never have grown wiser or kinder, or have matured into a man of anything like Richard Mason's humanity, but it was still a tragedy that he had been robbed of the chance. Sam's face was sharp in his mind. He was everything that Prentice was not. What he would have become was only a hope, his mother's hope because she loved him, perhaps felt responsible for his failures as well as protective of the good she knew of him, the ability to struggle, to feel pain. One defended one's own, it was part of the love that was belonging. It was instinct more powerful than reason, the passion that forgave, that never surrendered belief. It had saved many when nothing else could have.

Now was the time to change the subject and look at the photographs. He turned to them and regarded them quite openly. "It's a wonderful gift, to be able to have memories kept like this," he observed. "Happier

542

times caught and held for us. Is this Henley?"

He heard Judith draw in her breath.

Belinda followed her gaze. "Yes. It was a good time. The year before last, I think."

"A pretty young woman. Were she and Eldon close?"

Belinda looked at it more closely. "I don't think so. I remember I liked her. She was fun."

"Perhaps we should leave." Judith was standing close behind them. She was facing Belinda. "I know why you wanted to talk, but I think it's too soon. There'll be other times."

"I'll stay up for you?" Belinda said, her eyes eager. There was fierce, shy admiration in them.

"It'll be the middle of the night," Judith said wryly. "Are you sure that's still all right?"

"Of course! I couldn't leave you to find your own way." Then she blushed. "And I'd love to talk with you a little bit more, before you go back to see your sister."

"If I may, I'd love to," Judith agreed. "London's got to be more fun than Cambridge anyway!" She meant it as a joke, and after a second's hesitation Belinda smiled.

She accompanied them to the door, and bade them good night, hoping they would enjoy themselves. Judith hesitated before getting into the car on the passenger side, and Joseph closed the door firmly and went around to crank the engine and start up.

"No!" he said with a smile as he pulled out onto the road. "You are not driving. I don't care how much better you are at it."

She laughed, but it was hollow.

He glanced at her. There was a sadness in her face that was more marked now that she was away from the Prentice house, and the need to pretend. The shadows were more obvious in the passing streetlamps.

"Are you all right?" he asked softly, not because the question had any meaning, simply to let her know he was aware.

"No," she said huskily. "Now I'm sure it was my fault he was killed. That photograph at Henley is almost the same as the one I saw, and told General Cullingford about, but it's not exactly." She was looking away from him. "There was an older woman there — I expect it was his wife — and it's a different girl."

"Are you certain?" The implication was frightening. It seemed that the Peacemaker had reached this far, in this minute detail.

The original girl was indeed someone so close to him he could be identified from knowing who she was, and he had realized how Cullingford knew, and not only had he killed Cullingford, and probably Gustavus Tempany, but he had also substituted another picture for the one with her in it. The only other alternative was that it was all coincidence. Cullingford had been on a wild-goose chase, and died at the hands of some street thief with a knife. Tempany's death the day after was just one of those extraordinary chances of timing.

He did not believe that.

"I think I am," she replied. "That's proof the Peacemaker killed him, isn't it?"

"Yes, I think so." He reached out and put his hand over hers. "I'm sorry."

She sniffed and gulped. "I'll have a good cry about it later. I don't want to go to the party with a blotchy face."

"Of course not," he agreed. "We're all hiding some wound or other. Head up, eyes forward."

"How about you?" She turned to look at him. The tears brimmed over and slid down her cheeks, but she was searching to know if he was also hiding something too big and too heavy to bear.

"I know who killed Prentice," he answered, wondering why he told her. He had thought he was going to tell no one, but the decision he had made in the boat was now impossible to live with. He must face Sam, and he was almost certain what he was going to do about it. It would hurt bitterly, almost unendurably. But he had watched hundreds of men bear wounds they would have thought beyond any strength to survive, and yet they had done it with dignity; they were ordinary men, some of them little more than boys. Men sent their sons and brothers and friends into horror unimaginable, and did it without crying against fate. So could he. The loneliness afterward was the price for all of them.

"Who was it?" she asked.

He shook his head very slightly. "I'll deal with it. Let's go to the party. Put on our best faces, and pretend it's fun."

She smiled at him, and reached over to kiss him on the cheek.

The party was fun, in an absurd, dreamlike way. All the women wore beautiful gowns, but the colors were subdued. It was unseemly to wear reds and pinks, as if denying other people's loss, and yet everyone was pretending to a laughter and an ease they could not feel. Diamonds glittered, hair was perfect in the latest style, swept back, totally without curls except for the most discreet, just one on the brow, or at the nape of the neck. More would be unacceptable. The men were either in black, or uniform. Even though it was a formal dinner, nothing was more honorable than khaki, and Joseph was looked at with respect verging on deference.

The twenty guests were at one long table, so they might discuss information and ideas more easily. No attempt had been made to balance the numbers. There were fourteen men and six women. Their host was Dermot Sandwell, tall and lean, impossibly elegant in black and white, the light of the chandeliers gleaming on his fair hair.

"Good evening, Miss Reavley, Captain Reavley," he said warmly as they entered the room where the reception was held. "It was very good of you to come," he said to Judith in particular. "You will speak on behalf of a body of women we admire intensely. You have a nobility and a courage second to none."

"We have men, too, Mr. Sandwell," she reminded him. "Many of them are young Americans who came at their own expense, because they believe in what we are fighting for, and they care."

"Yes, I know. And we will do more to give you the supplies and the support that's appropriate," he promised. "That's why we need you here, to tell us exactly what that is. It's time to stop guessing, doubling up some actions and omitting others. There is so much goodwill in the civilian population, people willing to do anything they can to help, but it is desperately in need of organization." He turned to Joseph. "I see you are a chaplain. Are you home on leave?"

"Yes, sir, briefly," Joseph answered. "I return in two days."

"Where to?"

"Ypres." There was no indiscretion in answering. Chaplains were often moved from one place to another, and a cabinet minister like Sandwell probably knew far more accurately than Joseph exactly which regiments were where, and what their numbers were.

"Front line?" Sandwell asked.

"Yes, sir. I think that's where I should be."

"Were you there for the gas attack?" Sandwell's face was bleak, almost pinched. Joseph could not help wondering if he had lost someone he knew and loved in it.

"Yes, sir," he replied, meeting the wide, blue eyes and seeing the imagination of horror in them, and perhaps guilt, because he knew, and still had no choice but to send more men to face something he did not experience himself. Joseph wished he could think of something to say that would at least show he understood. For ministers and generals to risk their own lives helped no one. Their burdens were different, but just as real. Quite suddenly he felt an almost suffocating sense of loss for Owen Cullingford, not for Judith's sake, but simply because the man was gone, and he realized how much he had liked him. "Yes, I was there. It's a new kind of war."

"I'd give anything not to have to send men to that!" Sandwell said quietly, his voice shaking. "God in heaven, what have we come to?" He took a deep breath. "I'm sorry, Captain. You know better than I do what the reality is. Perhaps you would be kind enough after dinner, when we address the subject more seriously, to tell us anything you think might assist us to be of more help, and more support to our men?"

"Anything I can," Joseph agreed.

They moved further into the room, side by side, acknowledging people, being introduced, making polite remarks. After a little while they separated, Judith to talk to one of the other women, Joseph to answer questions from a bishop and member of the House of Lords on conditions and supplies that might be helped by civilian donations.

It was only as they were going in to dinner that he heard a voice he recognized with a stab of memory so sharp the sweat broke out on his skin and he felt cold the instant after.

"Virtuous and no doubt commendable, but naive, Miss Reavley."

Joseph spun around and saw Richard Mason talking to Judith. They were standing a little apart from the stream of guests moving toward the dining room. He still looked tired, his skin, like Joseph's own, chapped by the wind, eyes hollow, as if Andy's death were with him all the time. Also he had been at Gallipoli longer, and was perhaps more profoundly shocked by it than Joseph, who was used to Ypres. His dark hair had been properly cut and was smoothed back off his brow, and the power in his face, the carefully suppressed emotion, was naked to any observer who had ever been racked by storms themselves, or known feelings that overwhelmed caution and self-preserving.

"I have seen as many wounded men as you have, Mr. Mason!" Judith retorted icily. "Don't patronize me."

His eyes widened slightly and there was reluctant admiration in them. It could have been for her spirit, or the fact that she drove an ambulance. Or it could simply have been that she was beautiful. Anger and grief had taken the bloom of innocence from her and refined the strength. Cullingford had awoken the woman in her, and scoured deep with loss, all in the same act. Perhaps Mason saw something of it in her, because another kind of certainty had gone from his eyes, and whether she was aware of it or not, it was she who had caused that.

Without waiting for his reply, she turned and went through the doors to the dining room, leaving him to follow or not, as he wished.

Joseph found himself smiling, even though he was overtaken by a wave of fierce and consuming protectiveness toward her, and a knowledge that he could never succeed; no one could protect Judith, or be protected from her.

He followed after her, awed, proud, and a little frightened.

★ ★ ★

As always, he could smell the sour stench of the Front before he heard the guns, or saw the lines of troops marching, the broken trees, the occasional crater beside the roads where heavy artillery shells had fallen. There was a terrible familiarity to it, like reentering an old nightmare, as if every time sleep touched you, you were drawn back into the same drowning reality.

Like anyone else, he had to walk the last few miles. He was passed by Wil Sloan, driving an empty ambulance. He stopped, but not to offer a lift; it was forbidden and Joseph knew better than to hope.

"How's Judith?" Wil asked anxiously, sticking his head out of the side and trying to make himself smile. "I mean . . ." He stopped awkwardly, memory sharp in his eyes.

Joseph smiled. "Last time I saw her she was making mincemeat out of a top war correspondent," he answered. "She looked gorgeous, in a long, blue gown, and she was going in to dinner at the Savoy."

Wil looked uncertain whether to believe him or not.

"Actually," Joseph amended, "that wasn't the last time. I did take her to where she was staying after that."

Wil relaxed. "She's going to be all right?"

"In time," Joseph told him. "We all will be, one way or another." He stood back, waving him on, to avoid the embarrassment for Wil of having to explain why he couldn't offer a lift, even to a chaplain.

Wil smiled and gave a little salute, then slipped the ambulance into gear again and moved forward. Joseph watched him drive into the distance on the long, straight road with its shattered poplars and the ditches on either side. The fields were level, a few copses left. One or two houses were burned out. There was a column of smoke on the horizon.

It was dusk and the heavy artillery was firing pretty steadily, sending up great gouts of dark, sepia-colored earth, when he reported to the colonel.

"You look rough, Reavley," Fyfe observed. "Leave doesn't agree with you. Feeling all right?" He asked it casually, but there was a genuine anxiety in his face.

"Yes, sir."

"Are you sure?"

"Yes, sir. I ran an errand to Gallipoli. Bit of bother on the way back."

Fyfe raised his eyebrows. "Bother?"

"Yes, sir. Ship I was in got stopped by a

German U-boat. They let us off before they sank it, but rather more rowing than I care for."

"Are you fit to be here? You look stiff!"

"Yes, sir, but not too much." Deliberately Joseph used the words he had heard from so many wounded men. "I'm a lot better than many of those who are fighting."

Fyfe gave the ghost of a smile. "True. Glad to have you back. Morale needs you. Lost one or two good men since you've been gone."

Joseph nodded. He did not want to know who they were yet. "Do you know where Major Wetherall was moved to, sir? I need to see him."

The colonel looked surprised, then curious. He looked at Joseph's face, and read absolute refusal to speak. "I don't know where he went, but he's back. Been here a few days. He's probably in the same dugout as before. Are you going to tell me what it's about?"

"No, sir."

"I see. I suppose your calling allows you to do that."

"Yes, sir."

"Go on, then. If you go to the front line, take care. It's going to be a rough night."

"Is anyone going over on a raid?" He gulped. It was too soon. Far too soon. Yet what difference did it make? Whenever it was, it would come, and then that would be the end. The sweetness and the burden of friendship ached inside him like a physical pain. It would serve nothing to delay it.

"Are you sure you're all right, Reavley?" Fyfe repeated.

"Yes, sir."

The colonel nodded and made a small gesture with his hand. "Glad you're back. The men need you. Young Rattray was wounded. Not too bad."

"Yes, sir. Is he still here?"

"Hospital in Armentières."

"Thank you. Good night, sir."

"Good night, Reavley."

Outside in the dark he walked over the mud to the beginning of the supply trench and down the steps. It must have been raining again because there was water under the duckboards and he heard the rats' feet scuttling and the heavy plop and splash of their bodies as they slid off.

He made his way west toward Sam's dugout. He half hoped he would not be there. It would delay what he had to do. He passed the Old Kent Road and turned along Paradise Alley. Now and then a star shell flared up, lighting the trenches ahead and then he heard the stutter of machine guns. He recognized the pattern.

He went down the familiar slope and called out.

Sam came to the door, pushing the sacking curtain back, his face in the glare alive with pleasure to see Joseph.

"Come in! Have some hot brandy and mud! I've got chocolate biscuits." He held the curtain open and stepped back.

Joseph almost refused. What if he put it off another day? He knew the answer. He would make it worse, that's all. He would have behaved like a coward, and Sam did not deserve that.

He went down the step into the small, cramped space he knew so well. The pictures were the same, the books, the windup gramophone, a few records he had heard a dozen times, and the red blanket on Sam's bed. The hurricane lantern was lit, warm yellow, touching everything with a golden edge.

"You look like hell," Sam said cheerfully. "I heard about Cullingford. That's a damn shame. He was a good man. Is your sister going to be all right?"

"In time." Joseph sat down on the pile of

boxes that had always served as a visitor's chair.

Sam was heating up tea in a Dixie can. He added a generous dash of brandy, then pulled open a box of chocolate biscuits. There were five left. He gave three to Joseph and took two himself. "And your brother?" he asked.

"Fine. I went to Gallipoli on an errand for him."

Sam's eyebrows shot up. "Gallipoli? No wonder you look like that. They say it's worse than here."

"No, it isn't. But it's as bad." Joseph had to be honest. "Well, maybe the chaos is worse. They don't seem to have thought before they ordered the attack. Poor devils didn't even know there were cliffs there."

Sam swore quietly, not with rage, but with pity at the waste of it.

Joseph could not turn back now. "I found a war correspondent out there. Outstanding writer, not a novice like Prentice."

Sam's eyes were wide. "And?"

"And he intended to write it up exactly as he saw it, no excuses, nothing softened," Joseph replied.

Now Sam was motionless, his body stiff, his hands clenched around his mug of tea.

"You say he intended to. He changed his mind?"

Joseph looked at him carefully. He could see the fear in his eyes, but he knew beyond any question that it was not for himself but for Joseph, for what he might have done that he could not live with. How well Sam knew him! And accepted him.

"I tried to persuade him not to in Gallipoli, and I failed," he answered. "He left and I caught up with him on board a ship from Gibraltar. We were sunk by the Germans, and ended up in the same lifeboat."

Sam continued to stare at him, waiting.

"I tried again to persuade him," Joseph said. "There was another man with us, a crewman, wounded, and one who died. Mason and I were rowing the boat, trying to keep it into the wind as long as we could. And when we couldn't hold it any longer, we turned and ran before the storm." He took a deep breath. He had to say it now. "When Mason said he would publish his story, I stopped rowing. I sat in the stern and watched him struggle with both oars. I'd have let him go down, all of us, the crewman as well, rather than have him publish it."

"But he changed his mind," Sam said

softly. "He must have, or you wouldn't be here. And you believe him?"

"Yes." He saw the doubt in Sam's face. "Not because of what he said. We got becalmed in a fog. A ship came by, destroyer, I think. Mason stood up to hail it. Andy yelled at him not to, but it was too late. Mason didn't listen. The wash of the destroyer caught us and Mason overbalanced and went into the water. Andy went after him." He found it hard to say, even now. "I had the oars. I turned the boat and went back. Got Mason out, but we lost Andy." His throat was aching and his voice was barely audible. "That . . . that's what changed Mason, not really anything I said. Andy was typical Tommy, his brother's keeper. . . ."

Sam nodded. He did not need to speak. Suddenly the dugout seemed very small and close.

"Sam . . . I know you killed Prentice," Joseph said in the silence. "And I know why. Mason told me what he was doing, because he didn't know he was dead. He said it was all in his schoolboy code — but you could read that, couldn't you!" He did not wait for an answer — it was in Sam's eyes. "I don't know whether I would have done the same or not. A fortnight ago I'd have said no. Now I'm not certain. I couldn't kill Mason with my own hands, but that's an equivocation. I was willing to stand back and let him die, which comes to the same thing. And I liked him. We tended the wounded together on the beach at Gallipoli. He was a decent man, not an arrogant, self-serving bastard like Prentice."

"But . . . ?" Sam's voice was hoarse, his eyes full of inner pain.

He did not deserve to have to listen to Joseph excusing himself, talking about Prentice's murder, as if that would make what he said any easier.

"But you killed him," Joseph said. "There are other men here, young men who are offering their lives to save what they believe in, a decency they trust, who know he was killed by one of us. I wish to God I'd covered it some way, but I didn't, and now it can't go unanswered."

Sam looked crumpled, hurt more than he knew how to deal with. "Are you going to turn me in?"

"No," Joseph said softly. "I can't do that. I can't even tell you that you were wrong, only that the army will see it that way. They have to." He had tried to think of the words ever since he had decided what to do the night he had visited Mrs. Prentice, but it was no easier. "Next time there's a big raid, like later tonight, you can go over the top with the others." His voice cracked, but he could not stop. "Find someone dead who looks near enough like you, or whose body is beyond recognition, and change identity tags with him." He was shivering. "You'll live, and Sam Wetherall will be missing in action." He wanted to say he was sorry, that he would have done anything he knew how, but none of it would help. He wanted to close his eyes, not look at Sam's face, but he could not do that either. "If I can work it out, so will others. Before that . . . please . . . go . . ."

Sam did not speak for several moments. He stared at Joseph, searching.

Joseph wanted to answer, but he could not go back on the decision, or all it meant. Nor could he tell Sam's brother the truth. No one else must know. It was not his own survival or morality that mattered, it was Sam's. With passionate, consuming intensity, he wanted him to live. He wanted the gentleness, the anger at wrong, the courage, the pity, and the laughter to go on.

"You'd have died to silence Mason?" Sam said at last. "And taken the crewman as well?"

"Yes." There was no hesitation.

561

The hunger eased from Sam's face. It was what he needed to know. He held out his hand.

Joseph took it and gripped it hard, so hard it hurt. Then he stood up and went outside, tripping over the step, his eyes blind with tears.

It was a big raid. Thirty men went over the top, through the wire and into the German trenches. Joseph advanced immediately to the front and spent the night on the fire-step until there were wounded. One of them was Plugger Arnold, but his was only a flesh wound in the thigh.

"Glad to see you back, Chaplain," Plugger said, gritting his teeth as Joseph tied the bandage tight and then hoisted him onto his back, his muscles screaming in protest. There was little room here to turn a stretcher, and Joseph could not carry one alone anyway.

Half an hour later it started to rain, then their own heavy artillery began. There was a lot of cursing, because it meant that the German heavy stuff would reply. They always did. This stretch of the line would get it hard. There would be casualties, and a lot of digging and shoring up to do in the morning.

The raiding party came back just before dawn, with three German prisoners, five of their own wounded, six dead. One of those was Sam. The lieutenant who had led the party told him.

"I'm sorry," he said wearily. "It was a hell of a mess out there. I know he was a friend of yours. The body's over there. I'm afraid he must have taken a pretty direct hit with a grenade or two. I only know it's him because of the tag. At least it was quick. Better than being hung on the wire." And he moved away to be with his men, the injured, the shocked, others who had seen their friends blown to pieces.

Joseph knew it had had to happen, and somewhere inside him he was at peace that it was accomplished. Sam had accepted and done what was necessary. But there was also a gnawing loss, an emptiness that was always going to ache, like a missing limb. But first he had to look at the body and still the horror in his mind that it could, in hideous irony, really be Sam. Sam was the only one who would have seen the black laughter in that! God! How he was going to miss him!

He found it hard to make his way between the stretchers and the bodies lying on canvas, or duckboards. His legs were shaking. It was almost daylight now. The sky above was streaked with light drifting banners of cloud.

The bodies were all badly injured, but one was so torn apart, both legs gone, one arm shattered and the head half blown away, that all one could be sure of was that he had been at least average height, and had had dark hair. It could have been Sam.

Trembling, sick with fear, Joseph picked up the dog tag and read Sam's name and number on it. Now his whole body was shuddering. He reached for the one good hand, the left hand. Would he recognize it? He stared at it, trying to be certain. Then he saw the pale indentation on the third finger where there had been a ring, a plain circle, a wedding ring. Sam had never worn a ring. Relief swept over him, breaking out in sweat over his body; he was dizzy, the makeshift room swaying around him.

Someone grasped him from behind, holding him up, steadying him.

"You all right, Chaplain? Pretty bad, eh. Poor devil."

Joseph wanted to say something, but his voice would not come. He gulped for breath, fighting the sudden nausea.

Someone passed him a cup of tea, hot and laced with rum. It was vile, made in a Dixie can that had held a Maconochie tinned stew as well. As he drank the tea, his balance returned.

"Thank you. I'll . . . I'll have some letters to write. Lots of letters."

He conducted all the funerals, just brief words over white crosses in the Flanders clay, a few quiet men standing to attention, the sound of guns in the distance, the banners of sky like lead above them, as if their shoulders held it.

Sam's was the last. Joseph stood there alone after the others had gone. He did not realize anyone else had stayed until he heard Barshey Gee's voice.

"Oi'm real sorry, Captain Reavley. The major was a good man."

"Yes." Joseph found it hard to speak. "He was my friend."

"Did you ever foind out who killed that newspaper wroiter?"

"Yes. It's taken care of."

"Knew you'd see to it," Barshey said quietly. "Debt settled then."

Joseph turned to look at him. There were tears on Barshey's face, but he was smiling. He stood smartly to attention, and saluted the cross that bore the words

MAJOR SAMUEL WETHERALL,
KILLED IN ACTION, MAY 25, 1915.

About the Author

Anne Perry is the bestselling author of two acclaimed series set in Victorian England. Her William Monk novels include *Death of a Stranger*, *Funeral in Blue*, *Slaves of Obsession*, and *The Twisted Root*. She also writes the popular novels featuring Thomas and Charlotte Pitt, including *Seven Dials*, *Southampton Row*, *The Whitechapel Conspiracy*, and *Half Moon Street*. Her short story "Heroes" won an Edgar Award. Anne Perry lives in Scotland. Visit her website at www.anneperry.net.

The employees of Thorndike Press hope you have enjoyed this Large Print book. All our Thorndike and Wheeler Large Print titles are designed for easy reading, and all our books are made to last. Other Thorndike Press Large Print books are available at your library, through selected bookstores, or directly from us.

For information about titles, please call:

(800) 223-1244

or visit our Web site at:

www.gale.com/thorndike
www.gale.com/wheeler

To share your comments, please write:

Publisher
Thorndike Press
295 Kennedy Memorial Drive
Waterville, ME   04901